Untainted Blood

Liz Mistry

Print ISBN 978-1-912175-56-7

Falkirk Community Trust	
30124 03096053 0	
Askews & Holts	
AF	£8.99
MK	

To Nilesh, my rock

and Ravi, Kasi & Jimi (the sprogs)

Restless Natives die

Whilst inky venom scores deep

Tattoos paint the sky

Have you read the other books in the DI Gus McGuire series?

Unquiet Souls

Uncoiled Lies

High Praise for Liz Mistry's D.I.Gus McGuire series

Unquiet Souls (Book 1)

"It is a dark and gritty read that will affect you. If you, like me, need to grasp what is happening, you will keep on reading and not rest until you are on the very last page."
Caroline Vincent – Bits About Books.

"It is a very complex story with many strands intertwined to make up a very gripping, adrenaline, filled book that has the reader turning page after page well into the night."
Jill Burknishaw – Books n AllI

Uncoiled Lies (Book2)

"For me it was a captivating read, and I felt so many emotions when reading this book, family really was at the heart of this story and how we are influenced by them."
Alexina Golding – Bookstormer

"Uncoiled Lies is just brilliant. The Author delivers everything I would expect from a crime novel and more. I was totally hooked from beginning to end."
Sarah Hardy – By The Letter Book Reviews.

Prologue

Look North 19th November 2016

'The arrest of Tory MP Clive Clementon and his subsequent resignation from the highly-contested Bradford Central seat has wreaked even more havoc on the city. Bradford's infamous Matchmaker Case earlier this year resulted in many high-profile celebrities, politicians and officials being investigated for their role in historic and current child abuse cases. Despite vigorous denials of his involvement in child trafficking, child abuse and paedophilia, it seems likely that Clementon is the latest in a long line of public figures to be brought to book for such crimes. A by-election early in the new year is a foregone conclusion amid speculation of a possible general election later in the year after Article 50 is triggered.

'The Bradford Central seat was created during a manoeuvring of constituency boundaries, cynically described by some as an obvious move to create more Tory seats in the North of England. Now, with the incumbent MP resigning, and Bradford in turmoil after a series of gang-related killings and the outcome of the Bradford Central by-election in question, we eagerly await confirmation of the candidates ... This is Binish Aziz, signing off for *Look North*, Bradford.'

February 2017

Friday

Chapter 1

03:30 The Kill Site

'I love frosty mornings like this one. They are so invigorating, energising, full of promise and hope for the future, don't you think, Tara?' I smile when she nuzzles against my neck, her breath warm on my ear as she blows gently.

The other two horses aren't interested in me and keep their distance. When I run my finger down her long nose, she tosses her head this way and that in response, making me laugh out loud. I know what *she's* after. She can smell it, I'm sure. Thrusting my hand into my pocket, I pull out a perfectly formed cube of sweetness. Placing it flat on my palm, I extend it and grin, as in a single lick, she scoops it off and devours it. Her head dips down for more, and I take the opportunity to sink my fingers deep into her flowing mane, scratching long and hard, just the way she likes it.

Resting my head against hers, I continue to scratch her, savouring the musky horsey scent that erupts around me. I speak to her as if she is my best friend. For sure, she's the only one I trust with *these* secrets.

'Two down, and still nobody any the wiser,' I say, laughing as her ears twitch at the sound of my voice. 'They've found the latest one's body. Not that it'll do them any good. Why would it? I'm smarter than them, and I'm doing God's work. The purification of the human race, bit by bit, little by little, that's my aim.

'If only more people would take up the mantle and join the struggle. We've sat back for too long and look what's

3

happened. They've overrun the city. No more. All it took for me to realise what had to be done was the election of their kind to our Parliament. They think they can represent me? No chance.'

I get out another sugar lump and give it to her. Tara sees everything, yet she keeps her own counsel. My secrets are safe with her. I pat her rump, not hard, barely enough to send her away. She doesn't like the noise. It makes her uneasy, skittish. Best if she stays over there, under her tree. It's funny how she never goes inside the old barn, except to eat her hay. Maybe she's warm enough with only her rug on. Maybe she prefers being out under the stars. Who knows?

My fingers tingle at the thought of what I'm about to do. I stretch them, loosening them up, ready to create my masterpiece. I have a torch in my pocket, although the night sky is clear, and the moon lights my way as I walk back inside the old farmhouse. It's so cold that I almost wish I'd kept my gloves on when stroking Tara. The shelter from the slight breeze that carries a promise of morning frost with it, is welcome. The prone figure on the floor looks up at me, struggling against the ties. I don't know why they bother. I really don't. All they do is hurt themselves even more and make the ties tighten around their wrists. Not that I care. I block out their demeaning pleas and busy myself getting things set up. This one came around quicker than the others, and that suits me. The sooner I get this done, the sooner I can dump him. Moving with speed, I pull on a white overall and a pair of nitrile gloves. No point leaving any trace evidence for the police, is there?

The traditional razor I've opted for is sharp, much more precise, and it fits so well in my palm, as if it was made especially for me. I approach him, savouring how his eyes widen and his squirming increases as I near. Placing the razor down on the plastic sheeting, I pull a Stanley knife from my pocket. Humming to myself, I slit up the seams of his T-shirt and then along the shoulders before tugging it loose. I've always been a tidy person, so I take the time to fold it before placing it on the floor. Next, after I've emptied his pockets, his trousers get the same treatment and then his boxers. I dislike this part, and more so when the smell of excrement hits my nostrils. Disgusting animal! Good job I'm wearing gloves.

Clothes folded, I carry them out to the van and place them inside. It's good to build the tension. I find my enjoyment is intensified with their fear. I go back inside and see that he's begun to struggle again. 'Tut, tut … can't you give it a rest? I know your sort lack the intelligence of the superior race, but even *you* must be able to see that struggling is futile.'

Blood trickles down his wrists, staining the ties a russet hue. His face is contorted, partly because of the bruising and partly with his struggles. I lift the razor and hold it in front of him. His eyes fill with terror, and I laugh, enjoying the fact he doesn't know what I'm going to do with it.

I lift an aerosol and spray shaving foam over his genitalia. He's really panicking now. His skin's all mottled and goose-bumpy with the cold. Happy, I begin my task. 'Save your screaming for later … *this* is the easy bit.'

Saturday

Chapter 2

Dr Fergus McGuire had lined up the post-mortem findings on the large screen in the morgue and was studying images of the tattoos that had been found on both Asim Farooq and Manish Parmar. His son, Detective Inspector Angus McGuire, had been handed the case when the second body was discovered. Two bodies in the space of a fortnight, both displaying the same tattoo on their groin, made it a case for Angus' specialist team. Neither tattoo showed any finesse, although the swastika was clearly discernible. Bruising around the area indicated they'd been applied ante-mortem. Such a waste! Dealing with death was the pathologist's job, and Fergus loved it. He loved the science of it all, the feeling his work could provide answers for the grieving families. Sometimes, he could not get his head around the evil that existed in society … this was one of those times.

He glanced at his son, who was also studying the images, and sighed. Angus was wan, and his eyes, normally so blue, seemed dull, almost lifeless. It seemed to Dr McGuire he was treading on thin ice with him at the moment. He couldn't seem to do anything right. He knew Angus still harboured guilt about Alice. He felt responsible, Dr McGuire understood that. After all, his son had inherited his mother's over-zealous conscience. However, at this rate, it was going to kill him.

Anytime he or his wife asked about the therapy, Angus cut them down cold, refusing to say anything. Instead, he

9

shut them out. He'd lost weight, and it was clear from the bags under his eyes that his insomnia was back. Even the sunshine streaks that threaded through his dreads seemed flat and drab, and his tanned skin had a yellow hue. If he didn't know that the lad jogged for hours around Heaton every day, he'd think his son hadn't seen daylight for months. He bit his lip. Why wouldn't Angus just reach out to them?

As if sensing his father's eyes on him, Angus exhaled and turned towards him. 'Same killer?'

Nibbling on a few stray whiskers, Fergus made a mental note to get the beard trimmer out that evening. Corrine didn't like it when his beard got too straggly. 'Although the second tattoo is marginally more evenly administered, I'd say that's more to do wi' the tattooist having had some practise than a second practitioner. The design is the same, only slightly smoother this time. A definite amateur. And definitely a form of torture, unless, of course, the victim was unconscious.'

Gus pressed his lips together and shook his head. 'No, I don't reckon our killer was of a mind to make it painless for them. I think making it hurt was a major element of his MO. Probably got off on it. I suspect they were fully conscious and aware the entire time, poor sods.'

'I tend to agree. Why choose that particular site for the tattoo, if you dinnae want it to hurt?' He pointed to the area around the ink. 'This extensive bruising is caused by the needle pricks penetrating deeper than they should. The skin in this area is particularly tender. If the tattooist wanted to administer maximum discomfort, they couldn't have chosen a better place.' Dr McGuire shuddered. The thought of the agony these men had endured made his scrotal sack wither. Didn't bear thinking about. 'Do you reckon it was sexual as well as racist?'

Gus' lips tightened. 'More than likely. Shaving and tattooing the groin must have a sexual significance, I'd have thought. I'll check with Professor Carlton.' Head to one side, Gus continued to study the marks. 'How does he snatch the men? He somehow gets them out of their cars, moves them to another vehicle, and presumably transports them elsewhere to kill before taking them to the dump site. Neither of these men were small.'

'Ah.' Fergus McGuire turned and flicked to another image. 'This is an injection site at the nape of the neck. The first victim had it too. I've sent bloods for tox results, although, as you know, many of thon date rape type drugs are undetectable after a few hours. I suspect the killer injected our victims from behind and then, whilst they were unconscious, applied restraints.'

He flicked a few images to show a ring of bruising around the arms and feet of both men. 'Restraint marks. Each of the two men struggled forcefully against the restraints, as you can see. Again, an indication they were conscious during the torture. They are consistent with bog-standard cable ties.'

'That explains how he gets them to stay still long enough for him to do it. Compo says it'd take a good half hour to apply that to a willing participant, so the men had to be subdued somehow.' Angus studied the images. 'Cause of death?'

Dr McGuire pulled up a close-up of the neck area. 'Asphyxiation. It's clear from the ligature abrasions and the resulting bruising in this area, the victim was strangled with some sort of rope. Again, similar to the first victim. I've extracted fibres which I've also sent to the lab. Looks like some sort of hemp as opposed to the more modern nylon ropes people favour nowadays.' He pulled up a series of other close-up images. 'Petechial dots in the eyes and swelling round the mouth and tongue.'

'Owt else?' asked Gus.

Dr McGuire clicked on a new image. 'Post-mortem hypostasis,' he peered at Gus over the top of his glasses, 'or livor mortis to you, indicates that the body has been kept in a horizontal position. Some strange striations across the back and going vertically up parallel to the spine indicate they've lain on a board, or something with three-inch-wide vertical columns, before being left at the scene. The columns appear to be joined together by a series of horizontal bars, each four inches wide. The deep purple lividity is, again, consistent with strangulation.'

Gus studied the marks. 'Looks like these were caused by whatever the killer used to move the bodies. Any idea how long the bodies were on this surface before they were moved to the dump site?'

'Well, the fact that those marks are fainter than the pressure points at the shoulders and buttocks indicate the victims were only on there a couple of hours before being moved. Full lividity takes about six hours, and I've put time of death at between three and six on Friday morning. So, I reckon he was moved no later than eight and, quite probably, earlier.'

'Can you give me anything else?'

Dr McGuire raised a finger in the air and smiled, 'There is one thing. I checked for debris from the nails and hair and so on, and came up with zilch. However, we may have been lucky, for it appears I've found some saliva specks on the victim's face. I've sent them off to the lab; mind you, it's no' open till Monday. Ah've no' put a rush on it. It may belong to the victim, but I've got my fingers crossed it's our killer's.'

It wasn't a lot, nonetheless it *was* better than nothing. Gus would get Compo to see what he could make of the lividity marks. He was good at sourcing things using his weird and wonderful databases. 'Swastikas, strangulation and Asian males displayed naked in a cross shape are not good signs. Not good signs at all, especially not in this political climate,' said Gus. Frowning, he drew his fingers through his dreads. '... and, of course, we're understaffed.'

Dr McGuire pretended not to notice his son's shoulders had slumped, and instead, he flicked another glance at the tattoos. He was on the point of suggesting they go for a drink or, at the very least, have a drink in his office, when Gus swung his bag onto his shoulder and walked towards the door with an abrupt, 'Got to get off. See ya later, Dad.'

Reaching out, the pathologist grabbed his son's arm, forcing him to stop. 'Och, you've surely got time for a drink wi' your old man before you go rushing off?'

Not meeting his dad's eyes, Gus said, 'I'm running late. Dr Mahmood waits for no-one, you know that.'

Torn between feeling glad Gus was going to see his psychiatrist and hurt he clearly would rather do that than share a drink with him, Dr McGuire released his arm. He waited until Gus was almost at the door before saying, 'What happened to Alice wisnae your fault, Angus. You've *got* to let it go, son. You can't carry everything on your shoulders.'

Closing his eyes for a second, Gus sighed, then, with a grimace, he said in a voice so hopeless, it sent chills down his father's back, 'Then whose fault was it?'

Fergus shook his head as his son left. *Sometimes, you just have to let them get on with it,* he thought, feeling as if his heart had been ripped out, as well as Gus'. Guilt was a terrible thing.

Chapter 3

Nemo was gone!

Gus, breathing heavily, leaned against the aquarium, hands splayed against the glass. Knowing it was futile, he peered through the too-cheery bubbles, hoping the hulking fish he'd named Nemo would swim from behind one of the ornamental rocks. Where was he? Nemo had been his companion for months now, his one ally in the psychiatrist's camp. He'd grown used to coming in and drawing his abstract patterns on the glass for Nemo to follow. It calmed him ... readied him for his session with Dr Mahmood, and now, it seemed Nemo was no more. How much more loss was he expected to deal with?

From nowhere, an almost uncontrollable urge to smash the glass engulfed him. He imagined the water gushing out, sending a tumble of rainbow coloured fish onto the waiting room's newly carpeted floor. His chest tightened, and as his breath turned to shallow pants, he knew he was dangerously close to having a panic attack. Stumbling away from the tank, he flung himself onto a cushioned chair and closed his eyes, trying to calm his breathing. The only thing he could see, though, was the damn tank without Nemo. He tried to force his thoughts to the safe place he'd established with Dr Mahmood. Like a boomerang, they stubbornly took him instead to the funeral, and his breathing became even shallower.

Sweat dripped from his dreads, onto his brow and into his eyes. The salt stung them, making them water. His hands balled into fists, as he struggled against the vision that was so vivid, it was as if he'd been transported back to that day in November.

It would have been marginally better if the snow hadn't turned to sleet, making the occasion even darker. Frost bit his fingers as he stood, straight-backed, trying to keep a hold of himself ... and he'd managed, just. It had been touch-and-go, but with his parents, one on either side of him like incongruous bodyguards, he'd gotten through it. Now, however, he was tortured by all the things he hadn't said to her ... all the thoughts he hadn't articulated ... all the times he'd remained silent. Now, it was too late ... she was gone.

Chapter 4

19:05 The Fort

The session with Dr Mahmood, even by Gus' standards, hadn't gone well at all. So, feeling edgy, he'd dropped his car outside his house in Mariners Drive and headed into Heaton Woods. A foray into the woods normally calmed him; not today, though. Despite the crisp air and a sighting of one of the wood's elusive deer, Gus' spirits remained low.

After strolling aimlessly for hours, he headed down to Sean's pond and hunched on the bench overlooking the small pool, ignoring the drop in temperature that signalled the prospect of snow. He wished his dog was with him. Bingo, though, was vacationing with his mum for the duration of Gus' investigation into the tattoo murders. He was working unpredictable hours, and it was easier for his parents to look after the dog. Besides which, Bingo loved spending time with his 'sisters' as his mother, much to Gus' amusement, referred to their dogs. If his parents' bull terriers, Heather and Meggie, were indeed Bingo's siblings, then Bingo was, without doubt, the runt of the litter. Nevertheless, his little West Highland Terrier was also the boss.

When Gus got home, he opened his fridge, found two cans of beer and a mushy cucumber and gave up on the idea of eating. He wasn't hungry anyway. He seemed to have permanently lost his appetite at the minute. He changed into his jogging gear, complete with the high visibility jacket his mother insisted he wore. Setting off, he took a circuitous route up Emm Lane onto Leylands and down Scotchman Road, before arriving at The Fort, sweating and wet from the sleet shower that was beginning to pick up. His run had left him shaky-legged and hadn't really done anything to calm him down. He knew the trembling was a combination of the after-effects of his panic attack, lack of food, too much activity and an excess of caffeine. He was dog-tired, yet he couldn't stop pushing his body beyond the realms of endurance.

Deep down, he knew something would give soon, and if he wasn't careful, he'd be in pieces and unable to function. His boss had warned him, as had his parents. He was on a downward spiral, one he had no control over, and he knew if he didn't get a grip soon, he was in danger of splintering into irreparable pieces. The dynamic talking therapy was hard work, and he knew he was resisting opening up. After Greg's death, it had taken him time, and as Dr Mahmood kept telling him, he had gone through a lot, what with the Matchmaker Case, followed soon after by the gangland murders. She told him he needed time, which was a shame because time was one thing he didn't have, and he refused to stop working. So, she'd upped his medication and was monitoring him. Every session now seemed to be about his feelings of guilt and letting those go. He ran up the front steps of the police station, a glower on his face. A homeless man who'd taken shelter on the top step jumped to his feet and ran down the stairs as Gus pounded up. *Shit. Now, he was terrorising the public.*

Inside, The Fort's air conditioning dried his sweat, making him shiver. He waved to the duty officer, who grinned back with a 'You back again? No rest for the wicked.'

Gus jogged to the changing rooms. When he got into the shower, he cranked the heat up until it almost scalded his aching body. It felt good, like he deserved it, so he stayed there for as long as he could bear it, until his skin smarted in the heat. He liked weekend evenings at the station. The quietness gave him a chance to think, as well as catch up on the interminable paperwork he was obligated to do. It was only at shift change that it got boisterous and loud, and for that hour, he could almost cope with the racket. Mind you, the uniforms were a nice lot. Gus respected them, and they, he hoped, respected him in return. Gus' philosophy was if you treated people right, they would repay you in kind. It wasn't often he was proved wrong. Recently, though, he'd found it hard to live by his own rules.

He got out, towelled himself dry and got dressed. With his dreads still dripping, he walked along to the investigation room and was pleased to see it empty for a change.

One of the hardest things for him was interacting with his team. The solicitous glances he often intercepted drove him wild; the concerned looks made him want to yell at his colleagues. He knew this was unreasonable. Knew, too, it was placing excessive pressure on Sampson and Compo. He was two detectives down and only too aware he was functioning below par.

Photos of the two murdered men were on the board, and Gus moved over to study it. When Asim Farooq's body had been found in a known dogging area outside Haworth two weeks ago, the media, in particular, Jez Hopkins from the *Chronicle*, had blown it up into a frenzy of self-righteous spin. The moral majority condemned the man for his supposedly 'alternative' lifestyle. The media focus had shifted away from the fact Asim Farooq had been murdered, and instead concentrated on deriding the victim and his relatives. His poor family had been distraught, not only by Asim's death, but by their community's reaction to where he'd been found. His pregnant wife had been unable to grieve properly in the midst of the scandal, and his parents and siblings had been denied the comfort of their community.

Gus had kept an eye on the case, suspecting it would, sooner or later, land on his doorstep. He consulted, on the quiet, with Professor Sebastian Carlton, the forensic psychologist from Leeds Trinity University he'd met the previous year. Carlton had trained agents at the FBI Behavioural Analysis Unit before opting for a quieter existence this side of the pond in Horsforth. His first suggestion had been to keep the tattoo out of the media, and Gus had agreed. They always needed ways of weeding out the few who falsely declared their guilt. Thankfully, the previous senior investigating officer had been of the same mind. Carlton had suspected Asim's murder would not be a one-off, and when Manish Parmar had been discovered in woodland near Pudsey, it seemed his suspicions were correct. Gus was glad the swastika tattoo had been kept from the press.

Apart from the tattoo, both men had been placed naked in a cross position, arms extended to either side, legs straight, and feet crossed at the ankle. Their clothes had been sliced off their bodies and folded neatly near their heads with their possessions on top. The forensic reports had come back with very little. This killer was forensically savvy, by the looks of things, and they still were awaiting the tox screen on Manish Parmar.

Since the previous day, Compo and Sampson had been trying to find links between the two victims. Neither had been killed at their dump site. The tattooing had been done ante-mortem, and Gus knew they'd been killed somewhere where their screams wouldn't be heard. He wanted his team to find the link between these two men as he was sure that would help them find the killer. Their paths must have crossed somewhere, although it wasn't clear where, as

Asim worked in Manchester as a financial consultant and Manish was a taxi driver. Both men lived in different areas of Bradford, Asim in Harden and Manish in Keighley.

Both men's cars had been discovered in areas with few cameras, making it difficult to establish the killer's possible vehicle. Their locations also supported the idea they led alternative lifestyles. One in a well-known, dogging area and the other in an area notorious for the 'alternative' sex trade; S&M and the like. The fact they'd also been dumped in similar areas made Gus suspect both victims had been stalked. He'd also got Compo to source a few tattoo experts in the hope they could shed some light on either the equipment used or the artist, and he'd managed to schedule a meeting with Mo's tattooist in the morning. With it being Sunday, he was grateful to his best friend for wangling this.

Slumping in his chair, legs crossed at the ankle and resting on the table, Gus studied the crime boards. This killer hadn't finished yet, of that he was sure. Not by a long shot. They really needed to get a handle on this and quick. So far, the uniforms had come up with nothing, and Gus was champing at the bit for information to propel the case forward. A sudden weariness made him close his eyes. *Only for a minute,* he promised himself. The gentle click of the radiator as it cooled and the buzz of the dodgy light in the corner of the room soothed him into a light doze … which was broken when the door was thrust open, and DCI Nancy Chalmers, skirt rustling as she walked, burst into the room. 'Just the man I *didn't* want to see!' she said, her tone business-like.

Gus started and pulled himself upright, blinking at her. The last person he needed to encounter right now was his boss. Despite her undoubted professionalism, at times, she fussed around him like a mother hen, and it really pissed him off. He wanted to be left to get on with his job. He didn't need her pecking her solicitous beak into his business. When he spoke, his tone was sharper than he intended. 'What!'

'Don't you take that tone with me, Gus McGuire!' She glared at him, and then, when he blushed, she shook her head and softened her tone. 'Get yourself home, Gus. You're knackered, and you're no good to me like this. GO HOME!'

Eyes flashing, Gus stood up and stretched. This was exactly the sort of crap he hated. An image of Nancy's expression if he told her to 'piss off' flashed through his mind, and he found himself more tempted than he should have been to blurt it out. He took a deep breath and banished the thought. He was being ungrateful. Nancy wasn't solely his boss, she was a family friend, and *she* hadn't had it easy either since the Matchmaker Case. Resigned to politeness, he said, 'I'm fine. Just grabbing a bit of shut-eye, that's all.'

Nancy strode over and positioned herself in front of his desk, hands on hips. Gus sighed. He recognised the implacable look on her face. No way was she going to budge on this, and to be honest, he didn't have the energy to argue. With a short nod, he moved over, grabbed his bag and some folders, and headed to the door. With his hand on the knob, he turned and studied her, taking in the paleness of her face and the wrinkles that had appeared there since the previous year. Feeling guilty for his earlier bad thoughts, he smiled and said, 'I'm not the only one who needs to get some sleep, Nancy. Why don't you drop me off on your way home?'

Nancy held his gaze for a few seconds, and then, shoulders slumping, she nodded. 'Yeah, you're right. I could do with an early night. I'll get my things.' She walked over to the door, and as she reached Gus, she grinned, a glimpse of her old humour in her eyes. 'What are we like? It's a Saturday night, and we're both heading home to a microwave meal, *Ant and Dec's Saturday Night Takeaway* and a lonely bottle of whisky. Not exactly jet-setters, are we?'

Gus grinned. She had a point, and in all the years he'd known her, first as a surrogate aunt and now as his boss, she'd never been wrong. Her close relationship with his mum often meant with Gus, she blurred the professional boundaries. Sometimes, like now, he hated it; then again, most times, he was glad to know she was in his corner.

'Mind you, some might say *I'm* past it; on the other hand, *you* should at least be getting a shag on a Saturday night, lad.' She stretched out her palm and held it to his cheek. 'You need to get over yourself and start living a little. Get yourself laid once in a while, instead of moping about Alice and Sadia, and taking all the blame for something you had no control over. As we both know through experience, life's too damn short for that.' She sniffed and headed for the door. 'I'll meet you at the car.'

She had a point. It had been months since Sadia. Still, he wasn't interested in that. Not right now. Especially not after the trouble he ended up in last time. No, things were too raw in that department. Following her from the office, Gus cast a last glance at the pictures of the two dead men before snapping off the lights. He'd do his best to get to the bottom of their deaths, but first, sleep. He needed sleep, and whisky! He grinned. A bit of Ant and Dec and a frozen lasagne would do him for tonight. Besides, he was meeting Mo the following day. Who said he didn't have any fun?

Sunday

Chapter 5

10:30 Hebden Bridge

Mo was like a kid on a trip to the seaside, bouncing about the car, chattering on about everything and nothing. It made Gus smile, and he knew that was Mo's intention. When he'd wakened, he'd been cold, and his leg was cramping from sleeping for half the night on the couch. It was his own fault. To avoid nightmares, he had taken to dozing on the sofa, instead of going to bed. The result was, most mornings, he woke up with an aching back and felt more tired than he'd been before he went to sleep. He knew he had to break the habit, and he promised himself next time, he would sleep in his bed.

He'd picked Mo up from his huge terraced house off Oak Lane in Manningham. His friend lived with his wife and children in the street behind his café, which was aptly named Mo's SaMosas. Unlike Gus' house, Mo's was homely, filled with scattered cushions and toys. The spacious kitchen was covered with paintings and drawings done by the children, and it had a lived-in feel to it. As soon as he'd arrived, he'd been pulled into their chaotic, loving existence. He'd given sweets and hugs to each of Mo's five girls, all of whom were as beautiful as their mother, Naila, and as kind and good natured as their father.

Gus loved them, and after being in their company for a mere ten minutes, his spirits lifted. He knew he should spend more time with them. When he and Gabriella had first gotten married, kids had been part of their plans. Hmph! He couldn't imagine having them now, though.

Couldn't imagine making that sort of commitment again. According to Mo, the girls were always asking after their Uncle Gus, and it seemed like ages since he'd taken them out. As they climbed over him, each vying for his attention, he was happier than he had been in months. Maybe Mo should hire them out as a therapy for depression.

Amid moans that he was leaving too soon, he promised them a trip to the cinema in the near future, an offer that was met with whoops of glee. Naila had grinned and said, 'You do know it'll cost you a small fortune, Gus? They'll milk you dry with their demands for popcorn and all.'

Gus grinned and ruffled the hair of Mumtaz, the youngest. 'If I can't buy the prettiest girls in Bradford some popcorn, then there's something far wrong.' At last, he managed to extricate himself from their hugs, and he and Mo had set off.

Today's outing, despite Mo's holiday mood, was a work trip. Mo, at Gus' request, was taking him to meet his friend the tattoo artist, Emily Gilpin. She'd applied all of Mo's many tattoos, and according to Mo, what she didn't know about the tattooing business wasn't worth knowing. Gus hoped she had a solid stomach, as the pictures he'd packed to show her were not for the faint-hearted. She'd agreed to meet them on a Sunday because of the urgency of the investigation, and he was appreciative of that. Feeling as if there was something Mo wasn't telling him, Gus shook off the faint suspicion his mate had something up his sleeve, and put his friend's giddiness down to the two of them spending time together for the first time in a couple of months.

As they drove down the steep slope into Hebden Bridge, with its Victorian sandstone houses apparently shaped on a whim to fit the landscape, Mo directed him past the pretty market square along the main road towards the canal where they parked up in a pub car park. Jumping out of the car, Mo told Gus after their meeting, lunch was on him, and then, the pair of them walked against the bracing wind to the canal. Despite it being Sunday, it was busy with dog walkers and families, and Gus was fascinated with the brightly coloured barges lined up along the canal. With quaint names hand-painted on their bows and smoke spiralling from their chimneys, Gus envied the owners' uncomplicated lives. A few hundred yards along, on a side street opposite the canal, were a series of artists' workshops, cafés and a bicycle hire and repair shop.

A busker, playing a guitar, belted out songs in a less than tuneful tone. Attached with strings to his instrument was a moth-eaten papier-mâché doll with mad woman's hair and clown lipstick. As the musician played, the toy bobbed up and down in a macabre dance. Gus, thinking it resembled something out of a *Saw* movie, gave the busker and doll a wide berth. Traumatic memories of his sister Katie's favourite doll, Gemma, staring at him with her googly green eyes had remained with him into adulthood.

Emily Gilpin's tattoo parlour had an intricate spray-painted sign outside. Mo rapped his knuckles on the door three times and entered without waiting for a reply. The waiting room walls were decorated with images in different shaped frames representing all sorts of tattoo designs from Celtic knots to floral displays and peace symbols, and from Indian gods and goddesses to birds of prey.

Gus made a mental note to suggest Dr Mahmood invest in some of this artwork for her rather twee waiting room. Maybe he'd buy one for her as a leaving present when she eventually signed him off as compos mentis. He grinned to himself. He reckoned it'd be a while before she thought he was anywhere near ready; in the meantime, one of these paintings would go a long way to making her waiting room less soulless. Thinking of her waiting room made him remember the demise of Nemo. He'd tried to appear nonchalant when he'd asked her about the massive dark fish with the trailing fronds coming out its head. Still, he sensed she'd picked up on his grief when she'd told him it had died. He knew it was only a fish; nevertheless, Nemo's absence left a hole in his gut. He'd grown used to using his brief interactions with the fish as a way to prepare himself for his sessions with the psychiatrist. What would he do now?

Taking a deep breath, Gus forced himself back to the real world and continued to study the frames. Even when Emily came out from the tattoo room, Gus was reluctant to drag his eyes away from the artwork. No sooner had he finished absorbing one image when another one caught his eye. However, this *was* work. He grinned at the petite woman before him. And then frowned. He'd expected her to be covered from head to foot in tattoos; instead, she had only a few visible. Each one was delicate, the colours and highlights bright and intricate. They were completely unlike the one he was about to show her and served to emphasise how barbaric the killer was. He had a momentary pang he was going to somehow taint all the beauty around him in the studio.

However, Mo jumped to his rescue, thrusting out his arm to show her how good her most recently applied Celtic knot tattoo looked, and Gus' uncertainty faded. He really needed any information she could give.

Emily led them into the inner room, where a chair and a bed stood with her tattoo equipment beside it. She pointed to the chair, and Gus sat down, looking around in wonder at the images that adorned these walls too. For the first time, he really appreciated how much of a craft it was, how skilled a good tattoo artist was. He'd always slagged

Mo off for being addicted to tattooing; now, having seen the delicacy of the artworks in this room, he could begin to understand his friend's compulsion.

It wasn't until Emily said, 'Roll your sleeve up,' that he realised she'd been setting up the machine, whilst something was printing off her computer. Hadn't Mo told her why he was there?

'Oh, no. I've not come for a tattoo. I only need some information.'

Emily frowned. 'You're booked in for a tattoo on your upper arm.'

Gus glanced at Mo, who smiled in what Gus recognised as his false, 'I'm innocent' expression. Scowling at his friend, Gus said, 'I'm sorry, I think Mo's misled you. I really only want to ask you about some tattoos.'

Mo exchanged a conspiratorial glance with Emily. 'What did I tell you? He's a wuss. A big, fat scaredy-cat.'

Gus glowered at him. 'No, I'm not, Mo. I just don't want a tatt. Besides, you've got more than enough to go around.'

As Emily watched their interaction with a bemused smile on her face, Mo folded his arms over his chest and snorted, 'Told you. Wuss!' His tone was full of derision.

Gus blushed. He knew that Mo was partly right. The thought of hundreds of little needles pricking his flesh combined with the memory of the swastika tattoos on the victims made him wince. There was no way he was going to rush into some foolhardy tattoo because Mo was calling his bluff. 'Look, it's not something you rush into, okay?'

'No, I know,' said Mo, his tone triumphant. 'That's why I've done this.' And he showed Gus the template of a small, three-inch square Bob Marley with his dreads made up of serpents. 'It's Greg's painting in miniature. Thought you'd like it. Emily says she can do it really nice. Mostly in black with a bit of red, green and yellow shading for emphasis. You know, Rasta colours.'

Gus considered the small printed image Mo had sent to Emily. It was perfect. He must have taken a photo of Greg's painting that held pride of place in Gus' living room. Tracing the serpents Greg had drawn to replace Marley's dreads, a lump formed in Gus' throat, rendering him speechless.

When his silence continued, Mo jostled from foot to foot, biting his lip. 'It'll fit right there on your upper arm, Gus. A nice tribute to Greg, you know? Although, if you really don't want to, that's okay.'

He made to take the template back, but Gus pulled his hand away. His heart swelled in his chest as he glanced from the miniature copy of the painting to Mo's expectant face. With a tight smile, he nodded once and rolled his right sleeve up until the top of his arm was exposed. 'This is the perfect tattoo for me. You're more perceptive than you look.'

Afterwards, armed with a tube of Bepanthen cream and plastic film wrapped around his throbbing bicep, Gus, Emily and Mo headed to the pub to talk about the swastika tattoos. Tossing the keys to Mo, Gus said, 'You're driving. I need a drink after that experience.'

Mo tossed them back with a laugh, 'Alcohol thins the blood, so it's not a good idea after you've been tattooed. Looks like Emily will be the only one drinking.'

Gus shook his head and then laughed. 'Can't believe I did this.'

With a rueful look, Mo nodded. 'No, neither can I. Naila's gonna kill me. She made me promise not to force you.'

Gus flung his arm round Mo's neck, then instantly regretted it, as he had nudged the tattoo. 'Ouch! You didn't force me, Mo. Just used your gentle powers of persuasion.'

Settled in a quiet corner of the bar near the fire, Gus explained about the current case and made Emily promise secrecy. He showed the close-up photographs of the tattoo and explained where they were located on the body.

She flinched. 'My God! That is pure torture. That must've killed.' Then, she grimaced. 'Oops, you know what I mean.' She picked up the clearest photo. 'It's quite obvious this was done by an amateur. The ink is irregular and lacks the delicate touch of today's machines. Whoever applied this tattoo exerted too much pressure, and,' she frowned, 'it looks like one of the old, two-coiled machines was used. Nowadays, we use electro-magnetic machines. However, at the beginning of the last century, they used two-coiled ones. The tatts they created were similar to this. Marginally better, in the right hands, than prison tatts. However, these,' she tapped the photos, 'would have caused a lot of pain in that area, even if a professional had applied them. In the hands of an amateur, those men must have screamed their lungs out.'

Chapter 6

20:30 City Hall, City Park

Light snow fell over Bradford's Mirror Pool. Each flake was translucent, a mere shimmer in the white LED lights, making the scene other-worldly. The Alhambra and the old Odeon building loomed, shapely turrets and domes like statuesque guardians, defining the skyline on the opposite side of the road. City Hall, its scaffolding removed, dominated the near side.

Graeme Weston smiled. For him, today *had* been other-worldly. Never in his wildest imaginings had he expected this. It was like a dream come true. All his hard work – all *their* hard work – had finally paid off, and he was almost overwhelmed. The series of events leading to this point could not have panned out better if he'd tried. He'd been longing to take up the mantle for Bradford since he was a teenager, and now, with the resignation of Clive Clementon, the climate had never been more in their favour.

The Greens were superfluous, the Labour Party jampacked full of Pakis and poofs, and the Tories totally discredited. Besides which, the city was in a mess. The Matchmaker fiasco last year had delivered a resounding blow to Bradford's law and order. People felt uneasy. Who could they trust, if their public figures were corrupt? That, combined with the recent gang murders, and the subsequent spotlight on the immigrants and the current spate of killings, had bled the city dry and brought drugs and prostitution to their midst. No wonder Bradford had voted for Brexit. In Bradford, the natives were restless. They were ready for a change, and *he* was ready to offer it. Hopefully, this by-election wouldn't be followed by an early general election. Who the hell knew what nonsense would occur after Article 50 was triggered?

His team had made sure the media were there, and every supporter they could find had been dragged out, so a sizeable crowd in winter coats, scarves and gloves huddled at the bottom of City Hall steps. Its regularly changing turret light illuminated the banners and slogans held by his party's supporters. He knew it would look great on the news and had high hopes of it hitting the national as well as local and regional outlets. The people of Bradford needed to hear his message loud and clear; he was there to fight for them. No more kowtowing to 'the ethnics,' 'the deviants,' 'the immigrants' and, of course, the PC wishy-washiness of Westminster.

The only slight cloud on the snowy horizon was he hadn't told Christine yet. She wouldn't be happy with him putting himself forward in the public eye. Not when they had Jacob to think about. He shrugged. They'd kept their secret this long, and he was sure they could keep it a bit longer. She didn't fully support his political agenda, so he'd left her in the dark. He'd have to tell her sooner rather than later. However, before he could come clean, he'd have to confront her about that other matter. His lips tightened. She'd disappointed him, let him down again, and he was gutted.

As the crowd began to chant his name, he put all thoughts of Christine to the back of his mind and stepped forward, both arms raised, waving at the five-hundred-strong crowd who had gathered for this announcement. At the back of the throng, he could see the media cameras aimed at him. Raising his head, he smiled his best smile. The one he'd been practising in the privacy of his bathroom for weeks, the one that would become his campaign smile and would be plastered over every newspaper in the country. If Farage and Trump could do it, then so could he. Turning this way and that, he basked in the attention, soaking up the positive vibes, playing the crowd and making sure the photographers had plenty of material to work with. He was good at this, always had been, and he intended to take full advantage of this opportunity.

At last, he stopped waving, and taking the microphone from his campaign manager, Michael Hogg, he waited for silence. From the corner of his eye, he saw police cars driving onto the concrete park and officers alighting. Hmm, that could work in his favour. Public opinion of the police wasn't very high at the moment, and if they made one mistake, a single misstep, it would work in his favour. Still smiling, he began to speak to his acolytes.

'There has been a wave of unrest in this fine city for many years. Our culture has been diluted, our economy shattered, our jobs looted, and our houses taken over by huge litters of foreigners. We, the *pure* Bradford folk, have been the ones to suffer.'

A wave of cheering made him pause for a moment. Adrenaline surged through his system at such a positive response. *This* was what he was made for. *This* was what he deserved. As the police drew closer, he pulled an envelope from his pocket and waved it in the air.

'This is my nomination to stand as Albion First's parliamentary candidate for Bradford Central.'

Resounding roars met his words. He felt like Chamberlain brandishing the signed Munich Agreement. The only difference was he would not make any appeasement pacts. He would stand strong for what his party believed in, for the good of this country. Waving the envelope again, his smile in place, he lowered it, waiting for the cheers and clapping to subside before continuing. 'This tsunami of *rioting* and *deviance* and *violence* must be avenged, and if Westminster won't do it, nay, if Westminster *can't* do it, then who will?' He raised his hands in the same way he'd seen his hero Adolf do, and the crowd erupted in a chorus of 'Weston, Weston, Weston!'

This felt *so* good. Bowing his head this way and that, he kept his arms raised, commanding their respect, their adulation. Everything was going exactly to plan. He grinned as the police edged even closer. His team had made sure the Pakis knew he was here and what he was doing. His supporters had wanted to incite anger in them, riling them up good and proper. Looked like they'd succeeded. A nod from Michael told him *they'd* been spotted converging on the park from the top end. Now, it was time for the carefully choreographed finale.

Grinning, he calmed the crowd, and as the first group of thugs approached, he raised his voice and said, 'The time is *now*. No more concessions to Islam, no more mosques and temples in our city. No more deviant behaviour. No more job stealers, benefit thieves and filth. No more immigrants. We ... are ... Christian! We ... are ... British!'

As the crowd erupted in cheers, groups of angry Asians began to run towards City Hall. The police, on alert, moved to divert the youth. Graeme Weston quietly moved off the steps and, flanked by his bodyguards, sidled to the side car park where the *Bradford Chronicle* journalist, Jez Hopkins, waited, as arranged.

As the angry clash between his supporters and the Asians erupted, Weston grinned. It was all part of the plan. His supporters had been instructed to back away. Not to respond. To let the Pakis throw the first punch. Hopkins' cameraman would record it all, and in the papers tomorrow morning would be vindication of his beliefs.

He glanced at Michael, who, face red with exertion, ran up to him. 'Well?'

Hogg grinned. '*Exactly* as we'd planned. Two Pakis arrested, and our lot are backing off. The police focus is on *them* now, and that's what will be reported.'

'Brilliant! You've excelled yourself, Michael.' And he thumped his second-in-command on the back, before turning to greet the waiting reporter. Extending his arms for a double-handed handshake, Graeme shook his head. 'Freedom of speech in this country, *and* in this city, is seriously at risk. Those people don't want to listen to what the majority say. They want to take over our city and make it into a mini Pakistan. Do you know what they call Bradford?' He shook his head, his lips curled in disgust. 'Bradistan, that's what they call our beautiful city. This is unacceptable. We need to reclaim it before it's too late.'

Chapter 7

21:30 Hawthorn Drive, Eccleshill

Coconut fragrance filled Christine Weston's bathroom. She inhaled the intense aroma as she lit each of the candles dotted around the spacious en-suite. Steam floated around her, and the gentle gurgle of water flowing into her bath soothed her. With a languid motion, she swirled her hand through the liquid, dispersing the bath oil and creating a luxurious flurry of bubbles.

Turning the taps off, she pulled her hair up into an untidy knot and began to undress. As she peeled her knickers down her legs, the musky scent of sex teased her nostrils. Remembering what she'd been doing only an hour earlier, she purred deep in her throat like a smug cat with an excess of cream. As she moved, her muscles protested, reminding her of just *how* athletic they'd been. Her smile widened as she inhaled more deeply, the smell arousing her again. Naked now, she lowered herself into the bath, gasping with pleasure as the warmth engulfed her. Leaning her head back against the plastic cushion, she flopped her knees apart, savouring the sensation of lapping water against her genitals. With a sigh, she closed her eyes and lowered her hand beneath the foam. Allowing herself to relive the experience, she shuddered, once more, to orgasm.

Afterwards, still glowing in the aftermath, her heart rate returned to normal. She soaped her body to get rid of the evidence. *Amazing how a bit of illicit sex can spice things up.*

Later, snuggled in her towelling bathrobe, the belt drawn tightly around her slender waist, she applied moisturiser to her face and body. After a quick squirt of Tiffany eau de parfum, she left her room, pausing to glance in at her son, who, headphones on, was oblivious to her presence at his bedroom door. He'd been poorly again, and she was glad that now he seemed happy, nodding in time to whatever Ed Sheeran song he was currently into. His body looked disproportionate, all angles and gangly limbs, as he waited to grow into his new adolescent frame. Despite tugging his fringe down to try to cover them, a smattering of angry pimples was visible on his brow. Jacob had many obstacles in his life, yet he coped with them all, displaying a maturity lacking in many adults. She was tempted to walk over and ruffle his tousled chestnut hair and drop a kiss on his head, but he wouldn't thank her for that, so she contented herself with one last glance.

She headed downstairs to wait for her husband to come back from whichever boring meeting he was at tonight. Switching lights on as she moved through the house, she entered the kitchen and opened the American-sized fridge. She took out the open bottle of white wine and retrieved the packet of Dairy Milk chocolate from where she'd hidden it behind the lettuce in the salad tray so Jacob wouldn't snaffle it.

Wine glass in hand, she reached over the sink to close the blind, and glancing into the garden, she was startled to see movement in the darkness beyond. The wine glass slid from her fingers and shattered as she strained to see what had made her jump. The sound of something banging into the recycling bin made her jolt again, and she backed away from the window, one hand to her mouth, the other clutching the top of her robe closed around her throat, as if that would offer protection from whatever was outside. Her eyes became more accustomed to the darkness, and then, with a relieved giggle, she saw the white tip of the fox's tail as it strolled into the middle of the lawn. It paused, turning its head back towards the side gate before running into the gloom at the back of the garden.

Ever since they'd moved into this house, Christine had been nervous on her own. It was one of her husband's property developer builds, and although she hadn't told him, she'd never liked it. She found the heavy foliage and giant trees around the periphery of the large garden oppressive. She'd have much preferred a smaller, less melodramatic home with a garden that didn't necessitate a monthly overhaul by a gardener who leered at her. However, such decisions were not hers to make. Her husband, keen to aspire to greater social class, placed great stock by such things. Instead, she'd diverted her anxieties into making the inner décor warm and welcoming for her son.

Feeling foolish, she shook her head and lowered the blinds before walking over to the alarm control panel by the back door. Hmph, as usual, someone, probably Graeme, had turned off the outdoor motion sensor. Typical bloody skinflint! He'd spend a fortune on a status symbol like Hawthorn Lodge yet, saving a few pennies was more important than her feeling secure in her own home. It wasn't the first time he'd done this, and it really annoyed her. He always said, he 'paid the bills.' As if *she* didn't work. As if *her* job wasn't worthwhile. Granted, her salary was nowhere near as large as his, but at least she wasn't idle. Sometimes, she thought that the only reason he allowed her to work was so he could moan about how little she earned.

She flicked the sensor on and was reassured when the external lights remained off. She shuddered. Surely, nobody was out there. She chided herself. Of course not. Why the hell would there be someone in their back garden on a Sunday evening in February? Anyone that was out there would have had to access their property via the alley behind the lower semis. The ones that Graeme had taken so much care to obscure. Then, they'd have to be determined enough to squeeze their way through dense bushes, work their way up the steep slope and climb the barricades he'd erected as extra protection from the unwashed masses beneath. Stupid. No-one in their right minds would do that. Despite Graeme's elevated sense of his own value, they weren't important enough … not rich enough.

With a sigh, she picked up the larger shards of glass from the sink and wrapped them in newspaper before placing them in the bin and washing away the tiny splinters that remained. Thank God she hadn't decided to use one of the crystal glasses. Graeme would have gone spare if she had. With any luck, he'd never notice this one was gone. She couldn't be bothered with yet another lecture about her clumsiness. Taking another glass from the cupboard and picking up her chocolate, she wandered through to the living room, dimming the lights as she went.

Snuggled in the oversized sofa, she activated the Bluetooth and selected her easy listening playlist before reaching over and picking up the remote control for the curtains. Still unsettled from her earlier fright, she peered out the window. The external lights remained off, yet she couldn't shake off the feeling of being watched. Pressing the remote, she was happier, more secure, when the curtains closed with a near-silent swish. No bogeyman could get her now! She grinned, poured herself some wine and unwrapped her chocolate. Might as well end the evening in the same spirit of indulgence as the rest of the day … after all, her peace would be spoiled as soon as Graeme got back.

Chapter 8

The Eccleshill streets are almost empty. The cold night-time drizzle has sent people indoors, and there is that Sunday night feel to the evening. Only a few groups of lads loitering outside the chip shop and a few couples, arms linked, walking back from the Craven Heifer pub, break the silence. Nobody pays me any attention as I edge along the street, head down and hood up. Earlier, I'd parked two streets away from the Weston's cul-de-sac, on the main road in front of the chippie. Sandwiched between a Land Rover and a Mercedes, my van isn't noteworthy. Heart still thudding from nearly being caught in the garden, I slide into the seat and flick the ignition on. The rush of adrenaline that had flooded my veins is wearing off now, and shivers are taking over.

Reaching over, I switch the heating on and breathe in a long sigh of relief. She'd been staring right at me through the darkness. I could see her clearly by the light from behind her, and when she'd been distracted by the dropped glass, my only option had been to sneak away like a thief through the night. It was very annoying, though, that the recycling bin had been in the way. Thank goodness the fox had been startled and run onto the lawn. It had been a close thing. A very close thing, but it was important to be sure Christine was back home where she should be.

In this game, timing is everything, and after her earlier indiscretions, it pays to be careful. She'd get her comeuppance, no doubt about that. Shame, though, that there'd be no witnesses to her retribution. Couldn't risk it again. She'd turned on the motion sensor, so there'd be no more prowling until it was turned off again … maybe the chance would come to do that tomorrow or the next day at the latest. In the meantime, a low profile is probably in order. Besides which, I have better things to do tonight. More important things. Things that will teach that silly woman a thing or two. Maybe then she'll appreciate what she has, and what she is risking.

Chapter 9

11:15 Hawthorn Drive, Eccleshill

She must have dozed off. The first thing that told her that her husband was home, was the sound of something slamming onto the top of the glass coffee table, sending her glass shuddering across it. Toppling over, it shattered as it hit the table top, sending a gush of wine onto the carpet. Heart thumping, Christine struggled to pull herself out from the depths of the plush sofa that was attempting to swallow her whole. Her eyes blinked at the sudden harshness of the living room lights that, presumably, Graeme had switched to full power when he had come in. Mesmerised, she watched the spilled wine as it pooled by the edge of the table before dripping slowly off the edge. *Thank God she hadn't chosen the red.*

Conscious that the belt of her robe had worked its way undone, Christine pulled the flaps together over her naked thighs and, with frantic fingers, nipped the collar together to cover her breasts. Flashing anxious glances from her husband to the still dripping wine, she struggled to sit up. It was then she noticed the brown envelope that had nudged the stem of the wine glass. Frowning, she glanced at her husband. His eyes flashed, and a scowl pulled his brows together, darkening his expression. He wasn't a big man, yet when he was angry, he had a tendency to puff out his chest like a bullfrog. His engorged body encroached on her space, dwarfing her. Right now, he seemed to fill the room. His blond hair stood out in angry spikes, his face was a ball of florid anger.

Christine still clutched her dressing gown, soothed by its softness and the fabric conditioner scent released by her touch. Her voice was tremulous when she spoke. 'What is it, Graeme? Is something wrong?'

Graeme Weston spun away from his wife and marched over to the drinks cabinet. With staccato movements that set her nerves even more on edge, he poured himself a large brandy before flinging himself into the chair opposite her. Poised now, on the very edge of the sofa, she forced herself to stop kneading her robe and instead placed her hands in her lap, one on each thigh. She waited as Graeme sipped his drink, his dark eyes never leaving her face. The colour rose over Christine's cheeks in a hot flush. She refused to ask again what was wrong. He wouldn't speak until he was ready.

Casting a sideways glance at the envelope, she wondered what was inside. Probably some manifesto or article he'd written about the dangers of jihadists in Bradford or Muslim immigrants and the Caliphate. She hoped he wasn't going to ask her to proofread it for him. The poison that dripped so easily from his tongue made her feel sick. Yet, she stayed with him; she had little choice. It wasn't as if she was strong enough to argue against him. Deep down, she despised herself for failing to challenge him. So, in order to cope, she compartmentalised. Sometimes, she wondered what the liberal people she worked with would think of her husband's toxic views. If only things were different. If only *she* was different.

She heard him release a deep breath. When he leaned back in the armchair and crossed his legs, she knew he was nearly ready to get whatever had put him in such a bad mood off his chest. 'Go on then, Christine, *darling*. Take a look.' He inclined his head to the envelope, his eyes never leaving her face. His voice was steady, although his tone betrayed his underlying tension. She'd seen him like this before, and it never ended well for her.

Heart beating faster, her palms started to sweat. She wiped them down her robe and hesitated. Whatever was inside the envelope was something *she* wasn't going to like. With a trembling hand, she picked it up. Maintaining eye contact with her husband, she opened it and slid the contents partway out. Flicking a glance down, she saw that they were photographs.

'Well, *love*. Have a proper look.' he said, his cloying voice at odds with his expression. To an outsider, Graeme would look very calm. Christine, though, knew the tell-tale signs. The narrowing of his eyes, the cynical half-smile, the way he tapped his fingers on his knee... she knew he was barely holding on to his temper. Her breath caught in her throat, and a sinking dread made her mouth dry. She turned the envelope over so the front of the top photo was visible and gasped. Whatever she'd expected, it wasn't this. How could this have happened? Where had Graeme got these foul images, and who had taken them?

Tears blurring her vision, she risked a peep up at him, and then, seeing his tight lips, she directed her gaze once more, at the photo. There, in front of her, was an image of herself, mouth half-open, head thrown back, throat exposed, eyes closed in mid-orgasm, as she straddled a man who was not her husband. Fighting against the panic that pounded in her chest when she saw her husband stand up, she, too, jumped to her feet. As her eyes darted upwards to meet his gaze, he backhanded her across the cheek, sending her head ricocheting backwards with the force.

'Stupid bitch! You couldn't even be discreet, could you?'

Monday

Chapter 10

02:30 The Kill Site

It is getting to be a habit, this sneaking away in the middle of the night; however, I am getting good at it. Nobody noticed, and I have to say, it feels good to be doing something proactive. Something productive and meaningful, for a change. This time had been easier than the others. He'd been walking back from the pub – oh, what a good Muslim *he* is; fornicating, committing adultery and drinking alcohol. The sooner he meets his Allah, the better.

I laugh, remembering his startled face as he walked past the van, and I jumped out. He was too drunk to react, and I was very quick. I've always been agile, and a drunk Paki is no match for me. This one was special to me, almost personal, in a warped sort of way. I knew he'd take the shortcut from the Old Boar in Thornbury, down the back alley behind his house and in his back door. I hid in the shadows of the wheelie bins and waited until he passed before injecting him from behind. Dragging him into the van, I tied him up in less than two minutes. One for *The Guinness Book of Records,* I would think. Don't suppose they monitor that sort of thing, though.

I'm getting fed up waiting for him to come around. Tara's a bit unsociable as well tonight. She's had her treat and is now rubbing her neck against the tree. Horses are fickle beasts – well, some of them, anyway. The other two horses have never been over-friendly. Only Tara sees fit to keep me company through the night. I had wondered if I was taking a risk driving right through the gate onto the field. Considering the entrance is so far from the main road and the track is rarely used, I think it's safe enough. As long as I am gone by daybreak, I'll be fine.

Anyway, I don't leave any trace behind. I bag up my ink cartridges, gloves and suit and dump them in different bins all over Bradford. Some I even fling in the canal, although I don't really like doing that – polluting our lovely waterways and killing off wildlife. Who knows what toxins are in those inks? After all, they are quite old. They'd come with the machine when I bought it from the old antique shop months ago, and they didn't have a sell-by date on them. Nowadays, according to the man in the shop, tattooists have all sorts of hoops to go through: sell-by dates on the inks, numbing wipes, sterile wipes, aftercare rules. Not that any of that stuff applies to me. My 'clients' don't need any aftercare, and I don't much care about the rest anyway.

He'll be waking up any minute, so I cast a last look at Tara and head inside to put my 'uniform' on. I'm looking forward to hearing Razaul Ul Haq's cries, and I've already chosen my dump site. This was going to be *so* much better than the others. I might not even wear my ear defenders for this one. Get the full benefit of his pain.

Chapter 11

Christine pulled into her usual parking spot in the school car park and leaned her head on the head rest for a second before giving herself a mental shake and sitting up. Flicking the sun shield down, she opened the mirror and checked her face. Her fingers moved over her cheek, and with lips tightening, she studied the slight bruising her foundation failed to conceal.

Despite the events of the previous night, she'd risen early and had chivvied Jacob to get ready for school. He'd been poorly over the weekend. His condition had flared up, and he'd been in a lot of pain, but it had eased now, and Christine was reluctant to let him stay at home. He was in Year Nine, and she knew he needed to be in school. He'd quizzed her about their argument the previous night, and she'd deflected, saying it was about the broken wine glass.

Satisfied she'd done the best she could to hide the bruise, she pushed open the door and slid from the car, at the same time as Mr Dhanjal, the physics teacher, got out of his.

Smiling, she sent a half-wave in his direction and was surprised when he frowned at her and hurried ahead. Looked like she wasn't the only one with family troubles. Turning to pick up her handbag from the passenger seat, she locked the car and headed towards the ultra-modern school building.

As she walked, she became aware of a couple of the sixth-form pupils staring at her and whispering. Recognising

Seema Patel, who was one of the students she mentored, she smiled and was surprised when Seema scowled at her and turned her back. Christine faltered, debating whether to stop and challenge the girl or wait until class. Then, seeing it was nearly registration time, and she still had to drop her bag in the staff room, she kept on going. Entering the reception area, she smiled at the receptionist as she signed in and was surprised when her greeting was ignored. What was going on? It was as if she was in a play, and everyone else knew the plot, bar her.

As she moved along the corridor, she was aware of whispers and snide glances and her heart started to quicken. Surely her indiscretion couldn't have reached the attention of the pupils and staff she worked with. Surely Graeme wouldn't have broadcast it. She gave herself a shake. What was she thinking? Of course, Graeme wouldn't broadcast *that*. Perhaps someone else had. Knowing her cheeks were flushed, Christine pushed open the staff room door and walked in to a babble of chatter. As soon as the teachers registered her presence, their chatter trailed off, and instead of their normal cheery greetings, some of them turned away, heads down, avoiding her glance. Others stared straight at her, their faces tight and scornful.

The smile faded from her lips as she realised even her closest friends in the school had made no effort to greet her. Swallowing, she took a step forward, ignoring the pools of sweat gathering in her armpits and said, 'Is someone going to tell me what's going on?'

A few of the teachers mumbled under their breath and moved to the side. Mr Dhanjal, on the contrary, stepped forward, waving a copy of the *Bradford Chronicle* in the air. His eyes flashed, and his voice shook as he almost spat at her. 'What's going on? What the hell do you think is going on? Did you expect us not to react to *this*?' He thrust the newspaper at her, forcing Christine to take a step back. 'How can you expect us to work with you now?'

Christine paled. Surely the *Bradford Chronicle* hadn't somehow got hold of those photos. Please, God, not that. Moving like a robot, she stretched out her hand and took the paper from him, almost not daring to look. Glancing round the room, she saw everyone was looking at her, waiting for her reaction. Closing her eyes, she took a deep, steadying breath, and then, opening them again, she flapped the paper so she could see the lead article. Lowering her eyes to the front-page headlines, she gasped. For a long moment, she remained motionless, blinking in disbelief at what she saw.

Her frown deepened as she absorbed the extent of her husband's treachery. This was the *real* punishment for her indiscretion. He knew she worked in the biggest and most diverse inner-city school in Bradford, and he'd left her to walk into the lion's den this morning unprepared and unaware of this headline. How could she continue to work here after this? Nausea rose in her throat, and she let the paper drop to the floor as she stumbled to the staff toilets, the newspaper headlines branded on her eyeballs. *'Graeme Weston, local business man, to represent Albion First in the upcoming by-election in newly formed Bradford City constituency.'*

Chapter 12

The early morning drizzle had, as promised by the forecasters, given way to snow at around nine o'clock and grown in intensity in the intervening hour and a half. Dr Fergus McGuire, muffled by a long scarf and wearing a huge overcoat, shivered as he glanced around.

The cordoned-off area was like a quagmire, having been trampled over by numerous booted feet. Trees, still stripped of their leaves, looked forlorn against the unaccustomed activity, whilst the few evergreens, with their branches bending under the snow, seemed to be bowing in supplication. His feet were cold in his wellies, and he wished he'd taken the extra few seconds to don the second pair of thick socks Corrine had proffered when he had gotten the call. You'd think, after thirty years of marriage, he'd heed his wife's advice. Corrine was seldom wrong. Perhaps her many years as a paediatric consultant had made her infallible, or perhaps everything she'd struggled against to achieve excellence in her chosen career had necessitated efficiency. Whatever it was, whether in the hospital or at home, his petite wife was a force to be reckoned with.

Slipping and skidding his way down the crude uneven steps from the top of Ashwell Road into the woods, he hardly noticed his surroundings. A waiting constable guided him to his left into the depths of the woods where the body lay, now covered by a crime scene tent. Dotted around the area were a series of markers and floor plates placed to protect evidence. As the crow flies, he was a mere ten-minute, strenuous trek uphill to his own house at the top of the woods behind Shay Golf Course, on the back road towards Cottingley, but it seemed like a different world.

He shivered. Never had the prospect of his study with its huge open fire been so appealing. Feeling a tickle at his nose, he plunged his hand into his pocket withdrawing a linen handkerchief, with which he barely managed to contain the explosive sneeze. Glancing around, he had the satisfaction of seeing at least two of the officers had jumped at the sudden noise. He grinned. Good to keep them on their toes.

'Sorry, boys.' Folding the hanky, he wiped his streaming eyes and reconciled himself to taking off his overcoat and replacing its snug warmth with the thin crime scene suit he so detested. If he could work effectively in his coat, he would, but he knew he'd feel too restricted. Besides which, he wasn't sure they had a large enough suit to cover both him and his bulky coat.

A young officer he didn't recognise appeared by his side wearing a smile that was far too cheery for the weather conditions. Offering a suit and shoe covers to the Doctor, he said, 'Body's in there. We're waiting for the DI.'

Fergus knew that 'the DI' would be Angus in his role as senior investigating officer, and he hoped his son had managed to get some rest since he'd last seen him at the morgue. He took his coat off and thrust it towards the officer before struggling into the overalls, saying, 'Make sure you keep that dry, laddie. I've already got a cold, and if it turns into pneumonia because I've had to put on a wet coat after hours wi' only a bloody bunny suit for warmth, I ken who I'll be suing, okay?'

'Yes, sir.' The officer, looking apprehensive, bundled the coat in his arms and stumbled through the snow in the direction of a crime scene van that had managed to drive into the woods through the Park Drive entrance. In the process, no doubt, it had obliterated foliage, churned up turf and ground leaves and mud into unsightly whirls. The Heaton Woods Trust wouldn't be happy about that, however, what was the alternative?

Pushing one wellied foot into the depths of the overall, whilst attempting to keep the rest of it off the muddy damp ground, was proving difficult. Cursing, Fergus hopped on one foot like a ballet dancing elephant in a tutu. He attempted to pull the suit up one leg to his groin before trying to shove the second in. Without warning, his rubber-soled boot slipped on a clump of squelching muck, and he skidded. Whilst maintaining a pincer grip on the body of his overall with one hand, he reached out with the other snatching at twigs on a nearby tree, and swearing as each one broke under his weight. At last, he managed to grab a sturdy branch and pull himself upright. Maintaining as dignified a stance as his ridiculous antics allowed, he ignored the giggles from the few officers who'd witnessed the event.

Leaning against the tree, his face hot with a combination of embarrassment and exertion, he manoeuvred his other leg inside, and with a series of wiggles, yanked it up over his rounded belly. Next, he thrust his arms through the sleeves, pulled it over his shoulders and zipped it up, before turning to face the still giggling men. 'Shut up, you lot! Never seen a man fall before? Well, let me tell youse: if I'd landed on my arse, and you lot had just stood there, wi' glaickit looks on your stupid puses, you'd be chortling on the other sides o' yer faces now.'

One of the officers shook his head and wiped the laughter tears from his eyes. 'That right, Doc? You and whose army?'

'Och, away wi' ye. You useless bloody galoot,' said Fergus, laughing now alongside them. Well aware his capers would have lightened the darkness of the moment, he didn't grudge them that.

As he'd been talking, the same PC who'd taken his coat approached. Taking two pairs of nitrile gloves and surgical mask from him, Fergus yanked the hood over his head, dangled the mask round his neck and pulled on both pairs of gloves. As he did so, he noticed Angus, dreads flaring out behind him, gambolling like a sure-footed lion down the very same steps he had traversed, somewhat less elegantly, minutes earlier.

Taking a moment to observe his son, Fergus was pleased to see his limp had almost gone. All his jogging and the hours spent at the gym were paying off. As the laddie neared, Fergus sighed. Shame the same couldn't be said for the boy's mental health. The lines in his forehead and his sunken cheeks showed he was clearly still wracked with grief, and his pallor indicated sleep had not been a large part of his weekend. Fergus would have been less concerned if he'd thought the lad had been out partying. How long could the boy continue like this? Still reeling from the loss of his best friend, Angus had been flung back into two traumatic cases, one after the other. What he needed was a holiday. A complete break away from all this for a while, but would he listen? Would he hell! He was as stubborn as his mother.

Raising a hand in greeting, he continued into the tent, knowing Angus would join him when he was suited-up and would, no doubt, be full of questions. He already knew it was the body of a young, naked Asian man, and what he wanted to ascertain was just how similar this scene was to the other two. Using the stepping plates set out already by the scene of crime officers, he approached the young man. What a tragic waste!

Straight away, he saw the body had been laid out like the other two men. The victim's feet were crossed at the ankles and his arms extended out at shoulder level. His clothes had been folded in a neat pile near his head. Presumably, they'd been cut off him in the same way as the other two; however, he'd wait until he got to the lab to look at them properly.

He nodded to a nearby SOCO. 'You can bag these now, if you like.'

He watched the SOCO open a plastic sheet onto which he placed the clothes. Opening each item, he shook it onto the plastic to catch any debris whilst another SOCO took photos of each part of the process. Didn't look like there was much forensic evidence there, but you never knew. They might get lucky.

'Sliced off, like the other victims?' asked Fergus, as the SOCO held up a shirt.

'Looks like it. Up the seams to the armpits and then along each arm.' Placing the shirt in a paper bag, he moved onto the victim's jeans. 'These have been sliced up the outer leg to the waist. Belt's here too.'

'Any ID?' asked Fergus.

'No, nothing.'

'Maybe DI McGuire will already have been notified of a missing person. That would certainly help speed up the investigation.'

As the SOCO repeated the process with each item, Fergus turned his attention to the prone body. Two scene of crime officers waited, one with a camera ready to document his examination, the other ready to assist, where necessary. Above their masks, their anxious glances told him they wanted him to crack on so they could get the body moved. Once they'd erected the tent around the body and searched the wider area, they were obliged to wait for him, before they could transfer the body to the morgue.

Kneeling beside the victim, Dr McGuire switched on his tape recorder and declared the victim dead. He then commenced his initial observation of the corpse prior to having it removed to the mortuary to await the post-mortem. 'Naked body of an Asian male, probably early thirties, lying prone in freezing conditions. Significant bruising to the neck, torso and limbs. Groin area shaved, with a fresh tattoo of a swastika inexpertly applied, above the penis. Injection site on neck.'

As Hissing Sid, the Head Scene of Crime Officer, approached, Dr McGuire nodded. Together, the two men rolled the body onto its front. The pathologist examined the back. 'Lividity is consistent with the body being moved here soon after death. Pressure marks in a grid type shape show the body lay horizontally elsewhere for a short time after death.'

He finished his examination, taking note of body temperature and doing as thorough an external check as he could. The rest would wait until he was back at the morgue. As he struggled back to his feet, the insidious cold making his movements stiff, the tent flap was pushed aside, and Angus walked in.

'Hello, Angus. Looks like we've got another one. Same puncture site on the neck; and the same swastika, inexpertly tattooed in groin area, probably ante-mortem; along with a similar dump site.'

Gus, his dreads covered by the hood of his 'abominables,' shuffled over and approached the body as Sid said, 'Can we wrap and pack him, Doc?'

Dr McGuire rolled his eyes. He was used to Sid's down-to-earth manner, although treating the victim like a slab of meat was really a wee bit too much. 'No, but you *can* wrap him and transport him to the mortuary as respectfully as possible, if ye like.'

Sid grinned. 'That's what I said, Doc, 'wrap and pack.'" And bending over to help his assistant transfer the man into a body bag, he released a thunderous fart.

Taking a step backwards, Dr McGuire banged a fist onto his chest near his heart. 'Your sensitive nature gets me here every time, Sid. You need to toughen up a wee bit, develop a thicker skin. Dinnae want you letting all this death get to you.'

As the noxious fumes filled the tent, Gus strode over to the door and opened the flap. 'For fuck's sake, Sid, get your stinking arse outside if you're going to do that.' As he spoke, his nostrils flared, and his lips tightened. 'I'm not telling you again. It's fucking vile ... and while you're at it, show some respect for the dead. I don't want to complain to your line manager; however, if you don't develop some professionalism, I bloody well will. Got it?'

Hearing the simmering anger in his son's words, Dr McGuire exchanged a quick glance with Sid and shook his head, intimating that the other man should let it lie. Angus didn't usually let the scene of crime officer get to him like that. He'd worked with the man long enough to accept his idiosyncrasies for the coping mechanism they were. His son's short temper was another sure sign things were not good for him at the minute; however, he needed to control it. He couldn't go mouthing off like that to his colleagues.

As Gus exited the tent, Dr McGuire laid a huge hand on Sid's arm. 'Sorry about that. Ye ken he's no' in a good place at the minute. He doesn't mean anything by it.'

Sid sighed. 'Yeah, I know, Doc. There's only so much we can take, though. It's not only me on the receiving end of his tongue, you know? He's had a go at most of my staff, and I pity any officers working with him. Don't know how Compo and Sampson cope. Get my drift?'

'Aye, I ken exactly what ye mean, laddie. He's no' coping very well. Grief's a hard thing to live wi'.' He bit his lip and sighed, wondering when Angus would move through this.

Sid nodded to his assistants, who'd lifted the body onto a stretcher. 'Yeah, well … he needs to get over it, for all our damn sakes.'

Chapter 13

12:15 The Fort

The February snow continued to fall outside the window as Gus, a mug of coffee in his hand, stared at the mesmerising swirl of flakes. The heat in the incident room was beginning to thaw out his frozen toes, and the coffee mug was doing the same with his fingers. He knew he'd been an idiot with Sid, and he'd noticed the exchange of glances between Sid and his dad. Shit, he was a complete arse, and he knew he deserved more than a few surreptitious glances for his behaviour. Sid did a cracking job in difficult circumstances, and he never *ever* moaned.

Sid's somewhat unorthodox humour was a coping mechanism, and Gus knew that. He'd been completely out of order. The more he tried to subdue the venom that sprung to his lips, the less able he was to contain it. The bitterness burst out against his will. It was as if he was goading them to get a reaction. He did the same with his parents *and* Sampson *and* Compo, and there was no damn excuse for it. It had to stop.

Turning from the window, he thrust his fingers through his dreads and took a deep breath. The two-month delay before the funeral had affected everyone, not him alone, and when it had finally happened, he had felt like she'd broken his heart all over again. Being so close to her and knowing he'd never share a conversation with her again … or touch her … or breath the same air as her, was unbearable. He'd very nearly snapped.

His dad kept banging on about grief and adjusting and everything. Gus knew it was more than grief … it was guilt. And no-one knew better than him how destructive guilt could be. Hearing Sampson and Compo approach from the corridor, he moved to the coffee machine, refilled his mug and was ready by the crime boards when they pushed the door open and entered.

Pretending to ignore the nervous looks they exchanged, Gus attempted a smile, which, he noticed, made them look even more nervous. Shit! He really did have a lot of making up to do. Trouble was, he wasn't sure he had it in him at the moment. Although Dr Mahmood had increased his medication, it made no difference. He barely had enough energy to function, never mind keep up with the niceties of being part of a team. He was no bloody motivational leader right now. Trying to ignore the flutter of palpitations in his chest, he sipped his coffee, hoping to get rid of his dry mouth, and began the briefing.

'Uniform have been able to identify the most recent victim as Razaul Ul Haq, a British Asian of Bangladeshi descent, who has lived in Bradford for all of his 38 years. Although we're still waiting for the PM, early indications show the same person is responsible for this man's murder. We need to work out where the three victims intersect, for I'm sure they do. They must have something in common. A common link between them and their killer.'

'You don't think its random then?' asked Sampson.

Biting his lip, Gus considered the question. 'No. I don't see how it can be. It seems pre-meditated to me. Like they've been targeted. The fact the abductions are so smooth, eliciting no attention from passers-by, smacks to me of organisation. Early reports indicate Ul Haq had been at the pub and was then taken from the alleyway behind his house. I'd say, he was followed.'

Sampson nodded and wrote a note on his pad, whilst Gus moved over and leaned against his desk. 'Ul Haq has twin daughters but was estranged from his wife. Unfortunately, we are unlikely to get much information from her, as she is currently in Lynfield Mount, sectioned under the Mental Health Act. The daughters, however, are seventeen and their guardians, Ul Haq's brother and sister-in-law, have given permission for them to be interviewed at their school, City Academy on Manchester Road. You'll come with me, Compo.'

Compo, mouth filled with a half-chewed bacon butty, tried to swallow; instead, he started to choke, coughing so hard, his eyes watered. Sampson jumped to his feet and hammered on his friend's back until Compo succeeded in swallowing the offending food.

Eyes still watering, he said, 'Me? Me? You want me to go with you? No, surely not, Gus. Not me. I'm rubbish at that sort of stuff.' He wiped the arm of his long-sleeved T-shirt over his still streaming eyes and shook his head.

Smiling, Gus said, 'You're a detective, Compo. I *know* your strengths lie in the techie stuff, nevertheless, I'd be doing you a disservice if I didn't train you up in other areas.' Gus could tell Compo was far from convinced. It made no difference; he was determined to extend the lad's skill set. He realised it wasn't only the change in role that was upsetting Compo. It was the prospect of spending time with Gus. Well, it seemed like he had his work cut out for him.

Splaying his arms in front of him and trying to smile in a non-threatening way, he said, 'This isn't a punishment, for Christ's sake, Comps. It's called 'professional development,' and you're doing it, okay?'

Compo opened his mouth to reply, but before he could release the barrage of protestations Gus knew was on the tip of his tongue, the door was thrust open. It banged against the newly painted wall, reverberating for a moment before stilling. Flecks of paint floated onto the carpet from the dent in the wall where the handle had connected. Three heads turned to the door to be greeted by a smiling face, followed by the diminutive body of their visitor.

Before he had a chance to respond to the interruption, Compo and Sampson, in a flurry of excitement, jumped to their feet and rushed over to greet the dark-haired woman. Incomprehensible chatter spouted from their mouths as they escorted her over to Gus' comfy chair. Feeling bemused and uncertain, Gus followed behind. From nowhere, it seemed, Sampson produced a mug of coffee, and Compo relinquished one of his coveted supply of Mars Bars to their visitor. With a satisfied sigh, she tore the wrapper off, took a huge bite and chewed. Her eyes sparkled with mischief as she watched them.

Gus ran his fingers through his dreads and bit his lip. A prickling sensation behind his eyes was making them water, and he didn't know what to say. He tried to speak, but his throat was clagged up, as if he were the one chomping on the Mars Bar. Stepping forward, he studied the woman. Eyes raking her pallid face, he noted the newly formed lines that flared out across her forehead. His gaze moved down her body. The sight of her too-big clothes hanging on her skeletal frame made his heart clench. He was unsure of himself. How should he react? He moved his eyes upwards again and met her gaze.

Jumping to her feet, she yanked him into a hug with a strength contrary to her fragile appearance. Almost immediately, she pushed him away at arms' length, and with a huge grin that lit up her entire face, Alice said, 'You miss me then, Gus?'

Swallowing the obstacle that clogged up his throat, he sniffed, and ignoring the muscle that pulsed in his cheek, grinned back. This was the happiest he'd been in months. 'Missed your damn cheek, that's all.'

Frowning, he realised no-one had told him she was coming. This worried him for he was sure she wasn't fit for a return to work yet. Guilt that he hadn't visited her in hospital, like the others had, gripped him. He was such a fucking coward. He should have been there for her, instead of wallowing in self-indulgent guilt. What sort of friend was he? When *he'd* been hurt, fighting for his life, Alice had practically parked herself at the hospital. Yet, when she'd needed *him*, he'd cowered away like the spineless bastard he was. Even when she'd been released, he'd avoided her, despite his mum and dad's nagging. Covering up his feelings made his voice come out all gruff and accusing when he said, 'Should you even be here, Al?'

Alice's eyes narrowed, and then, she shrugged. 'Looks like DCI Chalmers pulled some strings with Doc Mahmood.'

Gus' shoulders tightened, and he glared at her, his eyes narrowed. 'What the fuck do you mean, she pulled some strings with the Doc? I'm not happy with that, Al. You need to recover fully before you come back to work.'

Alice waved a dismissive hand. 'You can talk, Gus. Wasn't so long ago she did the exact same thing for you, didn't she?'

Her words hit home. Gus couldn't deny it; Nancy had pulled strings to get him back to work the Matchmaker Case.

'You and me are the same, Gus,' she said, 'We need our work to get us through this shit. You know it, and I know it. I *need* to be here. It's the best therapy for me. I'm physically fit too. More to the point, *you* need me.' She stared at him long and hard, her eyes serious for a change. 'I saw how you were at Sadia's dad's funeral, *and* I saw how she ignored you. Your dad says you're grieving, and your mum says you're wracked with guilt over what happened to me. Well, you can stop that bloody nonsense right now, okay?' She prodded him twice in the chest.

Gus shook his head. 'Ouch Al ... that hurt!' And, thankful she hadn't opted to hit him on the arm where his new tattoo was, he rubbed his chest.

She snorted. 'That's because it was meant to. You need to get on top of this stupid, self-pitying guilt shit.'

Aware Compo and Sampson were grinning like a pair of Cheshire cats, he walked over to pour himself more coffee. His gurgling stomach and the caffeine headache that throbbed at his temples, told him more coffee was the last thing he needed ... still. Alice was right. He was a mess. Losing Sadia, on top of nearly losing Al, had almost broken him. It was easy for her to tell him to get over it, though.

Following him, she placed her hands on her hips and glared. To Gus, she appeared like a more fragile, yet equally assertive version of her old self. Her tone was scathing. 'You're in denial, Gus. You barely visited me in hospital. I didn't want your damn flowers or chocolates; I wanted *you*. You, of all people, should have known that, especially after what happened with Greg and Billy.'

Gus bowed his head with a curt nod, however, Alice wasn't finished.

'You never even spoke to me at that bloody funeral.'

Gus' head jerked up, and his eyes flashed, betraying his annoyance. 'I wasn't exactly welcome there, Al. Sadia made that perfectly clear, so although I had to toe the police line and be there, there was no way I was going to hang around for the social niceties.'

He took a slug of coffee and scalded his mouth, cursing as he swallowed it, feeling it burn every inch of his throat on the way down, before continuing, in a quieter voice, 'You're right, though, Al. I *should* have been there for you. Should have visited you, should've been your friend. Truth is, I did feel guilty. It was *my* fault. We should have waited for back-up.'

Alice exhaled. 'Aw, get a grip. What's it with you? The only one to blame was the bastard who pulled the trigger, and if my memory serves me right, he's been dealt with. So, man the fuck up, Gus, and let's get on with this case.'

Gus held her steady gaze for a second more and then smiled. It was so good to have her back. So good to see that she hadn't changed ... not inside anyway. He knew she'd be fine. With a glance at Compo and Sampson, both of whom were trying to look as if they weren't listening, he sighed and, with a shrug, said, 'Looks like DS Cooper's back. Bring her up to speed please, Sampson.'

And as Sampson updated Alice, he turned to Compo. 'Looks like you're off the hook, too. Might be better if I take a woman to interview the Ul Haq girls.'

Compo whooped and did a dance around the room, high-fiving Sampson and Alice as he went. Gus, a slight smile on his lips, said, 'Don't think you've escaped this, though. You do need to extend your skill set at some point.'

Chapter 14

With a mega-sized mug of strong Yorkshire tea steaming on his office desk and the morning's *Bradford Chronicle* laid out in front of him, Graeme Weston was happy. His grin showed it. Not only had the announcement that he was Albion First's candidate for the upcoming Bradford Central constituency by-election made the headlines, but Jez Hopkins' article also spanned over pages two and three. He was in the spotlight, and so were Albion First.

Albion First had distanced themselves from the BNP over the past few years, and this was their first bid for national recognition. Weston was proud his party had seen him as the way forward. He was no Farage, all soft policies and beer swilling. No, Albion First was a legitimate force for change, and *he* was the figurehead. Fast tracking Article 50 and Brexit were only the first steps in their plan. It would be swiftly followed by the repatriation of all European scroungers, calls for higher tax codes for non-British citizens working in the UK, and ultimately, the repatriation of second and third generation immigrants.

Grinning, he toyed with the idea of reclaiming the term 'white wash' as a slogan for his repatriation policies. Maybe he'd run that idea by the Generals. He knew it was a long-term strategy, however, he was convinced the political climate had never been more right for this sort of national cleansing. British ideals were continually being diluted by the rise of the jihadist Islamic extremists. He knew at grass-root level, the voters wanted them gone. At rallies, people told him so. His party had researched it, and with Trump's ascension in the USA, Britain would fall into line.

His thoughts were interrupted by his office door opening. Marcia Hogg, his PA, slid into the seat opposite his desk, crossed her legs and rested one arm over her knee. He pretended not to notice the length of thigh her actions had revealed. He'd no time for the sort of antics Marcia's husband Michael was so fascinated by. Although Marcia had a great body, she was his best friend's wife, and that was that.

An indulgent half-smile on her face, she shook her head. 'She's on the phone again, Graeme. I'm getting no work done fielding her calls all the time. You've got to speak to her at some point.'

Graeme smiled. He'd been ignoring Christine's increasingly frantic calls all morning and wasn't ready to speak to her yet. She'd deserved what she'd got. He hadn't wanted her to take that job in that bloody school. Neither had he wanted her to go around screwing Pakis. Nevertheless, she'd done that, too … as the photographic evidence he'd found on his desk yesterday evening had proved. If it hadn't been for that, he'd have given her advance warning of his intentions. The stupid cow only had herself, and her inability to keep her legs shut, to blame. Not that he could confide any of that to Marcia.

Marcia leaned forward, her blouse gaping at the neck. 'What's she done this time? You'd think she'd be happy with how successful last night was, wouldn't you?'

Graeme smiled. He'd never discussed Christine with Marcia, and he'd no intention of starting now. It didn't matter to him their marriage had long been a sham. The obsession that had tricked him into marrying her had long since abated, however, she *was* beautiful ... a real status wife, and that's what counted, wasn't it?

He didn't actually care she had frequent affairs. All he cared about was she was discreet. Now, her discretion was even more imperative. He wondered who'd put the photos on his desk. One of the builders or a client? Hell, sometimes, the place was like Piccadilly Circus, the number of people who trolled through. Especially recently, when he'd been using it as campaign headquarters and the venue for various caucuses he'd wanted kept secret from the wider Albion First members.

Someone had been following her, and that someone clearly had his back. They didn't want to go public with the info; they wanted him to stop it before her actions damaged the campaign. Well, that's what the typed note had said, anyway. That made him wonder if it was Michael Hogg.

Michael was professional, nothing got by him ... and he was loyal. He'd do whatever it took to remove any obstacle standing in Graeme's way, and he was astute enough to cover his tracks. Michael would see it as his responsibility to make him aware of anything that could threaten the effectiveness of their campaign. Graeme was under no illusion; he'd expect him to deal with it efficiently ... even if it was his wife who was the threat. But Michael wouldn't go in for subterfuge. If he'd found out about Christine's clandestine bedroom antics, he'd have come straight out and told him. Subtlety wasn't his strong suit. Thank God Michael wasn't privy to that other little secret he and Christine were keeping well and truly under wraps. No point prodding a sleeping tiger. Michael would be told *only* if it became necessary, and Graeme hoped it would never become a necessity.

He grinned at Marcia. 'She can stew for a bit longer. Won't do her any harm.'

Marcia pursed her lips. 'Maybe not, though, it's not you fielding her calls, is it? I've better things to be doing with my time. Michael wants me scheduling in some radio and television appearances for you. Of course,' she tutted, 'some of the 'trendy lefties' are refusing to share a platform with you. So much for freedom of speech, huh?'

Graeme rubbed his hands together. 'All the better for us, Marcia, all the better for us. It makes them look foolish. The public want to, no, they *deserve* to hear a frank exchange of ideas. The lefties' obstinacy will only play in our favour, mark my words. Albion First are cresting a wave, and with you and Michael at the helm, I'd expect no less. Now, off you go. I suppose I better speak to Christine before she pops a blood vessel.'

'You are incorrigible, do you know that?' She smoothed her skirt down before standing and walking to the door. Pausing, she turned toward Graeme, her expression serious. 'Has Christine done anything Michael and I need to know about?'

Graeme flashed a tight-lipped smile in her direction. 'Nothing for you to worry your pretty little head about, Marcia. I'm on top of it.'

Watching her leave the room, Graeme shook his head. Marcia was such an intelligent woman, and yet, she put up with all of Michael's 'affairs' like an obedient lamb. He couldn't understand it. It wasn't as if Michael was subtle about it. He laughed. Mind you, he could talk. Look at what he was having to deal with at the minute. Maybe he'd have been better off settling for someone acquiescent, like Marcia. He picked up the phone and steeled himself for the conversation he was about to have with his wife.

Chapter 15

13:30 The Abduction Vehicle

The tattoo equipment really needs moving. Can't risk it being found. Not now, when discretion is so important. No doubt it won't be long before someone leaks the existence of the tattoos to the press. The box looks innocuous enough, although there's no guarantee some nosy parker won't decide to stick their neb in. There's always someone on the lookout for something to pilfer. Best to move things out of temptation's way. Shame it's so heavy.

The newer machines are so much lighter, so much easier to store and move. This one didn't look quite so heavy in the second-hand shop – but I wasn't really thinking about weight when I bought it. Never mind. The back of the car will do for now. With the number plates. Just until I find another hiding place. The problem is, it has to be accessible. You never know when it will be needed again. There is no doubt Ul Haq won't be the last to need tattooing.

Chapter 16

It had been like turning the clock back for Gus, as he drove Alice from The Fort to City Academy. She sat beside him, singing along to Ed Sheeran and Little Mix in her tuneless yet enthusiastic tones, nodding in time to the music as she looked out the window.

'Don't you love City Park in the snow?' she said, when they pulled up at the Jacob's Well traffic lights. 'Pity the Broadway complex has obscured the view of the Cathedral.'

He was so caught up in his own misery he'd barely noticed the Broadway construction taking shape. First, the Matchmaker case ... and then, the awful turf war with Dolinski and The Old Man. He glanced at it now and saw Alice was right. City Hall, with its tower illuminated by alternating green, pink and blue lights and snowflakes gently falling, was the perfect backdrop to the well-used City Park. With its Mirror Pool and a variety of eating and drinking establishments circling the busy area, it was becoming ever more popular. Although the fountains were inactive at the minute, it was picturesque.

'You had a chance to visit the Gin Bar in Sunbridge Wells yet?' he asked on a whim, as the lights turned green and he exited the roundabout onto Manchester Road.

Shaking her head, Alice said, 'Aah, the tunnels. No, I've not had the chance yet.'

'Right. After this interview, I'll take you for tapas followed by a gin. You can catch me up on your recovery without Sampson and Compo waiting for me to snap at them.'

She laughed. 'Yeah, they told me you've been a right miserable old sod since last year.' As the lights changed to green, and he moved on, she continued, 'You need to lighten up, Gus. This isn't like you. You need to let it all go. There's nothing you could have done about Sadia's dad *or* about what happened to me.'

Gus sighed. 'Yeah, I know, I know. You've made your point. Numerous times, in fact. Now, can we focus on this interview before I regret not bringing Compo instead of you.'

'As if, Gus, as if!'

After stating his business over the speaker at the entrance to the school's car park, he was allowed to pull in. Parking up, the two of them sploshed their way through snow that was turning to slush under their feet and mounted the steps leading to the main entrance. Alerted to their visit, the receptionist signed them in and took their photos for their ID badges; Alice in a ridiculous bobble hat she refused to take off, and Gus scowling into the camera.

The receptionist guided them through corridors filled with pupils' brightly coloured art work and a series of English grammar posters with statements such as 'I don't brother to use a grammar checker every dime.' When the receptionist knocked on the Head Teacher's door, a curt 'enter' made Gus straighten up and glance at Alice, who had responded in a similar way. He knew Alice's experience of school had been dire, and she hated visiting these establishments, even now.

Expecting to see a dragon of a woman inside, Gus was surprised to be greeted by a tall woman whose skin was the warm brown of a rain-drenched beach. Her eyes sparkled, and her smile was wide. As they walked in, she stood up. With her hand extended, she rounded her desk and walked towards them. Her clothes were stylish and accentuated her slender figure.

After shaking both their hands, she gestured to a quartet of comfy chairs at the side of the room, saying to the woman who'd brought them up, 'Coffee for three please, Cath.' Then, she quirked an eyebrow at Gus and Alice and grimaced. 'Oops, sorry, should have asked. Coffee okay? Or do you prefer tea? I forget not everyone's as addicted to the stuff as I am.'

Nodding, Alice mumbled, 'Coffee's fine.'

Recognising his colleague's discomfort, Gus cleared his throat and said, 'I take it Neha and Shamshad Ul Haq's uncle has contacted you regarding this meeting, Mrs …?'

As soon as the word 'Mrs' left his mouth, Gus could have kicked himself. He knew better than that. Knew better than to use gender specific titles when dealing with the public, unless they requested him to. His instincts told him, before she responded, he'd made a huge mistake.

Taking the time to cross her remarkably long legs, she leaned back in her chair. Seemingly relaxed, her brown eyes fastened on him. Gus blushed under her scrutiny, and the desire to squirm in his chair was almost overpowering. He knew he'd offended her as he waited for her wrath to fall. Placing extra emphasis on the first word, she said, '*Ms*, please … Patricia Copley.'

Alice snorted, and Gus' cheeks reddened even more. Gus saw Cath smirk as she left the room and felt even more of an idiot. This meeting had got off to a bad start, and he was dependent on Ms Copley's good will to get a sense of the girls' family situation. He shrugged and smiled. 'Look, I'm sorry. Don't know where that came from. Can we start again? I've got three murders to investigate, and I think Razaul Ul Haq's daughters may be able to give me some information. Anything you can share would be greatly appreciated.'

Ms Copley nodded once and got down to business, a slight smile playing about her lips. 'No harm done. Let me fill you in on some of the background of the girls before you meet them.'

Pleased that things had turned onto a more business-like footing, Gus smiled and leaned back to listen. Patricia Copley picked up two slim manila folders from the coffee table that sat between them and handed them to Gus. 'I've copied those records I was at liberty to share with you. I'm sure social services will be only too happy to fill in the blanks.'

She clasped her fingers together, rested her wrists on her knees and began, 'Neha and Shamshad are extremely clever girls who will do very well. I expect them to be amongst our top A-Level achievers when their results come out in August.' She tipped her head to one side. 'Of course, that's assuming their father's murder doesn't affect them too adversely.'

She bit her lip and hesitated as if gathering her thoughts. 'The girls have not had it easy. The break-up of their parents' marriage, prior to them starting secondary school, made their initial adjustment to life at City Academy … shall we say … difficult? They were withdrawn at times, and then, Shamshad became particularly disruptive, leading Neha to follow suit.'

Before Gus could inquire about the nature of the disruption, Ms Copley, seemingly anticipating the question, shook her head. 'Nothing terrible: persistent low-level interruptions such as throwing things, scraping chairs, singing and being generally annoying.' She flicked a glance at Gus. 'Initially, we kept them in the same form groups. Then, when things got bad, we split them into different forms in the hope that, away from Shamshad's disruptive influence, Neha would settle down. The strategy worked in so far as the disruption lessened. However, Neha became withdrawn, and her tutors noticed that, already a slim child, she was becoming even skinnier. Further investigation showed she was also self-harming.'

After a perfunctory knock, the office door re-opened, and Cath returned carrying a tray with coffee and biscuits, which she placed on the small table, before leaving with a smile.

Patricia busied herself preparing the drinks, as she continued, 'After consultation with various agencies, the girls themselves and their mother, we decided Neha would benefit by being in classes alongside her sister. Shamshad, in turn, realised, despite her youth, her sister needed *her* to be a different, less angry person. She rose to the challenge and modified her own behaviour somewhat. In effect, she became her sister's support mechanism.'

Sipping his coffee whilst Alice munched her way through a Breakaway biscuit, Gus thought about what the Head Teacher had said. It sounded like the girls been through the mill, and he was concerned this might knock them back. It seemed their bond was what held them together. A bit like how things had been between him and Katie … before she took off with his wife, that is. Anger rose in his chest, and he sat up straighter, focussing on the matter at hand. 'Was it solely the break-up of their parents' marriage that contributed to the twins' behaviour?'

Patricia sighed. 'Unfortunately not. The circumstances of the break-up were quite distressing. The girls' mother is a very devout Muslim, and their father was, by all accounts, a womaniser.' Her lips thinned. 'Apparently, on more than one occasion, Razaul Ul Haq infected his wife with an STI. As a result, Mrs Ul Haq became more and more, shall we say, disassociated from reality? When the break-up happened, Mrs Ul Haq couldn't cope and became obsessive about her religion, praying continuously, disciplining the girls for imagined slights to her or Islam by locking them in the cellar or whipping them.'

She took a sip of coffee. 'Ultimately, after various suicide attempts, Razaul Ul Haq's brother stepped in and took the girls in, whilst Mrs Ul Haq was sectioned. I believe she is still an in-patient at Lynfield Mount Psychiatric Hospital. Although Shamshad visits her regularly, Neha refuses to. Neither girl has had contact with their father, to my knowledge, although, on occasion, he has made attempts to contact them via social services. I am not sure what effect the death of their father, in these circumstances, will have on the girls. However, I have requested their social worker be present when you interview them. She is with them now and has, at the behest of their uncle, informed them of their father's death.'

Although slightly annoyed to have been blindsided by this information, Gus knew Ms Copley would have been negligent in her duty of care to the Ul Haq twins, had she not implemented the strategy she'd just outlined. Gus could only hope the social worker wasn't a jobsworth who would obstruct his investigation by molly-coddling the girls too much. After all, there was a murderer at large, and they needed to catch him quickly. Any information from the girls might be crucial.

When he felt the pull of tension between his eyebrows, Gus realised he was frowning and a quick glance at Alice, who shook her head at him, confirmed this. With a conscious effort, he widened his eyes, removing the frown, and hoped his displeasure hadn't been too obvious. Meanwhile, the Head Teacher appeared to be scrutinising him with an indefinable expression. He cringed. God, he was making a real hash of this. Much to his relief, a sharp rap on the door pulled her gaze away from Gus. 'Come in.'

The door opened, and a small woman entered carrying a large shoulder bag from which protruded the edges of two or three different coloured folders. A ready grin was on her face as she moved towards them. Ms Copley stood and with a smile, introduced the woman, 'This is the twins' social worker, Naila ...'

Gus jumped to his feet and wrapped his arms round Naila, releasing her only when the Head Teacher's intake of breath reached him. He turned, conscious he was blinking like a startled doe as he tried to keep his habitual frown from his face. *What was wrong with the woman? What had he done wrong now?*

Before he had a chance to respond to the look of horror on Copley's face, Naila spoke. 'What's up with you, Patti?'

Ms Copley, who, until then, had maintained a professional calm, became flustered, flapping her hands, shoulders taut. 'Some Muslim women are uncomfortable with men, other than their husbands, touching them.'

Gus cocked his head to one side and winked at Naila, indicating she should respond. She squeezed Gus' arm and lowered her bag to the floor beside the empty chair. 'Don't know why you're getting your knickers in a twist, Patti. Gus is Mo's best friend. He's like a brother to me. No need to get all aeriated.'

She turned back to Gus. 'Patti and I went to Belle Vue Girls School together many moons ago. She was a goody-two-shoes, over-protective mother hen then as well ... and too politically correct for her own good sometimes.'

Risking a glance at the Head Teacher, who had sat down again and was grinning at Naila, he thought he'd never seen anyone who looked less like a goody-two-shoes ... or, for that matter, a mother hen.

Naila sat down. 'Remember the argument about *The Three Little Pigs*? You were really angry when Mark told you they'd read it to his class at story time.' She turned to Gus and Alice. 'Mark's her brother. She was all for complaining to the school about it, because there were Muslims in the class. Took all my best efforts to convince her that unless Mark's teacher was forcing the Muslim kids to eat the 'little piggies,' it was okay to hear a story about them.'

Patti released a belly laugh, surprising Gus by its sheer raucousness. 'I'd forgotten all about that, Naila. How things have changed.'

Naila punched her lightly on the arm and turned to Alice. 'Good to have you back, Al. You look great. Love the bobble hat.'

Chapter 17

14:15 Hawthorn Drive, Eccleshill

Christine stared at the dusting of lily pollen that dotted the windowsill. She'd have already nipped the stamen off, if she hadn't been distracted last night.

Remembering, she prodded the slight swell beneath her eye and grimaced. Graeme had been so angry, and she couldn't really blame him. This was *so* much worse, though, wasn't it? How could he not have told her of his intentions? It was bad enough he was involved in all that stuff, but to actually publicise himself as their official representative for the by-election was beyond her understanding. Shuddering, she wrapped her arms tightly across her body. How could he have kept this from her? She'd put up with his sexism because he was a good father and provided her with everything she needed on a financial and material level ... *this*, though ... was something completely different. He was risking everything for the sake of his own over-inflated ego.

A tear rolled down her cheek, and with an impatient hand, she wiped it away. After she'd seen the headline in the *Bradford Chronicle* and calmed herself down, she went straight to Patti Copley's office. One look at Patti's face told her she'd already seen the article, and before she'd even uttered a word, Christine knew what the outcome of the meeting would be. Sure, Patti had re-iterated it was only temporary, 'til things died down,' but Christine knew she'd never walk back through those school doors again.

She was worried about Jacob too. How would he be faring at school? Would his friends know already? How would they and their parents react? No doubt, some would agree with Graeme's sentiments. Bradford voted for Brexit, so there had to be a fair few Albion First supporters crawling around in the woodwork. Although she knew that most Brexiteers weren't racists, she was also aware Albion First was gaining more and more supporters. Disagreeing with her husband's politics, she'd voted remain, although she'd never admit it to him. Best to keep those sorts of things secret. She grimaced. Mind you, someone had other ideas, didn't they? The bastard who took those damn photos was definitely turning the knife, and judging by Graeme's reaction the previous night, he was not impressed. In light of the paper's revelations, Christine understood why he'd been so incensed. Bad enough for the Albion First candidate's wife to be caught in an adulterous act on the eve of his public announcement, but for it to be with an Asian man was one step too far. Good job the papers hadn't got wind of it.

To her, it was obvious who was to blame, both for Graeme's deceit *and* for his reckless actions. It was bloody Michael Hogg. There was no love lost between Michael and Christine, although this was extreme, even for him. She could almost hear his fawning tones, stroking her husband's already elevated ego. Buttering him up, he'd plant grandiose ideas her stupid, vain husband was gullible enough to accept as truth. She hated Michel Hogg with a vengeance. He was despicable and lecherous. On more than one occasion, she'd had to fight him off at the Albion First parties. Sleazy little bastard always seemed to have half an eye on the dark corners where he could feel up one of his brain-dead acolytes. Didn't seem to matter most of them were married or, in her case, that she was the wife of his so-called best friend.

It was Marcia she felt sorry for, though. Poor sod wasn't stupid. Christine had seen the look on her face when she'd spotted Michael disappearing into a corner with some floozy or other. No, Marcia Hogg was well aware of what her husband got up to. Seemed like she and Marcia had something in common after all ... duplicitous partners. She wondered what guilty little secret Marcia had. After all, no-one was one hundred percent innocent, were they? Maybe she had a thing for her boss. It wouldn't surprise her; Graeme could be a smooth operator when he wanted.

Christine poured herself another glass of wine from the bottle she'd opened when she got home. It was nearly empty now; still, she didn't care. Its numbing effect was a welcome distraction from the pain. She hit redial on her phone, knowing it would go straight to voicemail. None of the men in her life seemed keen to talk to her today.

Chapter 18

Naila needed a private word with the Head Teacher, so Gus and Alice had agreed to wait outside her office. Now, he was beginning to regret it. Kids in coloured polo shirts, arms filled with books, chattering as they walked to their next class, made him feel old. A few of them eyed Gus and Alice with interest as they skirted around them. One smart-ass waited until he was level with them before pushing his friend. The hefty lad fell against Alice, who, in turn, banged her arm against the wall. Straightening, Gus scowled at the perpetrator who lowered his head and sped up, clearly anxious to put as much distance between them as he could.

He turned to Alice. 'You okay?'

'It'll take more than that little scrote to knock me down.' She reached over and squeezed his arm. 'I'm fine, Gus. Really, I am. You need to stop worrying about me.'

Thrusting his hands in his pockets, Gus shrugged. 'Don't flatter yourself, Al. I wasn't worried about you. It was him I was bothered about. Thought you might deck him, and how would I explain that to the very scary Ms Patti Copley, Head Teacher?'

Alice snorted. 'Don't give me that 'very scary Ms Copley' shit, Gus. I know you found her attractive. Hell, if I were to 'turn' for anyone, it'd be her.'

Gus nudged her with his shoulder. 'Inappropriate, Al … and,' he sniffed and bowed his head, his tone low, 'if I may say so, under the recent circumstances, just a tad insensitive, don't you think?'

From the corner of his eye, he saw Alice's head jerk up, and then, he was grinning. 'Got ya.'

'Idiot. I'd forgotten all about Gabriella and your sis. I'll back-track and take my size tens out of my mouth, shall I?'

'Don't worry. If you weren't putting your foot in it, I would think there was summat wrong with you.'

Looking indignant, Alice banged him on the arm. Yelping, Gus jumped, raising his hand to cradle his arm.

Alice frowned. 'What's up with you? I only tapped you.'

Attempting to look innocent, Gus pursed his lips. 'Nothing, you caught me by surprise, that's all.'

'Don't believe you. What's up with your arm?'

'Nothing, I told you.'

Hands on hips, Alice glared at him. 'I know when you're lying, Gus. You're like a two-year-old, and your face goes all beetrooty.'

'Beetrooty? Beetrooty? You're mad. How can someone with my 'deeelicious mocha complexion' look like a damn beetroot? Just not going to happen.'

Alice was not to be put off. She glared at him until he gave in. 'Okay, okay. Don't tell my mum, though, will you? Promise?'

Raising an eyebrow, Alice shook her head from side to side in slow motion. 'How old are you, Gus?'

He fixed his eyes on her face and folded his arms.

'Okay, okay … I promise.'

Gus leaned forward and whispered in her ear, 'I got a tattoo on my arm yesterday.'

Bursting out laughing, Alice shook her head. 'You nearly had me then … tattoo indeed.'

Looking indignant now, Gus narrowed his eyes. 'I did. Mo took me. I got a small image of Greg's Bob Marley painting on my arm, so there!'

Inclining her head, apparently convinced, Alice said, 'Well, well, well, so you're not such a wuss after all. You can show me it later.'

Gus opened his mouth to reply and was interrupted by Naila stepping out of Patti Copley's room. She led them a few doors down and, chattering nineteen to the dozen, opened another door. Gesturing inside, all three of them entered, and she closed the door behind them.

Although the room wasn't quite as big as Patti Copley's, it was equally calming. One of the Ul Haq twins sat on top of the Deputy Head Teacher's desk, the other on a comfy chair in front of a small coffee table with two unopened bottles of water on top.

The girl by the coffee table appeared to be nervous. Her slender fingers were clenched white in her lap. An ornate hijab framed the girl's face and one of the long-sleeved, floor-sweeping dresses, fashionable with Muslim girls, covered the rest of her. She glanced over at her sister as Gus, Alice and Naila entered and then lowered her head. Seemingly under the pretence of lifting one of the water bottles from the table, she avoided their greeting. Tilting her head, she looked at her sister and said, 'Sham?'

Sham, her legs dangling down, her heels drumming a regular rhythm against the wooden table, smiled at her sister and maintained her tattoo. Her shiny black boots were in danger of doing serious damage to the desk. She wore a pair of skinny jeans and a crop top, both in black. The top skimmed her pierced navel, its sleeves cut short above a tattooed Celtic band that circled her upper arm. From her upper lip shone a small diamante and a line of steel studs glinted across the top of each ear with a complimentary row fanning from her lobe backwards. Her hair was short, spiked and purple.

Naila gave her a look and gestured for the girl to join them. In one lithe movement, she jumped down and plonked herself down beside her sister. Snatching a bottle of water, she stared at them her look a challenge. She opened the bottle and flinging her head back, gulped like a greedy toddler, spilling water down her chin.

The other girl sighed almost silently and stretched out her hand to touch her sister's arm. 'Come on, Sham. Stop it now. I need you.'

Naila gestured for Gus and Alice to take the other two comfy chairs whilst she wheeled the desk chair over and sat between the girls. Gus took the time to observe the twins. In the back of his mind, he'd been concerned he may not be able to differentiate between the two and may end up forgetting which was which. He found it difficult to focus at the best of times without massive amounts of caffeine, frequent breaks and recapping, but the Ul Haq twins had made his job easy. They were so dissimilar he'd have no difficulty telling them apart. He glanced at Alice, sneaking a wink.

Patti had told them one of the girls had real issues, and he was nearly certain she'd intimated it was Neha who had the issues and Shamshad who held things together for them. His glance slid from one girl to the other. Either he'd got the names muddled up in his mind, or he'd need to readjust his perceptions pretty damn quickly. The girl in the hijab had called her sister 'Sham,' so, if he'd *not* misremembered, that would mean the goth was the stronger sister.

Before he had a chance to say anything, Alice, her tone excited, leaned forward on her chair and addressed Shamshad Ul Haq. 'Love your boots, Sham. Just love them!

You don't mind if I call you Sham, do you? I heard your sister call you that. Is it okay?'

Gus smiled and settled back. Alice, as usual, was working her charm. Her gushing chatter had put the girls at ease, and the way she identified with Shamshad Ul Haq was something he couldn't hope to achieve in a million years. As he watched, Alice flashed her smile at Neha and held out her hand to shake. Neha glanced at her sister and then, with obvious reluctance, extended her hand and touched Alice's fingers. Almost immediately, she pulled her hand away and thrust it inside the sleeve of her opposite arm, repeating the gesture with her right hand. As the fabric fell away, Gus saw the pale white slashes of self-harm on her wrists. To accord the girl her privacy, he averted his gaze and saw Naila watching him. Her sad smile acknowledged the deductions he'd already made. With a slight head shake, Gus turned to observe Sham and Alice.

Like her old bouncy self, Alice engaged the girl in idle chatter. Gus was relieved. After what she'd been through, he hadn't been sure what to expect. He still thought she'd returned to work too soon, yet he knew better than to voice his concerns too often. Instead, he'd keep a watching brief on her. Make sure she didn't over-stretch herself. Mind you, at the minute, she seemed to be having the time of her life, comparing tattoos and boots and suchlike. He was aware of Neha watching her sister with Alice. Her shoulders were hunched, and under the sleeves of her dress, she scratched her arms ferociously.

Leaning forward, Naila placed her hand on Neha's arm. When the girl turned to her, Naila shook her head with a gentle smile. The girl gave an almost indiscernible nod and pulled her hands out from her sleeves, resting them on her knees, where they kept up their earlier momentum, this time kneading together as she continued to watch her sister.

Sham, on the other hand, was sprawled in her chair, smiling as Alice continued her relentless chatter. Gus cleared his throat and waited until Alice stopped speaking. Sham sat up and leaned closer to her sister, her stare warning him that he had better not upset Neha. Smiling, Gus nodded in silent acknowledgement, before beginning.

'First of all, I want to say how sorry I am for your loss.'

Sham snorted and said nothing. Neha, on the other hand, made no sound. Instead, she increased the intensity of her kneading. Both Naila and Sham reached out to stop her, Naila withdrawing her hand when Sham scowled at her.

Still holding her sister's arm, Sham turned to Gus. 'My father's death is actually no loss to either of us, DI McGuire. He was a selfish, arrogant bastard, and we're well rid of him.'

Neha gasped. 'Sham, don't say that. Please don't say that. I know he was never there for us, but you can't *say* that.'

Patting her sister's arm, Shamshad said, 'Come on, Neha. You need to be strong. Really strong. You can't make him out to be something he wasn't just because he's dead.'

'He's not just *dead*, though, is he, Sham? He's been murdered.' And she broke down completely, her frail shoulders heaving, as great gulping sobs engulfed her.

Jumping to her feet, Shamshad bent over to hold her sister, while murmuring soothingly in Bangla. When at last, her sister was quiet, she pulled away, revealing a darker patch on her T-shirt, where Neha's tears had soaked through the fabric. She turned to them. 'Look, I know you've got to ask us stuff about him. The truth is, we really didn't know him. We haven't seen him for years. Clearly, my sister is upset.' She shrugged. 'I'm not, so I'll answer your questions. Only, let her go. She's getting anxious because she's missing her physics lesson.'

Gus had seen Neha flinch as her sister spoke. *I wonder what she's hiding from her sister.* He glanced at Alice. 'You know, Al, I wouldn't mind a drink. Maybe Neha could take you to the drinks machine on her way to her class.' He smiled at Neha. 'You don't mind, do you?'

The girl jumped to her feet, clearly relieved by the prospect of escaping. Shaking her head, she pulled open the door before Alice had got up from her chair.

Shamshad, her face screwed into scornful disgust, glowered at Gus. 'What the fff ...? Did you really need to do that? Typical bloody pig bullying tactics.' She folded her arms across her chest and flung her legs over the arms of the chair. 'Divide and rule, that's what this is.'

As Naila made to intervene, Gus shook his head. 'Really ...? You really think DS Cooper is going to bully your sister? Don't be daft! I sent them together because I didn't want Neha going on her own, when she's clearly so upset. I would much rather have sent you, but,' he shrugged, 'you volunteered to talk to me.' He waited. Sham refused to look at him.

'Ok, let's crack on. You say you haven't seen your dad for years? Can you be more specific?'

'Probably about three years, yeah, three years ago. At Eid time. We saw him a couple of times after Mum was put in the hospital, and half the time, he didn't turn up when he were supposed to, so we said we wanted nowt to do wi' him.'

'Any other contact? Letters, email, phone calls, anything like that?'

Sham shook her head. 'He tried off and on for a while, but we didn't respond, so he gave up. Bloody bastard couldn't even be there for his own kids. Too busy shagging white bitches.'

Now that *was* interesting. 'What do you mean by 'shagging white bitches'?'

'Duh? Do I need to draw a diagram?'

Stifling a grin, Gus said, 'No, I think the mechanics of your statement are pretty self-explanatory. I was meaning more, how do you know he was 'shagging white bitches,' and do you know which 'white bitches'?'

With a grin, Sham said, 'I suppose I deserved that … you know, the sarcasm and all.'

Gus returned her smile with a nod. 'And?'

With a sigh, she whirled her legs around until her feet rested on the floor and took another swig from her opened water bottle. 'He's always done it. Well, for as long as I can remember. I think we were around ten when we first realised he wasn't the perfect dad. Then, when my mum went loopy, she became indiscreet. She told us loads of things normal mums wouldn't have. S'ppose she'd nobody else to share it with 'cos she'd come straight from Bangladesh and hardly spoke English. Poor sod. Don't suppose it was her fault. But …' Her fierce eyes met Gus'. 'It was *his* fault. He shouldn't have got married to her. Shouldn't have brought her over here, *and* he *should* have kept it in his fucking pants.'

'You're right, Sham. He should have kept it in his pants, and he shouldn't have treated your mum or you in the way he has, however …' He held her gaze. 'He's been murdered, and we need to find out who did it. Whoever is responsible has now killed three men, and they need to be stopped. Anything you can tell us could give us a lead.'

Sham drained her bottle and, with remarkable accuracy, threw it into the waste paper bin beside the desk. She stood up and walked towards the door. Gus was sure she had something more to tell, yet clearly, she wasn't ready to confide, and he couldn't exactly force her.

He stood up, ready to follow her from the room, when she turned back, one hand on the door handle. With a grim smile, she said, 'Maybe there's two folk you should be checking out, Mr DI McGuire. Christine Weston. She's been screwing my dad for months now, and she works here at the school.' She clicked the handle down and opened the door an inch. 'Oh, by the way, her husband's the fascist bastard who's standing as MP for the Bradford Central by-election. That gives you something to go on, does it?'

Chapter 19

14:45 Bradford City Centre

What a triumph! Better than I ever could have imagined. They found Razaul Ul Haq. Not that they released his name or anything. PC Plod McGuire probably still has his finger stuck up his behind. Not that anyone would notice a bit of extra brown on the nigger … or even the smell. Dirty wog that he is. They all smell like shit anyway, don't they?

They've even given me a name. Some dozy bastard, more than likely a Paki, has leaked my MO to the press. The Tattoo Killer! Jez Hopkins has excelled himself this time! I smile as I drive through town, along Sunbridge Road and up past the Interchange. There is something very fulfilling about having your work recognised in the public arena. Something very satisfying indeed. Validation. And it is no more than I deserve. After all, I am performing a public service. Hopkins waxed lyrically in his article about the rise of Nazism and right-wing ideals in Bradford. He condemned the Tattoo Killer as a savage, narcissistic racist. What psychology book has that little idiot swallowed whole before regurgitating onto a bit of tabloid newsprint?

He is out of touch. Well out of touch. The Brexit referendum clearly expressed the views of Bradfordians, and the Great British Public. No more dipping our caps at the masters of immigration and the sordid defilement they bring to our city. We may be small, but we are great.

With glee, I lean my fingers on the horn, releasing an ear splitting, elongated paaap. The Paki in his stupid dress and prayer cap, his white beard nearly touching the floor, jumps a good few inches, his duffle coat whirling in the wind. Seeing I have no intention of braking, he speeds up, hobbling to the kerb as I drive past. In my rear-view mirror, I see him waving his walking stick at me. Serves him right, polluting our streets.

It irritates me that, in the fading light, I can see so many Pakis and niggers. That's not counting the Polish who came, pissing in their gardens and setting up Polski shops all over. Haven't they seen an indoor toilet? Scum! The women, with their dyed red hair and velour tracksuits, jabbering on unintelligibly, their fat bums wobbling like piles of lard as they walk. No wonder the British obesity rates are high. It's the damn immigrants and their unhealthy lifestyles. They always have a hoard of kids trailing behind, taking up places in our schools, using the resources paid for by *our* taxes. The men smoking like there's no tomorrow, covered in tattoos and smelling of cheap aftershave. Without a doubt, I'll be adding some of them to my list … and they'll deserve it. I just need to identify which ones.

Chapter 20

15:45 City Park

Despite Alice's moaning, Gus had parked in his usual 'free' parking spot on Vincent Street. The sky was beginning to darken. From the top of Vincent Street, a derelict textile mill and church dominated the landscape with Bradford College buildings cowering beneath.

Gus was standing on top of a hill surveying the place he called home. The old sandstone spoke to him of hard work and grit. Despite his parentage, he'd spent his formative years in Bradford. With all its rich history, and despite being Leeds's poor neighbour, this was his home in the same way that West Calder, in Scotland, was home to his old man. He was proud of it. Loved the brooding architecture that mixed with the newer builds to create a unique feel. He loved its hills and its dips. He loved the fact that a five-minute drive could take him into the Dales, and he loved the diversity of the people. In the great tradition of Yorkshire hospitality, Bradford embraced its children.

He frowned. It still puzzled him Bradford had voted for Brexit. He glanced at Alice who stood next to him, impatiently pulling her coat around herself to ward off the evening chill. She was muttering about how tight-fisted he was with references to moths and wallets.

He nudged her and said, 'Come on, the tapas bar in Sunbridge Wells closes at 16:00. If we're quick, they'll still serve us.' Still whingeing, she followed as he set off at a brisk march.

'You do know I'm newly back after a severe injury, don't you?'

He laughed. 'Yeah, thought you were done playing that. Hope I don't have to report to my superior officers that you're not fit enough to walk a couple of hundred yards downhill?' Seeing the dirty look she sent his way, he stopped, and when she'd caught up with him, he linked his arm through hers. 'The tapas are on me, Al, despite being, em … what was it? Oh, yeah, that's it. 'Tight as a camel's arse in a sand storm."

Keeping pace with him, she said, 'Oh, well, I was only joking about that. If you're buying, that's fine then. Let's go.'

Entering by The Little Shop of Soaps entrance off Sunbridge Road, Gus was kept waiting for a few minutes as Alice explored bath bombs and scented soaps, before coming out in a cloud of rose scent, clutching a paper bag. Opening the bag, she thrust it under Gus' nose, before snatching it back and burying her own nose in its depths. 'Isn't this gorgeous?'

Gus shrugged and marched off towards the steel stairs that would lead to the upper part of the tunnels. What did he know about smelly bath stuff? As Alice followed, he could hear her oohing and aahing at each new discovery. He couldn't blame her. The tunnels were a delight. He'd been a few times now and had still to explore all the nooks and crannies. Mind you, he had spent an inordinate amount of time in the Sunbridge Lounge and The Gin Bar.

Leading her into the tapas bar with its solid pine tables and views over Sunbridge Road, they spent ages perusing the menu before Alice finally decided what she wanted. Fed up with the length of time it had taken her to decide, Gus got straight to the point. 'What did you get from Neha Ul Haq?'

'Well, that was a turn-up for the books, wasn't it?' said Alice, sipping her drink. 'At first glance, you'd think Shamshad was the unstable one. On the contrary, it's definitely Neha. Poor kid was jumpy as anything. Seems like, apart from her sister, the only thing that keeps her sane is her studies. She refuses to visit her mother, yet despite all the bad press her dad has got, she was visibly upset by his death. More so than Shamshad, I'd say.'

'Hmm, difficult to say, Al. People have strange ways of dealing with grief. I suspect Shamshad Ul Haq isn't as blasé about it as she makes out. She carries a heavy load, that kid ... main support for her sister, seems she visits Mum regularly, and she's an A student to boot. Lot of pressure on her. Maybe that's why she rebels in other ways.'

Alice grinned. 'Oh, so you reckon her being a goth is a rebellion, do you?'

Gus inclined his head to Alice's dark clothing and her barely subdued black eye make-up. 'Well, isn't it?'

She shrugged. 'Maybe it once was. Maybe when I was a kid at school trying to fit in and being shut out because I was the one with no phone or laptop or trendy clothes, it was my defence mechanism. Not now, though.' She preened. 'Now, I choose my image because I look hot!' She clicked her fingers like some rap artist gone wrong.

'Yeah, okay, if you say so.'

'I do say so, and you needn't think I've forgotten about your tattoo. Let's have a look.'

'Here?' Gus glanced around the near-empty restaurant as if expecting a paparazzi attack.

'For goodness sake, show me the damn thing.'

Peeling his sleeve back, Gus revealed his tattoo and watched to see Alice's reaction.

For long seconds, she said nothing and then, 'Wow, Gus. It really is good. Such a nice tattoo and a lovely tribute to Greg, too.'

Pulling his sleeve back down, Gus said, 'Yeah, it was Mo's idea ... one of his better ones, I have to say.'

Changing the subject, Alice said, 'I think you're right, though, with Sham. It's definitely her coping mechanism. Her sticking two fingers up to the world.'

'Exactly! Did you see the way Neha flinched when Sham said they'd had no contact with their dad for years?'

Alice nodded, her eyes lighting up as the waitress arrived with plates of sweet potato bhajis, spicy chicken meatballs and stuffed peppers, which she placed on the hardwood tables. Alice pushed her glass of non-alcoholic beer to the side, making Gus smile at her eagerness to start eating.

Talking around a mouthful of meatball, she continued, 'She'd definitely had some contact with her dad, though when I tried to broach it, she became quite agitated, flapping her hands and breathing from her chest, like you do before you have a panic attack.'

Gus raised an eyebrow. He'd always thought he'd managed to either escape to privacy or to cover up the palpitations and tightness, when the first warning signs of a panic attack hit him. He thought nobody else had ever noticed. Apparently not, it seemed. However, now wasn't the time to explore this. He was more interested in Neha's reaction. 'Did she say anything?'

'No. Whatever she's not telling us, I think she'd also keeping it secret from her sister. Maybe she and her dad were in contact via Facebook or some other social media. I think if we give her time, she may open up. She's clearly working through some really tough issues. Anyhow, how about you? How did you get on with Sham?'

Gus filled Alice in on what Sham had shared with him about the Westons, ending with, 'Like her sister, I'm convinced she knows more. She may not think it's important, however we need to get as much info from her as possible.'

Looking thoughtful, Alice wiped her fingers on a napkin and sipped her beer. 'So, I suppose we better head over to the Westons then?'

Gus pierced a meatball with his fork and traversed it to his mouth. He chewed before swallowing it. 'Before I met with you in the hallway, I went back to speak to the Head Teacher.'

Alice sucked her cheek in and nodded in an 'I've got the measure of you' sort of way.

Gus, knowing *exactly* what she was inferring, chose to ignore her. 'I asked her about this Christine Weston.'

Alice cocked her head and waited until Gus had eaten a chunk of stuffed pepper.

'Turns out, she, Christine Weston, turned up at school this morning completely unaware her husband had done the press release last night or, in fact, that he was running for office. Apparently, after chatting, Patti convinced her it would best for her to make herself scarce 'til things had died down a bit. Seemingly, a lot of the staff and a sizeable proportion of the students were angry and didn't feel she should be in the school.'

Alice made an 'Eeks!' expression with her mouth. 'Shit! City Academy is a multi-ethnic school, so if Weston's husband is standing as an Albion First candidate, that's clearly going to impact on her relations with other staff members and the kids and parents. What does she teach?'

'She's a teaching assistant. However, what's interesting, Al, is two things. First, Patti had no idea Weston's husband is a racist. Secondly, she'd heard vague rumours Christine was having an affair, although she wasn't aware it was with one of her pupil's, or in this case, two of her pupils' parent. Thirdly, and this is very interesting, she told me Christine Weston had a recent bruise under her eye which she'd clearly tried to disguise. However, because she'd been crying, the make-up had washed away. Patti didn't ask her about it. She did say it looked recent and was also swollen.'

'Phew,' said Alice, excitement lighting her face. 'This could be the lead we need, Gus. Three Asian or black men killed, a racist candidate singing his vitriol from rooftops in City Park, and meanwhile, his wife's screwing the latest victim.'

'My thoughts exactly. We need to interview them both. The wife first, I think. Patti gave me her address.'

Gus signalled for the bill and was reaching for his coat, as Alice said, 'Did you get her phone number?'

'Yeah, her address and phone number. She lives in Eccleshill.'

'I didn't mean Christine Weston's number, Gus.'

Leaving Gus speechless and ever so slightly embarrassed, she flounced out of the restaurant. The fact was, he had found Patti Copley attractive … and also a bit scary. Alice was the last person he'd confide that to. He'd never hear the end of it. Besides which, it was irrelevant; he wasn't going to see her again. No, he wasn't going to go there. It was far too soon after Sadia, and judging by the way he felt right now, that wasn't going to change anytime soon!

Chapter 21

16:15 Thornbury

Neha Ul Haq had tried her best to hold it together all day. Ever since the police had arrived at the school, she'd been on edge. She was sure Shamshad suspected something was wrong, despite her consistent denials, and in the end, Sham had had no option but to back off.

Now, locked away in the women's toilets in the small mosque that served the Bangladeshi community in Bradford Three, she peeled back the sleeves of her dress, wincing as the fabric pulled against the bloodied scratches on her arms. Her eyes filled with tears. She plonked herself on the closed toilet, cradling each of her sore arms in the opposite hand and shut her eyes. She wasn't using a razor anymore and hadn't done so for ages. However, it seemed her fingernails could do nearly as much damage. Why, oh why, couldn't she refrain from this self-flagellation?

She wasn't a Shia Muslim, nor was she male, so she knew she had no business doing this. Her mum had always mocked the Shias in Bangladesh who still practised self- flagellation to mark the Ashura commemoration of Husayn ibn Ali's death. That was rich, really, because Neha knew there was more than one way to self-flagellate, and her mum had it down to a fine art. On a practical level, Neha knew she did it because she felt out of control and unable to express her emotions; that didn't help her, though. Sighing, she stood and moved over to the sink, turning the tap on. Using a damp paper towel, she wiped away the clots of dried blood, making her arms sting.

Outside the door, she heard the chatter of the primary school girls who'd arrived for mosque school. In a few minutes, she'd have to go out and settle them down, clear their heads of everything except their purpose in coming to mosque – to be better Muslims by memorising their *Sparas*. Today, this was the last thing she wanted to do. Normally, this connection to the children through her faith made her stronger, however, the burden of deceit she carried made her feel unworthy of the honour bestowed upon her by the Imam. She was not pure in mind or spirit, so how could she be a role model for these girls? How could she lead them by example in the way of Allah, when she, herself, was not without sin?

Chapter 22

17:30 Hawthorn Drive, Eccleshill

When she opened the door, Gus saw straight away that Christine Weston did indeed have a bruise on her cheekbone underneath her eye. He also saw she was well on her way to being very drunk. He showed his warrant card and introduced himself and Alice. Without waiting for a proper invite, he pushed the door open, forcing her to take a backward step.

In a pleasant voice, he said, 'Thanks very much for inviting us in, Mrs Weston.'

Not allowing her to gain her equilibrium, he walked through the hallway to the open living room door and stepped through, waiting for her to follow. On a large table in the corner of the room, a teenage boy, with dark hair and brooding eyes, sat with a pile of books open before him. Gus wasn't an expert at judging children's ages, but he thought this boy was around thirteen years old.

He smiled at him and said, 'Can you take your homework up to your room? We need to talk to your mum for a minute or two.'

The boy gave an exaggerated sigh and, stretching out the process, piled his books one on top of the other, before lifting the entire pile and walking towards the door. Meanwhile, his mother stood in silence, wringing her hands in front of her. Gus was unsure whether it was because of the alcohol or whether she was indecisive by nature.

As the boy reached the door, he turned to Gus and, in a voice full of scorn, said, 'You'll be lucky to get any sense out of her, 'cos she's pissed.' He hesitated, and then, lip curled in derision, he added, 'As usual … Good luck!'

His tone, or perhaps his words, seemed to penetrate his mother's fugue state, and she shook her head, her voice slurred. 'Stop it, Jacob. You know fine and well I rarely drink.'

The boy snorted and turned to Gus. 'See what I mean? She can't even talk properly, *and* she was supposed to be dropping me at the cinema. Selfish cow!'

Christine Weston blinked and took a wobbling step towards her son. Placing her hand on his arm, she said, 'Stop it, Jacob! Stop it right now! It's always me who ferries you everywhere, isn't it? Anyway, neither of us want to go out again today. Not after what your dad's done. You said so yourself when you came home from school. You told me you'd had an awful day. That your friends aren't speaking to you.' She shook him slightly. 'Well, that makes two of us … and it's all your father's fault, so *stop* taking it out on me!'

Jacob jerked his arm away and, with a tell-tale glisten in his eyes, ran out of the room. His feet thudded as he ran upstairs, and seconds later, they heard the slam of a door followed by subdued sobs.

Christine Weston seemed to be in two minds whether to go after her son or stay and deal with the police, so Gus took the decision from her by settling himself on one of the huge armchairs near the fireplace. Alice followed suit, leaving Mrs Weston no option except to cast a final glance upstairs before settling opposite them on the sofa, a glass coffee table between them.

Now that he had the chance to study her without Jacob to distract him, Gus saw her clothing was dishevelled, as if she'd been sprawled on the sofa for most of the day. Indeed, the sofa cushions were moulded into a body shape. From the black mascara streaks grazing her face, she'd clearly been crying. Her swollen eyelids and puffy cheeks suggested she'd been doing so for most of the afternoon. Gus glanced around the room. On top of the coffee table was one empty and one half-empty wine bottle, a glass with presumably wine dregs in the bottom and an A4 brown envelope.

In a cabinet that stood along the back wall were a series of family photos of Christine with her husband and son. Gus squinted at them, trying to see any trace of the suave, sophisticated woman from the photos in the unkempt heap that sat opposite him. It was hard, but he knew from the Head Teacher's earlier description, Christine had impeccable taste and was always immaculately turned out with full make-up and well-coiffed hair. *What a difference a few hours can make.*

In the largest photo, Jacob looked to be about a year younger. Despite his tanned skin, he carried the look of a boy recovering from an illness. His cheeks were sunken, and his eyes carried dark shadows beneath them. Gus imagined the arm Christine stretched around him was a protective one, not merely a pose struck for the photo. Graeme Weston, for Gus assumed that's who the man was, stood erect, with his portly belly bulging over his trousers. Gus imagined when he moved, he'd have the same swagger many small, yet cocky men carried. That almost rolling gait that seemed to inflate the space they occupied, tricking people into thinking them larger and more important than they actually were.

As he watched, Christine leaned forward and lifted the bottle. Before she could pour any into the glass, Gus placed his hand over the top. 'You've had enough, Mrs Weston. I need you to focus, for I have some bad news for you.'

He turned to Alice and handed her the glass and the wine bottle he'd extricated from Mrs Weston's unprotesting hand. 'Make some coffee, Al. I know I could do with some, and Mrs Weston certainly needs it.'

Christine's head jerked up, and for a split second, her glazed expression vanished, replaced by a look of sheer loathing. 'You're not going to tell me my husband's gone and got himself arrested, are you? Because, if that's why you're here, you're at the wrong house, for I couldn't care less. He can rot in jail, as far as I'm concerned.'

Alice and Gus exchanged a startled glance, and then, Alice made her way to the kitchen, leaving Gus to explore Mrs Weston's words. Gus hesitated, watching as she hung her head, refusing to meet his gaze, almost as if she were ashamed of her words. Drawing her sleeve across her wet eyes, she sniffed. 'What is it? Has Graeme got himself into some sort of trouble?'

Then, as if a sudden thought had sprung into her mind, she placed a trembling hand over her mouth, and eyes wide, she whispered, 'He's not been attacked, has he?'

Gus shook his head. 'As far as I'm aware, Christine, can I call you Christine?' When she nodded, he continued, 'As far as I know, your husband is fine, although I am interested to know what sort of trouble you think he may have gotten himself into.'

Shaking her head, Christine studied her hands.

Gus tried again. 'Did you think that maybe the statement he made at City Hall last night or the article in the newspapers this morning may have gotten him into some sort of trouble?'

Christine shook her head. When she spoke, it was in the precise tones of someone who knew they were drunk, but thought no-one else would notice. 'It's a free country, isn't it? He's as entitled to stand as anyone else. At least my husband isn't a dirty paedophile, like the last one was.'

Returning to the living room carrying a tray with three mugs of coffee, milk and sugar on it, Alice said in a quiet voice, 'No, he's a dirty racist with a hateful agenda.'

'Alice!' Gus' voice was sharp, but before he could continue, Christine laughed and inclined her head to Alice.

'Of course, you're perfectly right, DC …?' She waved her hand as if Alice's name and rank were unimportant. 'My husband is a racist, and within these four walls, I can admit I agree with you. His party's policies are hateful, and I, for one, will not be voting for him. But he *is* my husband and, more importantly, the father of my son.' She tried to push herself to her feet and failed. Seemingly resigning herself to remain seated, she continued, 'If you have something to tell me about my husband, please spit it out.'

'Earlier, you said your husband could 'rot in jail.' What might he have done that would warrant him being in jail?'

Alice handed a mug of well-sugared black coffee to her and then sat down. Christine sipped the scalding liquid, grimacing as it burned her lips. Setting the mug back down on the table, she sighed and rubbed her hair back from her eyes. 'I know the Albion First supporters can sometimes go off the rails a bit. Graeme *never* does. He's the political face of the party,' she snorted. 'Christ, he practises that stupid smile of his in front of the bedroom mirror. If he's got caught up in something, I'm quite sure he's innocent. He wouldn't jeopardise his public image, if he could help it. However, I'm the last person you should be speaking to. The person you need to talk to is his 'publicity guru,' Michael Hogg.'

Gus lifted his coffee and took a sip. 'Actually, Christine, this has nothing at all to do with your husband. This is about Razaul Ul Haq.'

Christine, in the process of lifting her coffee to her lips, jolted and dropped her drink, spilling it all over the white rug. Alice jumped to her feet, grabbed tissues from a box under the coffee table and tried, with little success, to mop up the dark liquid. Christine remained seated, her eyes fixed on the ever-expanding stain. Then, as if someone had remotely activated her 'on' switch, she jumped up, ran to the kitchen and returned moments later with a cloth. Sinking to her knees beside Alice, she frantically rubbed at the stain.

A sudden flash of his sister Katie, playing Lady Macbeth in a school play, jumped into Gus' mind: 'Out, damn'd spot, out, I say!'

He kneeled beside her and took the cloth from her unresisting hands and handed it to Alice. Christine raised her fingers to her temple and released a long sigh as if trying to focus her blurred mind. With no warning, she turned and fell against him, weeping against his chest. With little option, Gus put his arm around her, and with a glance at Alice, he held her until she was calm. At last, her sobs reduced to the occasional hiccup, he helped her to her feet and guided her back to her spot on the sofa, leaving Alice to finish cleaning the mark.

'You know Razaul Ul Haq?' he asked, his tone gentle.

With a deep breath, Christine nodded. 'Yes, I know him. Has Graeme gone and done something stupid?' As she spoke, she shook her head from side to side. 'No, he wouldn't. Not Graeme. He wouldn't do anything that would jeopardise his chance at election.' She frowned and, seeming almost sober now, said, 'Please tell me what's happened?'

'So, you do know Razaul Ul Haq?'

She gave an almost imperceptible nod, and Gus continued, 'What exactly was his relationship to you?'

Whimpering like a wounded puppy, Christine said, 'He's my lover. He's my lover, and Graeme found out. He told me last night.'

Gus glanced at Alice who'd sat next to Christine and put her arm around her to comfort her. 'Razaul Ul Haq is your lover?'

Christine nodded, and he continued, 'When did you last see Mr Ul Haq?'

Sniffing, Christine pulled away from Alice and turned to Gus. 'I saw him yesterday. We met up. I left him around eight o'clock last night. Is he alright?'

Gus sighed. He hated this part the most. 'I'm really sorry to tell you, Christine. Early this morning, Razaul was found murdered.'

'Murdered?' She frowned, her expression full of disbelief. Then, her hands fluttered up to her neck before falling back onto her lap. 'Murdered,' she said again.

Watching the woman's reactions with interest, Gus nodded. Christine Weston was either a very accomplished actress, or she was totally thrown by his revelation.

'No! No! That's impossible. I was with him only last night. Graeme wouldn't do this. He just wouldn't!'

As she spoke, the front door opened, and Graeme Weston walked in. 'What wouldn't Graeme do?'

Chapter 23

18:30 The Delius, Leeds Road

Perched on a bar stool, Shahid Khan scowled as, through the mirrored panel above the optics, he watched the expanding group of people gather behind him, high-fiving Imti and chattering in their stupid, chavvy accents. Sensing Serafina was watching him, he glanced up in time to catch her averting her gaze. She was always so nervous of him, and since everything that had happened before Christmas, Shahid was too exhausted, both emotionally and physically, to make any effort with the girl. It wasn't that he disliked her. She was okay, he supposed. More importantly, Imti loved her, so that should be enough for him. She flicked her eyes back in his direction, her smile shy. Shahid shrugged his shoulders and made a half-hearted attempt to smile back. She made his brother happy, so he should make the effort.

Instead of turning his attention back to his laptop, where he was attempting to bring some sort of order to The Delius accounts, he let his gaze drift back up to the mirrored panel. He didn't mind Imti hosting these meetings here. He'd rather he was here than somewhere he couldn't keep an eye on the proceedings. He was being over-protective, but he'd lost a lot in the past year ... he was entitled to be over-protective. Imti had been blunt in his accusations of his 'nannying.' Tough luck. He was Shahid's only living relative, and he wasn't going to let a repeat of last year happen. No bloody way.

Aware his brother cut him some slack because of what had happened to Trixie, Shahid suspected he was beginning to get annoyed. He sighed; he only wanted to protect him, and what with this bloody Weston character putting himself forward for Albion First slap bang in the middle of Bradford, Shahid could sense the natives were restless. He remembered what it was like to be young and impulsive, and he had a bad feeling. He knew the kids weren't thugs. Sometimes, though, you didn't need to be a thug to get caught in the crossfire. Imti and his mates just wanted to exercise their right to express their youthful outrage at a fascist candidate standing in inner city Bradford. He got that. Fuck, he was pissed off too. The city was on edge, and tempers were frayed. Then, there were the three Asian men who'd been murdered. Who knew what that was all about? He snorted, even the police probably didn't know. Anyway, it all combined to promote a feeling of fragility and an aura of fear.

Sighing, he hit 'save' on the laptop and swivelled around on his seat. The door opened, and two girls he'd never seen before walked in. His first impression was they made unlikely friends. One wore a hijab and had the demeanour of a mouse. The other was a goth with all the swagger of the kids that came to his Thursday Teens' Night. When she'd slipped off her jacket, he was sure he'd seen a tattoo on her arm. He smiled. She reminded him a little of himself: from a Muslim family, but determined to make a mark on the world as his own person. Yeah, and *that* had worked out so well!

The girls moved nearer, and as Imti moved towards them, they both smiled. *Shit! They're bloody twins.* Well, who'd have thought it? Bet the goth one drove their parents wild. He hadn't seen either of them around the area, and something about their features told Shahid they were probably Bangladeshi. There weren't too many Bangladeshis in Thornbury, and they tended to stick to their own kind, so it wasn't surprising he hadn't seen them before. He wondered how Imti knew them, when Serafina let out one of those girlish squeals that so annoyed him. She rushed over and flung her arms round the goth, before turning, and more gently, hugged the other twin.

Shahid watched as the girl with the hijab tugged on her sister's arm and whispered something he couldn't hear above the din from the other kids. He suspected, from the anxious glances she was sending round the room, she wasn't comfortable being in a place that sold alcohol. Curious, he moved closer, pretending to adjust beer mats on the nearby tables. She was speaking in Bangla to her sister, and he smiled when the sister replied in English. That was something he had frequently done with his stepmother. It was rebellion, pure and simple.

'Neha, you need to calm down,' said goth girl. 'You are doing nothing *haram* in being here. You're not drinking alcohol, are you?'

Neha's mumbled response was received with a snort from her sister. 'Look, we're here to plan a way to stop this fascist, Weston, from being elected, that's all. Most of the group are Muslim, Neha.'

Again, Neha spoke in Bangla and took a step towards the door. Her sister grabbed her arm and spun her around. 'For goodness' sake. Bradford is *our* city. We have a fascist standing in the by-election, and three Asian men have been murdered. One of them our own father, useless piece of shit that he was. Anyway, we need to do something, don't we?'

Neha closed her eyes and then, straightening her spine, gave an abrupt nod before moving back to join the group. Her sister glanced around and saw Shahid watching. 'Seen enough, or do you want a fucking photo?'

Shahid splayed his hands in front of him and backed off. So, the murdered man found in Heaton Woods was their father. What the hell were these girls doing here, then, if their dad had just been killed?

Tuesday

Chapter 24

Gus sat at his kitchen table, reading the news headlines. He was pissed off the tattooing had hit the news. However, he couldn't waste precious time looking for the leak. It could have been any of the uniforms or SOCO staff. It'd be stupid to direct resources to pursue such a fruitless task. Still, he was fuming about it. He hated it when journalists, like Jez Hopkins, gave these killers validation by naming them. The Tattoo Killer! How bloody sensationalist. As ever, the killer was getting more attention than the victims and their families. Nancy would be well fed up with that. *What the fuck!* Nothing like egging the bastard on. He'd got Compo to securely email all his files to Professor Sebastian Carlton and hoped, in light of the news leak, he'd get a quick response from him. He really could do with his help.

Grinding his teeth, he rinsed his coffee cup and upended it on the drainer before putting the milk back into a near-empty fridge. He really needed to get to the shops. There was no excuse. There was a small Sainsbury's around the corner. It'd take him all of two minutes to grab some bread and marg from there. He just couldn't be bothered.

He glanced around. Everything was in its place in the kitchen. Not because he was domesticated, rather because the only items he used in this room were the kettle and the table. The state-of-the art oven that Gabriella, his ex-wife, had insisted they install, stood idle. The posh microwave was used only to heat up his lavender-scented heat pack when he'd overdone it jogging. In one corner, a crumpled pile of clothes dangled from the washer in a tangle of colours and whites. He couldn't be bothered separating them, despite the odd mishap with bleeding dye. In the opposite corner, lay two empty dog bowls on a mat. Seeing them, Gus sighed. He really did miss Bingo. The sooner he got this case solved and went back to more regular hours, the sooner he could have his friend back.

Photos of Gabriella and Gus taken at various parties and events had long since been removed from the fridge and replaced with ones of Bingo looking goofy as a pup with a mega-sized bone in his mouth and more recent ones of him scampering about Heaton Woods. The only major addition, since Gabriella had wandered off into the proverbial sunset with his sister, was the dog flap in the back door. Gus had installed it when his father had first given him Bingo, and he'd secured the back garden and built a big kennel near the decking so his dog could have some freedom.

He admitted the rest of the house could do with a once-over with a hoover. What was the point? It was only him and Bingo rattling about the house ... and Bingo didn't care about a bit of dust. Once more, Gus glared at the offending article in the newspaper, and then, although he didn't feel like it, he donned his jogging gear and set off.

Running to work at a steady pace through Lister Park and up Oak Lane was more of a punishment than anything this morning. Neither Mo's nor The Chaat Café were open, so, when he arrived at The Fort, the only sustenance available were two leftover flapjacks his mum had dropped off the previous day. The fact that Compo, for some strange reason, had failed to gobble them up, was a pretty clear indication of how bad they actually were. Shrugging, Gus tipped them into the bin, then as an after-thought, shoogled the container until they fell to the bottom. There was no telling when his mum would call in, and the last thing he wanted was for her to be offended if she saw her lovingly prepared offerings in the rubbish.

Wiping sweat from his forehead, he started up the coffee machine and headed for the shower. He could survive on coffee for an hour; nonetheless, he made a point of leaving a message with the front desk for Alice to nip over for butties before briefing. No way could he conduct a briefing and hope to get any sense out of the team, and Compo in particular, if they didn't have some nourishment in their bellies.

Letting the water pound down on his bowed head, Gus experienced an almost serene pleasure at the bite of the scalding water. Tossing his head, sodden hair bouncing around, he turned the heat down a notch and began to soap his body. His hand lingered on the scars that stood out pink against his tan skin. Each one told their own tale, some more emotionally painful than others.

Casting his mind back to the previous evening, he recalled how he'd interviewed Graeme Weston. It appeared that, between the time his wife last saw Razaul Ul Haq and the time his body was discovered, Graeme Weston was fully alibied. Shame, really, the guy was a massive prick, and Gus would have loved the satisfaction of locking the supercilious, racist, bastard up ... at least for a while. Mind you, his alibi had to be verified, even if he was sure Weston was telling the truth, even if the man *was* an animal.

Gus had tried not to get wound up when Weston had referred to him as half-caste or when he referred to the 'smaller' brain capacity of 'Pakis and blacks.' The fact it had taken real effort *not* to react worried him. He'd encountered abuse before in his professional life and had dealt with it, taken it in his stride. Not that it didn't bother him; of course, it did. The difference was it didn't usually leave him so drained and lifeless afterwards. He knew he'd come close to planting one on Weston's ugly little face, and worse still, he knew Alice suspected how close he'd come. This wasn't like him. He was the one who kept his cool. The one who laughed in their face whilst maintaining an indefatigable calm. What was wrong with him? He was so tightly strung, he could snap. Maybe Dr Mahmood was right. Maybe he did need to attend some mindfulness classes or perhaps some of the meditation drop-in sessions at the Buddha Land Centre in Keighley.

He switched the shower off and stepping out, began to dry his body. He wasn't even half dressed, when a hand holding a bacon butty appeared around the side of the cubicle. Despite himself, he grinned, as the tantalising smell hit his nostrils causing an involuntary gurgle in his stomach. He snatched the bread roll and took a bite, before saying, 'You do know this is the men's shower room, Al?'

'Phoo, judging by the BO in most of the incident rooms, I suspect you're the only one who ever uses the showers, so I reckon The Fort's male population is safe. Besides which, none of them have got owt I've nae seen before.' For the last part of the sentence, she adopted a Yorkshire accent that had Gus laughing aloud as he pulled his jumper on. Grabbing the remains of his sandwich, he stepped out and joined her on the other side of the cubicle. 'Come on, Yorkshire lass, let's get this briefing done.'

Minutes later, Gus pushed open the door to the open-plan space that doubled as both incident room and their offices and stepped inside. Before he'd taken a further step into the room, he was greeted by the words, 'Unsub's accelerating!'

What? A glance around told him that, apart from Alice, who had entered behind him, the room was empty. Then, he saw a head appear over the edge of his desk, followed seconds later by the full figure of Professor Sebastian Carlton. Well, that explained the use of the American term 'unsub,' anyway. Gus opened his mouth to ask him what he was doing crawling about on the floor. However, he refrained when Carlton held up a pen in silent explanation, before sliding it into the breast pocket of his too small, well-worn jacket and tapping it into place.

Gus frowned. Three things about that struck him as strange. The first was the pen, now residing in pride of place in Sebastian Carlton's pocket, was only a chewed up old Bic. The second was he was sure he had knocked that very pen *off* his desk when he'd dumped his bag on top earlier that morning. And thirdly, despite his myopic gaze and thick specs, Sebastian Carlton must have the eyesight of a crow to have spotted it in the first place. Professor Carlton, it appeared, was a pen-pincher.

Alice said, 'Oops, I forgot to mention that Prof Carlton is here.'

Ignoring her amused grin, Gus moved over and poured coffee for all three of them. Handing Sebastian a steaming cup and trying not react to the psychologist's luminous pink trainers, which seemingly had replaced his previous, equally luminous, green ones, he said, 'So, to what do we owe this honour?'

Through bottle-thick lenses that sat lopsidedly on his nose – courtesy of the absence of one of the legs – Sebastian blinked at him. This made Gus focus on the remaining leg secured by mucky-looking duct tape. The man's image was almost enough to convince Gus that even the lowest ranking police officers must gross a higher salary than the Prof. However, over the past few months, he'd come to know Sebastian Carlton and knew it wasn't lack of money that made him dress that way, but rather a combination of lack of vanity and impatience with what he called the 'foppery of materialism.'

'Stupid bloody question, Gus, isn't it? Where else would I be?' He jerked a chubby thumb towards the crime boards. 'Got ourselves a bloody serial killer, haven't we!' He thrust both hands into his trouser pockets and rocked on his heels, grinning his infectious grin. 'Told Andrea I'd been called in urgently to assist the West Yorkshire Police.'

Gus knew Andrea was the Professor's long-suffering colleague, for whom he had the utmost sympathy. Carlton's grin widened, and his rocking increased in speed, reminding Gus of the retro Weeble his dad kept on his desk as a keepsake from his childhood in the 70s. He remembered both playing with the wobbly toy himself when he was a child and the refrain 'Weebles wobble, but they don't fall down.' He shook his head and re-focussed on what Sebastian was saying.

'Landed her with my Level Four class. Can't be bothered with their inane questions. Half of them will be bumped off the course by the end of first year, if I have my way. Can't be bothered prancing about like a fucking peacock, strutting and preening and shaking my arse to attract a fucking hen, in front of a load of deadbeats who don't listen.'

Blinking, Gus wished away the image that had immediately sprung to mind, whilst Alice giggled. She was rewarded with a myopic glare.

'I'm not joking, you know. My time's better spent drinking coffee, eating doughnuts and helping you lot.' Carlton glanced around, his expression woebegone. 'Well, it bloody would be, if there were any damn doughnuts!'

Smiling, Alice patted his arm. 'Don't worry, Sebastian, I'll get you your doughnuts.'

Gus was fond of Sebastian after his minor involvement in their previous case. Now, he was glad to enlist the help of someone who knew a bit about serial killers. He'd be sure to clear it with Nancy, though, just to be sure. Sitting at his desk, he stretched his leg in front of him. He hadn't warmed up properly before his morning jog, and now, he was suffering the consequences. His own fault. He continued to flex his leg to release the knots. 'What can you tell us, Sebastian?'

Professor Carlton raised a finger and began pacing back and forth in front of the murder boards. Suspecting they were in for some key information, Gus turned to Alice. 'Round up Compo and Sampson, will you. Thought they'd have been here by now ... oh, and get someone to nip to Tesco for doughnuts for 'his nibs.' I know they sell those Krispy Kreme ones he likes so much.'

As Alice left to order the doughnuts for their guest, Compo and Sampson came into the room. Sampson wore his usual grey suit and tie. This morning, his hair was still damp as if he was newly out of the shower, and he brought with him a wave of Paco Rabanne's Million aftershave. Compo, on the other hand, brought in a waft of bacon butties and fresh air. Today, he wore a Doors *Riders on the Storm* T-shirt over a pair of cargo pants and an aubergine coloured beanie hat. Gus smiled as Alice walked back in. His team was complete, and he was happy, well, happier than he'd been for a while ... albeit short-staffed. He could feel the niggling pinch of a headache beginning. That was all he needed.

'Right,' said Sebastian at last. He turned around, his face lighting up when he saw Compo. 'The cavalry's arrived, I see,' he said, eliciting a blush from the lad. For some reason, the two men had hit it off. Gus shrugged; nothing strange about that really. After all, they were both eccentrics and geniuses in their field. Not surprising they had become friends.

When Sebastian didn't expand on his previous 'right,' Gus prompted him, 'And?'

With a shake of the head, Sebastian paused, before speaking. 'The unsub's one sick fucker!'

Sampson almost managed to hide his grin. Alice bit her lip and avoided Gus' gaze, whilst Compo flicked his hand, making a sharp cracking sound with his fingers and said, 'I told you so! Didn't I, Sampson? Didn't I say he was one sick fucker?'

Unable to contain his grin any longer, Sampson nodded. Gus, however, was less amused. 'What the fuck, Sebastian? Is that an official diagnosis?' He jumped from the desk and ran his fingers through his dreads. 'I was expecting a bit more than that, I have to say ... oh, and while you're at it, can you quit with the damn Americanisms too. It's distracting.'

Pursing his lips, his tone calm, Sebastian said, 'No, it's not an official diagnosis. It's a human one. However, diagnosing this person isn't going to help catch them. It's clear the *unsub's* a psychopath with narcissistic leanings. Hell, where does that get you? No, what we need to be doing is working out what motivates him ... and no, I can't give up on the Americanisms. They're inbuilt now, so put up and shut up, or I'll put in a bill for my expenses. Then where would your flimsy budget be, huh?'

Gus' budget wouldn't stretch to paying a specialist consultant, which meant he had to keep Sebastian sweet. He shouldn't have been so snappy, anyway. What did it matter what they labelled the killer? His deeds were just as deadly, whether the Prof called him an unsub or Larry the effing Lamb. So, realising he was fighting a losing battle, Gus put out his hands palms upward in a placating gesture. 'Okay, okay. I'll put up with *unsub*. Get to the point, eh? Time's running on.'

Shuffling closer to the boards, Sebastian tapped each of the three photos in turn. 'Usually, serial killers target people within their own racial grouping. I would say, in this case, we can be sure that this unsub is *not* doing that. Clearly, the tattoo torture and the presence of the swastika indicate a racial motive, so I would say the unsub is most certainly white. Which is good, in that it eliminates a huge section of the local population.'

Having already deduced that for himself, Gus wished Sebastian would hurry up. In an effort to curb his instinctive, impatient snort, he took a sip of coffee and tried swallow his frustration.

Meanwhile, Sebastian strode back and forth, as if considering his next words. 'That said, he doesn't seem to have a religious bias. Manish Parmar was Hindu and of Indian descent, Asim Farooq was Muslim of Pakistani descent, and Razaul was of Bangladeshi descent, also Muslim. Whether that's because the victim is ignorant of the cultural and religious differences or whether he just doesn't care, I can't tell you … yet!'

Yeah, yeah, got that, thought Gus. Then, intercepting a look from Alice told him he'd sighed a bit too loudly. He moulded his lips into a semblance of a smile and directed it at Sebastian. 'So, is racism his only motive? Seems a bit extreme to me.'

'You're right, Gus. Quite clearly tattooing the victim on the groin area is likely to carry a sexual motive. It's possible our man's subduing his own sexual bias, or perhaps he's impotent. He certainly appears to have a problem with Asian men who are either bisexual, promiscuous or gay.'

'Couldn't his message be about procreation? And why lay them out in a cross shape?' Alice studied the crime scene photos of the three victims as she spoke.

'Again, a possibility. The cross position may be about Christianity being the superior religion. Another slight against the victims' religions.'

Sebastian turned back to the board. He pointed to a correlation map Compo had configured. 'The proximity of the dump sites in Harden, Haworth and Heaton indicate local knowledge, and I would be looking for a kill spot in this area.' He drew a circle with his finger encompassing Baildon, Shipley, Queensbury and Keighley. 'The choice of sites beginning with an 'H,' although alliterative, is unlikely to have any bearing for the killer.' He paused. 'Mind you, should the next victim also be dumped in a place beginning with the letter 'H,' I may revisit this.' By the time Sebastian finished speaking, Compo had inserted the circle via his computer onto the map, earning an appreciative smile from Sebastian.

Gus rose and went over to closer study the map. This was good. At least they had an area to focus on now.

'Okay, so that's the supposed area for the kill spot. Does that mean he also lives in that locality?' asked Sampson.

Sebastian grimaced. 'I'm inclined to say yes, although at this point, I wouldn't want you to limit your investigation based on that. I suspect our killer lives near both kill and dump sites, however, it *is* only a suspicion. On the other hand, I'm nearly certain the kill site is close to the dump site.'

He splayed his hands. 'This is based purely on the practicalities of subduing a victim, torturing them, killing them and finally dumping them, all in the space of a few hours. Believe it or not, the whole process will be exhausting for the killer, and he'll want to minimise the energy he has to expend. Our unsub has a vehicle ... although you already knew that.'

He turned to Gus, who nodded, his gaze still focussed on the map, and then continued, 'This is all good for you, as you have a narrower geographic area to work with. The torturing process will not be a silent one, so, if I were you, I'd be looking at places in that target area that are remote from their neighbours or have had recent building work done or are vacant or even in extreme disrepair.'

Sampson frowned. 'Building work?'

'Building work can mean extra rooms. Extra rooms can be sound-proofed, or, for that matter, existing rooms can be sound-proofed under the guise of renovations.' Sebastian scratched his nose. 'Serial killers are notoriously devious. This type of non-spree killer is the hardest to catch, for they earn their title by being able to kill multiple targets whilst eluding detection over a period of time. They plan, and they pay attention to detail. They make use of any and all resources available to them. Be prepared for more victims.'

'Can you tell us anything about the killer themselves, other than them being racially motivated and white?' asked Alice.

Sebastian steepled his fingers together at waist level and closed his eyes. When he reopened them, he began talking. 'Okay, some of this you'll have worked out for yourselves by implication, so forgive me for stating the obvious. Depending on other factors like proximity, et cetera, I would say the killer is fairly strong. However, that depends on how quickly they subdue their victim, what ruse they use, what transportation they have available, and so on. This killer is making a statement. The tattoo is that statement, and they may have accelerated because their declaration is not being acknowledged. The posing of the bodies in areas known for 'gay' activity shows the unsub has issues not only with non-whites but also with homosexuality, and this is borne out by the choice of tattoo and its positioning in the groin area. I also wonder if this indicates our killer is an acolyte.'

Gus rolled his eyes, as Sampson's hand shot up. *For God's sake, it's not like he's in school.* Realising he was being a bit mean, he kept quiet. This was not the time to be moaning on about stupid things. He really needed to lighten up.

Sebastian grinned, waving Sampson's question away before it was uttered. 'By that, I mean he may be posing the body and inflicting that particular tattoo in that particular place to demonstrate to someone else his commitment to a shared belief system.'

Now that was interesting, thought Gus. *The killer may be doing this to impress someone else.* 'Would the other person be participating in this?' he asked.

Sebastian shook his head. 'It's unlikely. Most serial killers operate alone. However, if proving their worth or superiority by being an acolyte is part of their fantasy, then that person could, inadvertently, encourage them to more extreme acts of violence.'

'More extreme than that?' asked Gus, pointing at the photos of the dead men.

'It's all relative, isn't it? I've seen far worse than this.'

Gus had too, but now was not the time to dwell on that. He thought for a second or two. 'I thought psychopaths are arrogant. Why would this one take on a subservient role?'

'Ah, good question. You're right, the killer's arrogance is the main motivator, but although I'm calling him an 'acolyte,' I doubt he would view himself that way. He's probably convinced himself it is *his* superiority that makes him carry out the killings in the way he does.'

He peered around the room before moving on. 'Although we've not had the autopsy, excuse me,' he rolled his eyes, 'I forget I'm back in the UK. The *post-mortem* on Razaul Ul Haq – it seems clear from the crime scene photos of the groin wound, that this was a more vicious torture so …' He turned to Gus. 'Either our killer's getting a taste for inflicting pain, or *this* kill was more personal than the others.' He sighed and yanked his glasses off. Holding onto the taped leg, and seemingly heedless of their fragility, he waved them around. 'The problem is, we won't know the answer to that until either you catch the bastard, or he kills again. No pressure, huh?'

The ache that had started, first as a throb at Gus' temple and then as a persistent thump, had accelerated to a pulsing pounding across his forehead. He knew it was caused by the combination of lack of sleep, too much caffeine and the tension of the investigation. Popping two co-codamol, he washed them down with the dregs of his coffee and then moved to the front to address his team. Sebastian had given them enough to go on for the moment, and he was grateful for that.

'Right, we really need to move on this. I've alerted DCI Chalmers, who has organised a press briefing for lunchtime. She will warn the public we are dealing with a serial killer targeting Asian men and confirm he is branding them with a tattoo. She will emphasise the importance for all non-Caucasian men in Bradford to be vigilant and will not release specific details about the tattoo. That information remains within these four walls. She will also ask all tattooists and suppliers in the district to be vigilant and to report anything they notice that may be significant.'

Turning to the now-circled map on the board, Gus said, 'Compo, I want you to focus on finding any likely properties using the criteria specified by Professor Carlton in this area. I will be attending the PM with Alice and follow up by re-interviewing Graeme Weston. Seems likely our killer has some things in common with our wannabe MP, and in light of the possible personal element to the attack on Razaul Ul Haq, that makes Mr Weston a definite person of interest. Also, keep tracking old fashioned and traditional tattoo equipment. We may be lucky and catch a lead through that means.'

Turning to Sampson, he continued, 'I'm expecting a new detective constable to join the team at some point today. You know what the powers-that-be are like. We've got a serial killer on our hands, and they're still talking budgets, despite us being short-staffed. When he or she arrives, bring them up to speed and get them to crack on reviewing and inputting information from the helpline calls. I want you to go back over all three victims' histories. Double-check with their families and friends. Was there some sort of secret life they were living that our killer cottoned on to? Is there some mileage in the newspapers' assertions the first two were gay? We already know that Razaul Ul Haq was a womaniser.

'Is our serial killer cleansing the world of non-white men who don't adhere to his moral code, or are they just chance victims? Get Compo to run deep background checks on all of them, and instead of approaching their families, why don't you take the newbie out this afternoon and re-interview some of the victims' friends? The fact we now have three victims may prompt them to be more talkative.'

Chapter 25

'Come on, come on, pick up!'

Sitting on the closed toilet seat in the girl's loos at school, Neha glanced at the time on her mobile, hoping that Shamshad, for once, would leave her alone and give her some privacy. Ever since they'd found out about their dad's murder, Sham had been following her everywhere, as if she expected Neha to flip again, like she had when their mum went loopy. What Sham didn't realise was her continual worrying made it impossible for Neha to share the things that really mattered to her. Although she knew her sister did it out of love, boy, was it wearing. Especially when she had things she needed to do in secret. Things that her twin wouldn't understand. With one ear listening for the opening of the outer toilet door, she heard the phone cut to voicemail for the umpteenth time since the previous day.

Something was wrong. She knew it. This was the first time he'd ever not answered her call, and right now, she knew he needed her more than ever before. Hell, they needed each other. The outer door opened, and Neha waited for Shamshad to call her name. When she heard two girls giggling together, she breathed easier. Sham hadn't followed her into the loos. She dialled the number again and waited. Still, no answer. An almost uncontrollable urge to throw her phone against the wall and scream engulfed her. Instead, she pushed her sleeves up, crossed her arms over and scratched and scratched until they were bleeding and raw.

Her fingertips ached, and her nails were clogged with blood and flesh. She could smell it and it made her want to gip. Memories of her heart thudding, her breath catching in her chest as she applied pressure to the blade, pressing it against her skin, pulling it downwards, splitting her flesh open like she was scoring an orange, flooded her mind. Next came the release. Her breath slowed, and as the deep thick liquid bubbled to the surface and oozed from the gash, a feeling of serene calm overcame her. Her heart rate fell, and she was at peace.

Neha blinked. She *wasn't* that person anymore. No, she *wasn't*, and she wouldn't allow her memories to lure her back to that place. Not now. Not when she'd been better for so long. This scratching was a blip, a temporary aberration. When things were calmer, she'd stop. Bending over, she lifted her handbag from the toilet floor, and resting it on her lap, she unzipped it and extracted a pack of wet wipes. With care, she wiped each arm clean, pressing the damp fabric against the scratches until the bleeding stopped, ignoring the sting that accompanied it.

Her sister thought she wore long sleeves in adherence to her faith, and although she didn't believe it herself, Sham said she respected Neha's right to her belief and her modesty. Neha sighed. Goodness knew what her sister would do if she could see the scratches running down her thighs and arms. She'd frog march her right back to the psychiatrist, no doubt. Neha laughed. She'd probably end up in the next room to her mother in Lynfield Mount. Best to keep her secrets from Sham … after all, the self-harm wasn't the biggest one she kept.

Chapter 26

09:30 The Fort

Gus had brought Nancy up-to-date on Sebastian Carlton's input. They'd agreed to downplay the 'Tattoo Killer' moniker Jez Hopkins had come up with, and instead were focussing on warning the Asian and Black communities to be vigilant. Having promised to brief her prior to the lunchtime press conference, should anything critical come from the post-mortem, he was winding up the meeting when Alice ran into Nancy's office without knocking. Waving copies of the *Yorkshire Post* and the *Bradford Chronicle* in her hands, she strode over the carpet, stopping next to Gus. One look at her face told him she was angry. Her eyes flashed, and her mouth was in a tight line.

'Bloody bastard's homed in on the fact all the victims were found in villages beginning with an 'H,' hasn't he?'

Gus grabbed the *Chronicle* whilst Nancy snatched the *Yorkshire Post*. 'Since when did that little scrote, Jez Hopkins, write for both papers?' asked Nancy, hefting her unshod feet onto her desk and leaning back to read the front-page article.

Alice breathed heavily, her face flushed. 'Since he's come up with a sensationalist headline and a mainly unsubstantiated, equally sensationalist story. You're going to have your work cut out at the press conference later, ma'am.'

Scanning the article, Gus' heart sank. Hopkins' tone was the height of irresponsible reporting. He'd given scant notice of the latest victim, choosing instead to hazard guesses as to where the fourth victim would be found. Worse, he'd misled the public by stating the victims were killed where they were dumped.

Gus read the *Bradford Chronicle* headline aloud. "The Tattoo Killer hunts for his prey in homely Bradford villages!' Shit. 'The serial killer who has Bradford police running around like headless chickens struck a third time in the small village of Heaton on the fringes of inner city Bradford. Have the police still not spotted the very obvious link between the kills? If not, let's 'spell' it out. Each of the bodies was discovered in a village beginning with the letter 'H' within the Bradford district. First Haworth, then Harden, and now Heaton."

Gus threw the paper on Nancy's desk. 'Idiot. He's drawn a link between the dump sites, *and* he's insinuated the victims were selected and murdered there.' As he reached over to take the *Yorkshire Post* that led with a very similar story penned by the same journalist, his phone buzzed. Glancing at it, he moved away from the desk and answered. 'Hey, Seb, what can I do for you?'

Gus listened for a minute then hung up. 'According to Sebastian, this jackass leading with this story could result in one of two things. Either the killer will go along with this, assuming that wasn't already his plan, and dump the next body in a different village beginning with an 'H.' Clearly, that will extend our investigative area, spreading our resources even more thinly. Or he will continue on his pre-determined plan, whatever that is. He also cautioned that by tagging the killer, Hopkins has elevated him above the victims. He says this could temporarily satiate his need to kill by appealing to his narcissism. However, on the other hand, it could pique his desires and set him on a spiralling killing spree. Either way, if we don't catch him, there will be a fourth victim sooner or later.'

Nancy crossed her right leg over her left knee. Leaning forward, she pulled at her stockings which had got stuck between her toes. 'Phew, load of bloody codswallop. How does any of that help us? Basically, all Carlton's told us is he might delay his kill or he might bring it forward ... Duh? Like we didn't know that! Or ...' Having finished prodding at her toes through her tights, she waved her hand in the air. 'He might dump his next victim in a village beginning with and 'H' or, wait for it ... then again, he might not. Load of bloody twaddle.'

She swung her legs off her desk and jumped to her feet. The absence of her usual heels made her of equal height to Alice, nevertheless, the glower she levelled at Gus was ferocious. 'Go out and catch this bloody racist killer. I don't care where he plans to dump the next body. Our job is to prevent that, okay?'

Feeling very much like a dog with his tail between its legs, Gus could only nod.

Chapter 27

G us' dad looked up from his examination of Razaul Ul Haq. On noticing Alice had accompanied Gus into the room, he squealed, in Gus' opinion, rather like a schoolgirl. 'Alice, my dear. When did you get back to work?'

Although both his father and his friend were wearing surgical masks, it was clear to Gus they were smiling at each other. He scowled. He hated this habit they had of mixing business with pleasure. It wasn't as if he hadn't spoken to his dad about it often enough; still, the old goat insisted on rabbiting on, instead of maintaining a degree of professionalism.

Turning to Gus, Fergus said, his words clipped and accusing, 'And why didn't you tell your mum and me Alice was back at work?'

'What?' Gus banged his forehead with his blue gloved hand. 'Of course, I should have dropped everything to tell you. It's not as if I've got three dead bodies and a serial killer to think about. God! How remiss of me.'

Alice nudged him with her elbow, and his dad glowered at him for a long second, a frown pulling his hairy eyebrows into a furry bush on his forehead. He shook his head. 'Sarcasm does *not* become you, Angus. Your mother would be very disappointed. She brought you up better than that.'

Mentioning his mum was a low blow, and Gus nearly said so. Instead, he inhaled. His chest filled with the formaldehyde fumes of the mortuary, and immediately, he wished he hadn't. Despite the fact his dad hadn't opened up the body yet, his stomach gurgled, and to make matters worse, he'd forgotten his Vicks VapoRub. He knew it didn't really work, but it was his prop. No way would he ask Alice if she had any, either. He'd never live it down if he did. He glared at his dad who'd turned back to the body, still shaking his head. He was still annoyed the old man had brought his mum into the equation. Talk about guilt-tripping him. Trying to breathe small breaths through his mouth, Gus took a reluctant step closer and surveyed the remains of Razaul Ul Haq. He was in his late thirties and appeared young for his age. He seemed, apart from being dead of course, to be in good nick, externally anyway. No doubt his dad would soon tell him if that was true of his innards.

'Here's the injection site, Angus.' His dad raised Razaul's head to show Gus and Alice the miniscule spot on his nape. 'Exactly the same place as the previous two victims.' He shuffled down the length of the metal table, and lifting first one arm and then the other, he pointed to his wrist. 'Same sort of bruising as before and on his ankles too. Probably cable ties, which won't narrow it down for you, I'm afraid.'

He drew back the cover to reveal the groin area, which Gus had already seen at the crime scene. 'It was clear when we first viewed him the killer tattooed him much deeper than the other two victims, but after I cleaned it up, the extent of the injuries is even more evident. This must have been excruciating for him, poor sod! Most tattoos go down barely a millimetre. This was applied so heavily, it penetrated almost three to four millimetres in parts.'

An uncomfortable sensation near his own groin area had Gus cringing. He could almost feel Ul Haq's agony, as his father dropped the light sheet back onto the body.

Fergus nodded. 'Exactly, makes you wince, doesn't it?'

'Sure does. It also makes me think this *must* be personal. The level of pain inflicted here is much more than on either of the other two victims.'

Alice looked at him. 'You thinking Graeme Weston?'

Gus shrugged. 'Maybe. He's definitely worth looking at. After all, he's got a very personal motive for killing Ul Haq. Just worries me he'd do it when he's making such a public bid for stardom.'

'Ah,' said Fergus, lifting the Stryker saw. 'Weston is that Albion First candidate for the by-election, isn't he? Perhaps it's not him doing it. Maybe it's one of his acolytes.'

Gus frowned. 'Funny you should say that; that's the very word Professor Carlton used.'

Chapter 28

10:15 Caroline Drive, Dudley Hill, Bradford

Villages beginning with an 'H.' Shouldn't even dignify that with a response. What does that stupid reporter know? He thinks he knows it all, whereas he knows nowt. Not a damn thing. He hasn't one iota of awareness in his entire body. Look around, Mr Jez Hopkins, see what's happening to our city? It's not about 'H' villages; it's about Bradford. Bradford and the stinking Pakis and Blacks and Eastern Europeans, and homos and paedos and the like. That's what the problem is.

It is warm inside the car. Too warm. I open the window to let a quick blast of air in but then I have to shut it again, pronto, before the stench of Paki food gets in. Is it too much to ask they don't cook their stinking curries in the chip shops? Polluting the environment, the clean Bradford air, that's what they've done over the years. Building their mosques and restaurants. Makes me want to puke. Feel sick at the very thought of the garbage they shovel down their throats. They act all holier than thou, too, as if they, with their Islam and their burkas, have some sort of access to God's heavenly sanctum.

I was right to think Ul Haq wouldn't be the last to need tattooing. It's easy to find them ... too easy! Once I've chosen them, it's not rocket science to find out where they go. They thought they'd been discreet, and this one is no different. Getting blow jobs from some crack whore off Thornton Road for a tenner, whilst his wife is laid up, ready to drop. Funny how it is so easy to find them. Funny how it is always the blacks and Pakis. Makes my skin crawl looking at them, watching them in the darkness, hearing them moaning for their cheap thrills, seeing them pervert God's will. Makes me sick.

This one though, he is special … special and so, so easy to snare. He'll be the simplest catch yet. The only question is when and, of course, where to dump the body. Would it be better to go along with the stupid journo's 'H' tag and choose the dump site accordingly? Or should I just do my own thing? No, this time, I'll make a stance. Make sure they all sit up and take notice.

There is time still, though. Time to make a final decision. I lay my head back, resting it on the headrest and wait, blocking out the jabber of Paki voices and the drone of their music and the rotting stench of their existence. After all, patience is a virtue!

Chapter 29

12:30 Hawthorn Drive, Eccleshill

Parked in front of the chippie along from the Weston's street, Gus stared in amazement at Alice as she stuffed ketchup-covered chips into her mouth – as if they hadn't, less than an hour previously, witnessed Razaul Ul Haq's post-mortem. What was it with the woman? Gus could still feel his stomach churning, and he couldn't shake the images of the tattoo that had been inflicted, somewhat inexpertly, on Ul Haq's shaven groin. The familiar watering at the back of his throat that preceded the act of throwing up, had him thrusting open the car door and breathing in deep breaths of not so fresh air. The coolness seemed to do the trick, for his nausea waned. Trust Alice to insist on fish and chips. The greasy smell had made his stomach roll, and he was not looking forward to re-entering the car.

The sound of the passenger window whirring down made him turn. Alice, still cheerfully stuffing her face, pushed a bottle of water in his direction. He took it, grateful for the chance to wash away the near sick taste from his mouth. 'You nearly finished, Al?'

Stuffing her last chip into her mouth, she balled up the wrapper and handed it to him through the window. Tutting, Gus accepted it, his lip curled downwards as he held it at arm's length and deposited it in the nearby bin. 'I'm going to walk round to the Weston's, Al. You drive, but can you keep all the windows open to get rid of that stink?'

Gus thought he heard the word 'wuss,' as Alice shimmied over into the driver's seat and started the engine. Grinning, he chose to ignore it and set off at a brisk pace. Eccleshill had once been a predominantly white area of Bradford, however now it was becoming increasingly culturally diverse. The Westons lived in the posh part, in a small street of newly built houses selling for in the region of three quarters of a million pounds. The building and property development trade must be soaring. The Weston's house was about halfway down the street and was a five-bedroomed detached with a double garage and, according to Google maps, had sizeable gardens to the front and the rear. The front garden was pristine with flowerbeds surrounding an immaculate, if wet lawn. Gus suspected they employed a gardener to keep it so. He couldn't imagine Christine Weston getting her hands dirty, and he guessed at this point in his career, Graeme Weston was a hands-off kind of guy. The sort who issued orders to his minions and expected everyone else to jump. Gus had been surprised when he'd phoned Weston on his mobile and was told to come to their home address rather than his works one in Bingley.

As he drew parallel to the house, Alice got out of the car and met him on the pavement before they both walked up the terracotta tiled path to the front door. The previous evening, Gus hadn't paid a lot of attention when he'd rung the bell, but today, the metallic tones of 'Rule, Britannia!' drifted through the door. Gus raised an eyebrow. *How predictable!*

The door opened, and there stood Christine Weston, looking a damn sight more groomed than she had the previous day. Gus noticed the dark shadows beneath her eyes and the remains of the swelling on her bruised cheek. Averting her eyes, she clutched the edge of the door, and stammering over her words, she invited them in. She led them through to the same room they were in yesterday, and apart from the absence of wine bottles on the coffee table, it appeared much as it had done then. Graeme Weston, dressed in horse riding gear sat, legs crossed, on one of the armchairs. The TV was tuned to *Loose Woman*, but on their entry, Weston switched it off. Jacob was curled up on the sofa in a grey faux fur blanket. He was pale and appeared feverish.

Christine stood by the door, glancing alternately between her son and husband. Licking her lips, she said, 'Can I get you something to drink?'

Before Gus or Alice could reply, Weston interrupted, 'Don't be stupid, woman, this isn't a social call. Why would we entertain them? They're public *servants* after all, paid for by our taxes.'

The emphasis on the word 'servants' combined with the sneering look he sent Gus showed clearly his opinion of him. Gus put his hands in his pockets to hide the way he'd clenched his fists, and plastering an insincere smile on his face, he moved over and, without being asked, settled himself into the chair opposite Weston. He was pleased to see Weston's mouth tighten, and responded by widening his smile. He then turned to Christine and said, 'Could you get a chair for my colleague please, Christine? We wouldn't want to disturb young Jacob here.'

Christine, bursting into a flurry of activity, ran across the room returning with a high-backed dining chair for Alice, who accepted the chair with polite thanks and a warm smile.

Turning to Weston, Gus said, 'Wouldn't have had you down for a horse lover.'

Mouth curling, Weston eyed Gus as if he didn't really care what the other man's thoughts were. Then, capitulating, he said, 'Not that it's any business of yours, my grandparents owned a stable over Haworth way. Michael was their neighbour. When they died, they left me one of their horses, and Michael is good enough to let it bunk up with his now.'

He sniffed. 'We're taking them for a run across Shipley Glen. That is, if you get a bloody move on, of course.'

Christine settled herself in the corner of the couch. After tucking the cover around her son, she ran her hand over his forehead and grimaced. With a sigh, she placed the back of her fingers on his cheek. When he jerked his head, she smiled and removed them.

Thinking the boy was a bit old to be squashed into a couch downstairs, Gus turned back to Weston. 'Is Jacob poorly?'

From the corner of his eye, he registered Christine flinched and was further intrigued when Weston barked at him, 'The boy's medical history is of no concern to you. It's irrelevant to your investigation, and I'll thank you to leave him out of it.'

Wow! That was a bit of an overreaction. Even Jacob had stirred at his father's tone. Inclining his head, Gus watched Christine Weston. She held her hands in her lap, her fingers so tightly clenched, they were white. She kept sending surreptitious glances in her husband's direction, and a small tic at the side of her eye told Gus how agitated she was. Maintaining a level tone, he said, 'I wonder why you're so aggressive about what was a very simple solicitous question regarding the welfare of your son, Graeme.'

The other man tensed, and Gus knew he'd hit a raw nerve.

'Jacob's welfare is of no concern to the likes of you … and *you* can address me as Mr Weston.'

Knowing Weston had barely managed to prevent himself from adding the word 'boy' to the end of his sentence and realising exactly how rattled the older man was, Gus leaned back and crossed his legs. He was beginning to enjoy himself. Maintaining a mild tone, he asked, 'When you say the 'likes of you,' are you referring to me as a British police officer or me as a black man?'

The colour that suffused Weston's face was that of an aged Burgundy wine, and Gus watched with amusement as it darkened to a Merlot as he struggled to come up with a response. 'Take it how you like,' he said at last, almost spitting the words at Gus. He then turned to his wife. 'Take the boy upstairs, Christine. Now!'

Christine jumped to her feet and shook her sons shoulder, gently rousing him. The boy was pale, and if Christine hadn't inserted her arm under his armpits, Gus was sure Jacob would have fallen. As he left the room, each step seemed to drain the boy even more. A flash of rage surged through Gus, as Weston leaned back and watched his wife struggle with their son. What sort of man would behave like that? Fair enough, he was angry with his wife … who wouldn't be? His own experience made it easy to imagine how Weston felt; however, to allow his wife to struggle on like that was plain nasty. Seemed like this politician didn't necessarily possess the manners to go with his aspirations.

Barely concealing his emotions, Gus said, 'Do you have any tattoos, *Mr* Weston?'

Clearly put off balance by the question, Weston gawped, 'What?'

Enunciating each word with care, Gus repeated the question.

Weston frowned. 'Well, yes, I do, although I don't see the relevance.' Then, as if a light had gone on, he nodded his head and laughed. 'Oh, you're asking because of that lunatic who tattooed Razaul Ul Haq. Saw it on the news. Well, I hate to tell you, despite having tattoos, I've never applied any. You need an expert for that.'

Gus continued to smile. 'Yes, I know that. I merely wondered if *you* had a tattoo like his one.' He flung a close-up photograph of the swastika applied to Razaul Ul Haq onto the table. It had been taken at such an angle the area of the body it was applied to was unclear.

Weston gave the photo a cursory glance and shook his head.

Christine Weston, who'd returned from escorting her son upstairs, gave an audible gasp and averted her eyes at once. Covering her mouth with trembling fingers, tears sprung to her eyes. Gus was sorry he'd had to inflict this pain on her in order to provoke a response from her husband.

Alice leaned over, and resting her hand on Christine's arm, she squeezed. Christine exhaled and then eyed the photo again. Gus studied Weston, who was watching the byplay with a smirk on his face. He tapped the photo. 'Well?'

Weston screwed up his mouth and rolled his eyes. 'No, I don't.'

Christine gasped again, and Gus swung his gaze to her. 'Do you disagree with your husband?'

For a moment, Christine's eyes drifted towards her husband, and Gus was certain she was going to denounce him. Then, she glanced away shaking her head. 'No, he hasn't.'

Gus stood up and walked out of the room, Alice following.

Weston stood and called after him, 'Is that it then? Are you done with us?'

Gus waited until he reached the front door before responding, 'Not by a long chalk, *Graeme*. Enjoy your ride.'

Chapter 30

13:30 Hawthorn Drive, Eccleshill

Graeme Weston paced up and down in front of the fireplace whilst Christine cowered on the sofa. She was distraught. She could hardly believe Razaul was dead. How could he be? She'd only been with him on Sunday night. During the last two days, she'd lost her lover, and now, it seemed, she was in danger of losing both her husband and her son.

Graeme knelt in front of her and clasped her hands in his. 'You understand what's at stake, Christine, don't you?'

Feeling numb, she nodded. What else could she do? Graeme smiled and patted her hand. 'That's my girl. All we need to do is keep quiet, and make sure that nobody finds out about the lad.' He stood up and slid onto the sofa next to her and put his arm around her. 'We've kept it on the QT all this time, we can manage a few more years. At least until I'm elected, yeah?'

Tired of the lies and deceit, but too exhausted to protest, Christine nodded again. Smiling, he pulled her closer and began nuzzling her hair. The insistent pressure of his erection pushed hard against her thigh, and when he thrust his tongue into her mouth and his hand up her skirt, she thought she would vomit.

Chapter 31

14:40 The Fort

S ampson felt like he was drowning in a never-ending pile of paperwork. He was going stir crazy and had even snapped at Compo twice in the past hour for singing 'People are Strange' by The Doors. It wasn't like him. Normally, he'd join in, even if he didn't know the words, which was the case, in this instance. He glanced over at Compo, who every so often allowed a few words to escape his lips before, seemingly conscious of upsetting his colleague, clamped his mouth shut and resorted to miming the lyrics instead. Sampson had never been able to fathom why Compo put one or sometimes two tracks on repeat and listened solely to them for hours on end. It would drive him crazy, but Compo said he chose the track that fitted the job in hand and stuck with it until the task was complete. Whatever task matched the 'People are Strange' song was taking him a substantial amount of time.

Sampson grinned. It was surprising Compo didn't use that track every week bearing in mind the sort of people they came into contact with. He rummaged in the bottom of his drawer, found what he was looking for, and laid his findings on the desk in front of Compo. Compo stilled. A moment later, he looked up at Sampson, his round face breaking into a grin, as he grabbed the Mars Bar and ripped the wrapper off. 'Thanks, Sampson. Was nearly dying without my sugar rush.'

Sampson laid a hand on Compo's shoulder and smothered his smile, aware Compo had, only a few minutes earlier, devoured a bag of crisps and a Creme Egg. Having had enough of computer work, Sampson took a note of Asim Farooq and Manish Parmar's friends' addresses and was about to head out, when the door opened, and a head poked around.

'DI Gus McGuire?'

'He's not in. Can I help?' asked Sampson, as the young man entered the room. To Sampson, he seemed about fifteen, with barely a shadow of a moustache on his baby-soft face. He was one of those lads who were short but burly. He slouched into the room, his arms bent at the elbows and grinned. His eyes sparked with good humour, and Sampson was instantly drawn to his understated charm.

Flashing a set of perfect, white teeth, the lad held out his hand. 'I'm Talvinder Bhandir. People call me Taffy.'

Sampson shook his hand. 'You don't sound Welsh'

'Nah, I'm not. I'm Yorkshire,' said Taffy, his tone serious, the slight frown on his forehead telling Sampson he'd missed the joke.

'Yeah,' said Sampson, drawing out the word, 'I got that. I was joking. Welsh folk are sometimes called Taffy.'

The frown disappeared. 'Oh, well, it's my nickname, 'stead of Talvinder, like.'

Sampson grinned. All Taffy needed to do was to wipe his sleeve over his nose and he'd look exactly like one of Sampson's many nephews. Introductions over, Sampson saw Taffy look at the crime boards with rather more interest than he was comfortable with. Wary of confidentiality, he asked, 'Was DI McGuire expecting you?'

'Oh, yeah, I'm the new DC. First day on the job. Can't wait to get cracking, like. Done six months as a PC after my degree and got fast-tracked here. Shall I get doing summat?'

Remembering Gus had told him to expect a DC, Sampson nodded. He'd expected someone a bit older. Bearing in mind Alice had thought *he* looked young when he'd first joined the team, he decided to give the lad the benefit of the doubt. At least he seemed eager and had no airs and graces like some of the fast-tracked DCs he'd come across. It was unfortunate he'd missed the briefing, but Sampson reckoned he could fill him in on their way to interview the victims' friends. He checked Taffy's warrant card and phoned through to DCI Nancy Chalmers for the go-ahead before leaving the incident room in Compo's capable, if extremely sticky, hands.

The first of Asim Farooq's friends available to chat was a friend from university who worked at the Yorkshire Building Society in Bradford and could spare them a few minutes. Sharon Kelly was tall, with flaming red hair and a wide smile. She wore a whopping engagement ring and mentioned her fiancé at least five times during their conversation. Turned out, she'd known Asim's wife more than she'd known him. Her impression was he was a nice guy, despite the current rumours. Asim had met her friend Humairah at university, and they'd dated throughout their time there. When pushed to expand on the rumours, she shrugged looking embarrassed, and in the end, all she would commit to was the news reports after his death backed up some of the rumours from their time at university. Not, she hastened to add, that she could confirm anything.

Sampson came away feeling as if his questions had only served to fuel the already over-worked gossip mills. With Taffy in tow, he persevered, and by the end of the afternoon, had managed to pinpoint two men who admitted to having sex with Asim Farooq and one woman who told him she knew Manish Parmar was into S&M in a big way, but purely heterosexual. Sampson got the impression she was his dominatrix, and that's why she was saved in his phone under the name Dom.

'What do you make of all this, Taffy?' he asked. He'd soon realised although he considered Taffy to be younger than himself, they were actually the same age. The only difference was Sampson had joined the police straight from school, and Taffy had gone to university to study criminology first.

Taffy scratched his head. 'Well, it's not unheard of for folk to lead a double life, is it?' He shrugged. 'Sometimes, the culture gets in the way of people leading the lives they want to. Can be a real conflict for some.' He met Sampson's eye. 'I'm not only talking Asians, though, you know? Every family has its own culture. Its own way of doing things, its own 'code,' if you like. I had gay friends at uni who kept their sexuality secret from their families because they knew they wouldn't accept it. Fundamentalist Christians can be as bad as fundamentalist Muslims or Hindus or Sikhs.'

Sampson nodded. He knew only too well firsthand how hard families could be on one another. His sister had gotten pregnant fifteen years ago, and because the bloke wasn't a Catholic, his parents had kicked off something chronic. All sorted now, of course ... babies had a habit of making things alright, didn't they? He tried to imagine what it would have been like for Asim Farooq to have family pressure to get married and to deny his true sexuality. He also empathised with his wife and family, who now had to deal with the aftermath of his secret life in the public eye. It was a complete ball-ache.

It seemed each of the three victims had lived an 'alternative' lifestyle to a greater or lesser degree. Of course, that leant itself to Professor Carlton's belief that each victim had been targeted by the killer. Now, they could start to cross-match to see if they could work out exactly how they'd come to the attention of their killer.

Feeling that they'd been productive, Sampson was happy to call it a day and head back to The Fort.

Chapter 32

15:00 The Hare and Hounds, Toller Lane

Rather than head back to The Fort, Gus had elected to try to unwind a bit after his interview with Graeme Weston. Merely being in the man's presence made Gus want to shower, a feeling he was aware was entirely mutual. He wanted to bounce a few ideas off Alice, so they sat in the pub's alcove near the real wood fire, nursing two mugs of coffee. Deposited on each saucer, in lieu of a biscuit, was a handful of chocolate Smarties. Their crisp coating bled a rainbow of colour through the droplets of coffee in their saucers. Alice's eyes lit up at the sight of the sweet treat, and without asking, she helped herself to Gus's share.

Outside, heavy snow clouds flitted across the darkening sky, and already the cars on Toller Lane had their headlights on. For a short while, they sat in companionable silence. Gus used the opportunity to study Alice. She was pale, and her ready smile seemed to take more effort than usual. It wasn't surprising, considering this was only her second day back. If they hadn't been in the middle of such a big case, she'd have been able to build up to full-time hours. As it was, she'd been thrown in at the deep end. He was amazed at how well-adjusted she seemed. Unlike him, she didn't appear to lapse into periods of brooding or struggle to interact. She seemed upbeat, just like she'd been before she was hurt. How could it be that she was so resilient, and he'd fallen to pieces?

As if she sensed what he was thinking, Alice kicked him under the table and said, 'Don't get all maudlin on me now, Gus.'

Rubbing his shin where her boot had connected, he grinned. 'I suppose I should be grateful you didn't wallop me on the arm.'

'If you don't stop worrying about me, I bloody well will whap you on the arm ... hard. Now, get the bloody Bepanthen out, and I'll put some on for you.'

Fumbling in his bag for the elusive tube, he said, 'Ah, Alice, it's good to have you back.' Withdrawing the cream, he pulled his jumper off and yanked his T-shirt down from the neck so she could apply the moisturiser. With gentle fingers, she spread it over the tattoo, enthusing again over its appropriateness. 'Don't think your mum will like it, though.'

Gus grimaced. The mere thought of his mother's reaction made his stomach muscles clench. 'You promised, Al.'

Laughing, she pulled his T-shirt back up. 'Secret's safe with me, Gus. Lips are sealed, and all that. She's going to find out though. She's sure to. You can't keep it hidden from her forever. Anyway, for goodness sake. How old are you? Twelve? Man up. It's *your* body.'

Gus rolled his eyes. 'You know how she is – relentless. That's the only word for it. She'll go on and on ... and bloody on.'

Alice snorted and flung a Smartie in the air, catching it in her mouth. 'Idiot!'

Shrugging his sweater back on, Gus glared at her. 'Great, say it as it is, why don't you? Nice to have your sympathy, Al. Don't know what I'd do without that.'

She clicked her fingers. 'Knew it. You missed me. Can't cope without me. I'm an integral member of the team. The cog without which no machine can run, the –'

'Alright, alright, you've made your point. Now, shut up and listen. What do you think is wrong with Jacob Weston?'

Alice frowned. 'Don't know. I was wondering that. He looked feverish and in pain ... flu?'

Gus shrugged. 'Suppose it could be … Didn't you get the impression they were being cagey about it?

'God, yes! Christine was as jumpy as a flea on a porcupine's arse. She couldn't settle. Didn't know where to put herself. She's clearly grieving the loss of her lover, but she also seemed to be worried sick about Jacob. As for that arsehole, referring to him as 'the boy.' It's pathetic. He's pathetic.'

'Hmm.' Gus sighed. 'Jacob looked fine on Monday, so what happened overnight to make him flake out like that, and why would they need to be secretive? Why not just tell us if he's got flu or a tummy bug or whatever?'

Alice waved at a little girl who was sitting in a highchair opposite. 'There's something dodgy about Weston. I don't care if his alibi is solid; there's something off with the man, and as for Christine … why, when your husband's a member of an extreme right-wing fascist party, would you have an affair with a Bangladeshi man? It's plain stupid. Especially on the eve of his announcement as election candidate. Very dodgy.'

'We really need to speak to Michael Hogg, his election manager, Al.'

Alice clapped her hands. 'Yippee, can't wait. Hope he's as nice as his boss!'

Gus laughed and finished the dregs of his coffee. 'Come on. I'll buy you another coffee to fill the time. I reckon I know where Michael Hogg will be in about an hour or so's time.'

Chapter 33

15:30 Hawthorn Drive, Eccleshill

Dressed in a white terry bath robe that barely skimmed his knees and was loosely tied at the waist, revealing his substantial paunch as well as his manhood, Graeme Weston sat, legs apart on the sofa, speaking into his mobile. His hair was still damp from the shower he'd just had. The overpowering aftershave he'd splashed on filled the room. 'Well, I think it's important I show face. Can't kowtow to pressure from jihadists, can we? Bradford City is mine, and City Park is at the centre of the constituency I want to represent. They cannot and will *not* scare me away, Michael.'

He listened for a minute and then smiled. 'That's settled then, you'll sort it. Let's make those idiots look like the amateurs they are.'

He lay back on the sofa, a smile on his face. Those bloody lefties could do their worst ... Michael had it all in hand. It was all going to backfire on them and serve them bloody well right too.

Slipping the phone into the pocket of his robe, he made a mental note to dispose of it at the earliest opportunity. The thing about being part of a much-maligned political party on the fringe of society was that you had to be cautious. Throwaway phones were a part of his party's day-to-day operations. No point giving anyone ammunition against you ... and definitely *not* when you'd just planned an illegal act with your second-in-command.

He laughed and yelled up the stairs for Christine to make him a sandwich before he set off for City Park. She'd need to apply extra make-up again to cover the matching bruise on the other side of her face. No more than she deserved, but she could do her repair work after he'd gone.

Chapter 34

It was hard to believe despite the falling snow, they'd still managed to fill City Park with more than three hundred protestors. Imti was stoked. They'd worked overnight to create banners and placards, and Shahid, despite his irritation, had mucked in and helped. Imti still worried about him. He hadn't been the same since his girlfriend's death, and he was pleased to see his big brother participating in something that didn't involve The Delius. He even carried a 'No to Albion First!' placard, and for once, he was actually smiling. Maybe things were improving for them, and about bloody time.

After Sunday's announcement by Graeme Weston that he was representing Albion First in the upcoming by-election, the various youth groups in Bradford had mobilised quickly – from Woodcraft to Young Labour to various religious youth groups representing all of Bradford's faiths. Imti had heard many of the youths who had been ineligible to vote in the Brexit referendum express their anger that Brexit had led to this. He'd also heard some of the people here today had voted for Brexit and were angry with the racist backlash that had occurred in its wake. Bradford had taken a bashing over the past couple of years with the Matchmaker scandal followed by the gang warfare that had resulted in many deaths. Imti did not want his city to be a testing ground for the likes of Graeme Weston and his fascist cronies.

Imti grinned at Serafina who was supporting the other end of a 'No to Racism, No to Weston!' banner. He'd never done something like this before. In truth, he'd never really thought about what he believed in, until he'd met Serafina. Now, seeing how strong she was, made him want to make her proud. She'd been through so much, and yet, she was still here, holding her head high, getting on with her life, thinking of the future and what she wanted to achieve. As far as he could see, things were looking good.

People from Bradford's African-Caribbean communities were dancing as if it was carnival time, and the huge papier-mâché puppets, normally used in the lantern parades through Lister Park, bobbed about, colourful and flamboyant. Drums and whistles made it feel like a street party. Passers-by stopped to watch, smiles on their faces, as the dancers weaved among them, engaging them, entertaining them.

Weston hadn't even showed his ugly face and nor had any of his band of thugs – well, not as far as Imti knew, anyway. Despite a few dodgy-looking characters being around, no-one had been overtly hostile. All they wanted to do was make a statement that Bradford Central ward was not up for grabs by racists and homophobes in this by-election. The left-wing parties had jumped on the bandwagon, and there were a few Socialist Party members selling their newspapers. The local Labour councillor had agreed to speak later on the steps of City Hall, and so far, the police had kept a watching brief, leaving them to protest peacefully. No-one wanted a repeat of the Bradford riots of 20:01.

Then, as if from nowhere, there was a sudden silence that lasted for a few seconds followed almost immediately by shouting and cries. People had stopped, were pointing fingers. All at once, they surged towards the Mirror Pool.

Imti couldn't see what was happening at first then … he saw it. On the grassy bank that covered the roof of the café stood a large group of people. Some had covered their lower faces with scarves, and many of them were holding banners displaying Union Flags, St George's Crosses, and swastikas. Right at the front, the burly forms of Graeme Weston and his sidekick Michael Hogg were clearly visible. Their faces were uncovered, and Weston's trademark smile was in evidence, as he raised his arms in front of him like a priest in a pulpit, addressing his congregation.

The mood of the crowd below changed as rage simmered and bubbled through them as if by osmosis. This was not good. Not good at all. As the jeers and jostling began to pick up a malevolent tempo, Imti rolled up his banner and pulled Serafina close to him. The protestors surged forward, their chants resonating across the park, and from their elevated position, Weston's supporters responded in kind, whilst Weston himself stood still, hands held aloft. Around the periphery of the crowd, tense-looking police officers began to move forward in an attempt to place themselves between the rival crowds. All the while, they spoke in sharp tones on their radios, and with extendable batons drawn, they edged themselves through the tightly grouped bodies. The earlier party atmosphere had dissipated, replaced by the heaviness of fear and anger. The protestors continued to push ahead, angered by the way the Albion First supporters towered like avenging soldiers above them.

All the time, Imti scoured the crowds looking for Shahid, but he was nowhere to be seen. Sensing Serafina's fear, he smiled down at her before continuing his search. Then, as if from nowhere, someone was pulling Serafina from him and shouting something unintelligible in his ear. At first, he struggled against it, then he recognised DI Gus McGuire and DS Alice Cooper.

As Alice led Serafina towards the Broadway Shopping Centre away from the park, Gus shouted, 'Who are you looking for, Imti?'

Relieved to see his girlfriend heading for safety, Imti glanced round and realised the friendly police, who had been dotted around earlier, had been replaced by officers in riot gear. His heart began to thud in his chest. Things were getting more threatening by the second.

'Shahid,' he yelled. 'I can't see Shahid. He was here a minute ago.'

In a panic, he craned his neck, pushing against the force of the throng, trying not to be swept into the centre as he searched for his brother. The crowd had got ugly, and as he watched, he saw a hooded figure standing near the café entrance. As if in slow motion, the figure lifted an arm high and with barely a pause to take aim, had thrown something into the crowd standing in the empty Mirror Pool. Imti frowned. He'd seen the man in the crowd earlier and thought he was dodgy. He'd sidled past Imti and Serafina with his hood up and his head low. His eyes had cast side to side, as if scoping out the crowd, and Imti had ducked down on pretence of tying his laces and had looked up into his face. When their eyes had met, the other lad had frowned and swerved away from Imti, keeping his head and face averted.

The missile arced over the heads of those nearest to the front, heading straight to the centre of the bunched-up people. Imti caught sight of a flame, bright against the fading light. It was a Molotov cocktail. Panic thudded against his chest, as he cricked his neck upwards to follow the trajectory. Was Shahid in the middle of the throng? He couldn't see him, yet he had a sense of foreboding.

Gus tried to pull him back, away from the inevitable explosion, but Imti had just seen a placard bearing the slogan 'No to Albion First!' He struggled to free himself from Gus' grip. There was a sudden moment of silence, as the crowd realised what was happening and tried to reverse their forward momentum. It was too late. The homemade bomb exploded, and the air in City Park was rent with shrieks of pain and horror.

Chapter 35

17:00 The Fort

Shuffling along the corridor as fast as she could, DCI Nancy Chalmers slammed open the door and propelled herself through the door, narrowly missing being hit on the face as it rebounded after slamming against the wall. 'Riot in City Park. All officers needed. Peaceful protest gone awry. We need to be on top of this.'

As if realising she was talking to a near-empty room, she stopped and glanced around. 'Gus ...?' Seeing the look on Compo's face, and the way Sampson had jumped to his feet at her words, she exhaled and counted to five before saying, 'He's there, isn't he?'

Sampson, grabbing his coat, nodded and halfway across the room, shouted, 'And so is Alice. I'm on my way. I'll let you know when I find them.'

A small man Nancy had never seen before followed behind Sampson, saluting as he passed. 'I'm DC Taffy Bhandir, ma'am. I'll help DC Sampson.'

Bemused, Nancy observed Compo, who, face taut with tension, had his fingers flying across the keyboard.

'Compo ...?'

'Shh!' said Compo, waving his hand in the air in uncharacteristic rudeness.

Nancy moved over and stood behind him, watching over his shoulder as he worked his magic.

'Accessed the CCTV from City Park. We'll at least have eyes on what's going on.'

Nancy placed her hand on his shoulder and squeezed. 'Thanks, Compo. Let's see if we can keep tabs on what's happening from here as it's unfolding. Get communication up with Sampson so we can co-ordinate with him when he gets there. The riot police will have their own comms up and running, but any extra can only help.'

With another few key strokes, Compo transferred the grid images from his screen onto the whiteboard, and he and Nancy watched images from the six cameras.

'You take the top three, ma'am, and I'll take the bottom three.'

Nodding, Nancy scoured her three frames for sight of either Alice or Gus and was finally rewarded when she saw Gus heading towards City Library with a young lad by his side.

With a sigh, she sat down on Gus' chair. 'Got eyes on Gus, Compo. He seems fine.'

Thank God. *How in heaven's name does that boy always seems to end up where there's some sort of trouble?* She took her phone out and punched in a number. When Gus' mum answered, she said, 'Don't know if you've seen the news about City Park, Corrine, but he's fine. Gus is okay.'

Corrine erupted into a series of questions, and across the line, Nancy could hear her moving around. Then, the sound of the muffled voices told her that her friend had switched the TV on to see for herself what was happening.

Nancy smiled. Corrine was ferocious when it came to protecting either of her two children. She may be small, but Corrine McGuire had the survival instincts of a tigress. She'd had to, having suffered abuse as a child before being taken into foster care in Scotland. Nancy's smile faded as she recollected that those childhood experiences were not the only trauma her friend had suffered. Despite all the odds, the mixed-race Scottish girl had excelled in her chosen field, and until she'd taken early retirement, had been a renowned paediatrician. Nancy listened to Corrine for a few seconds more, a faint smile alleviating the tension from her face, then promised to get Gus to phone her when he got back to The Fort before she hung up.

Chapter 36

17:15 City Park Bradford

Fire engines, screams, ambulances, tears, police sirens. The noise was deafening. However, what was worse was the smell of petrol fumes, and the overlying stench of singed flesh that clogged up Gus' throat. He had bodily dragged Imti away from the blast, and within ten minutes, the police in riot gear had cleared the area of everyone, except the injured. In record time, two fire engines drove straight onto the park. The City Library had opened its doors as a base for triage, and the surrounding restaurants and cafes distributed hot drinks to the emergency services and those in shock.

As he'd pulled Imti away, Gus had spotted Shahid towards the back of the crowd, looking as desperate as his younger brother. He'd managed to reunite the brothers, and now, the three of them were helping the paramedics do triage. The most serious injuries had been whisked off to BRI, but many people with non-life-threatening injuries remained in the library where, at least, they were warm.

Gus suspected an investigation into the bomb would establish some combustive commodity had been added to extend the effects of the explosion. Imti had told him he saw who had thrown the bomb, and he said it had come from the protestors' side. One of the riot squad had stated various witnesses had reported seeing the bomb in the hands of one of the protestors in City Park. It didn't make a lot of sense, and it would be a nightmare to prove until the fire investigator had done her full and thorough investigation.

As they worked in the freezing conditions, Gus was aware of Jez Hopkins and the other journalists snapping photos and trying to interview people. On the parapet above the café, Graeme Weston delivered an interview which, no doubt, would lead on most national news channels as well as local news. A few words drifted downwards, and Gus' body tensed as he realised Weston was using this to paint a picture of an immigrants' riot.

Behind him, he overheard one firefighter say to another, 'If I'd known that Brexit would release the floodgates for scum like him, I'd never have voted for it. All I wanted was independence from Europe, not a bloody race war.'

Unfortunately, many people Gus came across during his working week held similar views, and he knew they would be horrified with this outcome. Looking around him at the broken people, with their heads bowed in defeat, a wave of anger wracked his body. The delicate balance of his city was at risk, and whilst these people licked their wounds, Graeme Weston and his cronies stood, Union flags stretched between figures in balaclavas, too cowardly to reveal their true identities to their neighbours. Their fists raised in cheers, as if this had been some sort of victory for them. It made his skin crawl.

At least with UKIP, most of their members were accountable for their views. Most expressed their views honestly and openly. The worry with the Albion First members was that many of them were under the police radar. Their insidious beliefs and propaganda were covert until ... like now ... they weren't. Until, like now, they fanned the flames of unrest from behind their balaclavas and voiced their vitriol, with only their topmost ranks brave enough to show their faces. It was sobering to think you could be living next door or sharing a drink, or working with one of them, and not know just how deep their hatred was. *Deep enough to murder?* wondered Gus. Was one of those faceless figures responsible for the deaths and torture of three men? It was a scary thought.

Chapter 37

18:05 Caroline Drive, Dudley Hill, Bradford

It was amazing and *so* damn simple. All eyes had been focussed on the wogs, Pakis and gay sympathisers gathered in the Mirror Pool. Their man had got himself into position early. Then, arm up and over, leaving a trail of flames like a huge firefly, as it sailed through the snow and landed – *plop!* – right in the middle of them. Lambs to a slaughter. Couldn't have been planned any better. The idiots didn't even realise they'd been herded into a corner until it was too late, and like the animals they were, they squealed and ran; headless chickens in a slurry of flames. Brilliant! The scent of flesh burning hung heavy in the air; a delicious winter barbecue, and, like Gods on Mount Olympus, we watched them burn.

I could have watched all night, but after the initial rounds of interviews and playing-up to the media, it was time to go. Strutting our stuff – showing the reality of the protestors trying to discredit us – that was fine, but when they'd got things under control beneath us, the police turned their attention our way. It was time to leave.

Thank God for a quick getaway! I escaped from City Park by walking briskly over the road, up past the Alhambra Theatre and into Sir Titus Salt Wetherspoons. No rushing. No drawing attention to myself. Just a measured getaway. After a quick trip to the toilets, I emerged, having pulled a dark woolly hat over my forehead and black scarf around my mouth. My reversible jacket was duly reversed too. Everyone in the pub was staring at the huge wall-hung telly, where journalists were already on scene outside City Hall reporting on the devastation. The interviews were being played on a loop, interspersed with footage of the clean-up.

Nobody noticed me exiting Wetherspoons from the upper level. Nevertheless, heading up past the ice rink and around the corner to the National Science and Media Museum car park, I kept my head down until I reached my car. Didn't want anyone to realise that, whilst their expressions were full of horror, *mine* was full of joy.

Thinking about it even now makes my heart beat faster ... the last remnants of adrenaline still course through me, making me hungry for what I've got planned for tonight. That's why I've come here. I've been smart, though, and have driven a circuitous route. No point in taking chances. Now, outside the row of shops, in the comfort of my vehicle, I replace my reversible jacket with my heavy coat, and with the engine running, I'm warm. When I parked up, I turned the radio down a notch and slid over into the passenger seat. Anyone wondering why I am parked there with my engine running will just assume the driver is in one of the shops. I've grown wise over the past few weeks. Been a fast learner, and with three targets already disposed of and the next one within my sights, a warmth gushes through me from my stomach up to my chest.

Settling in for the long haul, I pull off my gloves and flick the radio on. As expected, all the local stations are harping on about the 'protest gone wrong' in City Park. I smirk, lean my head back on the seat, and listen.

Through the window, I see my target pull into his drive and alight from his brand-new BMW. More than likely bought with the proceeds of drug transactions. That's how most of them make their money, isn't it? Bringing their trash to our streets! He turns and reaches back into the car, pulling out his briefcase, and that's when I see it... a big scrape down his cheek and a bandage round his hand. A wave of pure pleasure ripples through me, giving me goose bumps. He'd been at City Park! He'd been hurt at City Park! I hadn't seen him, but it is good to know he'd been there. Proved my point. People like him take the moral high ground when it suited, yet they are happy to behave like animals in secret. I frown. Good job he'd not been one of the ones seriously hurt … that *would* have messed up my plans.

Head drooping, he limps towards his front door, and then, it's flung open and his pregnant wife appears, her bulk making her movements clumsy as she descends the steps and wraps her arms round him. Dropping his briefcase, he embraces her, raining kisses on her hair and cupping her face with his injured hands. My skin tightens, and I taste bile at the back of my throat. Cracking open the window, I breathe in the cool air. It calms me until I hear her relieved sobs as she helps her husband inside. Vile creatures. My skin crawls, and I want to do it right there and then. I want to smash their happy little family to smithereens. Twisting around in my seat, I rest my forehead on the side window and allow its delicious coolness to soothe my flushed face. Knowing she thinks he's had a narrow escape gives me a rush. It makes the promise of her devastation when I'm done with him all the more delicious. Anticipating her destruction, I laugh out loud.

A voice I recognise filters through the radio, so I flick the volume back up and listen to his smooth oratory performance. Slow, definite phrases describe the scene in City Park. Faultless delivery. The tone perfect. Leaves the listeners in no doubt the Molotov cocktail had originated from the protestors. Expressing sadness that anyone had been hurt, emphasising the point that, if the perpetrator had had a better aim, it would now be Albion First supporters lying injured or in Bradford Royal Infirmary.

The interview continues, 'Make no mistake! It is Albion First who are the victims here. It is my supporters who were the targets of this heinous attack, and many witnesses saw that the firebomb originated in the hands of the protestors. The events in City Park today were appalling. As you know, I am a great believer in free speech, having had my own rights, in that respect, denied on many occasions. It pains me to see that same right denied to the people of Bradford by the Asian and Black communities that protested my legal right to stand as a candidate for Albion First in the upcoming Bradford Central by-election. Having arrived with a few of my supporters in City Park to have a civilised conversation, I was shocked to witness the tragic event that unfolded there this afternoon.'

Another voice interjects, 'For those of you have just tuned in, we are here in City Park, Bradford, and I am Jez Hopkins, speaking to Graeme Weston, the Albion First candidate for the by-election in this ward. Mr Weston, could you tell us more about what happened in City Park today?'

'It is with a heavy heart, indeed, I have to say these words, Jez. Today, I witnessed yet another indication of the unrest that the ethnic minorities provoke in our city. Today, I personally witnessed one of the protestors hurl a lit Molotov cocktail into their own group. I have no doubt whatsoever this act was either a conscious and malevolent one aimed at casting the blame on my followers or a misguided attempt to hurl the bomb at my followers who stood on the balcony. Fortunately, the claim that the homemade bomb, aimed at – and I make no bones about the use of this word – terrorising the people of Bradford was thrown by one of my supporters, has been widely refuted by many witnesses most of whom were part of the protesting group.'

'Isn't it true your decision to attend the protest was a spontaneous one which casts doubt on the pre-meditation of the protestors?'

Tut! Smarmy-voiced jackass! I cross my arms wishing I could punch that Jez Hopkins. What *is* he playing at? It was quite clear who was to blame for the bomb! What more did Hopkins want? It was all a media conspiracy to discredit Albion First.

'Ha, ha, ha! Very amusing, Jez! I do admire your tenacity in trying to discredit me and my party. Albion First are a legitimate political alternative to the hypocritical ineffective mainstream parties. Since my decision to stand in this fine city, Albion First have increased their membership both locally and nationally. My message is clear to Bradfordians. Albion First will represent you. We will return Bradford to its former self. We will pull Bradford from beneath the skirts of its sister city, Leeds, and we will put Bradford on the map. First stop: Bradford, next stop: the rest of the UK!'

What a save! What an inspired response. I raise my fist in an air punch. How's that for a sound bite. Tell it how it is! Then, realising I've attracted the attention of a group of people waiting at the nearby bus stop, I duck my head. My heart speeds up when, from the corner of my eye, I see an old woman place her handbag on top of her wheeled trolley bag and rummage inside. When she withdraws a pen and a small notepad, my stomach flips. What is she doing? Talking a note of my number plate because I punched the air? I shake my head. I'm being paranoid. Why would she take a note of my number plate? Anyway, even if she has, it won't do anyone any good. I swapped the number plates with an old Polo in Keighley. Time to make another swap though. No point in taking unnecessary chances. No point in risking being recognised. Not now. Slipping back over to the driver's side, I drive off. In my rear-view mirror, the old bitch isn't even watching me. I laugh, amused at my own paranoia.

Chapter 38

19:35 The Fort

The smell of burning human flesh and petrol fumes had gotten into Gus' nostrils. So much so that now, he inhaled with relish The Fort's institutional lemon scent overlaid with eau de grease. This was the same aroma he moaned about with monotonous regularity, but this evening, it was like a bouquet of roses. The TV was on in the corner when he arrived with Alice, and when they entered, three heads turned from the screen as one, before Compo, Sampson and Taffy, who'd made it back minutes earlier, jumped to their feet and let loose with a barrage of questions.

Gus grinned and waving them to silence, grabbed the controls and turned up the volume on the TV. 'Let me listen to this, guys, then we'll talk.'

He and Alice joined the other three to watch the interview with Graeme Weston. It had been on the car radio as they drove back to the station. Now, he wanted to watch the man's body language as he spoke. Weston had changed his clothes for the demo, and instead of the riding gear he'd worn when Gus had interviewed him, he now wore a suit and tie.

Maybe Weston knew there'd be a photo opportunity, thought Gus, not bothering to quell his cynicism.

Where Graeme Weston was concerned, Gus was sure a healthy dose of scepticism should always be applied. The man interviewed well. He had all the charisma of Farage without any of his 'comic' characteristics, and judging by the crowds watching the televised interview in City Park, he was amassing quite a crowd of supporters.

As the news anchor in the studio began to list the details of those injured and the one boy who'd died, Gus switched it off. He turned and studied Taffy. 'You my new DC?'

Taffy nodded his head and thrust a hand in Gus' direction. 'Talvinder Bhandir, most folk call me Taffy.'

'You Welsh then?' asked Gus, deadpan.

Before Taffy could reply, Sampson laughed. 'Don't go there, Gus. The lad's got no sense of humour. Completely missed the joke when I asked earlier.'

Taffy grunted. 'Actually, it was your delivery that was poor, Sampson. DI McGuire's was spot on!'

Alice laughed. 'Oh my God, we've got ourselves an arse lick! What'll we do with him, Compo?'

'Make him get some food in?' replied Compo, his tone hopeful.

Alice shook her head. 'Christ, Compo, Gus and I have been in the thick of it for hours in the freezing cold, in the driving snow and wind, dealing with distraught victims and relatives, whilst you, on the other hand, have been cosying up with your computer *all* afternoon, and all *you* can do is think of your belly?'

Compo's mouth drooped. 'I'll take that as a no, then, shall I?'

'Damn right you will.'

'Okay, children,' said Gus, raising his voice. 'Welcome to the team, Taffy. Just muck in, and if you're unsure, give us a shout.' He turned to Compo. 'I've ordered food from Mo. He's delivering it in a bit, okay? Meanwhile, let's get updated before we eat. I'm cold and knackered, and I want to go home. Who's first?'

Sampson brought Gus and Alice up-to-date on the interviews with the victims' friends ending with, 'So, it looks like maybe the link is that each of our victims breached our killer's 'moral code.' That would tie in, too, with each of the dump sites being known for 'illicit' goings on.'

'Keep on that tomorrow. Taffy will help you with that.'

Sampson put a note in his book and said, 'What about Weston? Any progress either incriminating or eliminating him or any of his lovely sidekicks?'

Gus shook his head. 'He's a sleazy bastard, no doubt of it, yet his alibi holds up. We were heading to interview his campaign manager, Michael Hogg, when it all kicked off in City Park. Truth is, I don't think he's a stupid man. The question is, would he risk putting someone up to this at this critical time in his political career? That's not to say he doesn't have a rogue supporter acting on their own. I want to get the measure of this Hogg guy. Anytime I've seen him being interviewed, he seems less polished than our man. More of a thug, maybe more unpredictable.' He shrugged. 'Who knows.'

Wandering over to the small fridge in the corner of the room, he took out a can of Irn Bru, saying over his shoulder, 'Tell them about the son, Al.' He took a long swig, savouring the way its coolness caressed his raw throat as it went down. Maybe it would get rid of the scorched taste in his mouth.

Alice filled them in on Christine and Graeme's reaction to Gus' innocent enquiry about Jacob's health, but the other detectives were as stumped as they were.

Gus drained his can and said, 'I reckon if we don't make headway soon, we could try to get Christine on her own … I think she's fragile enough to break the party whip, so to speak.'

After clearing his throat, he began to speak again. 'Today, in City Park … it was awful. Many people were hurt. Most of them were kids. Imti and Serafina were there, for God's sake. Imti reckons he saw one of the protestors throw something into their crowd. He's convinced it was someone from Weston's group trying to make trouble for them, and I have to say, word from the bobbies backs that theory up. When the statements are compiled, they're going to send copies to us.

'I don't know if there are links between this and Weston and the deaths, but I want us to keep on top of it. When they come in tomorrow, I want you, Sampson and Taffy to go through them with a fine-tooth comb, okay?'

Compo, who'd been watching the door with eager eyes, presumably for signs of their samosa delivery, burped, and then, as if the burp had released some inspiration, he jumped to his feet, dashed across the room and started typing on his PC.

'Comp?' said Gus.

Not taking his eyes off the screen, Compo said, 'I've got something. Give me a minute, huh?'

Just then a knock signalled the arrival of Mo with the samosas. Gus was amused to see the look of consternation that crossed Compo's face, as he jumped from one foot to the other, leaning over his PC at an awkward angle, his chair pushed to the side, clearly torn between finishing the task in hand and grabbing a samosa. Taking pity on him, Gus popped two meat and a veg samosa on a plate with a dollop of raita and a squirt of chilli sauce and deposited the plate, accompanied by a handful of napkins, next to Compo. To be fair, Compo barely glanced at the food as he continued to type, eyes on the screen as he worked. Gus hoped whatever he was doing would bring some results, for they were getting nowhere fast.

Before Gus helped himself to a samosa, Mo grabbed his arm and, head to one side, said, 'Well?'

Gus was stumped. 'Well, what?'

With an exaggerated sigh, Mo rolled his eyes at Alice and said, 'Can you believe this one?'

Alice bit into the flaky pastry and shook her head. 'I know. He's useless. I've had to remind him all day.'

Puzzled, Gus splayed his arms. 'Done what? What have I not done?'

Like a magician pulling a rabbit from a hat, Mo, with a flourish, produced a small light blue and white tube from his pocket and presented it to Gus. He was like an excited jeweller displaying a ring to his would-be fiancée. 'Voila!' he said in an accent that made Gus cringe.

'Okay, okay, I've been a bit remiss in the Bepanthen department today. Thanks for setting me up, by the way, Al.'

Alice helped herself to another samosa and shrugged. 'No probs, Gus. Always a pleasure.'

Glowering, Gus grabbed the tube from Mo, shrugged off his jumper and began to unscrew the lid. He nearly jumped when Mo shouted, 'NO!'

'Shit, Mo! What's wrong with you?'

Mo grabbed the Bepanthen tube back. 'Go and wash your hands first, Angus McGuire. Right this minute!'

Eyes narrowed, Gus studied him, then, as Mo pointed to the sink, he slunk over, ignoring the laughter that accompanied him. After drying his hands, he pushed his T-shirt sleeve back revealing the scabbed tattoo and put out his hand for the tube. Whilst Sampson, and Taffy gathered round to admire his tattoo, Gus applied the cream, making sure he didn't blow his street cred by wincing.

However, moments later, when a high, sweet voice broke over their conversation, Gus did jump. The colour drained from his face as he tried to pull his sleeve over the tattoo, but he was too late.

In what could have been a parody of Mo's earlier tone, Corrine McGuire spoke, 'What *exactly* have we here, Angus?'

Gus hung his head and extended his arm, knowing from his mum's tone any arguing would be futile. Next to him, Mo stood looking equally shame-faced. Corrine McGuire moved over and with a frown stood on tiptoes to fully consider the tattoo on her son's arm. 'Hmm.' She glanced at Mo, her lips tight. 'Your idea, I suppose?'

Mo and Gus responded at the same time. 'Yes, Ma McGuire, I'm so sorry. It's all my fault.'

'No, Mum, it wasn't Mo's fault. It was all my idea.'

Corrine, hands on hips, glared from one to the other, shaking her head, 'Look at you both. Grown men, and you still behave like a couple of naughty school boys. What am I going to do with you?' She homed her steely gaze on Mo. 'Does Naila know about this?'

Gus glanced at his friend and saw he, too, had paled.

Mo's brow wrinkled, and he shook his head from side to side like an adamant toddler. 'No, No. Naila doesn't know. Please don't tell her, please don't.'

Aware of his team trying to cover up their amusement, Gus pulled his sleeve down and began to put his jumper back on. 'Can we talk about this later, Ma?'

Corrine reached out a hand and stopped him. With soft hands, she pushed his T-shirt back up and studied the tattoo again. 'This is Greg's painting, isn't it? The one in your living room?'

Gus nodded.

His mother's lips twitched, and with gentle fingers, she pulled his T-shirt sleeve down, being careful not to smudge the cream. 'Hmmm! It's quite lovely.' She turned to Mo, whose face had broken into a big grin. 'I'm still not sure I'm going to keep this secret from Naila. Maybe *you* should confess before I bump into her next.'

Mo nodded. 'I will, Ma McGuire, I promise.' Then, as if to himself, he said, 'Don't see why everyone's so protective of *him*. Naila never moaned when I got *my* sleeves done.'

Mrs McGuire patted Mo's arm and said, 'That's because we all know Angus is a wuss and can't stand anything remotely medical. You did well to get him to do it.'

She turned to Gus and studied him. Seemingly satisfied with what she saw, she exhaled. 'I only came to make sure you were okay after what happened in City Park. I did tell Nancy to get you to phone, but I know what you're like when you're busy.'

Gus' shoulders slumped. 'Sorry, Ma.'

Mrs McGuire snorted and, depositing a box of, probably inedible, home-made cookies on the table, headed out. 'Take care of yourself, Angus.'

Compo ambled over, gazing towards the door that was just sliding shut, his expression disappointed. Around a mouth filled with samosa, he said, 'Did I hear your mum's voice, Gus?'

Laughing, Alice nudged him and pointed to the tub of cookies. 'Don't worry, Comps, she left you some snacks.'

Visibly brightening, Compo swallowed his mouthful and pulled the tub towards him. 'Great, choc chip, my favourite.'

Glancing into the box, Gus said, 'I think you'll find the 'chips' are just burnt bits.'

Nonetheless, Compo took a bit and chewed. 'Nah, definitely choc chip. Shall I share my brainwave now?'

Feeling tiredness wash over him, Gus plonked down behind his desk, and in an effort to stave off his fatigue, he swivelled his chair back and forth with his foot whilst Compo explained what he'd been doing.

'I remembered you saying maybe the killer stalked the victims … so, I thought if that *was* the case, the killer may have paid multiple visits to the vicinity of each of the victims' homes in the weeks prior to their deaths. You with me?'

Gus wasn't completely sure where this was going, but rather than interrupt Compo's flow, he nodded.

'So, because we've got no witnesses to any of the snatches, I thought we should track any vehicles that frequented the areas around each victim's home, and see if we can place any of them at or around the snatch and dump sites.'

Gus frowned. 'That's good logic, Compo, but how on earth can we do that? We've no make or colour or reg number or anything?'

Compo grinned. 'Well, you know Bradford has one of the most widespread distribution of active cameras and that over one hundred thousand images are taken per day?'

Nodding, Gus crossed his arms and, leaning back against his desk, waited. He had complete faith in Compo and was happy to let him come to the punchline in his own time.

Pausing, Compo dragged his samosa through the raita and the chilli sauce before transferring the dripping pastry to his mouth. Seeming not to notice the dot of yogurt sauce on his nose, he chewed briefly before swallowing. A quick glug of Pepsi, and he continued, 'That's why I'll write a programme that will collate the Automated Number Plate Recognition records for vehicles returning more than once, to a within a two-mile radius of the victims' homes in the month prior to their deaths. I've set the programme, in the first instance, to eliminate any cars registered to family members, close friends and neighbours as per our working hypothesis that these are stranger killings. I've also set it to eliminate any vehicles registered to black or Asian owners, by linking it up to the DVLA database.'

Taffy, who'd been listening intently, said, 'But how will your computer programme know who's black or Asian?'

Not taking offence at being questioned by the younger man, Compo said, 'All our driving licences have photo images, don't they, Taffy? Facial recognition will do it for us, if I set the parameters.'

Gus thought about the information Compo had imparted and then sat up. 'Won't that generate thousands of hits?'

Compo grinned. 'That's where things get all fancy. Each locality and timeframe will generate, as you say, thousands of hits. These will be narrowed using the criteria I've already outlined, but will still be in the thousands, I reckon. I've then put in a filter to get rid of vehicles registered to addresses outside Bradford and those that only make the ANPR once in the given time frame.'

A bubble of excitement rose in Gus' chest. He could see that – by the second –Compo's programme was narrowing things down. He glanced at the rest of the team and saw they were equally riveted. 'Go on, then. What else?'

Taking another bite from a cookie and wafting his hand around, Compo sent a sprinkle of crumbs down his front and over the desk. Words slightly muffled by the contents of his mouth, he continued, 'Well, after the programme has completed that for each of the victims, we can cross-reference for vehicles that have popped up at every locality … again, narrowing the list.'

'How narrow will the list be, Compo?'

Screwing his face up, Compo frowned. 'That's the thing, Gus. I won't know 'til I get the results how many hits we'll get. Truth is, it could still be too unmanageable, but my gut tells me it won't be.'

Tapping his fingers lightly on the desk top, Gus grinned at him. 'Okay, that's good enough for me. When will we get the results?'

Again, Compo grimaced. 'I'm not sure. It's a new programme. I'll stick with it through the night, try to speed it up, like, but it'll run 'til it's done.' His face fell. 'I'm sorry, Gus.'

Gus stood up and banged him on the back. 'Don't be daft, Compo. No need to be sorry. You've given us the possibility of a lead we may well never have got. Just do your best. That's all any of us can do. Here, have another cookie.'

Perking up, Compo accepted the cookie with a smile. 'If we narrow it down enough, we'll be able to find the vehicles and their owners pretty quickly, though, Gus, *and* they may well lead us straight to the kill site.'

At last! It looked like they may be getting somewhere. Not knowing how the killer had lured the victims away, nor how he'd subdued them, had been a major obstacle to their investigations. Thanks to Compo, that obstacle may soon be removed.

He grabbed his coat, ready to leave, when he had a sudden thought. 'Hey, Compo, can you link your programme to CCTV, too, or would that be stupid?'

Head to one side, Compo considered the suggestion. 'Right now, I think we stick to the ANPR, then when we've narrowed it down, we can link to CCTV to see what that throws up. If you can think of any other parameters to narrow the criteria, that would be good. If we don't get any hits, we can always play around with it.'

Gus nodded. 'Come on, Taffy, let's get to know one another. Come with me to interview the delightful Michael Hogg.'

Taffy's eyes opened wide, and his jaw slackened, but he jumped to his feet, grabbing his coat and notepad as he did so. 'Brilliant, thanks for the opportunity, sir.'

'Drop the 'sir,' Taffy. My name's Gus, and so you know, I only chose you because you're Indian. Michael Hogg won't like two 'brown' people turning up on his doorstep, will he, eh?'

Rubbing his hands together, Taffy laughed. 'Great. I'm all for ruffling a few racist feathers.'

Chapter 39

Neha was grateful to her aunt and uncle for taking them in, but they had three children of their own, and the house was crowded. She shared a room with Shamshad, which had its good points ... it also had its bad ones. Both sisters studied hard, and they helped each other with that. Sham was messy, and often had run-ins with her very traditional aunt and uncle, who despaired of her fashion sense and lack of piety, which was offset by her devotion to their mother. A devotion Neha could not and did not want to share. Her mother had deserted her when she needed her most, and though Sham seemed able to forgive her, she couldn't. Not even knowing the teachings of her faith indicated she should forgive her mother as many times as she, herself, expected Allah to forgive her would change her mind. She hoped Allah could forgive her this one lapse.

She knew things Shamshad didn't know. Things she could never tell Sham. The burden was heavy, but Neha saw it as her duty, and regardless of the emotional strain it placed on her, she would carry it alone. She'd lost weight again. Not that she had much to lose in the first place, but the past few weeks had been difficult, and she'd started to make herself sick again. To cover up, she'd begun to wear extra layers to pad her emaciated body out so no-one would notice. She knew if her arms weren't so shredded, she'd be able to see the tell-tale signs of added hair growth, one of the side effects of being underweight.

This afternoon at City Park had been the final straw. Shamshad had been so close to the bomb when it exploded and had been lucky to escape with only minor cuts to her face, but she'd been shaken. They both had. It was a sign of the times, and it terrified her. To see her brave, outgoing sister so cowed in a place where they had shared many happy memories hurt Neha. Of course, the backlash from Syria and now Brexit meant that walking down the street had become a major challenge if you were brown or wore a hijab. Worse, still, if you wore the burka.

Every non-Muslim you passed in the street could be a potential threat or could see you as one. She couldn't blame them, not really. Syria, terror attacks, trucks mowing people down in the name of Islam. It made her so *angry*. This wasn't Islam, but how did you reassure the frightened? The ignorant? Those wanting to place blame? Those wanting to protect their own. The simple fact was, you couldn't; and the existence of people like Graeme Weston made things worse. His sort created a climate where people got hurt just as much as the terrorists using Allah's name falsely did. Now, Bradford even had a serial killer targeting Asian men. Where would it all end?

She snuck out whilst Sham was in the shower. Her nerves were frayed. She was tired of thinking three steps ahead so she could keep all her secrets hidden. She hated subterfuge and deceit, but this was necessary and not only for her own sake. Tonight, at least for a little while, she could breathe easy … be herself. Hell, she might even manage to eat some popcorn without throwing up afterwards. She paced back and forth in front of the Odeon building. He was late, but she didn't mind waiting. It was more difficult for him to get away than it was for her. She was thankful he'd finally managed to contact her.

Car headlights lit the car park up, and for a moment, Neha thought she saw him walking towards her. Then, he was gone, and she realised she'd been mistaken. Her eyes were sore, and the bright lights from the car had momentarily distorted her vision. Even now, she could see black shapes dancing in her peripheral vision. She reached out her hand to steady herself against the wall. Someone walked past her, brushing against her, making her bang her elbow on the concrete, spinning her body around like a weightless ragdoll. She took a deep breath. Maybe it had been a mistake to come out on her own at night in the dark. Maybe the cold air was affecting her ... that and the residual shock from City Park. She was dizzy ... light-headed, faint. Please, hurry up! Come on. Please, just get here. The automatic doors creaked open behind her, as someone exited the cinema complex. The sound made her jump, and then, she was falling ...

Chapter 40

20:35 Canal Lane, Bingley

Gus had let Taffy drive the pool car to Bingley. The earlier snow had melted to nothing, leaving a shimmer of frost as the temperature plummeted for the night. As Taffy manoeuvred down the cobbled street, which as the name suggested was adjacent to the canal, the faint drone of traffic on the by-pass faded. Three large detached sandstone cottages, each with their own large garage attached, stood proud. A sizeable stretch of land separated each from its neighbour. They smelt of privilege. In the one bordering the Hogg's home, Gus could barely make out the outline of two large horses, tugging on what looked to be a netted bale of hay. So, this was the Hogg's paddock? Seemed like self-employed, central heating engineers made a buck or two. He made a mental note to get Compo to check out the Hogg's finances.

Five minutes away, an overcrowded estate with mostly boarded windows and a children's playground, now locked up against graffiti artists, drug users and the homeless, crawled with activity, whereas here, the silence stretched so deep, it knocked you flat. Sometimes, life just didn't seem fair.

Gus wasn't sure if it was his knowledge of Michael Hogg that clouded his impression of this idyllic little area or some deeper introspective inferiority complex. All he knew was he felt uneasy here in the same way he had in school when someone questioned his genetic relationship with his dad. Or when he'd been passed over for something and couldn't quite quell the persistent thought that his ethnicity was to blame. His common sense told him he was gearing himself up for the coming interview with Hogg. He'd encountered racists before, and he would do again. However, Hogg's positioning himself at the front of mainstream politics in Bradford, alongside Graeme Weston, had all the symbolism of a changing tide. It seemed Brexit and Trump had validated racist attitudes, and Gus feared for the future of his home city, if hatred won. In one fell swoop, a carpet had been pulled out from under them, and the UK, indeed, the world, still had to stabilise.

'You okay, Taffy?'

The lad nodded and got out of the car. Gus noticed him straightening his back and holding his chin up and realised he'd done exactly the same. They approached the door, and Gus lifted the heavy copper knocker and let it fall with a clatter. For long seconds, there was silence, and then, the faint shuffling of someone approaching the door made Gus drop his hand before knocking again. The door was opened, and from behind a chain, a pair of blue eyes glowered at them. 'Yes?'

Gus showed the woman his warrant card and introduced himself and Taffy before asking if Michael Hogg was at home.

The woman repeated her previous word, 'Yes,' but made no move to open the door.

Hiding his annoyance, Gus smiled, keeping his voice pleasant, 'And you are …?' which prompted a different response.

'None of your business.'

Anticipating she was about to close the door on them, Gus inserted his foot in the gap, and despite the pain of her squashing the door against it, he maintained a neutral expression. 'We are police officers, Mrs Hogg. I presume that's who you are, anyway. We have come to speak to your husband. We've shown you the necessary ID and would be grateful if you would inform your husband we're here.'

Gus kept his eyes on her face, refusing to flinch, even when she exerted a final pressure on the door, squashing his foot even more. With a derisive glance, she relented and eased the door open, and in silence, she removed the chain. At last, she opened it wide. Stepping away from them, as if reluctant to share the cramped space with them, she pointed to the matt on the floor. 'Wipe your mucky feet.'

Taffy and Gus did as she asked, and when they'd done so, she walked down the hallway, leaving them to follow. At the end, they entered a room which proved to be the kitchen. Once inside, Mrs Hogg moved over to the table and stood behind her husband who sat reading the *Bradford Chronicle* article about Graeme Weston that was on the front page of today's edition. Michael Hogg, bald and burly, glanced at them, and then, with deliberate slowness, shook the paper at arm's length before folding it in half and placing it on the table in front of him. He then lifted his thick, tattooed arms over his chest and tucked his hands into the opposite armpit before speaking. 'In the whole of the Bradford, police couldn't they find two *British* officers to come here?'

Refusing to be baited, Gus smiled and inclined his head, hoping the pulse throbbing at Taffy's temple wasn't a sign that the lad was about to lose it. 'Both DC Bhandir and myself are British, Mr Hogg, as I think you well know, because, if we weren't, we wouldn't be in the *British* police now, would we? I suspect that what you're trying to ascertain is why two non-white officers are knocking on your door, am I right?'

Hogg released a bellow of laughter and flexed his biceps making his swastika tattoo dance as if taunting them. 'Well, you've got spirit, I suppose. Now, let's get right to it. The sooner this is done, the sooner you can leave, and I can get the air freshener out.'

Clenching his fists inside his pocket, Gus smiled. In his mind's eye, he imagined slamming his fist into Michael Hogg's face. The resultant sore knuckles would be worth it, but he wouldn't give Hogg the satisfaction. Gus was better than that. From the corner of his eye, he saw Taffy extract his notebook from his pocket and flip it open. He hoped he hadn't overestimated the lad's ability to hold it together in the face of this sort of provocation. Hogg was an arse. A sudden memory of his dad years ago calling a racist colleague a 'bawbag' to his face made Gus' lips twitch.

'Something funny, *boy*?' said Hogg, eyes narrowed, his face reddening almost as if he could see Gus' thoughts.

Gus curled his lip. 'Was thinking how good it would be to get out into the fresh air myself. Now, can we start?'

Thrusting his chest out, Hogg glared at him. 'This about that Paki, Razaul Ul Haq, is it? Graeme told me you lot might turn up here asking about him. What do you want to know?'

Keeping his tone neutral, he led Michael Hogg through a list of questions that confirmed Graeme Weston's alibi for the time of Razaul's abduction. Taffy scribbled frenetically in his notebook, with only the occasional derisive glance at Michael Hogg in response to some racist comment or other.

Finishing up, Gus said, 'I have a witness who asserts someone matching your description threw the Molotov cocktail that caused the death of one boy and injured many more in Bradford today. Can you confirm your whereabouts during the protest in City Park this afternoon?'

Hogg laughed, his eyes crinkling in amusement. 'Good luck proving that one. Yeah, I was there. In case you didn't know, I'm Graeme Weston's campaign manager. We were both there. We'd planned to try to reason with the protestors, but then, that bomb went off, and after Graeme fulfilled his public duty by speaking to the press, I made sure he was escorted to safety. That's my job. Countless people will vouch for me.' He snorted. 'All of them will tell you I was at Graeme's side the entire time on the balcony over the café. I suspect there will be plenty of video footage to corroborate that.'

Gus nodded. 'And you've got nothing to add about either the bombing this afternoon or about the murders of three young Asian men who were forcibly violated with tattoos very similar to the one you have on your arm.'

Hogg snorted. 'If that's all you've got, good luck. You'd be surprised how many people in Bradford and indeed, the UK, share my views about *your* sort. A lot of them will have similar tattoos. Don't make them murderers, though, does it?'

'No,' said Gus, 'Just arseholes!' And with Taffy struggling to hide his smirk, he turned on his heel and walked towards the door. Mrs Hogg followed on their heels, as if making sure they didn't steal anything on their way out. Before he opened the door, he turned to face her, aware her husband stood in the kitchen doorway at the end of the corridor. 'Were you in City Park today, Mrs Hogg?'

Stretching past Gus, she opened the door, swinging it wide open, before standing back to let them pass. 'Yes, I was there with my husband and Graeme.'

Gus nodded but didn't move. Instead, he stepped closer to her. 'Do you share your husband's political views?'

She tensed and stepped back from Gus, her mouth mangled in a look of distaste. 'Of course I share my husband's political views. I work for Graeme Weston, and as far as I'm concerned, Bradford would be a far superior place without immigrants and scroungers.'

'Well, that's good to know, Mrs Hogg.' He glanced back along the hallway and nodded. 'Mr Hogg.' He walked outside, where the sudden blast of cold air had never been more welcome.

Chapter 41

Shamshad was sweating like the proverbial pig. Her uncle had dropped her at BRI when she got the phone call about her sister. He had stayed with her for a while, but he'd needed to get back to her auntie and the babies. To be honest, she was glad he'd gone, leaving her on her own to think. Sometimes, she felt so much older than her seventeen years, and sometimes, like now, she was ill-equipped to deal with everything life threw at her.

She'd seen the looks they'd given her when she came in demanding to see her sister. Now, looking at her reflection in the bathroom mirror, she could understand why. Her hair was mussed, her face covered in small scratches from the explosion earlier, and she hadn't had a chance to remove her make-up, so there were long streaks of mascara stretching from her eyes down to her chin. She was a mess, and she felt *exactly* how she looked. Reaching over, she grabbed one of the coarse green paper towels and dampened it before scrubbing her cheeks, ignoring the sting as she reopened the fragile glass cuts on her face.

Neha had still been unconscious when she'd arrived, her face pale against her black hair. The contrast was doubly startling to Shamshad, because she rarely saw her sister without her hijab. Beneath blue-veined lids, Neha's eyes were in perpetual motion, tormented by who knew what. A drip stand stood like a solitary guard by her bedside. Its clear liquid making its way into Neha's dehydrated body. Both her arms were bandaged from the wrists to the elbows.

The nurse who'd spoken to Shamshad had explained that some of her sister's wounds had become infected and needed urgent treatment. They'd asked her if she knew her sister self-harmed.

Dazed and confused, Shamshad had nodded, saying in a helpless whimper, 'But she'd stopped. She told me she'd stopped.'

The nurse had smiled and patted her arm. Then, she'd gone, leaving her alone looking at her sister in her washed-out hospital gown, her skinny arms jutting out, all bone and veins, from jagged shoulders. She hadn't known what to do. When the nurse returned, minutes later, with a cup of sugary tea, Shamshad had taken it, grateful for the warmth that suffused her freezing fingers.

The nurse sat beside Shamshad and explained about Neha's injuries and what they could do for her. She didn't know whether to be relieved or shocked or even angry that her sister hadn't used a razor to slash her skin this time. Was it any better she'd used her own fingernails? That she'd been so upset and tortured she'd clawed her skin so much it had become infected? She'd been told it wasn't only her sister's forearms but also her thighs.

God, Neha, couldn't you just have fucking confided in me? I didn't know you were drowning. Didn't know you were in such pain.

Neha had been wearing six layers of clothes under her dress. The nurse had shown her. They were piled up in the small cabinet next to her bed. The tools of her deceit. A classic tactic to avoid being questioned about her weight loss. Shamshad *knew* that. They'd been through it all before, and Neha had got better. She'd helped her get better.

Sham lifted her eyes to the mirror, and for a split second, she wanted to smash her fist through it. That's when she knew *she* needed help. Someone she could trust to sit with her, before all the professionals came and told her they'd need to take her sister away from her again. She took her phone from her jacket and dialled.

Chapter 42

22:15 The Delius

The Delius was almost empty, which wasn't unusual for a Tuesday night. Shahid, however, made it policy to remain open, regardless of how many punters graced his bar with their presence. Tonight, only a couple sitting in one of the booths and a few lads playing pool in the back room were present. Fluted, easy listening music played at a low volume. This gave the couple in the booth a semblance of privacy for the low-level argument their tense bodies and flashing eyes told Shahid they were having. Turning his gaze back to his brother, he nodded and continued to dry the few glasses he'd just washed.

'Look, I'm telling you, Shahid,' said Imti, his face serious, 'it wasn't one of *our* lot who threw the bottle. I saw it with my own eyes, and I've told Gus too. It was a deliberate move to sabotage our peaceful protest. It was one of Weston's crew, I reckon. I mean, it stands to reason, doesn't it? Who else could it have been?'

Imti turned to Serafina, who nodded and laid her hand on his arm. 'I believe you, Imti, but what good is *knowing* this if we can't prove it? DI McGuire said the fire investigators will examine the crime scene, and that they will measure up angles and things. Your story will be corroborated and …' she splayed her hands, '*then* we'll go to the press and expose Weston for what he is. A devious man with an agenda.'

'That's just it, Serafina, if the fire investigator proves it was thrown from the middle of *our* group, Weston will say 'I told you so.' Unless I can find the bloke who threw it and *prove* he was planted by Albion First to discredit us, Weston will win.' He paced back and forth in front of the bar, his voice loud and indignant. 'I'd recognise him again, you know? I'm certain I would.'

Shahid had been tidying up, drinking whisky and listening to the two kids discussing it for hours now. He wanted to tell Imti to forget it, to be grateful he and Serafina had escaped unhurt, but he knew his words would fall on deaf ears. Imti was incensed, and to be honest, a slow burn rose in Shahid's gut too. It was a strange feeling for him. He'd not felt much of anything for months now. And he'd certainly never been political before, but something had changed. Imti had grown up and was forcing Shahid to confront his narrow-mindedness, his blindness to what was going on around him. Working beside Gus McGuire in City park earlier had been strange. A mere few months ago, they'd been on opposite sides. Now, after everything that had happened they were, if not friends, then at least not enemies.

Okay, he was never going to get citizen of the year award, but at least he was trying to be a better person, to live up to Imti's expectations. Maybe the fact he'd very nearly become a father the previous year had changed his outlook. People said fatherhood changed you. Maybe the prospect of it, even if had been wrenched away from you, did too. From left field, his chest tightened, as if someone had gripped it and was squeezing the life out of him. Shit, not this again. He recognised it for the grief it was and hated his own weakness.

Turning to replace the dried glasses on the shelves, he took a few deep breaths. Thank God, Imti was too involved in his discussion to notice, but a quick glance told him his temporary show of emotion had not gone unnoticed by Serafina. She smiled and nodded, letting him know his secret was safe with her. He inclined his head in acknowledgement, slid back into the seat behind the bar, picked up his glass and focussed on his brother.

They kept going around and around in circles. Personally, at that precise moment, Shahid couldn't have cared less who'd thrown the damn bomb. He'd been relieved Imti was okay. For a good few minutes, until he heard Gus McGuire calling his name and looked up to see him with Imti, he'd thought he'd lost his brother. And that sense of loss was an all-too-familiar feeling for him.

Sensing Imti was all for trying to find the bloke on his own, Shahid intervened. The need to protect his brother was strong, and the easiest way to do that was to placate him. 'Look, Imti, I agree with you. We need to find the bastard who threw the bottle-bomb. But rather than you go off half-arsed trying to find him, why don't you ask McGuire if you can watch the police footage of the protest? McGuire said although *you* saw his face after he threw the bomb, he took care to angle his face away from the City Park cameras. That tells me it was deliberate. Maybe earlier on, he wasn't so careful. He might have slipped up.'

Perching on a bar stool, Imti grinned at Shahid. 'You're not as daft as you look, big bro. I'll text Gus now and head into The Fort tomorrow. We *need* to catch this bloke.'

Relieved he'd diverted Imti from going off like an avenging angel, Shahid poured himself another whisky. 'You know, I bet somewhere in The Fort, they keep images of extreme right and left-wing activists. Maybe if you find the bloke on the footage, that computer geek, Compo, might be able to match it to those photos.' Maybe all that stuff the previous year with Dolinski hadn't been entirely in vain after all. At least they'd made a few acquaintances – 'friends' would be too strong a word to describe them – up at The Fort now.

Thumbs flying over his phone screen, Imti sent off a text to Gus. Seconds later, he looked up triumphant. 'Gus says to come in tomorrow.'

He put up his hand to fist bump his brother, whooping 'Result,' as their knuckles met. Whistling to himself, Imti moved round the bar to get a coke for Serafina and himself.

Shahid saw Serafina glance at her boyfriend before speaking in a low tone. 'I know you worry about him, Shahid, but *he* was worried about *you* too. He thought he'd lost you today. You should have seen him when he saw the banner you'd been holding near the explosion. Gus could barely restrain him.'

Shahid, trying to keep things light, winked at her. 'Thanks, Serafina. Good to know'

She grinned and, leaning over, took his glass away, 'And so, knowing that your brother worries about you too, you should stop drinking for tonight. You've had more than enough.'

Shahid opened his mouth to protest, then seeing the way her fingers caressed the cross she always wore round her neck, he realised she was nervous. Speaking to him like that had taken a lot of courage. He grinned, and then, when her phone vibrated on the table top, he said, 'You better get that, love. I'm off to bed. Make sure you two lock up after yourselves, when that lot have gone.'

Serafina smiled and picked up her phone.

'Is that your mum?' asked Imti, pushing a glass over the bar towards her.

Serafina bit her lip. 'No, it's Shamshad. I've got to go.'

Chapter 43

Shamshad was slouched in a chair in the empty waiting room, when Serafina, accompanied by Imti, walked in. The contents of Neha's bag were strewn in a messy heap at her feet. One look at the other girl's face told Serafina she was in shock. If there was one thing Serafina had been used to dealing with over the past few months, it was people in shock. She turned to Imti and pushed him out the door. 'Find somewhere to buy a drink for us all. Make her one with lots of sugar.'

Then, she turned and sat beside Shamshad, trying to ignore the tingling in her limbs and the churning stomach that being back in hospital triggered. Taking a deep breath, she relaxed her shoulders and told herself, right now, her friend's need was greater than hers. 'What happened? How is Neha?'

Shamshad blinked and then exhaled. 'Right, well, em, yeah ... Neha will be okay physically ...' She explained about her sister's condition. She added she hadn't yet had a chance to talk to her. Pointing a trembling finger at the bundle of things on the floor, Shamshad said, 'That's her stuff.'

Serafina recognised Neha's bag and had assumed the items on the floor were also hers. She took in the conglomeration of pens, rubbers, notebooks and tissue packs that were scattered at Sham's feet. What had Sham been looking for in her sister's bag? Unless, of course, she'd tipped it over by accident, although to Serafina it didn't appear that way. Kneeling down, she began to pick the things up and put them back into the bag.

'I found this,' said Sham, her tone abrupt.

Alerted by her friend's strained voice, Serafina stopped what she was doing and looked up at what Sham held in her hands. The other girl pushed it towards her, and with a puzzled glance, Serafina took it. 'What is this, Sham?'

Shrugging, Sham bit her lip, and a tear rolled down her cheek. With an impatient hand, she brushed it away. 'Open it. Look.'

The other girl was clearly distressed, and Serafina couldn't begin to imagine what was in the envelope Shamshad pushed so insistently towards her. This was so unlike Sham. Her friend was a rock. Strong and indestructible, and it frightened Serafina to see her so upset, so fragile. Her mouth dry, she moved back into the seat beside Sham and turned the envelope over. There was no name on it, and it was grubby and creased in places, as if it had been handled on many occasions. The flap had no stick left, so she knew it had been opened previously.

Reluctant to open it and look at the contents without having at least some idea of what she'd find, Serafina said, 'What is it, Sham? What's inside?'

Sham shook her head and shrugged. Her eyes remained fixed on her hands which lay cupped in her lap. Realising her friend was beyond speaking, Serafina lifted the flap. With a sinking heart, she slipped the contents out until she could cradle them in her hand. They were documents. Open mouthed, she stared at the top one, then using her index finger, she flicked through the rest of them. When she'd finished, she sat in silence. Then, not quite believing what she held in her hand, she repeated the process, before saying, 'What the heck does this mean, Sham?'

Sham laughed a mirthless laugh. 'I think it means my sister has a lot of explaining to do, don't you?'

Wednesday

Chapter 44

01:15 Ingleby Road to Dudley Hill, Bradford

It doesn't take long to find another vehicle to swap plates with. The Mother Hubbard's car park on Ingleby Road is busy. A quick drive around shows a marked absence of cameras. When I see the old bloke head inside the building, clutching his car keys and wallet, I pull in behind him. He's perfect. Doddery old fool probably wouldn't notice if I spray-painted his car fluorescent pink. My heart beats faster as I sneak from my vehicle and glance around. It's dark enough to hide what I'm doing, and nobody's looking in my direction. I slip on my gloves, and two minutes later, the plates are swapped. I check that the mud obscuring my front number plate is still there, and then, I'm sorted.

Humming to myself, I head to Caroline Drive and park up outside his house. Now, all I have to do is wait. If *he* doesn't go for a ride tonight, I'll get him next time. After all, patience is one of my many virtues. Doesn't matter to me how long I have to wait; the end result will be the same.

My fingers tap along to Heart FM, and despite the cold, I feel warmth suffuse my body. It's been a tiring day full of emotion and excitement, but I am ready now. The successes of the protest in City Park have buoyed me up. The interviews were inspired, and our cause is now very firmly in the public arena.

The hallway light goes on in his house. Is this it? Is he leaving for one of his illicit little assignations, or is he locking up for the night? I lean forward, hugging the steering wheel, and peer through the dark. Then, I see the porch light flick on, and a chink of yellow hits the steps. He is coming out. He glances at the house, probably checking to see if the bedroom lights are still off. Poor cow is probably sound asleep. Getting into his car, he backs from the driveway. I follow, not putting on my lights until I join the main street after him. As I expected, he heads straight to Thornton Road. I know exactly what he's doing there. Dirty pig! I follow, keeping my distance, as he takes a circular route driving up Tetley Street, along Sunbridge Road and back down Lower Grattan Road. He drives this route twice before pulling into the kerb on Tetley Street.

A skeletal figure darts from the shadows of the deserted buildings and makes a beeline for his car. She passes under a street light, and I see her in all her sad glory; she looks about eighteen going on fifty. For a mere second, I pity her, wonder what tragedy has driven her to this ... servicing the likes of him in a stinking alley for a few quid and the chance of catching something terminal. I shudder. They've got so much to answer for, that lot.

As I drive past, she skips around to the passenger side. For all her scrawniness, I notice the gentle curve of her belly. Her pregnant state makes what she's about to do even more distasteful, and for a second, I consider intervening now. Right this minute. If I acted straight away, I could save her this indignity. Then, I come to my senses. For the greater good, I would wait ... that's the right thing to do. I mustn't let myself be distracted.

She climbs in beside him, and he continues his circuit ending up in a disused car park off Sunbridge Road. I slide to a halt in the street opposite the car park and see the glimmer of his tail lights as he pulls up in the farthest away corner and brakes. For a moment, the glare of his headlights reflects back off the building edging the area, then they're doused. In the half-light, I can see only the outline of his vehicle, but I don't need a spotlight to know what's going on inside. I wait until the girl gets out. She wipes her mouth and pockets her cash before slipping through the still night, down a side street and, presumably, back to her 'spot.' As soon as she's out of sight, I make my move. Sliding into gear, I edge forward, the engine barely purring as I drive between the dilapidated gates.

It's ridiculously easy, really. When I'm lined up, I accelerate and flick my lights on full blast. Blinding him, brakes squealing, I ram his BMW with my old van. His lumbering frame half stumbles out of the vehicle. Still blinded by the harsh gleam, he approaches, hands splayed before him. I'm more agile than him, so I jump out quickly. The increased tempo of my heart seems to buoy me up. Its rhythm matching my staccato movements, *thurrump, thurrump, thurrump.* I've done this before. I know my routine by now. I get out of the van, taking care to flick the switch on the extra strong lantern I wear round my head. He can't see a thing. I move fast. The syringe is ready prepped in my hand, and in it goes, smooth and easy. He doesn't have a chance to react as he slides to the muck.

I pull his legs together, smirking at the mud that spatters his trousers. He is one big bloke. I get the trolley from the van. No need to be gentle, so I force the metal scoop under his buttocks and lay the trolley flat. He's heavier than I'd anticipated, but finally I manage to drag him on. The first time, with Asim Farooq, I'd immobilised him straight away with the cable ties. That had been a disaster. He'd been hard to manoeuvre with his hands and feet tied together. With Manish Parmar, I'd adapted my technique. Instead, I'd got him onto the trolley first before putting on the cable ties and that worked better.

Pulling his feet together at the ankles, I pull the tie tight, until it cuts right in, his socks bulging out over the top. I tie a rope round his middle to hold him in place, and then, I raise the trolley. Soon as I've done that, I drag his arms behind the trolley, and using another tie, I bind them together attaching them to one of the metal cross bars. It's taken a matter of a few minutes. That's all. I look around, but I'm fairly sure the activity has gone undetected. Who would want to be in this area in the middle of the night?

I lower the ramp at the back of my van before wheeling the trolley over, and once it's in place, I raise it up and in. The beauty of my trusty trolley is it lies perfectly flat ... for what I'm going to do, I need a flat surface. For a second, I study the inert body in the back of my van, and as my heart rate slows, a slow smile lifts my lips. Humming to myself, I slam the door shut, and after a quick glance to make sure I've left nothing behind, I climb into the driver's seat and head off.

Chapter 45

02:15 Marriners Drive

Gus accepted the excess of coffee he was pumping into his body wouldn't help. It was either that or crack open a bottle of whisky, and *that* would definitely *not* bode well for a productive day. The facts of the cases kept churning around and around in his mind. He *felt* Graeme Weston was guilty of something, but he didn't know what. He *sensed* Michael Hogg knew something, but, likewise, *he* wasn't telling. He *knew*, without doubt, Christine Weston had secrets she wanted to share but was too scared. Whether any of that was related to his serial killer was the big question.

When he'd checked in with Compo, his programme was still running the data. Nancy's press conference earlier had initiated a few leads that the uniformed officers were following up on. Now, the City Park bomb had put the serial killer momentarily on a back burner ... at least until he struck again. It was this last thought that worried Gus. Everything pointed to the fact the killer would act again soon. He clearly had a racist agenda, and that was being fuelled by the day's events. According to Professor Carlton, whether or not the Tattoo Killer was directly involved in Albion First, their actions were a tacit green light for him to continue. Gus hoped he wasn't 'continuing' whilst he sat in the comfort of his living room, over-dosing on caffeine.

He hit the dimmer switch, rested his head on the back of his sofa and looked at the portrait of Bob Marley painted by his best friend Greg … the friend he'd been forced to kill. He sighed.

'What do you reckon, Bob? What else should I be doing?'

For the third time since he'd arrived home that evening, Gus peeled his sleeve back to reveal the tattoo on his upper arm. It was still raw and crusty, but the shape was well defined. He compared it to the larger painting on the wall and grinned. He was happy with it, and Mo, bless him, hadn't told anyone he'd nearly fainted … well, not so far, anyway. It *had* been sore but not unbearable. It wasn't the pain that had got to him; it was the sight of the needle moving so fast and the sound, and the little pinpricks of blood Emily kept wiping away with a tissue. He was pleased he'd done it, but he definitely wouldn't be having another one applied anytime soon. Getting out his tube of Bepanthen, he applied it to the tattoo. Its coolness felt soothing against the warmth of his skin. He exhaled, knowing their sadist tattooist wouldn't think twice about aftercare or being gentle. He shuddered at the thought of the pain he'd gone through for his paltry little tatt, magnified a hundredfold. It didn't bear thinking about. What kind of person did that sort of thing?

Chapter 46

03:30 The Kill Site

Through the shadows of the trees and bushes, lit only by moonlight, the slight swish of Tara's tail tells me she is waiting for my signal to tell her it's safe. I open the van window. Whistling in a low tone, I imagine her trembling body calming, her ears falling back and her nostrils quivering in the night air, searching for my familiar scent in the breeze. I sense, rather than hear, the bushes rustle, as her magnificent splendour moves towards me. She'll be anticipating the treat I always carry for her in my pocket. I smile and draw to a halt near the old barn. The van is out of sight of the track. Not that anyone would be about at nearly four in the morning.

I jump out, and Tara comes right up to me, her nose butting against my back, her teeth nibbling my pocket trying to tease out the sweet treat. Her breath is warm against my hand as I give in and take the cube from my pocket before offering it to her, in my palm. She inhales it without pausing, and then, looking at me, she demands to be stroked. Running my gloved fingers through her thick mane, she puffs her pleasure against my cheek, nuzzling my neck. For minutes, we stay like that … as one. Savouring each other's company. Until I pat her rump lightly, whisper promises to return later and send her back to her shelter in the copse of trees. Tara is the only witness to my dark deeds, and, lucky for me, *she* can't tell a soul.

Readying myself for the next stage, I take the syringe in my hand and swing open the doors. A dull light illuminates the man still secured to the trolley. Hmm, something is different … no movement. Usually by now, they are starting to come around. I release the hydraulic step and climb in, wary in case he is trying to trick me. Syringe poised, I creep closer and prod him. No reaction. I move closer, and then, I see his dark eyes staring up at me. Mocking me! Whoever said the eyes were windows to the soul was quite right. They are. I look right into his eyes, and all I see in their emptiness is darkness and perversion.

I cradle my head in my hands, my fingers raking my hair, and sob. Tears wash down my face, and stabs of anger course through my body until finally, with only Tara's anxious whinnies to soothe me, I drive my fist into his face. Then again … and again … and again until those evil eyes are no longer mocking me. He might have escaped the pain, but I am damned if he escapes my message. I take out the tattoo kit, and there, in the silent night, I brand him with the symbol of purity.

Chapter 47

Nursing the worst hangover of all time, Jez Hopkins slouched into the offices wearing the same clothes he'd worn the previous day. A large Starbucks latte with extra sugar in one hand and with his bag over the opposite shoulder, he stumbled towards his desk. Ignoring the knowing looks and sarky comments from his colleagues, he eased himself onto his chair. Taking care not to jolt his head too much, he closed his eyes and waited for his world to settle, before taking a tentative sip of his drink. Satisfied his stomach could handle it, he took another longer sip, and feeling the caffeine course through his alcohol suffused veins, he opened one eye. *Ouch! Too bright!* He closed it again and leaned back in his chair groaning.

'Anyone got some co-codamol?' he said, whispering on account of his headache. He heard a rustling from the desk behind him and half-smiled. Angie always had painkillers, thank God! He heard her swishing towards him, her heels clacking just a little too loudly on the linoleum floor. 'Fuck's sake, Prentiss, keep it down!'

He was rewarded with a slap to the back of the head which made him wince, followed by the sound of the painkillers being slammed down on the desk in front of him, then the words, 'You stink like a bloody brewery. Couldn't you at least have showered before you came in?'

Ignoring her, Jez focussed his attention on his dizziness as a wave of nausea drifted over him. Not for the first time, he thought he may have to use the metal bin next to his desk, for there was no chance of him negotiating a path to the men's loos in time. At last, it passed. Unwilling to risk a reoccurrence, he put out his hand without moving his head or opening his eyes and groped around for the pills. There they were. Lifting them, he transported them to his mouth, and with the minimum of head movement, he downed a couple with a swig of coffee. At the same time, he vowed never to touch another drop of alcohol again in his life.

Settling back into his chair, with tentative movements, he swung his legs up and rested his feet on his desk. He'd deserved to celebrate last night. He'd had a few action-packed days of top stories, rounded off by the bonus of being the only reporter on hand when the bottle-bomb had been released into the crowd in City Park. And, of course, he'd risen to the occasion like the professional he was. Not only had he snagged a radio interview with Graeme Weston, but because the *Calendar* crew couldn't get in quickly enough, he'd managed to snare a TV one too. He smiled. It had been repeated ad infinitum all night; his face plastered all over the country asking insightful questions of Bradford's newest and most controversial politician. He'd been in his element, and he hadn't let Weston off lightly. Oh, no! He'd made sure to cast doubt on Albion First's claims the protestors had hurled the missile.

He sighed. One day of rest after all his recent achievements wasn't too much to ask, was it? After all, he was sitting on some pretty darn good career prospects right now, and the big bosses had better take note or their golden boy might head down south or, at the very least, to North Yorkshire. He was in a prime position to out-manoeuvre his opponents and cut a once-in-a-lifetime deal.

Half an hour and a snore-filled snooze later, he was interrupted by the arrival of the post. Groaning, he accepted his pile which looked like the usual junk: invitations to boring gallery openings and previews of this or that boring amateur production. Nothing that couldn't wait until he got his head straight.

He was about to toss the lot on top of the existing piles of junk mail on his desk when he saw it. A brown sealed envelope, marked in crabby small writing in ballpoint, 'For the Urgent Attention of Jez Hopkins.' There was no postmark, so it had clearly been hand-delivered. He turned it over in his hands again, and then, decision made, he ripped it open, spilling the contents over his desk. 'Whoa!'

For a second, he was immobilised. What he was seeing didn't register at first. Then, realising the implication of this delivery, he swept everything back into the envelope. With a quick glance around the room to make sure none of his nosy neighbours had eyeballed it, he stood up. Hangover gone in an instant, he grabbed his bag and tossed his Starbucks cup into the bin. 'Working from home for the rest of the day, Prentiss!' Shouting over his shoulder, he exited the building, ignoring his colleagues' cat calls and jeers branding him a 'lightweight' and suchlike.

Sod them! What he had in that envelope was a passport to the big time. A way out of Bradford with a wad of cash in his back pocket and the bright lights in sight. This was bigger than North Yorkshire. This was his ticket to the tabloids.

Chapter 48

'Right all, listen up! Here are the actions for today. Compo, how's your programme doing?'

'Getting there, Gus, maybe by lunchtime?'

'Ok. Taffy, Sampson, follow up on interviews with the victims' friends. Also, Imtiaz Khan is coming in today. He's going to go through footage of yesterday's City Park protest to see if he can identify the man he saw throwing the bomb. If he does, put the face through our facial recognition programme. Imti thinks he's one of Weston's thugs, so we should have him in our records.'

He turned to Alice. 'I want you to focus on identifying and alibiing any known right-wingers with a penchant for violence. This afternoon, you and I are going to visit the premises identified by Compo as being within our parameters as kill sites. Nancy is going to put out another appeal to the public, reiterating our request for information in anyone expressing recent interest in tattooing techniques, and warning the targeted group, young Asian men, to be ultra-vigilant.'

Alice stood up. 'The forensics are in, Gus. Looks like our tattooist is using Propofol to knock the victims out.' She clicked through the reports on her computer screen, 'Yep, Asim Farooq's tests show Propofol levels at 2.4µg/mL, Manish Parmar's were at 1.4 µg/mL and Razaul Ul Haq's at 2.3µg/mL/.'

'Propofol?' Gus tapped his lip. 'Isn't that the drug that killed Michael Jackson? What did they call it? They had some catchy name for it, I seem to remember.'

Compo's fingers had been flying across his keyboard as they talked, and he now turned the screen so the rest of the team could see his findings. 'Milk of Amnesia! That's what they called it, for obvious reasons. It acts as a short-term anaesthetic lasting between ten and fifteen minutes. For our killer's purposes, it's very quick acting. Knocks them out in seconds. And,' Compo screwed up his face, 'can you believe it? It's not a controlled drug, which probably means it's relatively easy to obtain.'

Sampson groaned. 'Just what we need.'

Alice, who'd continued to scan the toxicology report, said, 'This is interesting. The results indicate the Propofol used on Razaul Ul Haq was compromised. There's evidence of bacterial growth. Apparently, because it's a liquid emulsion, it's more susceptible to being compromised if it's not stored properly, that is, in a fridge. Maybe our killer's getting sloppy.'

Gus grinned. They'd caught a lead, and it had come at exactly the right time for them. This could be the breakthrough they needed to narrow down their seemingly bottomless suspect pool. As he glanced around at the team, he could see from their expressions that their spirits were lifted. About time too! 'Right, Compo, I want to know who has access to Propofol, if it's obtainable on the black market and how. Where did our killer get this from? Is he a professional who has access to it?'

Again, Compo had some of the answers before his boss had finished speaking. 'Looks like it's widely used as part of a drug combo for human general anaesthesia, so most hospitals will stock it. With it not being a controlled drug, who knows how well monitored the usage and supplies of it are. It's also used in animal surgery, so vets will have access, and recent newspaper articles indicate it is becoming more widely used as a recreational drug of choice … bit risky, really, bearing in mind its main function is as a muscle relaxant, and what's the body's most important muscle?'

Taffy, jumping up and down on his chair, looking like a school kid eager to please his teacher, blurted out, 'The heart, it's the heart, isn't it?'

Gus had an urge to tap him lightly on the back of the head, but instead said, 'Never heard of the term 'rhetorical question,' Taffy?'

The young man frowned, then sighed, the smile falling from his lips and his eyes widening. 'Oh no, I thought Compo was really asking. My bad.'

Biting his tongue at the annoying Americanism, Gus began a slow count to ten. Next the kid would be saying, 'missing you already' and 'have a nice day,' and that would *really* piss him off. Before he had a chance to continue, Taffy was off again. 'Always been a bit too gullible, me. Once, when my mum went to India to look after my *dadi*, that's granny in Punjabi, you know?' He barely waited for Gus' nod before continuing, 'She asked me to look after her plants. They were her pride and joy, so it was a *big* responsibility.'

Seemingly oblivious to Gus' growing impatience, he continued. 'One of them started to wilt, and my mates told me it was bunged up and needed its system cleaning. They gave me a bottle of Syrup of Figs and told me to give it a spoonful day and night. By the end of the week, it were dead.' He looked down at his hands, 'My mum were well pissed off when she got back.'

Taffy rubbed the back of his head, making Gus wonder if the lad's mum had employed the tactic he himself had been tempted to use earlier. Unsure of how to respond to this story, Gus was relieved when Alice let out a shriek of laughter and said, 'You're a right bloody wally, Taffy.' She walked over and tapped the lad lightly across the back of his head, saying, 'Syrup of Figs! Idiot!' as she did so.

Taking it in good grace, Taffy, a big grin on his face, said, 'Ouch!' and, once more, rubbed his head.

'Sir?' A uniformed officer popped his head round the door. 'Got a young woman on the phone, says her husband went out to get her some ice cream last night and didn't come back home. She's pregnant, like, and fell asleep waiting for him. The thing is, I thought you'd be interested because he's black, and his car's not in the drive. I know the others were Asian, but thought it was a bit too much of a coincidence, eh, sir?'

'Shit!' said Gus. Then, with a nod to the officer, he added, 'Good work. Put her through to me now. I'll gather the details.'

Ten minutes later, Gus hung up and turned to Alice. 'You're driving. I think we've identified another victim. Wonder where he's been dumped?'

Gus stiffened his spine as he and Alice headed out to the car park. At some point during the day, the chances were, he would be informing this woman her husband was not only dead, but that he'd been murdered in a brutal and horrific manner. To top it all, she would discover her husband and the father of her unborn child was, more than likely, targeted because he had some sort of predilection for illicit sex she knew nothing about. That made the task of interviewing her all the more traumatic. Anger at being forced into this position by the killer made Gus want to slam his fist into a wall. The only thing that stopped him was knowing the victim had suffered unimaginable pain already, and his family were about to suffer far more. Life was a fucking bitch!

Chapter 49

Jez Hopkins turned the shower to as hot as he could bear it for ten seconds and then down to cold for five, before switching it off. He shook his head, sending water droplets splashing against the white tiles before wrapping a towel around his waist and wandering through to his open-plan living area.

En-route to the shower, he'd stripped his clothes off, dropping them at his feet as he moved towards the bathroom. Now, seeing them lying there, creased and stinking, marring the flat's virginal plains and revealing his inner slob, his mouth curled in disgust. With rapid movements, he bundled them together and shoved them into the washer. He glanced at his desk to check that the envelope was still there – it was – and then walked to the window.

Despite the under-floor heating and triple-glazed windows, the mere sight of snow falling outside brought him out in goose bumps, and his nipples tightened. From his flat's position on the top floor, which as it happened was only three doors down from the one occupied by mighty DI Gus McGuire's sister and his ex-wife, he could see The Fort opposite. If he strained his neck to the right, he could see right down Oak Lane and over to Bolton Woods. Today, the view didn't interest him. He was too busy trying to work out what to do with the anonymous gift he'd been given.

He half wondered if he should share them with DI McGuire's team. Maybe that would earn him some brownie points from the delectable Detective Sergeant Alice Cooper. Then, he remembered *just* how much of a ballbreaker she was and realised it'd take a damn sight more than a few saucy pictures to get into *her* knickers. No, that wasn't going to happen anytime soon. Wandering through to his bedroom, he rummaged around in his dresser and then pulled on a pair of boxers followed by jeans and a T-shirt. Barefoot, he went back into the lounge and picked up the envelope. Plonking down onto the sofa, he spilled the photos out onto the pine coffee table that had come with the flat and fanned them out.

This was one huge scoop for him, and he had to play it just right. The only problem was, did he go national or keep it local? He was a big fish in a little pond at the *Bradford Chronicle*. He'd built up some loyalties there over the years, whereas with the nationals, he'd barely made a ripple to date. This would be the equivalent of a tsunami for him, however with the nationals, it was hard to judge for just how long the aftershocks would line his pockets. They were notoriously close-ranked, and he worried if he sold to them, he might have burned his bridges nearer to home for no long-term gain.

He picked up one of the images at random and turned it this way and that to get the best view. Phew! Christine Weston was one athletic bird and bloody naughty to boot. Wonder if old Graeme knew she'd spread her legs for an Asian ... well, he soon would. He glanced at the range of snaps, and grinned – she'd done it in such a variety of ways *and* with such evident enjoyment.

He picked up the last image, his hand already, in response to his hard-on, tugging open the zip of his jeans, when he stopped. His hand halted, and his erection withered to nothing. This was the only photo with a clear view of Christine Weston's lover's face, and it changed everything. Yanking his zip back up, Jez jumped to his feet, blood pumping through his veins. *Shit!* He glanced at the time stamp on the photo and cursed again. Now, he definitely had to take this over the road to McGuire.

Feeling the blood return to his groin area, he smirked and picked up a different photo ... he didn't have to go right away though, did he?

Chapter 50

09:30 Caroline Drive, Dudley Hill

From the outside, the house was like any other in the street, neat and well-maintained under the spattering of snow that dusted the front lawn. The expression on Alice's face said it all as they pushed open the gate and began to walk up the path. Her face was taut and tension lines spread out from her usually smiling mouth.

Gus acknowledged he probably appeared just as serious. Nudging her, he said, 'Try to lighten up a bit, Al. No point in taking our emotions inside too. They've got enough on with their own, right now. Time enough later, when we've got something definite, to burst their bubble.'

With a curt nod, Alice exhaled and relaxed her facial muscles, and squeezing her arm, Gus followed suit.

Two cars, neither of them belonging to the missing man, were parked in the drive. They seemed like they'd been abandoned there in a hurry and probably belonged to relatives or friends come to support the pregnant wife. Bracing himself, Gus rattled the letter box and was pleased to see it opened almost immediately by Janine Roberts, the family liaison officer he'd contacted. Her presence accounted for one of the vehicles. 'You got here quick, Janine.'

Keeping her voice low, Janine stepped outside and pulled the door closed behind her. 'Yeah, felt I should be here for when ...' She shrugged. 'You know.'

Gus did know. He'd have done the same in her shoes. Best, if you had the chance, to get the initial introductions over with before that raw pounding grief set in. Before death was confirmed, as he had no doubt it would be in this case. 'How is she? Got anyone else with her?'

'Her mother-in-law. She told me when she speaks to you, she wants to do it *without* the mother-in-law present. Think she's got something she needs to tell you she doesn't want her to know about.'

That sounded ominous; however, with any luck, whatever it was would provide them with a lead of some description.

Reopening the door, Janine stepped back into the house and led them down a hallway lined with pictures of an arrestingly handsome couple in various wedding type poses. They reminded Gus of the ones of himself and Gabriella that he'd not long since removed from his own walls. Every picture hid a story. He smiled at his cynicism as they entered a pleasant and spacious front room. An oversize leather sofa stood against the back wall. This was matched by a humungous TV that dominated the space. *Good Morning TV* played out in a series of silent images. Clearly, Sandra Gore wanted quiet. Two matching chairs stood on either side of the cast iron stove, which blasted out welcome heat. A bundle of baby blue wool with two needles protruding from its depths lay on one of them. A large image of Sandra and Lewis taken in Lister Park had pride of place above the fire, and Gus couldn't help notice the frequent glances the room's sole occupier cast that way.

Sandra Gore sat in the middle of the couch, a jumble of multi-coloured cushions supporting her back and knees. Her feet rested on a small footstool. Gus noticed her ankles were swollen and remembered Mo's wife's ankles ballooning with her second pregnancy. He hoped her current worries about her husband weren't adding to her pressure. On top of a small glass-topped table lay a couple of well-thumbed women's magazines. A discarded mug stood next to them on a coaster. It was one of those plastic personalised coasters, like the one Mo had given him at Christmas with his kids on it. Gus couldn't see the image on this one, but judging by the others dotted around the shiny surfaces, it was of her and Lewis on their wedding day. She had worn traditional white with a voluminous veil cascading down from her corn-rowed hair, whilst Lewis wore a dark grey suit and bow tie. They were radiant, their hopes for the future displayed for all their guests to see. Gus' heart contracted.

Smiling at her, Gus introduced both himself and Alice. Considering the fact that, after their earlier conversation, Sandra Gore appeared to have no doubt her husband was the latest Tattoo Killer victim, she appeared calm. Although her eyes were puffy, Gus assumed from tears shed earlier, she radiated composure.

The door adjoining the room opened, releasing a delicious aroma of cooking meat into the room. Sandra groaned and covered her mouth. Clearly, the smell made her nauseous. Alice walked over and closed the door behind the large woman who'd just walked in.

'You gonna find my son?' the older woman demanded, glaring at Gus, her eyes raking him from top to toe.

Gus smiled and indicated she should sit down. 'That's the plan, ma'am. And you are?'

'Monica Gore. Lewis is my baby.' Sitting down, she turned to Sandra and gripped the hand that rested across her swollen abdomen, nodding towards the bump. 'This little one will be my fourth grandson.'

Sandra smiled and patted her mother-in-law's hand. 'We don't know the baby's sex yet, Monica. Lewis didn't want to know. You know that.'

'Psst, you're carrying him low. Same as I did wi' Lewis. He's a boy. No doubt about it.'

As Sandra's eyes clouded over, her bottom lip quivering, Janine intervened, 'Come on, Monica, let's get that curry cooked, shall we? Leave the officers to talk to Sandra on her own. If they need us, they know where we are.'

Monica glanced at Sandra, her face a mask of concern. 'You sure, baby? Maybe I should stay.'

Sandra smiled and patted her mother-in-law's hand. 'No, Monny, you get that curry ready. I'll be fine. When I'm finished here, I'm going up for a lie down.'

Monny's eyes raked her face, and then, she leaned over and kissed Sandra's cheek. 'Ok, sweet girl. I'll leave you to tell Lewis' secrets to the Detective.'

She turned to Gus and waved her finger. 'Don't you dare be upsetting that girl any more than you need to, alright?'

Gus, sensing a woman after his own mother's heart, just nodded and held her gaze, hoping his sincerity shone from his eyes. Seemingly satisfied, Monica Gore hefted her substantial frame upright and, hips sashaying to her own rhythm, left the room.

Sandra sighed and said, 'Sit down. You must appreciate my mother-in-law is very upset *and* very protective.'

Gus waved her comments aside and sat down opposite her, leaving Alice to sit on a chair at the dining table that nestled in an alcove overlooking the back garden.

Sandra frowned. 'Come and sit here, Detective Cooper.'

Alice smiled, 'If it's okay with you, Mrs Gore, I'd like to use the table to lean on to take notes.'

Perched on the edge of the chair, feeling that if he wasn't careful he might fall backwards and be unable to get back out, Gus leaned his elbows on his knees, his hands clasped. 'You gave us most of the information we needed during our phone conversation this morning. I want you to know we activated an immediate search for your husband and his vehicle. So far, nothing has been found, but we're still looking.'

Sandra looked him straight in the eye. 'Are you looking for my husband's BMW or a dead body, Inspector?'

Gus, refusing to flinch in the face of her bravery, ran his fingers through his hair. Her words, although not a hundred percent accurate, showed she was well aware of the chances of finding her husband alive. They were, in actual fact, looking for his car and were prepared for the worst. He admired her courage. Every passing hour would drain what little hope was sustaining her now, and he was glad she had her mother-in-law's support. 'We're looking for anything that may help us locate your husband.'

She glanced away with an abrupt nod and then said, 'There's something you need to know about Lewis. Something very important.'

Chapter 51

Serafina had sent Imti home, and she and Shamshad had talked for hours about what the documents could possibly mean and why Neha had them in her bag. Finally flagging, Serafina had hugged Shamshad and gone home, leaving her alone with her thoughts. Sham was drained and anxious. The lead weight sat in her stomach seemed to slow her motions. Even lifting her hand to her brow took all her energy. Her head throbbed, and her eyes were sore from crying.

Overnight, a huge gulf had appeared between her and Neha, and she didn't know how to bridge it. She'd thought they shared everything. She'd have sworn to it, if necessary, but this? It was a double whammy. First, she'd been oblivious to her sister's self-harm. They shared a room, and *still*, she hadn't noticed Neha had lost weight – again. That she was covering up in extra layers to hide her skeletal frame and concave stomach. Sham had been so pleased her sister appeared to be eating normally. She'd dropped her guard and stopped being vigilant. Since the psychiatrist had signed Neha back into primary health care, Sham had gradually stopped looking for signs she was failing.

She'd stopped searching Neha's face for signs of disgust when her aunt brought food to the table. She no longer counted how many bites her sister took of each meal or wondered if she was moving food around her plate to deceive them into believing she'd eaten. She'd stopped hovering around in the hours after meals to prevent her from flushing all the nourishment she'd just consumed down the toilet. *How* had she let this happen? Why had she stopped spying on her sister as she undressed for bed – looking out for signs of new cuts on her arms and legs? For months, she'd not checked the inside of her clothing for blood or the outdoor bins for razors or bandages, and look what had happened! *She* was responsible for Neha, and she'd failed.

Watching the steady rise and fall of her sister's breathing and the slow movement of saline crawling down the drip into her sister's arm, she wondered if Neha would ever forgive her ... she wondered if she'd ever forgive herself.

The urge to scream bubbled in her chest, constricting her breathing, making her dizzy. She rose and moved over to the small sink in the corner of the room. Turning the tap on, conscious she should not disturb the other patients, she splashed some cold water on her face and patted it dry with a paper towel. The intravenous antibiotics had worked. Neha's fever had abated a little, and as she slept, sustenance was being pumped into her body. Sham almost envied her sister's oblivion.

Plonking herself down in the other chair, she opened the near transparent curtains that provided scant privacy from the rest of the ward. Despite their flimsiness, she'd been claustrophobic huddled up behind the fabric with only her sleeping sister, the backdrop of hospital white noise and her own thoughts for company. The sights of the ward coming to life around her were a welcome distraction.

The nurses had allowed her to stay overnight., Their sympathetic glances and soothing tones made Sham want to shrivel up into a ball and hide. Past experience told her they'd soon make her go home. Concern for *her* health would compel them to call her uncle to collect her. She wished Neha would wake up so she could ask her about the documents in her bag. Why did she have copies of someone else's birth certificate and medical records? Who was this person, and what connection did they have to her sister?

She'd read the medical records, but hadn't understood them. If the signal in the ward hadn't been so bad, she'd have Googled some of the words. She made a mental note to do that later. In the meantime, she couldn't help thinking her sister was in some sort of trouble. The sort of trouble that had driven her to abuse herself again. To punish herself. Worse, though, was the realisation she hadn't asked *her* for help. Never mind, she didn't need to ask now. Sham would insist. There was no way she'd allow Neha to keep any more secrets. She tried in vain to come up with answers to the various questions that had hummed in her brain all night. At last, the rhythmic ebb and flow of the ward soothed her, and she drifted off into a deep sleep.

Chapter 52

10:35 Tetley Street, Bradford

Gus was aware of Alice casting little looks in his direction as she drove. He was mulling everything over in his mind, so despite knowing she was desperate to discuss what Sandra Gore had just told them, he ignored her.

The bombshell that Lewis' wife had dropped had repercussions for *all* of Bradford's police. As soon as she'd said it, Gus had been on the phone, first to Nancy and then to Lewis Gore's handler, for the secret Sandra Gore had not wanted her mother-in-law to hear was, Lewis, working undercover, had infiltrated an international drug ring. Gore's handler revealed his contact was a prostitute called Gloria Styles, and their meet up point was just off Thornton Road.

They weren't talking little operations, like Shahid Khan or Bazza Green's. No, this time, they were talking about a multi-million-pound international operation that was happy to use Bazza and Khan as cover, without them even knowing it. This organisation had established 'houses' up and down the length of the country and exported internationally. They supplied to legitimate businessmen and focussed on the leafy suburbs of each city, where the real money was, rather than the inner city. They used their contacts in inner cities as drug mules. Bradford had become a hotspot for them – cheap labour, willing pushers and discontent. That was how they kept under the radar.

Lewis Gore, though, had been working as part of the covert operation to infiltrate the organisation. According to his wife, Gloria Styles had set up a meet with Lewis the previous evening. He'd promised to return with a McDonald's Cadbury chocolate McFlurry for her, but she'd fallen asleep, and only realised he hadn't returned on waking this morning.

Just as they were leaving the Gore house, after reassuring Sandra they would keep her updated, a phone call came in, telling them Lewis' BMW had been found in a disused car park off Tetley Street near Thornton Road. The previous victims' vehicles had also been discovered in similar areas and combined with the fact Lewis was black, Gus was pretty sure Gore had been abducted by the killer. He quickly gave instructions for Gloria Styles to be located and interviewed straight away.

Approaching from the bottom of Tetley Street, they nearly missed the small entrance into the parking bay. Had it not been for a police officer positioned at the entrance, who guided them through, they would have driven past. Slowing down, Alice turned into a pot-holed road. Gus smiled as she cursed under her breath about the fate of the suspension on her beloved Mini Cooper.

Proceeding over sludge-filled ditches as slowly as she could, grimacing each time her wheels hit a particularly bad one, Alice said, 'Next time, we take a bloody pool car, ok?'

The end of the narrow lane opened up into a sizeable tarmacked area which extended to both sides. Gus saw that the crime scene tape had been stretched from a fence post on their right to a corresponding one to their left. A number of police cars, marked and unmarked, were parked up. A uniformed officer supervised two kids with skateboards near one of the police vehicles.

As Gus stepped out of the Mini and stretched his back, another officer approached, his hand extended in greeting. Gus gripped it, listening as the other man explained the kids, bunking off school, had decided to ride their skateboards in the parking area. Apparently, they'd done so before and found the potholes, old pallets and discarded rubbish a challenging obstacle course to test their skills. When they'd seen the BMW with its 66-plate abandoned in the far corner, they thought it strange, but dismissed it as none of their business. It was only when they approached the vehicle and saw it had been bashed in at the back and left with the driver's door ajar and a wallet discarded on the floor that they decided to tell someone. So, they'd phoned it in.

Gus thanked his lucky stars the boys had possessed a degree of honesty. The previous victims' vehicles weren't discovered until after their bodies had been found. This way, at least, they had a bit of a head start. Gus had already asked Compo to add Lewis Gore's details to the programme he was still running.

Ducking under the tape, Gus approached the scene. Whistling under his breath, Hissing, Sid dusted for prints. Gus had a momentary pang of guilt as he remembered the way he'd spoken to the other man at Razaul Ul Haq's crime scene. Sid, on the other hand, appeared to have forgiven him, for he winked as Gus approached. 'Doubt we'll find anything much. There's a bit of white paint lodged in the scrapes at the back of Gore's car. If you can find the vehicle that rammed him, we'll be able to match it. As long as it doesn't get its bumper repaired in the interim.' He wafted his hand in the air in a circular motion. 'I had a look around, and there are no cameras or owt here to give us many more details. Looks like we'll have to rely on good old fieldwork.'

Gus grinned, relieved his relationship with Sid hadn't been affected by his bad temper. 'Any tracks or anything?'

'Just a mishmash of sludgy indecipherable tracks, except for this …' He took Gus over to where a dog turd lay squashed to the side of Lewis Gore's BMW.

Sid was beaming at him, so Gus rose to the bait. 'Okay, I'll bite. What have you got?'

Seemingly oblivious of the shitty stench that Gus could smell from a standing position, Sid knelt beside the excrement, his nose inches from the offending article as he spoke. 'Fortunately for us, whoever walks their dog here, A, doesn't pooper scoop and B, owns a rather huge dog.'

'You've lost me, Sid. I don't get the relevance. You think this dog walker saw something?'

Sid laughed and gestured Gus to move closer. Pointing with a pencil at the large squashed turd, he said, 'Looks like a tyre ran over it.'

Seeing the tracks that Sid pointed to, Gus grinned. 'Brilliant … and you can match them to a vehicle, can you?'

Sid sighed. 'Well, no. Not a vehicle. They're too thin to be from a vehicle … and they're not textured enough to be from a bike. My reckoning is a trolley or wheelbarrow of some description.'

Gus studied the proximity of the dog crap track to where the marker indicated Gore's wallet had been found. What did this mean? Had the killer used a trolley or barrow to move Gore, who, by all accounts, was a large bloke, to his own vehicle? Did the trolley even belong to the killer? Perhaps they were snatching at things … perhaps not. 'Any database on these sort of tracks, Sid?'

Still studying the poo, Sid shrugged. 'Of course. Later on, we'll get you a match to the type of trolley this belongs to. We may even get a brand name too.' Stretching his hand out, he pulled Gus' trouser leg, indicating he should come closer to the smelly pile. When Gus closed his nostrils with two fingers, Sid snorted. 'Thought you'd be used to worse than this by now. Anyway, *this* is where you just got lucky, Gussy boy. This nick here is quite distinctive ...'

Gus studied the mark that showed this particular tyre had a small nick in it, before speaking in a nasal tone. 'So, what you're saying is, if I find you a killer who owns a trolley with a tyre matching that distinctive nick –'

'– and bearing traces of this shit. Then, yes, you've got him.' Sid followed through on his statement with a rumbling fart that made Gus groan.

Standing a couple of feet away from them, Alice shook her head and took a step back. 'You're an animal, Sid. Do you know that?'

Gus, moving away from the combination of canine and human toxic smells, said, 'Good work, Sid.'

Sid nodded. 'Oh, not going to rip me a new one today then, Gus?'

Dipping his head, Gus exhaled a long slow breath and stepped towards Sid. 'About that. I'm really sorry. I was out of order the other day. Won't happen again.'

Sid waved his blue gloved hand. 'Forget it, Gus. I have. We all overreact on occasion. Look, I'll keep myself available on this one, you know? Until we find him.'

Ignoring the fact that had Sid forgotten his bad behaviour, he wouldn't have felt the need to mention it, Gus nodded. This was the other man's way of offering support, despite feeling miffed. Gus still had some work to do to make up for it. He reached over and squeezed Sid's arm. 'Appreciated, mate.'

As he walked back towards the tape, he saw that Alice was now talking to a girl in jeans and trainers, with a hooded coat that stretched over her distended abdomen. She'd pulled the hood up over her hair and was smoking a cigarette. Gloria Styles, he presumed. By the time he joined them, Gloria had given Alice all the information she had ... which was zilch.

She'd met Gore by appointment and driven to this spot, as they did every time. She'd given him the names of two business men she'd heard the other girls taking about, and they'd hung out for fifteen minutes to make it look like she'd done business with him. When she left, she'd cut through the side street that led back out onto Thornton Road where she continued her shift. She hadn't noticed any other vehicles or anyone hanging about. Gus told her to hang on until Gore's handler came along so she could update him, but to all intents and purposes, she had nothing more to offer him.

'Come on, Al, let's get cracking on that list of secluded premises Compo compiled. The sooner we find Gore, the more chance we have of finding this sick fucker.'

Neither of them voiced the words they were both undoubtedly thinking; that Lewis Gore was well and truly dead by now.

Chapter 53

Compo had come up with nine possible secluded buildings in the targeted area. The plan was to extend the criteria if none of the nine panned out. Alice and Gus had taken three of them, Taffy and Sampson another three, and two uniformed officers had been charged with looking at the final three. Time was of the essence now, and Gus didn't want the trail to go cold. Judging by the times of death for the previous victims, he was sure they were looking for a dead body rather than a live one. However, if there was even the slightest chance Lewis Gore was still alive, then Gus would move mountains to find him.

Deciding to drive to the furthest point first, Alice headed along Thornton Road through Denholme and onto Haworth moors, where they took a winding lane to the disused farmhouse identified by Compo. It sat on the very edge of the moors. The rain had brought out that foliage smell Gus always associated with Bronte country; windswept and raw. He took a deep breath, savouring the freshness through the half-open window, as he gazed out at the uneven moor.

As Alice drove over three separate cattle grids, she spoke in soothing tones to her Mini, 'Come on, Minnie. You can do this. I'll make it up to you at the weekend. We'll have a spa day, you and me. A nice bath and a massage. Hell, if you're lucky, maybe the firefighters in Bolton will be out with their hoses doing a charity car wash.'

Used to Alice talking nonsense to her vehicle, Gus butted in, 'Don't listen to her, Minnie. She's full of false promises and wishful thinking. There's no way the Bolton firefighters will be out doing their charity *thang* in this weather.'

Alice braked and threw him a look which told him in no uncertain terms she was pissed off with him. He laughed and unfolded his legs from the car. Their way was blocked by a padlocked metal gate attached to a barbed wire fence that appeared to skirt the property.

Joining him, Alice examined the wilderness of bracken and gorse that spread out to either side of them. 'Very Heathcliff,' she said and peered under the chassis to check the suspension.

Gus approached the gate and rattled the padlock. It seemed old and rusted, but secure. He doubted that anyone had opened it in a long time. Jumping onto the lower ring of the gate, he craned his neck until he could see the dilapidated farmhouse that stood just beyond a curve at the end of the overgrown track. He cursed. 'Looks like this one's a dead end. Compo's map shows this is the only entrance to the property.'

Alice nodded and turned to head back to the car. However, a yelp from Gus followed by a muffled curse, had her spinning around. Gus glared at her. 'For fuck's sake, don't just stand there gawping at me with that stupid grin on your face, come and help me then.'

He'd jumped onto the gate, swung one leg over and, repeating the process with the other, had managed to get his trousers caught on the padlock. Balancing on one leg, he had gripped the top bar with both hands and tried to kick the fabric free. This, in turn, caused him to wobble even more.

'For goodness sake! Can't you even climb a simple gate without getting in bother?' Huffing and puffing, Alice wandered over and yanked at his trousers. This action caused Gus to sway even more on top of the fence.

'Watch my bloody chinos, Al. They're new.'

As a loud ripping noise rent the air, Alice's mouth tightened in an insincere 'I'm sorry' sort of expression as she said, 'Oops, oh dear.'

Gus narrowed his eyes, and swinging his freed leg over, he jumped down onto a clump of urine coloured grass. Mouth curled, he glared at her. 'Thanks very much. Glad you were there to help.' Looking towards the distant building, he continued, 'Thought whilst we're here, we should make doubly sure.'

Ignoring the hand Gus extended towards her, Alice climbed onto the gate and, with rather more finesse than he'd managed, swung her leg over and jumped down beside him. 'Nobody's been here for months, Gus. You can tell by the way the grass is all springy. Look, it's grown up over the bottom rung of the gate. I doubt we could open it, even if we had the key.'

'You're probably right, but let's just check.'

Shrugging, Alice followed him as he walked the short distance to the old house. It was completely uninhabitable, with holes in the roof and partly collapsed walls. Gus walked through the open door into a dank smelling room which must once have been the kitchen. Alice was right. This place wasn't the kill site, but now he was here, he might as well do his job properly. Taking his phone out, he activated the torch and began to explore. The ground floor rooms were empty, and as the stairs had buckled, there was no way to check upstairs, and no point, either. He couldn't imagine the killer bundling his victim over that gate and transporting him along the uneven track to tattoo him.

'Come on, Al. We can cross this property off the list. Let's head to number two.'

Once back in her Mini, Alice reversed all the way back down the track until they reached the main road. Next stop was a small, disused industrial plant outside Harden. Gus suspected this property wasn't quite remote enough for the killer's purposes, but it was worth checking anyway. When they arrived, he saw immediately it was a no go. It was too close to the main Harden road, and apart from that, a trio of travellers' caravans had parked up outside the empty building. According to the oldest man present, who appeared to be their spokesperson, they'd been there since November. There was no way they would have missed someone trundling up with subdued bodies and a boot full of tattoo equipment.

'Another one struck off,' said Alice, with a sigh. 'Last one for us and then back to The Fort.'

Gus put his seat belt on and nodded. 'Okay, on we go.'

The final disused building on their list was a barn just outside Wilsden. It stood in the top end of a series of fields on the opposite side of the road from a small row of houses bearing the delightful street name Bay of Biscay. Its distance from civilisation made it slightly more promising than the other buildings. Still, Gus didn't hold out much hope. The barn was remote, and it did have secluded access via a side road, but it was barely accessible and easily missed. On top of that, three horses occupied the field, making it likely there were regular visitors to look after the animals.

Alice drove up and stopped at a latched gate. A mish mash of tyre tracks showed Gus' expectation of regular traffic to the field was accurate. They got out, and as they approached the gate, Gus was pleased to see it wasn't padlocked. No need for a repeat performance of his earlier indignities. As they walked through, closing it behind them, a large brown Shire horse, with eyes to match, shied away from them and joined two other horses standing in a copse of trees further down the field.

'What do you think?' asked Gus.

Alice shrugged. 'Not sure. Let's have a proper look in the barn. It's accessible enough, and look, there are tracks leading towards it.'

'Probably the vehicle that drops off the horses' food,' said Gus, pointing to the corrugated roofed lean-to that adjoined the barn.

Inside the sizeable structure, three netted bales of hay were hooked onto the brick wall. A trough of water stood outside, presumably to harvest rain water for the animals. The muddy ground was pitted and churned by horseshoe marks which obliterated the evidence of any human presence in the form of boot treads. A heady horse manure smell hung heavy in the air, and the absence of too much dung in the vicinity confirmed the horses were well tended. Very unlikely to be the kill site! Gus suspected their killer would not want his activities interrupted by the horses' owners. Unless, of course, he was their owner. 'Has Compo got details yet on who owns these fields?'

'On it,' said Alice, opening her phone and texting.

Gus surveyed the field and barn. 'It's accessible, and clearly, it is well-used.' He pointed at tracks in the churned-up muck. 'Let's head inside the barn itself. See what we find there.'

As they moved round to the gap where a door should have been, the Shire horse sidled up, its wise eyes watching their every move. The other two horses, with studied indifference, ignored them. Gus watched as Alice approached it. He'd never been comfortable around large animals. As a child, summertime farm trips with his parents and sister, Katie, had been fraught with fear for him. Even now as an adult, despite the disparity in size being diminished, he was uncomfortable … disadvantaged. It wasn't just the animals' size, though. It was something about their wildness, their unpredictability. He'd seen a herd of cows stampeding as a child and had the sense nothing human could stop them. Once, at Knowsley Safari Park, he'd seen the elephants thunder from one end of the enclosure to the other. It had petrified him. All that dust swirling in the air, and their bellows long and, to him, rabid sounding. He'd clutched his dad's hand so hard his father had seemed to sense his terror and lifted him into his arms, squeezing him tight.

In fact, one of the last arguments he'd had with his ex-wife, Gabriella, had been because of his refusal to go on a Kenyan safari with her. Why the hell would he want to go to Kenya to see animals that were not only enormous, but possessed claws and teeth sharp enough to eviscerate a man? No chance! In his job, he'd seen enough people eviscerated by human animals without tempting fate by putting himself in the way of a completely different, but equally unpredictable, species.

At first, the big animal shied away from Alice. Then, as she continued to talk softly, it allowed her to approach. From a safe distance, Gus saw its ears twitch and its nostrils quiver. He also saw the huge rippling muscles in its legs and imagined the power of its jaws. He shuddered. Soon, Alice was rubbing her palms along its nose and burying her fingers in its mane. Shoving his fists in his pockets, Gus headed toward the barn itself. With any luck, she'd think his haste was more to do with an eagerness to crack on, than a nervousness of horses. Who was he kidding? Alice was as sharp as a bloody tack. She'd know exactly what was driving him inside the barn right now. Hearing her low laugh, he turned, just in time to see the horse bumping her with its nose, telling her not to stop scratching. Despite himself, he smiled. Cute!

Continuing into the barn, he peered around, using his phone for light again. There was nothing to indicate it had been used as a kill site. The concrete floor was damp in patches where flurries of snow had drifted through the open door and melted. There was nothing to show the building had been used for anything other than shelter by the horses ... and most telling of all ... no tattoo machine and no Lewis Gore! He heaved a sigh of relief and exited the barn.

Alice left her new friend and joined him as he walked back to the car. 'No tattoo machine covered by a tarpaulin lurking in the corner, then?'

Gus shook his head. '... and no body either, thank God.'

'Shall we count this one out?'

Gus hesitated and peered around again. He bit his lip. 'No, not yet, Al. Let's be thorough. We know it's been accessed recently; we know it's remote enough for our killer's purposes. Let's investigate this a bit further. Find out who owns it, who owns the horses and see if they've seen anything strange, before we cross it off our list.'

'Yeah, you're right. The other two were definite no-nos. This, though, is a possible maybe.' She got into the Mini. 'We've made some progress, Gus.'

Gus nodded. 'Maybe ... although we haven't found Lewis Gore yet.'

As far as he was concerned, *some* progress wasn't enough. Not for Lewis Gore and not for his family!

Turning around in her seat to reverse out of the lane, Alice said with a smile in her voice, 'And you needn't think I didn't spot you edging away from the horse, Gus. Big bloody baby, scared of a little gee-gee.'

Gus spluttered, 'Little? ... Little? Bloody great hulking thing is more like it.'

Chapter 54

12:35 The Fort

The weather had taken a turn for the worse. From nowhere, a dark cloud had scurried across the sky skidding to a halt directly above Bradford. Right on cue, it released its load in a torrent of pelting rain at the exact moment Alice and Gus parked up in The Fort car park. Laughing, they made a mad dash for the door and, like a couple of bloodhounds, shook themselves off in the doorway before taking the stairs up to the incident room.

They'd no sooner got in and warmed up with mugs of coffee when Taffy burst through the door, his dripping hair splattered across his forehead. Clenched in his hand was a somewhat sodden copy of the *Bradford Chronicle*. Panting, Sampson followed the younger officer into the room, wiping rain from his face as he stopped in front of Gus' desk. Amused, Gus watched as Taffy bent over, rested his hands on his knees and inhaled huge gulps of air. A quick glance at Sampson's serious expression wiped the smile from Gus' face. Realising his officers' hurry had something to do with the newspaper, Gus strode over and snatched it from Taffy's unresisting hand.

Still breathing heavily, Taffy said, 'Thought you should know, ASAP.'

Tension gathered across Gus' shoulders as he unfolded the newspaper to read the headline. Alice stood behind him, peering over his shoulder. 'What the fuck,' she said, her voice reflecting Gus' horror. 'Who leaked that?'

Voice tight, Gus said, 'Who, indeed?'

Having finally caught his breath, Sampson said, 'That's not the worst of it, Gus. Turn to page three where the article's continued.'

Wondering what could be worse than the garish headline on the front cover, Gus pulled the sodden pages apart. His heart sunk. It was worse than he'd imagined. It was clear the photo had been cropped and manipulated to make it suitable for inclusion in the local newspaper, nevertheless, it left little doubt what Christine Weston and Razaul Ul Haq were getting up to.

Gus closed his eyes for a second. What a bloody nightmare. Last thing he needed was for this to have exploded when they still had Lewis Gore to find. His mind flashed to Razaul's twin daughters. The feisty gothic one, Shamshad, and the more reserved Neha. What would having that crap in the public domain do to *them*? Bloody irresponsible ... no, it was more than that ... much more. It was deliberately malicious. No doubt he'd have Weston hammering on his door in a minute, demanding he sort out the media bias. God only knows what that thug would do to his wife – he'd already hit her once, to Gus' knowledge. What a massive fuck-up this was! Nancy would have a mega fit.

He flipped back to the front cover. 'Jez fucking Hopkins,' he said, reading the by-line aloud. 'What the fuck does he think he's doing? He should have come to me with this. Where did he get these images from?'

Alice, angry red blotches on her cheeks, slammed her hand on the desk. 'Bloody immoral paparazzi. No fucking concern for the Ul Haq girls and their extended family or the Westons, for that matter ... Bloody toxic. 'Wife of Albion First candidate Graeme Weston Gets Up Close and Personal With Murdered, Razaul Ul Haq'? Makes me sick.'

Samson nodded. 'And the subheading's worse.'

Alice scowled. 'Ugh. 'Sleeping with the enemy takes on a whole new meaning for the Westons.''

Gus had listened to his team in silence. A vein pulsed on his temple betraying his anger. As he read the article, his chest tightened, until without warning, he took his mug and hurled it at the wall. He raked his fingers through his dreads while pacing round the room like a caged lion. Alice gawped at him, open mouthed, whilst Taffy, after a quick glance at Sampson, shuffled his feet. Sampson stood stock still. Each pair of eyes moved from the broken mug and the liquid that rolled in rivulets down the wall, to their boss. Silence pounded in Gus' head as he realised what he'd done.

Alice took a tentative step towards him. 'You okay? Come on, sit down. Everything's getting a bit intense. You're under a lot of pressure at the minute, what with Lewis Gore still missing and a killer at large, to say nothing of Weston's links to both the bottle-bomb in City Park and Razaul Ul Haq.'

Taking their cue from Alice, Samson rushed over and began to pick up the broken mug, whilst Taffy grabbed a wad of kitchen roll and began wiping the wall down.

Gus exhaled and stretched his neck back, rolling it to release the knots that threatened to strangle him. 'Shit, guys, I'm sorry about that. That was uncalled for.'

He rubbed his forehead. Then, realising his hand was shaking, he thrust it into his pocket instead and moved over to his desk. Embarrassed by his display of temper, he tried to rein in the anger that had erupted from nowhere. Truth was, he'd allowed the frustration to build up all day. From the minute he'd taken the call from Sandra Gore, he'd been trying to hold it together. The knowledge that Lewis Gore was lying dead somewhere ate at him. He felt helpless and responsible. If he'd caught this killer already,

Lewis Gore and his wife would be looking forward to the birth of their new baby without a care in the world. He knew he'd not been coping well for months. This seething anger wasn't new … wasn't just the Tattoo Killer case or Jez Hopkins' article, although this had certainly exacerbated it. Maybe he wasn't up to the job anymore – maybe he'd burnt out. He'd seen it before, albeit usually with older officers. Maybe he should just walk away from it all. This bubbling simmering tension was … different. Worse than he'd been after Greg. At least *then* he'd not had this unpredictable anger to control. Fuck, what was he doing? He'd acted out in a way he'd never done before in front of his staff. *That* was unacceptable.

The tension in the room was palpable. No-one knew what to say … they avoided looking at him, instead sending furtive glances to each other, their faces strained and pale – and *he* was the cause. What sort of leader was he? The kind who has an outburst when reading a bloody newspaper article by some tosser? In his mind, he tried to formulate an apology … words that would express his feelings without making them pity him. The last thing he needed was their pity. They'd all, bar Taffy, been through the mill over the past few months. Each of them had suffered media scrutiny and public condemnation. They deserved better.

Hell, Alice had nearly lost her life, and here he was, acting like a spoilt child. He hadn't had it any worse than they had, so why was it so difficult for him to hold it together? Needle pricks jagged at the back of his eyes and tried to blink away the tears before they became visible to his team … how humiliating would that be, on top of everything else? Swallowing hard, he accepted the steaming mug of coffee Alice had brought to him and opened his mouth to say something … anything to stop them all looking at him like that.

He didn't have the chance, though. The door burst open yet again. Nancy Chalmers, in high dudgeon, as his father would say, strode through, a copy of the offending article held high in her hand. She glared at Sampson, and her frown deepened. He was holding the base of the broken mug filled with ceramic shards and had a sheepish look on his face. She turned to Taffy who, with a brown stained pile of soiled kitchen roll, still dabbed at the wall. Her mouth tightened. Lowering the paper, she glanced round the room, her eyes narrowed, assessing. Honing in on the discomfiture that resonated between them, she said, 'Right, what's gone on here?'

Her gimlet eyes raked over each of them in turn, resting finally on Gus. Knowing he had to own up, he opened his mouth to explain the coffee stain on the new paintwork. However, before he had a chance to speak, Sampson stepped forward. 'Taffy and I were mucking about, and I tripped and dropped my mug.'

Taffy glanced at Samson and nodded, looking too terrified to speak. Sampson continued, 'It smashed against the wall, ma'am. Don't worry, though, Taffy and I are going to clean it up.'

Before Gus had a chance to refute Sampson's words, Alice's small hand clenched around his arm, just where his tattoo was, and squeezed. He turned and saw the warning look in her eye at the same time as he registered the slight increase in pressure around his tender arm. Her eyes narrowed. Turning to Sampson, he was greeted by another almost imperceptible nod. Then, the younger man tossed the broken ceramic pieces in the bin. 'No harm done,' he said.

Nancy, apparently still attuned to the tension in the room, seemed unconvinced. However, she shrugged and let it go. 'Hmm, well, we've got more important things to worry about than that.' She slammed the paper down on Gus' desk. 'What the hell is this about?'

Still feeling off-kilter, Gus examined the newspaper for a second and then turned to Sampson. 'Get uniforms to bring in Jez Hopkins.'

Hardeep Singh, the duty officer, popped his head around the door. 'No need. He's just walked in demanding to speak with you, Gus. I've put him in interview room two, that okay? Thought after that shit he's published, you'd want to turn the screws on the little bastard.'

Gus smiled. 'Thanks, Hardeep, you did the right thing.'

He turned to Nancy. 'When we've got a minute, Alice and I will speak to him.'

Nancy, her face stern, walked back over to the door. 'No rush. Let the little fucker sweat.'

Chapter 55

Shamshad had gone home to shower and change. She'd barely had the chance to speak to Neha before she'd left. There would be time for that later. Besides, in her sister's absence, she wanted to take the opportunity to search their room. She wanted ... no, she *needed* to know if Neha was keeping any other secrets from her.

So, bottling down her hurt, she shut their bedroom door and leaned against it, surveying the room with a calculating eye. She hadn't had to spy on her sister for a long time now, but the tricks she'd learned before flooded back to her in that instant. She knew exactly where to look, where to find any secrets Neha wanted to keep hidden. Later, when she had the chance, she'd search her school locker too.

Ignoring the feeling she was violating her sister's trust, Shamshad told herself Neha had betrayed *her* first. That she was only doing it to protect her sister. Steeling herself, she started. First, she skimmed her hand under the mattress protector, pushing her arm under as far as it would go. Then, she pulled the sheets off and flipped the mattress on its side. With a practised eye, she checked it thoroughly, looking for signs Neha had created a hiding place in the wadding ... nothing. She progressed to the headboard. Next, the pillows and duvet... again nothing. No microscopic slits to store razors or other secrets. So far so good.

Next step – her sister's books. She checked the spines of each for evidence Neha had concealed a razor inside, and her heart sank when she felt a slight lump on the spine of Neha's physics book. Using tweezers, she prised the spine away from the book, and inserting the tweezers, she fumbled about until they gripped something. For a second, the item resisted the pressure, and then, it plopped out, expanding in the space of its new-found freedom. Her brow knitted together. It was a photo that had been folded into six. With gentle fingers, Sham opened it out on their shared desk. Flattening it with the palm of her hand, her frown deepened. Her lower lip trembled as she drank it in, and tears welled in her eyes. Then, she placed two fingers to her lips and kissed them before pressing them to three of the four faces in the photo; her sister, her mother and her father.

She hadn't known Neha had this family photo. They had barely been three when it was taken. She and Neha wore identical pink shalwar kameez ... sparkly two-tone ones with sequins covering the yoke and around the bottoms of the shalwar. Their mum had scraped their dark locks back into ponytails and they each had intricate floral clips in their hair. She and Neha held hands and grinned at the camera, without a care in the world. If you looked close, you could see Henna patterns decorating their small arms, meandering up past their wrists. It must have been a family wedding or Eid or something like that to warrant such detailed mehndi.

Their parents had all the freshness of youth in their smiles. Her mother wore her hair down, her head uncovered. Shamshad couldn't remember a time when her mother had been so carefree. A time when she hadn't covered her hair. She wore make-up. Lipstick shone on her curved lips, and her eyes, looking up at her husband, were warm and smiling. Her dad had one arm on each of his daughter's shoulders, and he wore a traditional suit too. His smile was direct and charming. How things had changed in fourteen years.

Whilst Sham, understanding it had been beyond her mother's control, had forgiven her for the things she'd done to her daughters, Neha had not. For a long time, Neha had pinned her hopes on their father. Sham had never held onto that hope. Their father had been unwilling or perhaps unable to commit to them, and so it had fallen on their uncle to take them in. Their father had let them down repeatedly. Trips and outings cancelled at the last minute. Promises to pay for school trips were reneged on. His daughters were left to watch in silence, heartbreak hidden behind their quiet stoicism, as other children visited museums, farms and shows organised by their schools. So, finally, Sham had treated her father like a boil and lanced him from their lives.

During Neha's illness, she had blocked the few moves he'd made to see her sister. Now, Sham wondered if her sister had been seeing him in secret. Curling up on her sister's unmade bed, her duvet pulled around her, breathing in her scent, Sham cried and cried, all the time wondering where she'd gone wrong. All she'd ever wanted to do was protect Neha. Seemed like she'd blown it, and now, they were back to square one. Only this time, it was different. Neha had secrets, and Sham wasn't sure her sister wanted her help anymore. Right now, she wasn't even sure she wanted to give it.

Finally, she got up and tidied the mess she'd made. With one last, lingering look, she folded the photo and returned it to its hiding place. Tired of it all and feeling sticky and dirty, she headed to the bathroom for a shower. Half an hour later, Sham was in her bedroom getting dressed. Studying her face in the mirror, she was pleased to see the cuts she'd sustained in City Park were healing. She picked up her brushes and began applying her make-up. Boy, did she need to do that, because without it, her skin was wan and tired. It was then she heard raised voices coming from downstairs. Her heart sank. Her aunt and uncle rarely argued, and experience told her when they did, it was usually to do with her parents.

Feeling the familiar butterflies in her stomach, she wondered what had happened now as she added the final flick to her eyeliner. Giving her face a last once-over and deciding she looked marginally more human than before, she braced herself to go downstairs. Whatever had happened couldn't be any worse than what they'd been through over the last couple of days.

The paper was lying in the middle of the kitchen table when she walked in. Her aunt's face was drawn, her eyes dull with shock. Sham glanced at her uncle who nodded towards the paper. 'I'm so sorry, Shamshad, *beti*. You should not have to suffer this on top of everything else.'

Sham held his gaze for a second, and then, her eyes moved to the newspaper. At first, she couldn't see its significance. She glanced at her uncle, one eyebrow raised in question. His mouth drew into a line, and he pointed at the paper. 'Read it, Sham.'

Sham picked it up. As she read the headlines, her hands began to shake, and the colour drained from her face. Taking a deep breath, she turned the page and groaned. Oh no! Not this! How much more were they expected to face?

She pulled a chair from under the table and sank onto it. Looking from her aunt to her uncle, she whispered, 'I'm sorry.'

Her aunt got up, and moving as if her body was weighted down by something heavier than mere gravity, she walked around the table. Pulling Sham's head to her chest, she smoothed down the hair Sham had just spent ten minutes spiking to perfection. Uncaring, Sham moulded herself to her aunt's frame and sobbed. When she finally stopped and wiped her eyes, her uncle, head bowed, appeared sadder than she'd ever seen him.

Her aunt held her hand. 'This will pass, Sham. I promise. And you and Neha will be stronger for having suffered it.'

Shamshad glanced at her uncle and realised he, too, was crying. She put her hand on top of his and squeezed. 'We have each other, and we haven't done owt wrong. We can still hold our heads up high, can't we?'

Wiping the sleeve of his kameez over his eyes, her uncle smiled. 'Insh'Allah, we will be fine.'

Her aunt smiled at him, then turned to Shamshad, 'Go and redo your hair and put that awful make-up back on your face. You've got ten minutes, okay? Your uncle will drive you to the hospital. You'll need to prepare Neha for this.'

Sham jumped up, and in an uncharacteristic show of affection, she kissed first her aunt's and then her uncle's cheek, before moving upstairs, her feet like lead, to re-apply her make-up.

Half an hour later, walking into BRI with the offending newspaper hidden in her bag, it was like everyone's eyes were on her, judging her and finding her wanting. She was glad she'd taken the time to put on her armour. Entering the ward, she saw Neha was sitting propped up against a sea of white pillows. She seemed frail. Her hair, unconcealed by her hijab, was spread out making her look like an awake version of sleeping beauty. Her head was angled towards the window, and her eyes were shut. Sham stopped and just stared at her.

Sudden panic thudded in her chest, and she wanted to spin on her heel and run. Then Neha, as if sensing her presence, turned her head. Sham had no option but to do as she always had ... deal with shit!

Chapter 56

12:35 The Kill Site

Tara seems to sense the anger that reverberates off me. The weather matches my mood. I don't care that rain trickles down my back, or that the wind whips my hair. Both things serve to fuel my ire, and I welcome it. Tara sidles up, and her front hoof gently paws the mushy dirt. I'd hiked over three fields to get here, not wanting to be seen in the daylight, but it was worth it. Her gentle presence soothes me. With her, I don't need to pretend, don't need to cover up my feelings. Just as well, because right now, I'm having a job covering up my rage.

I'd only nipped into the Co-op to get a pint of milk and some cigs. I nearly died right there on the spot when I saw it. I wanted to slam my fist right through the flimsy sandwich board and kick it into the road. Don't know how I stopped myself. Maybe it was the funny looks the woman behind the counter kept throwing my way. I ducked my head down in case she recognised me. No point in taking chances. Mind you, I wanted to smack the stupid bitch in the face when she sniggered and made some smart-ass comment about the article. If they couldn't talk in proper sentences, they shouldn't be inflicted on the general public. Who was she to take that job when there were loads of deserving Brits queued up at the job centre?

As she handed me my change, I let my anger at her go. More important things to worry about. The humiliation of those photos was insurmountable, and I didn't know how to react. That's why I'd hotfooted it here. I knew I needed to calm myself. Try to think straight. God, it was one fiasco after another!

My main concern is *who* leaked it to the press? I'd made sure only to send them to Graeme. To warn him to keep his tramp of a wife in line. So, he could make sure her dirty little affairs wouldn't jeopardise the campaign, and now, some idiot had sent them to the *Bradford Chronicle!* I flick it open again and look at the photo. Had she done it out of malice? Had that stupid cow he called his wife done it to discredit him? After all my hard work sorting out Ul Haq, cleansing the streets to make things easier for Graeme, had she gone and made it all for nowt?

Breathing heavily, I feel Tara pull away from me with a sharp whinny. Realising I was tugging too tightly on her mane, I ease my fingers open and offer her an apple to soothe her. For a second, she seems hesitant, and I persist, forcing myself to be calm, trying to let the tension go. Then, she gives in, her rough tongue scoops the treat into her mouth, and just like that, all is forgiven. If only life was like that.

Well, at least when they find the body that will distract everyone from the Weston article. Not that the stupid cow doesn't deserve to have the entire world know how sluttish she is.

I move away from Tara, studying the paper again. The headline is seared on my retinas, and the anger wells up inside me again. I open my mouth as wide as I can, fling my head back and yell against the wind, ignoring the teeming rain that pounds my face.

Chapter 57

12:35 Hawthorn Drive, Eccleshill

Like clockwork, the clatter of the letterbox accompanied by the paperboy's off-tune whistle, signalled the arrival of the newspaper. With his rolling strut, Graeme Weston, feet bare, walked from the kitchen and along the hallway to the door. Bending down, he picked up the paper, frowning when he saw his name in the headline. What was that little toe-rag Hopkins saying about him now? Probably some follow up from yesterday's bottle-bomb in City Park. He grinned; that had worked out quite well for him. Michael's plan of planting one of their supporters among the Pakis to throw the bottle had been inspired. He'd taken the moral high ground. Been able to expose them for what they were … a bunch of idiots not worthy of calling themselves British.

With one hand, he flicked the paper open to see the headline and froze. What the hell was this? He scanned the page, his florid face losing colour as he read. Then, licking the tip of his index finger, he turned to the next page. His jaw tightened when he saw the photo and scrunching the paper up in one hand, he threw it to the floor and yelled, 'Christine!'

He turned and kicked open the living room door, making it slam against the wall before it rebounded, narrowly missing him as he barged his way into the room. Without stopping, he lifted his arm, and using the momentum from his motion, he swung it, backhanded, towards his startled wife as she stood holding a vase of lilies. His ring caught her on the cheek, and her head jerked backwards. With an animalistic grunt, he continued through with a shove that sent her toppling backwards towards the glass coffee table. The vase flew from her hands spilling water and flowers, before shattering. Her head followed, cracking onto the corner with a resounding thud that hung like a thunder cloud in the air for a second ... and then ... she was still. Curled up like a wilted petal. Blood mixed with water, drenching the white rug. It covered her hair and soaked into the pile leaving a stain like a ruby coloured tiara, discarded and askew, near Christine Weston's head.

Chapter 58

13:00 The Fort

When Nancy left, Gus walked around to the front of his desk. Feeling like an idiot, he opened his mouth to speak and then closed it again. He had no idea what to say. He thrust his fingers into his dreads and racked his brain for inspiration ... none came, so he settled for, 'Thanks, guys!'

Sampson, Taffy and Alice shrugged his thanks away. Compo, who'd spent the entire episode with his headphones on, nodding to his own beat, chose that moment to tune in to the real world. A slight frown creased his forehead as he said, 'Thanks for what?'

Alice grinned. 'Nothing, my darling.'

Taking her words at face value and clearly excited about something else, Compo nodded. Jumping up, he grabbed a pile of paper the printer had just spewed out and thrust it at Gus. '*You* can thank *me* for this, Gus,' he said, adding in an only half joking sort of tone, 'Preferably with donations of food.'

One look at Compo's grinning face told Gus he'd come up with the goods. 'Is this what I think it is?'

Burgundy beanie nodding ferociously, Compo rocked on the balls of his feet, his hands clasped behind his back as if he'd been called to the front of the class to receive a special award. His enthusiasm and excitement were contagious, and unable to hold his own in check, Gus released a 'Whoop woo' that would have made Compo proud.

Alice jumped and then smiled at Gus. 'For God's sake! Will you make up your mind if you're clinically depressed or just going off the rails?' She rubbed her ears. 'That hurt.' Moving over to join them, she added, 'Can't be doing with your damn mood swings.'

Despite her light-hearted tone, Gus detected the seriousness behind her words. He grabbed her arm and squeezed. 'Thanks, Alice. I owe you all one,' he said, before turning to Compo.

Compo pressed a button on his PC, and the sheets came up in the whiteboard for the rest of them to see. 'That's the names and addresses of all the people who have been ANPR'd in all of the first three victims' localities. The records show activity for the month prior to their murder.'

The list was about twenty-five or so names long. Compo pressed another key. 'And these are the ones that made multiple journeys around that area.'

Gus nodded, impressed. The list had shortened by about ten names, and he was just about to praise Compo, when the man himself pressed yet another key bringing a third much shorter list onto the screen. 'And these are the ones who made more than four visits to these localities.'

There were nine names on the list. Gus and his team studied them and their addresses, hoping a name would stand out for them ... none did. That didn't matter. This was a move in the right direction. Gus could feel it in his bones ... things were moving now. They had another direction to go in.

'Right, I want a team of uniforms to interview each of those on the list. Keep it light ... routine enquiries ... you know the drill. However, if any flags fly, we bring them in ASAP. Don't forget we still haven't found Lewis Gore ... he's our priority.'

Taffy lifted his gaze to Gus. 'Surely he's dead by now, sir.'

Gus stilled and then regarded the lad. 'Look, Taffy, as far as I'm concerned, 'til we know otherwise, Lewis Gore may still be alive. If he is, I don't want our killer startled into doing something stupid.'

Red-faced, Taffy nodded and turned back to his desk.

Gus called his name and waited until he'd turned around, before continuing with a smile, 'It's Gus… remember?'

'Gus,' Compo sounded a bit wary. 'I applied the programme to Lewis Gore's locality as well, and something interesting came up.'

Gus frowned. 'What?'

'Well, only five of those nine ANPRs pinged for Lewis' locality. I just wondered, bearing in mind we've not found him yet, if we should prioritise those five.'

Gus moved over and fist-bumped Compo. This was even better. 'Right, Sampson. Get moving on those five names now!' He turned to Compo. 'Well done, Comps.'

Compo still stood there, grinning at him. 'I've got summat else, too.'

Running his finger through his dreads, Gus attempted to hide his impatience to be off following up their leads. 'Okay, spill.'

'Whilst you lot were off gallivanting this morning, Imtiaz Khan came in. You'll never guess …' Wiggling his eyebrows, he waited, presumably for Gus to guess.

Realising it would be quicker just to humour him, Gus splayed his arms in front of him, palms up, and said, 'No idea.'

'Well, he bloody went and identified that bugger wi' t' bomb in City Park from the wider footage. I've been running the photo against the facial recognition database and look … here he is!'

The face of a man, perhaps in his early twenties, appeared on the screen. He was laughing and had the look of any other young lad out for a good time on a Saturday night. That impression lasted all of two seconds, because next to his smiling face, Compo had added a list of his misdemeanours going back to his early teens, which included GBH, theft, vehicle theft and arson.

'Name's Niall Boyle. Lives in Holme Wood estate and is currently on probation. He'll not be a happy bunny when we catch up with him.'

'Again, well done, Comps. Get this passed on to the officer in charge of the City Park investigation, alright?'

When Compo nodded, Gus turned to Alice. 'See to it the uniforms tasked with interviewing the vehicle owners are briefed, Al. Meanwhile, Sampson and I have got a scumbag journalist to interview.'

Chapter 59

13:20 Bradford Royal Infirmary

Shamshad took the newspaper from her bag and laid it on her sister's lap. Neha moved her still bandaged arm, as if it weighed a tonne. Using her thumb and index finger, she moved the paper so she could see the headline. She flinched as she read, her mouth curled in disgust, and then, with an effort, she manoeuvred the tabloid until she could open it to read the rest of the article.

When she saw the picture of their father, Sham expected her to thrust the paper away or cry out or something, but instead, Neha just stared at the photo, and then, letting her head fall back on the pillows, she whispered something that sounded very much like, 'So, he did it then.'

Puzzled, Sham moved closer, flicked the paper from her sister's lap and put it back in her bag. 'Who did what, Neha?'

Neha just smiled and shook her head. 'Nobody.'

The lie struck her like an arrow to her heart. She was so helpless. This wasn't *her* sister. Not the one she'd nurtured and cajoled and bullied back to health by sheer force of spirit. Not the one she'd fought for, put her life on hold for, not the one she loved beyond all else. This was an imposter. Anger gripped her, and she leaned forward and pressed lightly in Neha's bandaged arm. 'Tell me!' she said, her voice a croak.

Neha winced and tried to pull her arm away. Ignoring her, Shamshad increased the pressure just a little. She didn't care if she hurt her sister. She deserved it. 'You will tell me, Neha. I've had enough of this. The lies and deceit. The secrets! How do you think I feel right now? If you weren't so fucking poorly, I'd kill you.'

Uncaring of the tears coursing down her cheeks, she glared at Neha. All the worry and anger she'd kept inside floated to the surface. She could see the hurt in her sister's eyes, but she didn't care, as she ranted on. Everything she'd been feeling about her father's death and Neha's secrets came spewing out, and she couldn't stop it. To be honest, right at that moment, she didn't even want to. 'You've let me down, Neha. I've always been there for you. Done fucking everything for you, and *this* is how you repay me.'

Releasing Neha's arm, she flung herself back in the plastic chair causing it to scrape against the floor. Poking at a hole in her jeans, she continued, 'Oh, how the mighty have fallen, Neha. Miss bloody prim and proper, Insh'Allahing every two minutes, and now, look at you. You're a liar! A fraud! Where in your Islam does it say that's okay, huh?'

Realising some of the other patients were watching them, Shamshad took a deep breath. It took all her willpower to do it, and when she next spoke, her tone was calmer. 'Then, you go and get poorly again.' She snapped her fingers. 'Just like that ... you forget all about me. You're so fucking selfish, you know that?' She ran her fingers through her spiky hair and then rubbed her cheeks dry. 'Well, you know what, Neha? I've had enough. Enough of your petty little secrets, enough of your self-pity and self-destruction. Do you think I haven't suffered? Do you think you're the only one who lost their mum? The only one who lost their dad, the only one who feels alone? Well?' She clicked her fingers in front of Neha's face in a zig zag motion.

'Reality check! You're fucking not. I'm the one who is alone. I was alone when you nearly starved yourself to death last time. I was alone when you cut yourself, and I was alone last night when you did it all over again, because poor little Neha is in pain. Well, fuck that. I'm in pain, right? Right now, *I'm* in fucking pain!'

Sham wasn't aware her voice had escalated to a shout, or even that she'd stood up, or that all the other patients and visitors were looking at them.

She spun on her heel, banging into the nurse who'd come to see what was going on, and had taken two steps from the bed when Neha spoke.

'I'm sorry, Sham. I really am. I didn't want to burden you, so I kept it to myself. I'm truly sorry.'

Sham stopped, took a deep breath, and then turned back to her sister who was looking at her, her eyes filled with tears.

'Please don't give up on me yet, Sham, please don't!'

Sham studied Neha's face; her hollowed cheeks, her sad eyes and the tension lines radiating from her mouth. The nurse, seemingly sensing Sham's tirade was over, stepped back. Sham walked slowly back to the plastic chair that had been her home since Neha had been admitted. She stretched out her hand and linked her fingers with her sister's, squeezing gently.

'We need to talk about these, Neha.' She pulled the envelope out of her bag and spread the contents over the bed.

Neha scanned them and then nodded. 'Okay.'

Sham released the breath she'd been holding and allowed her shoulders to slump. At last, she'd get to the bottom of her sister's secrets.

Neha put her palm on the pile of paperwork and began to talk. 'When I was really ill, I used to see dad. He'd visit me at the centre during the day when you were at school. Things between him and mum weren't the way she described, you know, Sham. She was always sick. Even before we were born, she had mental health issues. And, well, the community, being what it was years ago, couldn't understand it. So, they ignored it, and nobody got her help. Then, we came along, and for a while, she was okay; and then, she got ill again.' She lifted her face to her sister, pleading, 'Ask Auntie and Uncle. They'll tell you I'm speaking the truth.'

Sham nodded for Neha to continue.

'He had an affair when we were about three. It was someone he'd known since school. His family wouldn't let him get married to her, so they split up. When they met again years later, she was in an unhappy relationship, and so was he. Mum had begun to hit him, and a few times, he found glass in his food. She said if he didn't leave, she would hurt *us*, so he left. Then, she started telling the Imam he'd brought a disease to the home.'

'The STIs?' asked Sham.

Neha nodded. 'Yeah, the STIs ... it wasn't true. She made it up, and she kept making things up until he was ostracised. The only people who believed him were Auntie and Uncle. Then, the school found out about the things she did to us. That was a blessing in disguise, really, because she was diagnosed, and she got the help she needed, and we were safe.'

Sham frowned. 'She's ill, Neha. She never wanted to hurt us.'

Neha, suddenly looking older and wiser than Sham had ever seen her before, smiled. 'I know that. The fact remains, though, she *did* hurt us. I can't bear to see her again. Can't bear to feel that pain again. You're a better person than me, Sham.'

Sham frowned and studied her sister with sudden understanding. 'You took most of the beatings, didn't you? You took the blame for everything to protect me. Sometimes, you even pretended to be me, didn't you?' Half-forgotten memories flooded her mind. 'I couldn't understand why you always got hit more than me, but *that's* why, isn't it? You were protecting *me!*'

'And since then, *you've* protected me, Sham. When I was ill, *you* fought for me. We look after each other.'

Sham knew whatever had been released from her memory today would continue to haunt her for a while. Right now, though, she couldn't think about that. Visiting time was nearly over, and they hadn't discussed the papers.

'Why do you have this birth certificate and those medical records?'

Quietly, Neha explained to her sister, and by the end of it, the two sisters were clinging to each other like they would never let go.

Chapter 60

13:30 The Fort

Jez Hopkins came across as pissed off when Gus marched into the interview room with Sampson. Sitting down at the table, Gus leaned over towards him, invading his space. He was pleased to see Hopkins lean as far back as he could in his uncomfortable chair, sneaking nervous glances towards the door. Slamming his palm on the table, he grinned. 'Nobody's coming to rescue you, so you better give me all your attention.'

Hopkins bristled, and when he spoke, it was a bluster that was not backed up by the nervous tic under his eye. 'Don't know why you're being so aggressive. I came to you, didn't I?'

Gus took a deep breath and modulated his voice to a low snarl. 'Yeah, after the article was released to the entire Bradford population. Good one!'

'Look, I came here voluntarily to tell you what I know, okay? I've done nothing wrong.'

'Actually, pillock, you have. You've obstructed my investigation by not sharing sensitive information, ASAP.'

Hopkins shrugged, laying his hands out before him in a placatory fashion. 'Okay, okay, I get it! Let's just move on from this. We're on the same side, aren't we?'

Gus snorted and flicked his eyes in Sampson's direction. 'He says we should move on from this. Says we're on the same side. What do you think, Sampson?'

Sampson leaned back arms across his chest and laughed. 'Yeah, right. Same side. As if!' He grinned at Gus, seemingly enjoying his role as a baddy. 'Or we could just arrest him for endangering the public!'

Gus held out a hand, and they high-fived. 'Good one, Sampson. We could do that.'

Hopkins threw annoyed glances between them. 'Aw, come on. Quit the comedy act, and let me show you what I've got. They arrived anonymously at work.'

He bent down and began rummaging in his bag. When he straightened, he held an envelope which he upended on the table between himself and the two officers.

Before looking at the photos, Gus snagged an evidence bag from his pocket, took the envelope by the corner and popped it inside. He then took the time to study the writing on the envelope. 'What do you reckon, Sampson?'

Sampson shrugged. 'Looks like a kid's writing to me. Either that or some anally retentive sexual deviant.'

Gus turned to Hopkins and said, 'We'll need a handwriting sample from you.'

Hopkins blinked, startled. 'You think I took these?'

Gus didn't, but he wasn't going to tell Hopkins that. He was enjoying having him dangling like the worm he was on the end of his hook. He shrugged. 'The lab will tell us, won't it?' He agreed with Sampson that it looked like kid's writing. Then again, sometimes, his dad's writing resembled a ten-year old's, so who was he to judge? Maybe they'd get some saliva from the envelope, which luckily wasn't the self-seal type.

'Hand-delivered, was it?'

Hopkins squirmed on his chair and nodded. 'Yeah, to the *Bradford Chronicle* offices at Hall Ings.'

'External post box?'

Hopkins nodded.

'CCTV on the box?'

This time, he shrugged. 'Don't know, never thought to look.'

Gus nodded to Sampson, who jotted something down. 'Note?'

'What?' said Hopkins, looking visibly rattled now by Gus' near monosyllabic rapid-fire interview strategy.

Sighing, Gus elaborated. He pronounced each word slowly and precisely, as if he thought Hopkins was lacking mental capacity. 'Was ... there ... a note ... with ... the photos?'

The journalist's expression cleared. 'No, no note. Just the photos.'

Taking a pen from his pocket, Gus moved the photos about on the table, his mouth turned down, demonstrating his disgust at the violation of privacy.

Hopkins pointed at the date stamp. 'Dated the night Razaul Ul Haq was abducted.'

Gus glowered at him. 'You do realise I'm a detective, don't you?' He waited for Hopkins' nod and then added, 'So shut up with the Miss Marple, if you don't mind.'

Donning a pair of gloves, Gus gathered the photos together and slid them into an evidence bag. 'Got your jollies off over them, did you? Before you came in?'

Hopkins' face reddened, and he shifted his buttocks on the chair making an involuntary squeaking sound as he moved.

Dirty little bastard, thought Gus. *Got his rocks off looking at the photos of a dead man being intimate.* Turning to Sampson, he said, 'Ask them to check for evidence of bodily fluids as well as prints.'

Smirking, Gus winked at Hopkins and pulled a cotton bud in a test tube from his pocket. 'You don't mind, do you? For elimination purposes, you understand.'

Face paling, Hopkins swallowed hard and, with a brief nod, opened his mouth.

Chapter 61

Gus had tried to contact both Christine and Graeme Weston by phone, but to no avail, so he and Alice jumped into her Mini and hotfooted it over to the Weston residence in Eccleshill. As they drove, Gus phoned Weston's campaign manager.

'I'm busy right now,' said Michael Hogg, not bothering to conceal his annoyance. 'Fitting a boiler. Can't this wait?'

Nancy Chalmers had once told him when having a difficult conversation with someone, smiling made your tone less antagonistic. Gus wasn't particularly bothered about Hogg's opinion of him, and any other time, he'd have relished the opportunity to antagonise the man. However, for the purpose of getting a quick answer, he pasted a smile on his face and hoped it shone through in his words. 'Do you know where Mr Weston is, or how I can get hold of him, please?'

Tone gruff, Hogg responded in his usual abrupt manner. 'Nope … and if I did, I wouldn't tell you now, would I? Your lot are as bad as the press; hounding him and invading his privacy. Unfair treatment, I say. Just because he's a man of principle, not afraid to say it like it is.'

Gus pictured Hogg's chest inflating like a balloon in righteous indignation, and the desire to deflate one little prick with another was almost overpowering. Instead, feeling like a less agreeable Joker from the Batman films, Gus widened his smile. 'Well, that *is* a shame, sir. I take it you've seen the *Bradford Chronicle* today? In light of the article, it might be an idea to share his whereabouts with us, don't you think?'

Hogg hesitated, then extending the sound of the first consonant, he gave an elongated reply, flicking his pitch up at the end. 'Nnnnnope.' He added, 'Graeme will show up when he's good and ready.'

Although he sounded full of bluster, Gus detected an edge of concern amongst the bravado. Michael Hogg was clearly keeping his anger on a tight leash. Gus wouldn't want to be in Weston's shoes when Hogg finally caught up with him.

Next, he phoned Weston's offices where his PA, Marcia Hogg, answered. Gus recognised her voice from their meeting the previous evening. Seemed like Weston and Hogg were linked in business as well as politics, if Hogg's wife was Weston's PA. When he introduced himself, it was easy to imagine her thin lips tightening as she spoke. She made no effort to disguise her disgust and was barely polite. Irritated by her pettiness, Gus prodded her.

Finally, she said, 'Look, all I know is, every six weeks on a Wednesday, regular as clockwork, Graeme keeps his diary clear. He's marked today off on his calendar.'

Was she a little prickly about divulging that information? A bit fed up, perhaps, that she wasn't privy to his whereabouts? Gus pushed her. 'So, where might Mr Weston go on those pre-booked Wednesdays, Mrs Hogg? Care to hazard a guess?'

Marcia gave a brittle laugh. 'He's my boss, not my partner. I suspect he needs 'me' time every so often to unwind. After all, he *is* a very busy man.'

Unwind doing what? wondered Gus. Maybe Weston's wife wasn't the only one in flagrante. Maybe Weston had a regular six-weekly assignation with someone other than his wife. Mind you, a six-week gap didn't exactly speak of high passion, did it? More a clinical scratching of an itch than lustful uncontrollable shenanigans. Gus smiled at the thought of the rotund Graeme Weston, golden boy of Albion First, submitting to his basest instincts.

'You must have some idea though, Mrs Hogg. You *are* his PA. You've got your finger on the pulse. I would imagine there's not much passes you by.'

The silence from the other end of the phone was palpable. Gus wondered if she'd hung up on him. 'Mrs Hogg ...?'

Her sigh drifted over the line. 'Was there an actual question in there, Inspector?'

Touché! Maybe she *should be the politician.* Annoyed by her obstructiveness, Gus added an edge to his tone. 'Have you seen today's *Chronicle*?'

She snorted. 'Garbage! That newspaper is just garbage. It's all a conspiracy to discredit Graeme. We all know the newspapers and the police are at the heart of a smear campaign against Albion First. I have no doubt whoever leaked those ...' she swallowed before continuing with a quiver in her voice, '... those abominable images to that immoral Hopkins man has his own agenda. An agenda that is not for the people of this city. One that will protect those who seek to steal our jobs and snatch our houses from us. Graeme Weston should not be judged by his ...' she hesitated, and it seemed she was struggling to find the words to end her sentence. As the gap lengthened, Gus could hear her laboured breaths drift down the line until, at last, she said, '... *wife's* actions.'

The word 'wife' had *not* been her first choice to describe Christine Weston. Gus' eyes narrowed. Was that a touch of jealousy amongst the anger in her tone? If it was, it threw up an interesting scenario. He wished he could see her face right now. How rich would it be if Hogg's wife was in love with Weston? Whatever else Marcia Hogg was keeping secret, she clearly did not like Christine Weston one little bit, and judging by her well-rehearsed dogma, she shared her husband's racist views fully. No surprise there, then!

'You'd think, though, in light of the damage that article could do to his political career, he'd have been in touch with his campaign manager, wouldn't you?' said Gus.

She snorted again, so Gus pushed the knife in further. 'So, he's not been in touch with your husband *or* yourself, and you've no idea where he disappears off to on a Wednesday afternoon, every six weeks?'

Again, his words were met by silence, prompting him to sharpen his tone. 'Well, would you say that's accurate, Mrs Hogg?'

He could almost feel the venom as she said in nipped tones, 'Yes!'

Feeling well and truly fed up with the antagonism from the Hogg couple, Gus ended the conversation with, 'So, it sounds very much to me like he's as dishonest as his wife. Maybe Mr Weston's having an affair too. Wonder how *that* would go down on top of today's revelation?'

Gus hung up, wondering where Graeme Weston took himself off to, and if his wife knew where he went.

Chapter 62

'Pick up! Pick up, for God's sake!' When Graeme Weston's phone went to voicemail for the umpteenth time, Marcia walked over to her office door, opened it, and with all the force she could muster, she slammed it shut. The release of aggression made her feel better, but her breath still came in sharp pants as she scrolled through her phone before hitting another number.

Where the hell was he? It annoyed her his whereabouts on these periodic Wednesday absences was unknown to her. She'd got used to his secrecy in that department and was prepared to overlook it. After all, in all other aspects of his life, he was remarkably transparent. It wasn't that she hadn't tried to find out where he went ... she had. It seemed wherever it was he went, it was with his family. Or at least on the few occasions when she'd tried to spy on him, he was always with Christine and Jacob. So, despite the wog officer's innuendos, it didn't seem Weston was having an affair. Mind you, it would be no more than that bitch deserved if he was.

She had no idea why he stayed with that woman ... none at all, and after the revelations in today's *Chronicle*, she was even more dumbfounded. For such an intelligent man, he was remarkably thick when it came to his wife.

Finally, the number she'd dialled was answered. 'Where the hell have you been? I've been trying to get in touch with you for hours. That darkie police officer's been on the phone. You know, the one who came to the house last night? He's looking for Graeme. Do you know where he is? Have you heard from him?'

She flinched at her husband's clipped response. 'I've no damn idea, Marcia. Bloody idiot's switched his phone off. Don't even know if he's seen that fucking article yet. He's supposed to be contactable twenty-four seven. Doesn't he realise we're running a campaign here?'

Marcia's lip curled up at Michael's words. Did he think she came across the channel on a banana boat like some bloody immigrant? Thanks to the wonders of phone tracking, she knew *exactly* where her husband was at this precise moment and campaigning was the last thing on his mind. She could guarantee that!

Chapter 63

14:55 Hawthorn Drive, Eccleshill

By the time they reached the Weston's street, dread gnawed at Gus' gut. Bad enough that *he'd* been unable to contact them in the wake of the newspaper article, but that Weston's campaign manager and PA had also been unable to was worrying. As they drove into the street, a jostle of journalists scurried over to them, vying to reach them first. Gus scowled. Half of them he didn't recognise, and the others had not been among his allies during the Matchmaker Case or last year.

Pulling up at the kerb, Gus noticed Weston's car was in the drive. He jumped out and elbowed his way through the crowding press.

'Can you comment on the photos revealed in the *Chronicle* this morning, Detective?' 'Would you say that makes Graeme Weston prime suspect in the Razaul Ul Haq murder?'

'Could Graeme Weston be the Tattoo Killer?'

'Do you think you'll find Lewis Gore alive?'

The last question threw him. He'd hoped Gore's name would escape the attention of the press until he'd been found. The words 'dead or alive' echoed in his brain, taunting him. *Bloody parasites!* Dipping his head, Gus allowed his dreads to obscure his face. No point in giving them easy access to his expression. They'd give him enough bad press anyway.

With Alice following close on his heels, he strode to the door in silence. Then, turning to face them, he said, pointing to the front garden, 'Private property. One step through that gate, and I'll have you. Clear?' He caught the eye of a uniformed officer who was trying to herd the journalists backwards and nodded. The officer grinned and nodded back, before turning with renewed effort and forcing the mob further up the street.

Gus pressed the doorbell and waited. His worried feeling intensified when there was no response. 'Weston should be in.'

He rang the bell again, bracing himself for the tinny rendition of 'Rule, Britannia!' to play out as they waited. Still no response. Unwilling to initiate an encore, he rapped his knuckles on the glass door. Now that the press had been herded away and the final tones of Weston's signature tune had faded, he could hear sounds from inside the house ... the TV or perhaps the radio. Still, nothing to indicate someone was making their way to the door.

The thoughts he'd been trying to subdue since he first saw the article, returned with a vengeance. What exactly would a man like Weston be driven to, after seeing the disgusting photo of his wife in flagrante for all the world to see? He was already under immense pressure with his political campaign and the after-effects of the bottle-bomb the previous day. What would it take to push him over the edge?

A quick glance at Alice showed his own worries reflected in her face. 'Try his phone and then Christine's again, will you?' he said, before lifting his fist to hammer again. He had just connected with the glass, when he felt an elbow in his ribs. Glancing at Alice, assuming she'd got a reply, he saw her nod towards the gate. Spinning round, he saw a red-faced Michael Hogg lumbering up the path, his jacket flying open.

One hand raised in a near Nazi salute, he yelled, 'Oi, stop that!' at the top of his voice.

Gus stared the other man down as he watched him approach. For someone who'd supposedly been at work fitting a boiler fifteen minutes ago, Michael Hogg was remarkably well-dressed in a suit and shirt. As the man drew close, he stretched his neck towards Gus, mouth open in a sneer. 'What do you think you're doing? That's harassment, that is.'

Having endured an antagonistic phone conversation with both Hogg and his wife not an hour earlier, Gus was in no mood to pander to the man's attitude. He was doing his job, and he was damned if a smarmy little upstart like Hogg would stop him from doing so. Gus leaned closer and sniffed the air in an exaggerated manner. 'Always slather yourself in eau de toilet for work, do you? And dress like that to fit boilers?'

Alice sniffed and cocked her head to one side. Using an exaggerated phonetic enunciation, she said, 'I think it's *Pour Homme*, no less.'

Grinning at the obvious mispronunciation, Gus nodded and raised an eyebrow. 'Look, I don't care what you're wearing … or for that matter, who you're wearing it for. Just get Weston to open the damn door. We need to speak to him.'

As if he'd heard Gus, the door opened, and Graeme Weston stood there, a glass of amber coloured liquid in his hand. From the pavement, cameras flashed, and the journos yelled a series of questions.

'Mr Weston, did you know of your wife's affair with murder victim Razaul Ul Haq?'

'Where does your wife's affair with Bangladeshi murder victim Razaul Ul Haq leave your political aspirations, Mr Weston?

'How can the people of Bradford take Albion First seriously, after their leader's wife is shown in compromising photos with one of the Tattoo Killer's victims?'

'Would you refute claims that you are now the police's number one suspect in the Tattoo Killer investigation?'

Hogg stepped in front of Weston, using his bulk to shield him from the barrage of questions. Side-stepping both men, Gus pushed the door wider and gestured for Weston to retreat. As Weston turned and walked back indoors, Gus, Alice and Hogg followed him inside.

With the door shut behind them, Hogg spun around and getting right into Gus' face, began mouthing off. 'You've forced your way into Mr Weston's property. You'll be hearing from our solicitors. This is unacceptable.'

Ignoring Michael Hogg's blustering threats, Gus stepped back. 'Thanks for inviting us in, Mr Weston.'

'What!' Michael Hogg yelled. 'You weren't invited! You pushed your way in against Graeme's wishes.'

Lowering his voice, Gus glared at Hogg. 'What are you on about? You *really* think suing us is top of your list of priorities? In case you haven't noticed, the only parliamentary candidate for Albion First, an openly racist organisation with some members who have been arrested for hate crimes, has just had a photo of *his* wife shagging an Asian murder victim plastered all over the newspapers, and *you* want to sue the police?' Gus pushed past him, saying, 'Pulease!'

During Gus' interlude with Hogg, Graeme Weston had wandered over to the drinks cabinet. After refilling his glass with shaking hands from a half-empty bottle of Glenfiddich thirty-year-old malt, Weston turned around, sloshing half the liquid onto the carpet.

Gus' eyes narrowed as he noticed bloody marks across Weston's knuckles. Then, as his eyes followed the direction of the whisky droplets falling towards the rug, he noticed the blood stain near the table. A quick glance at Alice told him she, too, had noticed the stain. Drowning out Hogg's whingeing tones, Gus stepped forward and removed the glass from Weston's hands. 'Where are your wife and son, Mr Weston?'

Weston blinked as if unsure of the question. Gus repeated it, his words slower in an attempt to penetrate the other man's drunken fugue.

'Where exactly are your wife and son, Mr Weston?'

Graeme Weston sank onto the sofa, head bowed, with his arms resting on his knees. He began to laugh, the sound getting louder and louder by degrees. Gus moved forward, gripped his shoulders and shook him. Not hard; just enough to bring him back to reality. Blank eyes gazed up at Gus, and then, releasing an alcoholic fumed breath, he ran his injured hand over his eyes and then down past his mouth.

Gus' concern for the welfare of Christine Weston and their son Jacob intensified. It was clear Weston had punched someone. It was also clear someone had bled substantially on to the floor. He needed to get Weston to respond. He knelt beside him, infringing on the other man's personal space, forcing him to return his gaze. 'You need to start talking, right fucking now.'

Towering over Gus, Hogg, hands on hips, glowered. 'You can't talk to him like that.'

Without turning his head, Gus said, 'Watch me! Now, you fuck off and let me do my job.'

Alice moved forward and laid her hand on Hogg's arm. 'Come on, Mr Hogg. You need to leave now. This is a possible crime scene, and you can't be here.'

'Crime scene? Fucking crime scene? If the likes of your fucking nigger boss would do his job right, this wouldn't have happened. It's that little bastard Hopkins you should be talking to, not upstanding citizens like Graeme.'

Not of a mind to employ any more placatory techniques, Gus spoke, his anger reverberating in every word. 'Get that slimy little bastard out of here, Al. We need to talk to Weston without his puppet master.'

Weston began to laugh again. Three sets of eyes turned to him. With no warning, he leaned forward and vomited all over Gus' shoes. For a moment, Gus could only stare in disbelief, and then, the stink of regurgitated alcohol hit him. He jumped to his feet trying to put distance between himself and the smell. Realising it wouldn't happen, he swallowed back the bile that rose in his own throat. Then, his instincts kicked in, and he began to employ the technique he normally reserved for the morgue; breathing in shallow pants through his mouth. Lips curling, he glowered at the drunk man. The urge to punch him in the face had never been stronger.

Weston, seemingly sobered after his purge, grinned and winked. 'No fucking comment, black boy.'

Nostrils flaring, Gus abruptly turned on his heel. 'Get the SOCOs in, Al. They need to rip this place apart ... oh, and arrest this joker for obstruction.'

Stepping through the door, Gus welcomed the cool air on his cheeks. He knew he'd lost it inside, but he didn't really care. He was too worried about what might have happened to Christine Weston. Scowling at the journalists who moulded themselves around the gate, the urge to raise a finger in a swivel-on-it motion was strong, however, he refrained. Instead, muttering under his breath, he ignored them and stalked over to the tap attached to the side wall. Balancing on one foot, he slipped the opposite shoe off. He held his breath against the stink and ran freezing cold water over the shoe to dislodge the puke, before repeating the action with his second shoe.

Alice appeared at his shoulder and pushed a packet of wet wipes into his hand. 'Wipe it with this now. At least it'll get rid of some of the smell.'

Some of the tension left Gus' shoulders, as leaning against the wall, he took the wipe and rubbed it over his shoe. He was still too tense to speak. He hoped to hell Christine and her son were ok.

Alice sniffed. 'I only gave you that because I couldn't stand you stinking out my car. By the way, a preliminary search of the house discovered nothing untoward.'

Relief that neither Christine Weston nor her son were lying dead in a corner made Gus laugh. 'That's a relief.' Then, handing the pack of wet wipes back, he winked at her. 'Thought you were going soft, Al.'

Journalists' voices, raised in a barrage of questions, alerted them to the fact Graeme Weston was being escorted to a squad car. Gus watched as the reporters fought for access to the First Albion leader. Lips tightening, he heard one of them say, 'Care to comment on the graze mark on your knuckles, Mr Weston?' *Observant bastards!* Well, at least now he knew what the headlines would be.

Putting his sodden shoes back on, he and Alice walked through the gap left by the journalists who had followed Weston from the house.

Alice held her hand out palm upwards. 'Bloody rain's started again.' Speeding up to avoid the downpour, they dodged into her Mini without being spotted. As they drove off towards The Fort, Gus' phone rang. He listened and then said, 'Change of direction, Al. Glen Road, Shipley Glen. They've found Lewis Gore!'

Chapter 64

15:30 Shipley Glen

Pelting rain pounded against the windscreen as Alice put her foot down and drove along Harrogate Road towards Shipley Glen. Mesmerised by the water pouring down the window, Gus used the twenty-minute drive to gather his thoughts.

Graeme Weston was in custody, and his wife Christine was missing after being revealed publicly to have had a sexual relationship with their third victim. Weston's alibis for all three of the previous victims had checked out, although there was a possibility one of his racist cronies had worked under his direction. Gus didn't think that added up. Weston seemed too smooth, too organised, too focussed to have risked his carefully planned political career by something as wild as abducting and tattooing black men. That just didn't make sense.

Gus was under no illusion, though. He knew that the sort of rhetoric espoused by West and his followers could contribute to the sort of hate crimes they'd witnessed. Whoever was targeting these black and Asian men didn't seem likely to stop anytime soon.

What he couldn't get his head around was Christine Weston. What on earth had prompted her to have an affair, never mind to choose an Asian as her suitor? It seemed totally and absolutely mad. Why would she risk her cushy life with her openly racist, wannabe politician husband for a bit of slap and tickle with Razaul Ul Haq? Weston seemed controlling, so Christine seemed to be playing with fire there. And where was the boy, Jacob? When they'd arrested Weston, Alice had searched the house very quickly, and there was no sign of him or his mother. Still, Weston refused to say anything. Arrogant sod!

Gus didn't believe in coincidence, and everything seemed to be linking up. He now had a definite link between Weston and/or Albion First and his third victim. The bombing at City Park demonstrated Albion First were not averse to committing violent racist acts, despite their so-called desire to become a legitimate political party. However, Gus, having been on the receiving end of a fair amount of racism growing up, knew there was a huge difference between random racist attacks and the targeted abduction and torture of non-whites.

He wondered if, although he had no concrete evidence to support this, the Tattoo Killer was a part of Albion First rather than a lone vigilante psychopath. It seemed too co-incidental to ignore that the meteoric rise of Albion First's public profile and the start of these killings came at the same time. He couldn't put all his eggs in the one basket, though. Albion First was despicable; on the other hand, this killer may have nothing to do with them. The challenge for Gus' team was to narrow it down.

On the plus side, the City Park investigation team had arrested the thug responsible for the bomb. They were sure he would eventually be persuaded to give up the brains behind the attack, because in one officer's words, 'that little fucker is a few currants short of a fat rascal.' Gus stomach rumbled at the thought. He'd not eaten for a while, and he could demolish a fat rascal as quickly as Compo right now.

Having driven through Idle and Shipley, the skies darkening by the minute, they neared their destination. Through the rain, Gus could just about distinguish the distorted blue lights of police vehicles, as Alice indicated to turn onto Glen Road, which ran adjacent to the area of Glen where Lewis Gore had been found. Huge slabs, like giant stepping stones, punctuated the bracken covered gorge. Puddles of mucky water, like trenches made by massive feet, made the ground marshy. Winter had scared away all hint of greenery, leaving defeated brown grass struggling to stand to attention against the wind and rain. As they pulled in, an ambulance, lights flashing, siren shrieking, screeched off in the opposite direction.

'Shit,' said Alice, mirroring Gus' thoughts. 'Hope no-one's hurt. The weather will have made the ground treacherous.'

Grabbing the old fisherman's jacket he'd tossed onto the backseat earlier, Gus shrugged into it, breathing in its waxiness as he flipped the hood up over his head.

'Wellies?' asked Alice.

Gus snorted. 'No point in bothering for me. My shoe's squelching after that pillock threw up all over them ... And my trousers, thanks to your clumsiness, are shredded too.'

Failing to hide her smirk, Alice put her coat on and toddled round to the boot from which she extracted a pair of black wellies with purple flowers that matched those adorning the bonnet and roof of her Mini. They were far too cumbersome for her delicate frame. Gripping Gus' arm, she tossed her leather boots into the car, one at a time, replacing them with the wellies. All the while, Gus peered over her head at the scene on the edge of the Glen. The weather made it difficult to see anything, but the white-suited figures shone through the dimness. Gus could see they were focussed on a spot about fifty metres or so off the main road.

As Alice released Gus, he strode off, leaving her to struggle after him as best she could. One of the uniformed officers handed him a torch and a protective suit. With practised ease, he got into it, donning booties and gloves too. As he neared the focus of the attention, he saw they'd erected a tent. Looking towards Sid for permission, he swept the canvas flap open and entered.

The SOCOs had erected a light, so Gus, standing on the raised platform at the entrance, could see the entire area. He frowned and turned to Sid who stood just behind him. 'Where's –'

'The victim?' asked Sid, his chest puffing out as he rolled back and forth on the balls of his feet. 'He's gone.'

Gus bit his lip, and a scowl furrowed his brow. This was unacceptable. The body should have been kept *in situ* for him to view.

Sid grinned. 'Nobody's told you, have they?'

Gus' frown deepened. 'Told me what?'

'He was alive. They worked on him here, got him stabilised, and they've just taken him off to BRI. Didn't you see the ambulance?'

'He's alive?' Gus could hardly believe it. All this time, he'd been preparing himself for another body, yet, somehow, against all odds, Lewis Gore had held on. Which, of course, raised the question, why had he been allowed to live? What had gone wrong? As soon as he was finished here, Gus would contact Professor Carlton to see what he thought.

Sid grimaced, 'Yeah, just about. Groin's a mess, and his heart's fucked up. The paramedics don't know how the hell he kept going. Hypothermia. His heart stopped twice whilst they were here, but they brought him back. It's touch-and-go whether he'll make it or not.'

Sid nodded towards a large, thickset man. Without a jacket, his shirt and trousers were sodden. He watched the SOCOs working, seemingly oblivious to the rain dripping from his flattened hair onto his face. 'That's Gore's boss,' said Sid. 'You'll want to speak to him, no doubt. First, let me tell you what we've got.'

Knowing exactly what the man was going through, having nearly lost Alice a few months ago, Gus thought he'd give the man some time to come to terms with what had happened. He turned his gaze away from him, and seeing Alice had her notebook out, he nodded at Sid. 'Shoot.'

Indicating they should follow him out, Sid showed them a block where a piece of earth had been covered. 'We got a bit of a print here. From a tyre. Must be a van of some sort because it's deep, which is the only reason we were able to get it. The rain had only just started when we got here, and we covered it up quick. Looks like your killer drove right onto the glen, again indicating a van of some sort.'

Gus agreed. Anyone driving off the road onto the glen itself would need to be in a van or a four-by-four. The vast rocks interspersed with hardy grasses and bracken made it near impossible to drive over, yet their killer had managed to get to that spot.

Sid stood up, and moving back over to the tent, pointed to a yellow marker with a number two. 'That's the same print as I took from the dog shit in the car park. We've sent samples. We'll see what we come up with. I've taken a mould. Gore's clothes were cut off as per the previous victims. They were folded and laid here.' He pointed to a number three marker. 'We've bagged them up, however, we did discover something.' He walked them over to a durable plastic box containing evidence bags and sifted through until he found what he was looking for. 'This!'

Gus peered at it and saw a long hair, just as Sid farted. 'For God's sake, Sid. I'm trying to concentrate here.' Trying to ignore the odious stench, Gus said, 'Our killer's got long brown hair?'

Laughing like a teenage prankster, Sid said, 'Oops, sorry, don't know what came over me! Nah, or rather, neigh. Your killer's not the owner of that hair … but maybe the killer has come into contact with the owner.'

Gus frowned. 'You're doing that thing, Sid.'

'What thing?'

'That fucking thing where you're being an arsehole and pissing me off. Just tell me the damn significance of the hair.'

'Horse …' said Alice, with a grin.

Sid scowled at her. 'I wanted to tell him, Alice.'

'Not a damn competition, children,' said Gus. 'Just give me the info I need, okay? Is it from a horse?'

'Yes. I'll be able to tell you a breed later, and, of course, you find the horse, and I'll match the hair to it.'

Alice looked thoughtful.

'What's up, Al?' asked Gus.

'What about that horse we saw this morning? In the field near the Bay of Biscay.'

Gus frowned. Although there were loads of horses in Bradford, it *was* a coincidence. Pretty far-fetched, perhaps, however it was the one horse they'd come across in the course of their investigation. He frowned. Something was niggling him, but he couldn't put his finger on it. It'd come to him, if he left it alone. 'Yeah, worth trying out. I'll send a uniform up there to get a strand from its mane.'

'Don't worry.' said Alice, 'I picked about three off my coat when I got back into the car and put them in my little binny.'

Gus shook his head, 'Bloody binny, indeed,' he muttered, then grinned. 'Well done, Al. Sid …?'

Sid was already sending one of his techs over to Alice's car, saying, 'It's that silly little Mini with the floral monstrosities all over it.' Alice cast him a dirty look and then followed the tech, beeping it open with the key as she ran.

Chapter 65

Gus had spent the journey to the hospital catching up with Sampson and Compo. He knew they wouldn't be able to talk to Lewis Gore, but he wanted to touch base with Lewis' wife and make sure she was okay.

There had been no word about Christine Weston, and according to Sampson, Graeme Weston was snoring 'like a buffalo in labour' in a police cell. No doubt the alcohol was to blame for that! Other than the blood stain on the carpet and some skin cells and hairs on the corner of the coffee table, the SOCOs had found no evidence of wrong-doing in the Weston's house.

Gus hoped Christine Weston and her husband had had a bust up, and that she'd walked out. If that was the case, Gus would be very angry with Graeme Weston for wasting police time. Wasn't like they didn't have a fucking serial killer to catch, was it?

When they parked up, Alice took a deep breath before pushing her door open and getting out. Gus understood how she felt. He'd been the same the first time he'd returned to BRI after his own brush with death. It was a combination of fear, relief and guilt all balled up together. It got you right in your gut. He caught up with her and slipped his arm through hers, giving it a quick squeeze.

She turned and smirked at him. 'Don't you get all bloody soft on me now, McGuire. Can't be doing with that shit.' Pulling her arm away from him, she straightened her back and marched ahead.

Well, that'll teach me to get in touch with my feminine side, thought Gus, following at a slower pace. The biggest hurdle for her would be walking through the doors, so he kept an eye on her as she approached them. Not that there was anything he could do to make the process easier.

As Alice walked past the smokers' fug and up the disabled ramp leading to the automatic doors, they opened, and a woman came out. Although she was half-turned away from them, talking to someone behind her, Gus recognised Christine Weston. What the hell! He'd had officers looking for her all afternoon, and here she was. Maybe she'd come to get whatever injury her husband had inflicted on her seen to. He frowned. He'd given explicit instructions to check all the hospital A&E departments, and they'd come back clear. Quickening his step, he moved over to the stairs to cut-across Christine Weston's path. Alice, head down, didn't notice the woman, who turned to go down the steps with her son.

'Mrs Weston, wait,' called Gus, causing Alice to look back at him and then spin around to locate the target. Running up the last few feet of ramp, Alice, instead of going through the doors, turned to the steps and began to descend, just as Gus reached the bottom of the stairs. Christine Weston was sandwiched between them. First, her gaze was directed at Gus and then back at Alice again. Her shoulders slumped, and her face took on a hunted look.

Realising how threatening it must appear to have one officer in front of her and another behind, Gus smiled. 'We just wanted to have a quick word, Mrs Weston.'

Now that he was up close, he could see a large dressing at her temple, and a large bruise swelling out from under her right eye and down towards her cheek. His eyes narrowed. The thought of Weston inflicting this sort of injury on his wife, no matter what she'd done, made Gus want to punch him. He sighed. This sort of violent thought was becoming a bit too frequent for comfort. He needed to keep a lid on it. It didn't matter he knew he wouldn't carry it through in reality. The fact he'd had the thought at all disturbed him.

Seeing Christine hesitate and glance at her son, her eyes wide and pleading, Gus said, 'Why don't we find the canteen and have a drink?' He turned to Jacob. 'They do a mean hot chocolate there, if you fancy one?'

Jacob look swivelled between Gus and his mother. 'You do realise I'm not ten, don't you?'

Gus' lips twitched. Jacob was right. He had tried to bribe him as if he were a child, not a teenager.

The boy shoved his hands into his hoodie pockets and turned to walk back inside the building. 'Hope you're here to stop that bastard hitting my mother again.'

Gus smiled. That was a change in attitude from the first time he'd met the boy. Then, when Christine was drunk, he'd lashed out at her. However, looking at Jacob's expression, Gus could see whilst he'd lashed out at his mother through love, he seemed to have a much less benevolent attitude to his father. If Gus wasn't mistaken, Jacob Weston hated his dad.

Christine gasped, and her hand reached out to grip the handrail as if she thought she might fall. Gus, somehow managing to maintain a neutral expression, said, 'Well, we want to chat to your mum, Jacob. Let's see what she says first, huh?'

He stepped towards them, forcing Christine to either barge past or turn and follow her son. She hesitated for a fraction of a second and then turned, making her way back inside the hospital. Alice stepped aside to let mother and son lead the way. Once inside, Gus kept pace with Christine, whilst Alice attempted to distract Jacob. From what Gus could hear, Jacob was not one for being mollified.

He smiled. He was much the same in his early teens. Thought he was an adult and hated being excluded from 'adult' things.

At some point, either he or Alice needed to phone in they had found Christine and to call off the search for her.

Deciding to postpone the big conversation until they were sitting in the canteen, Gus said, 'Are you here visiting someone or getting your injury dressed?'

Christine cast an anxious glance back at Jacob and said nothing.

Glancing back, Gus saw the boy's angry gaze was piercing into his mother's back. *What's all this about?* wondered Gus, as they moved into the canteen. Manoeuvring Christine to a table in the corner, Gus sent Alice and Jacob to the counter to buy drinks. Jacob, despite his obvious reluctance to comply, stared at his at his mother, his gaze intent, and then stalked over to join Alice at the counter, his entire body bristling with annoyance.

Once seated, Gus studied Christine. Her fingers clasped and unclasped on the table top, she kept sending worried looks towards her son. Biting her lips, she spoke, 'Graeme *didn't* do this, Inspector McGuire. I fell.'

Gus inhaled and leaned towards her. 'Look, Mrs Weston. I've seen abusive men and the things they do to their wives on many occasions, and the one thing I know beyond a doubt is, once they've gone down that path, they will not stop … not ever.' He waited until she glanced up and held her gaze before continuing. 'You don't need to put up with that.'

She lowered her head, and when she spoke, her voice was quiet. 'I deserved it, though. Didn't you see the newspaper?'

Gus sighed and lowered his voice in response. 'Yes, I did see the article, and although he's got every right to be angry, he does *not* have the right to hit you.'

She sniffed and fumbled in her pocket. At last, she drew out a tissue and blew her nose. Wiping her eyes, she said, 'You don't know everything. It's easy to sit on the sidelines and judge him, but he's a good man.'

Gus shook his head. 'I don't understand. You clearly don't share his views, and yet, here you are defending him.'

She glanced over to where Alice and Jacob were now queuing up to pay for their drinks. 'I don't *have* to share anything with you. I don't *need* to do anything. My husband had a right to be angry. He didn't hurt me. I, on the contrary, did hurt him. Whoever sent those pictures to Graeme said they were only to tell him about my behaviour, not for public consumption.' She shrugged. 'They must have changed their minds.'

'Are you telling me you'd already seen those images?' Gus could barely keep the surprise from his voice.

'My husband showed me them on Sunday night. I promised I'd end the affair …' Fingers shredding her tissue, she focussed on her moving hands. 'I didn't need to, though … Razaul was found dead the next day.'

Gus gave her a moment to compose herself. He'd assumed the photos had been sent to Jez Hopkins first, and from Hopkins' responses at interview, so had he. The question of who had sent the photos remained, and now, another question was raised. Who sent the images to Graeme Weston, and was it the same person who'd delivered them to the journalist?

'Do you have any idea who sent those photos to your husband? Who took them?'

She shrugged. 'They're taken through Razaul's living room window. Whoever took them was spying on us.' She shuddered. 'Makes me feel unclean. Could it have been the Tattoo Killer? The one who killed him?'

'We don't know, Christine. It may have been. I want you to think really hard. Who else would have taken the time to follow you and wait to take compromising images of you with Razaul?'

Eyes wide, she shook her head. 'It's all so awful.' She exhaled and then went on. 'I suppose, it could've been any one of his Albion First cronies. None of them were happy with what they considered my lacklustre support for my husband's political aspirations.' She inclined her head to one side, a slight smile on her lips. 'Truth is, I didn't even know my husband was standing in the by-election until I saw the newspaper on Monday. He didn't bother telling me. He keeps his political life away from me.'

'Isn't that unusual?'

She laughed. 'Very. The rest of them are all in it together. Husbands and wives attending their meetings and rallies and demonstrations ... taking the kids along, shouting racist and homophobic abuse ... teaching them to hate.' Her fingers pulled her tissue to bits as she spoke. 'I found it distasteful. So, Graeme and I agreed to differ.'

Gus could not understand what made this woman so loyal to her racist, bigoted husband. She clearly didn't support his political views, and yet, here she was, defending him, although distaste was written all over her bruised face. 'So, you have nothing to do with the Albion First members?'

'Of course I do. Michael and Marcia Hogg are family friends. Marcia works for my husband. We have dinner parties, and occasionally, there are social events I attend.'

'Do you like them?'

She laughed. 'The social events or Marcia and Michael?'

'Both.'

'No to the social events. Michael tends to use them as an excuse to rub his vile body over his friends' wives, once he's had a few, and Marcia throws daggers at Michael and whichever woman he's salivating over at the time. Generally, she's an insipid little thing, but if she imagines a woman is a threat to her marriage, then she can be toxic.'

Bundling the fragments of used tissues together, she continued, 'Look, I really don't have anything more to tell you. I'm ashamed of my behaviour, and I've ruined my husband's chance to further his political career. Michael will find it difficult to put a positive spin on those pictures. Even if he did, there are some in the party who believe in extreme measures, and I'm sure I will be on their target list. Maybe Graeme will disown me. That's the only thing he can do, given the circumstances.'

'And his son?'

A strange expression passed over Christine's face, one that Gus struggled to put a label on, then she smiled. 'No matter what, Jacob will stay with me.'

Gus sensed he was missing something important. Christine was hiding something, and he needed to get to the bottom of it. He thought for a moment and then said, 'Do you know where your husband goes on a Wednesday afternoon once every six weeks or so? Does he have a regular appointment?'

Christine jolted, her hand jerked to her mouth, and then, she straightened. 'Yes, I do know, Inspector. He spends time with Jacob and me. That's what he does. He's a family man.' She looked him straight in the eye, and her gaze didn't falter.

What the hell did that mean? It didn't seem likely, from his experience of the man, Graeme Weston would book a regular slot for 'family time.' Yet, his wife seemed quite definite about it. He shrugged and let it go ... for now.

Alice and Jacob approached and sat down. Alice distributed the drinks. Shrugging off his hoodie, Jacob reached forward for his. His sleeve rode up his arm revealing a small plastic band round his wrist. Almost before Gus noticed it, Christine jumped to her feet and grabbed the boy's hoodie. 'Put this back on Jacob, we need to head off. Take your drink with you.'

Jacob looked as if he was about to object until he caught his mother's eye. He glanced down at his wrist and then jumped up, shrugging his hoodie on as he did so. Christine left her drink steaming on the table, whilst Jacob, a quick glance at first Gus and then Alice, grabbed his hot chocolate takeaway cup and followed his mother.

'Anyone would think the Hound of the Baskervilles was after them,' said Alice, watching Christine usher her son through the café exit door.

'Or a delegation of Albion First supporters, pissed off he's discredited their golden boy,' answered Gus.

Alice sipped her drink. 'What *was* all that about?'

Gus frowned. 'Not entirely sure, did you see the band 'round his wrist?'

Alice shook her head. 'No, what sort of band?'

'A hospital one. It had a ward number on it, and I intend to find out which ward young Jacob Weston visited as an in-patient today and why. Strange that they're being so secretive about it, don't you think?' He slurped his coffee and grimacing, pushing it away, 'Yeuch, that's awful coffee … really bad.'

Alice grinned. 'It's tea, actually. Thought you'd had enough caffeine for one day.'

Gus peered into the offending cup and shook his head. 'I'm not convinced. I think it's dishwater. Come on, drink up so we can check on Lewis Gore.'

They found Lewis Gore in a private room in ICU, with his heavily pregnant wife and his mother taking turns to sit with him.

Gus and Alice stayed only for a brief time to ascertain he was being monitored, and that there was an officer on the door. Lewis seemed to have suffered some sort of reaction to the drug his abductor administered. *Probably Propofol,* Gus thought. His heart had stabilised now, and as he drifted in and out of consciousness, he spoke a few disjointed words here and there.

According to his wife, he seemed to be intimating his abductor had thought he was dead. It seemed Lewis had tried to keep immobile all the time he was being tattooed. It would be a couple of days before they'd be able to question him fully, but that was interesting information. Gus had wondered why they'd found Lewis Gore alive. He wondered how the Tattoo Killer had reacted to thinking his victim had died before he'd had the chance to torture him. Another question for Sebastian Carlton.

Before leaving the hospital, Gus and Alice made a detour to see which ward Jacob had been on that day. On finding the right ward, Gus went in and had a chat with the nurses. Although they wouldn't give information about specific patients, a flash of his badge got him a general description of the sort of things people attended this ward for.

As Gus left the hospital, his head buzzed with ideas. Things were getting curiouser and curiouser.

Chapter 66

17:45 The Fort

On the short drive from the hospital to The Fort, Gus phoned Sebastian Carlton and was relieved to learn the other man was already heading into Bradford. He'd no sooner hung up than Compo rang.

'What's up, Comp?'

Despite Compo sounding like he was chewing cardboard, Gus could just about make out his excited words. 'I've got something for you. How close are you?'

Peering out the window, Gus saw they had just turned off the Duckworth Lane roundabout. 'Two minutes away, Compo. Get the coffee on, will you. Alice has got me on a reduced caffeine diet, and I'm flagging.'

Some static came over the phone line, and then, the sound of running water. Gus assumed Compo was filling the coffee machine. 'Hurry, Gus, this is good ...' Gus was left with a disconnect tone buzzing in his ear.

By the time Gus and Alice arrived back at The Fort, Compo was all but bouncing on his chair. As soon as Gus walked through the door, he catapulted from his chair and dashed over. 'We got a hit on the ANPR. My programme correlated it down to one in that area. Registered to a seventy-five-year-old man named Jack Froud. I checked and couldn't find any links to neo-Nazi organisations or anything. No previous convictions. He looks like he's led a blameless life.'

All of Compo's words seemed to run together in one long stream, and Gus had to concentrate to realise what he was telling him. 'You've narrowed the cars in the vicinity down to one possible?'

Compo grinned. 'That's it!'

Gus thought for a moment. The possibility of the Tattoo Killer being a seventy-year-old man hadn't been in Sebastian Carlton's profile, and it certainly hadn't crossed his mind either. Something seemed off to him; still, you had to follow the leads. He frowned at Compo, who was still grinning like an idiot.

'Any links to Graeme Weston?'

Compo shook his head and bouncing on his toes like an inebriated rabbit, his face glowing, he grabbed Gus' arm. 'Nope, no links to Weston, or to any of our victims. On paper, the old guy's a saint. I despatched uniforms to check him out.'

His bouncing increased in tempo. Gus frowned, quelling the urge to grip him by the arms and force him to stillness. Aware of Alice looking on in amusement, he said with more patience than he felt, 'Compo, I know you've got something else, so do us all a damn favour and spit it out.'

Compo's arms lifted in the air, as if he was conducting an orchestra. 'Uniforms were smart. They mentioned the areas he'd been seen in, and the old bloke categorically denied it. He even provided proof that, on one occasion, he was out of the country. So, the uniforms had a look at his vehicle and what do you think they found?'

By this stage, Gus guessed where Compo was going with this. Rather than burst his bubble, however, he shook his head, hung his jacket up to dry and kicked off his sodden shoes. Pulling off his socks and chucking them in the bin, Gus walked barefoot to his desk, and from the bag underneath it, he pulled out a towel, a pair of dry socks and his trainers, and began to dry his feet before putting on his dry socks. 'Go on then, Compo. What did they find?'

'The number plates had been swapped.' Compo grinned. 'You get it? It means that my programme worked. Must've been the Tattoo Killer who swapped the plates, yeah?'

Gus nodded, wondering where this left them now. 'Yeah, good work, Compo. I presume you've –'

'Yep, the plates on Jack Froud's car were registered to a vehicle that's been sent for squashing. So, that doesn't link to our man. However, the net's drawing in.'

Gus sighed. It wasn't drawing in quick enough for his liking. 'Keep on it then, Comps.'

Re-commencing his earlier bouncing, Compo burst out. 'I've got a new lead though.'

Gus raised an eyebrow. 'And?'

'Well, I re-did the whole rigmarole focussing in on only two areas this time. Lewis Gore's house and Tetley Street where he was abducted from – and I got two hits. An octogenarian called Trevor Blackhurst, and a sixty-year-old called Ishmael Mahboob. So, I sent uniforms to them, and guess what?'

Gus pulled a face. 'I sincerely hope you've got something concrete, Compo, with all this rabbiting on you've been doing.'

Compo took a bite of a Mars Bar that had appeared seemingly from nowhere and continued nodding his head. 'Yeah, yeah, we did. After Mr Mahboob checked out. He lives two streets from Lewis Gore and works in a garage off Tetley Street. His plates are intact and I reckoned, like, with all the racism and that, we're probably looking for a white bloke. I moved onto the second candidate. Assuming Mr Blackhurst couldn't be our killer, I got uniforms to check his vehicle and guess what …?'

Again, his arms stretched out like a demented conductor. *All he needs is a bloody baton,* thought Gus, beginning to think if Compo didn't speed up his delivery, he'd strangle him. Aware of Alice's snigger, he said, 'Hurry the fuck up, Comps.'

Compo's face fell for a second, and then, he grinned. 'Mr Blackhurst doesn't drive his car at *all* … except for on a Tuesday night, when he goes to get fish and chips from Mother Hubbard's on Ingleby Road. Otherwise, it's secured in his garage. So that's the *only* time the plates could have been switched. I'm waiting for CCTV footage from Mother Hubbard's to be sent over as we speak.'

Gus heart rate increased, and the desire to strangle Compo was replaced by an urge to promise him a year-long supply of bacon butties. A quick mental calculation of the number of bacon sandwiches the younger man could get through in a year made him swallow the promise. Never mind, though. He knew they were onto something. This was great news. Within a few minutes, they could have footage of their killer in their hands.

'Bloody great. You're a star.'

Alice and Gus were discussing Compo's findings, when the door opened. Professor Carlton exploded into the room like a grenade, saying, 'Update.'

Blinded by his rather 'out there' burgundy suit, banana yellow tie and his lime green trainers, Gus gawped at the Professor, before shaking his head and gesturing for him to sit down. Although the police activity on Shipley Glen had made it onto local news, Gus had so far managed to keep a lid on the fact Lewis Gore was still alive. He wanted to discuss it with the psychologist before coming to any decisions and had ordered a complete press blackout. He and Alice brought Sebastian Carlton up-to-date on the car and Lewis Gore.

Sebastian jumped to his feet, thrust one hand into the pocket of his vibrant trousers and strutted back and forth. 'This is all quite interesting. There are two separate things to consider here. Firstly, he thought Gore was dead. So, what effect will the fact our killer was unable to play out his entire 'torture scene fantasy' have on him? Secondly, how will he be affected on discovering he was wrong about Gore, and, just as importantly, that Gore is still alive?'

Gus glanced at Alice and rolled his eyes. What the hell was it with these experts? First, he had Compo grandstanding to him, instead of getting to the damn point. Now, it was Sebastian Carlton's turn. Couldn't they just blurt it all out, like normal people?

Turning on his heel, Sebastian glared at Gus through his lopsided specs. 'You want to know what I think?'

With difficulty, Gus managed to confine his response to a nod, which appeared to be enough encouragement for the psychologist to continue.

'I think our killer is beginning to unravel. The fact he made a critical mistake shows this. He played out his fantasy on a dead man. If he wasn't unravelling, he would have discovered his mistake at some point and been able to yank it back in his favour.'

Another myopic stare, this time at Alice. 'No, he's unravelling faster than a ball of wool on an alpaca. Thing is, what will he do now? He'll have other targets in mind. My feeling is, he'll go with the next one pretty damn fast. You need to shut this down.'

Gus got to his feet, but before he could respond, Alice stepped in front of him. 'In your considered opinion, Professor, should we release the information Lewis Gore is still alive or not?'

'Not. The killer is unstable and is on a downward spiral, which, as I've said, will result in an acceleration of his plans. Any hint he has left a living witness will increase that acceleration. We need to get as close as we can, before flushing him out. However, although not ideal, I do think you need to issue a public warning.'

'What do you mean by 'not ideal'?' said Gus.

Sebastian shrugged. 'It will no doubt infuriate our killer, however, on the other hand, people need to know. Mention his next victim will have been stalked already. You know the victim profile ... the public even know the victim profile, thanks to the press. Use it. Get people thinking about a stranger loitering in their neighbourhoods.' He took off his specs, pulled his shirt loose from his trousers and used it to wipe the lens. 'My experience with the FBI shows when these killers unravel, they do so big style. They become more unpredictable. It's a balancing act between not needlessly aggravating him and making the public aware. A vigilant public may thwart this guy's plans. Appeal for information about where our killer acquired the tattoo paraphernalia. It's clearly not state-of-the-art equipment, so maybe he got it second-hand. Mention the racist motives. It may contribute to his unravelling; perhaps on balance, it may also save a life or two.'

Gus considered the Professor's words. Sebastian was right. The public already knew what the press had leaked about the Tattoo Killer. It was time for the police to build on that.

Sebastian putting his specs back on, flung himself into a seat and rolled it across the floor to where Gus leaned against his desk. He sighed. 'I know you don't want to hear this, Gus, but I think you should head up that public appeal.'

Gus was already shaking his head. No way was he going to do that. Nancy was much better at these things than Gus. He hated the limelight. All he wanted to do was focus on catching the bastard. Nancy would do a better job than him.

Sebastian gripped his arm. 'Listen. I'm suggesting this for a good reason. I know you don't want to do it, but this isn't about you, is it?' He released Gus' arm. 'With the killer targeting blacks and Asians, you are the perfect choice to deliver the appeal. The killer's perception is non-whites are inferior, unworthy. By using *you* as the police spokesperson, we will be doing two things. One, we'll be playing into his warped belief these deaths are inconsequential. To him, it will seem the police are not prioritising this investigation.' He grinned at Gus. 'He'll see you as an inferior detective, and it'll pacify him a little. Two, your photo has already been in the media regarding this case, so it won't seem unusual. If I were you, I'd use that young lad Taffy as your sidekick.'

Cursing under his breath, Gus raked his fingers through his hair. 'Don't have fucking time for this!'

'He's right though, Gus,' said Alice. 'Just bite the bullet and do it.'

Gus turned, and picking up his desk phone, he contacted DCI Chalmers. As he explained the situation to her, he half hoped she'd veto the Professor's advice. Deep down, though, he knew she wouldn't. Nancy believed if you asked for expert advice, then you damn well used it when it was proffered. With Nancy agreeing to the press conference, he left her to set it up for 18:30. No point in hanging around. He'd rather get it out of the way.

Turning to Alice, he said, 'I want an increased presence around the black and Asian communities like West Bowling, Manningham and the rest. Nancy has sanctioned overtime, so we need feet in the streets to coincide with my press conference and to continue in eight-hour shifts 'til we shut this down. I want them talking to the communities. Get more admin staff in, too, for the hotlines. I'll be making a direct plea for information, and we need to facilitate the public getting through to us quickly. I also want all the key Albion First Generals under observation. I know it could well be one of their foot soldiers or perhaps someone outwith the organisation. We need to be sure.' He turned back to Sebastian Carlton. 'Will you brief me again?'

Carlton grinned. 'That's my job!'

Gus stood up and rolled his shoulders. 'Right, let's crack on.' Then, noticing Alice still standing nearby, he said, 'What's up, Al? You look thoughtful.'

'Yeah, I've been thinking about something, too. I think it's worth following up.'

Gus, conscious of how little time he had to prepare his appeal, made a rolling gesture with his hands to hurry her up.

'You know the horsehair that Hissing Sid found today?'

Gus nodded and waited for her to speak.

'Well, we know Graeme Weston has a horse. He told us the horse was kept at a paddock owned by the Hoggs, didn't he?'

'That's it. That's what was niggling me earlier. The horsehair. Graeme Weston has access to a horse, and his sidekick owns some. Good catch.' He smiled at Alice. 'You're thinking the horsehair could be from Weston's or the Hoggs' horse, not from that horse we came across at the Bay of Biscay?'

Alice shrugged. 'Maybe … maybe not. Worth looking into though?'

'Certainly is,' said Gus. 'After this bloody thing, we'll head down there, and see if we can get ourselves a couple of hairs to compare to Sid's sample.'

Chapter 67

18:30 The Fort

In contrast to the drizzling snow of the past few days, rain now fell in sheets, bouncing off the pavement, soaking on the way down and on its rebound. Street and car lights slashed through the torrent as rush hour slowed to a drizzle. From inside The Fort's entrance, Gus watched with satisfaction as a four-by-four swished past a tad too close to the kerb, sending a deluge over the waiting journos. Some had come prepared with umbrellas, although most seemed to prefer getting wet and having their hands free for gesticulating and holding their recorders. 'Drookit craws!' would have been his dad's pithy observation of the cluster elbowing each other out of the way like a nest of cackling chicks vying to stay safe inside their haven. He saw Jez Hopkins join the group ... the cuckoo in the nest. Gus hoped some other cuckoo would come along and oust him before too long.

Taffy joined him, hair damp and flattened down over his forehead giving him the appearance of a teenager. Just the sort of image the Prof wanted them to portray for the benefit of their killer ... young, inexperienced, incompetent. 'You all set, Taffy?'

Grinning, the younger man shrugged. 'As I'll ever be, I suppose.'

Well, that makes one of us, thought Gus, wishing the entire thing was over. He waited whilst the corrugated canopy was rolled over to protect them from the torrent. At least he wouldn't get soaked, and maybe the adverse weather would encourage the unprotected reporters to speed up their questions. He and Taffy would stand under it with a podium bearing West Yorkshire Police logo and contact details and a microphone in front of them.

As he pushed open the glass door and walked the few feet to the lectern, his knees shook, and he hoped it wasn't visible to the crowd. There was a momentary silence.

Gus saw the journalists look at one another. A whisper of surprise spread through them, and then, one of them, a male reporter from one of the nationals, said, 'Where's DCI Chalmers?'

Here it was, the first hurdle. Gus took a deep breath. 'I am Detective Inspector Gus McGuire, and on the authority of DCI Nancy Chalmers and in my position as senior investigating officer in the so-called Tattoo Killer investigation, I am here to brief you on updated information regarding the abduction of Lewis Gore.'

Gus risked a glance down from his elevated position on the top step and saw the reporters appeared to be listening intently to his statement. All heads were tipped towards him, and Taffy, who stood to Gus' rear, hands clasped behind his back, a solemn expression on his youthful face. Over the drum of rain on the makeshift roof, he heard the unmistakeable click of camera lenses shutting, and the rustle as the reporters huddled closer to hear his words.

'Earlier today, the body of Lewis Gore was discovered on Shipley Glen. At this point in time, we believe the perpetrator of this murder to be the same person responsible for the unlawful killings of Asim Farooq, Manish Parmar and Razaul Ul Haq. Our investigation is ongoing, multi-faceted and complex. With this in mind, I wish to enlist the assistance of the public.'

As he'd rehearsed with Professor Carlton, Gus stopped and glowered directly in the camera of the BBC reporter stationed at the front. He paused and gathered his thoughts, glad the pooling of sweat under his armpits was obscured by the suit jacket he'd borrowed from Sampson. Resisting the urge to yank at the tie, also borrowed from Sampson, he swallowed and continued.

'This killer is targeting non-white citizens of Bradford. Therefore, it is imperative that people in these communities remain vigilant. This attacker *will have*, on numerous occasions, visited the areas where his targets live. He *will* have staked out their homes, and he *will* have followed them as they went about their day-to-day business. We believe, despite an increased police presence in these communities, he *will* strike again.'

Gus paused once more, as rehearsed, and moved his gaze along the rows of reporters.

'I appeal to Bradford's ethnic communities to look after each other. Be alert, be strong and above all else, be careful. If you lead any sort of alternative lifestyle, be extra vigilant. There is safety in numbers ... stay in groups. These are the things I want you to watch out for.

'1. A white vehicle, probably a van, with an occupant inside, parked up for any length of time.

'2. Repeat sightings of strange vehicles in your neighbourhood.

'3. Any sense of being followed or of seeing the same person in repeated locations.'

Gus gathered up the papers he'd placed on the podium. He drew a deep breath, and knowing this was the part where he allowed the vultures to peck his eyes out, he said, 'Any questions?'

The immediate barrage that erupted from the crowd would have thrown him backwards, had he not been holding onto the lectern. Instead, thankful when Taffy stepped forward to stand beside him, he raised his voice and spoke into the microphone. 'If you want to ask a question, raise your hand. DC Bhandir will indicate when you can speak.'

Taffy pointed to a woman in a long raincoat, clutching a pink and white spotty brolly in one hand, her recorder held aloft in her other. 'Lesley Smithson, *Channel Five News*. Bearing in mind how high profile the Tattoo Killer case is, I think we're all wondering why it is only a Detective Inspector and a Detective Constable leading this press briefing. Why is DCI Chalmers not here, reassuring the people of Bradford the police are on top of this investigation? Perhaps the minority communities in the city would be right to wonder if this case is not high priority.'

Despite knowing this was exactly the sort of response they had aimed for, Gus' hackles rose. The murmur of support for the questioner was clear, and Gus wished he could lambast them. Instead, he bowed his head and counted to three before raising his eyes and focussing on The Chaat Café on the other side of the road. 'I am the senior investigating officer on this case, and I am co-ordinating the investigation of a series of leads. These murders are West Yorkshire Police's top priority, and we are confident we will make a breakthrough soon.'

'Aliya Qureshi, the *Telegraph and Argus*. In light of the Albion First leader Graeme Weston's arrest yesterday, is he or anyone in his party, a suspect in these clearly racially motivated attacks?'

Another murmur went around the mob, and Gus groaned. A flurry of hands went up before he'd even attempted to respond. 'At this moment, Graeme Weston is assisting us with our enquiries, and I am unable to speculate on any ongoing lines of enquiry.'

Questions bombarded him as harshly as the rain that hit the pavement. Their tone seemed venomous and unforgiving, like the howling of jackals. He put up both hands in a placating gesture, knowing he'd done the job the Prof had wanted him to do. 'I can't take any more questions at this time.' And, feeling like a coward, despite knowing that that was precisely the desired effect, he shuffled back inside The Fort, Taffy on his heels.

Minutes later, having taken the elevator upstairs, Gus loosened his tie and shrugged off his jacket before handing both back to Sampson with thanks. Alice had set up the TV and as *Channel Five News* began, Gus, Professor Carlton, Nancy and the rest of his team settled down to watch his performance. Critical of himself at the best of times, Gus realised any soupçon of street cred he thought he had had just drained into Bradford's sewage system with the rest of the rain. What a fiasco. Yet, as he stood embarrassed in front of his colleagues, having just exposed himself as an idiot on national news, he knew he'd do it all again, if it helped buy them more time from the Tattoo Killer.

The one thing he hated, though, was giving the impression West Yorkshire Police were side-lining this investigation because of race. There were some dicks on the force, course there were. However, not nearly as many as there had been a few years back and none on his team. He didn't tolerate that.

Chapter 68

19:15 The Tattoo Killer's Home

What. A. Joke. Gus McGuire, senior investigating officer and clueless fool. He has no more control over the investigation to find me than Christine Weston has over spreading her legs.

Laughing, I help myself to another whisky. There's always something nice about being at home with the curtains shut and the rain battering against the windows. After that sorry excuse for a press conference, I think a little celebration is in order.

They'd found Lewis Gore. That still rankles, however not as much as it did earlier ... before the press conference. No, seeing McGuire so clearly out of his depth, so clearly flummoxed, asking the communities for help, has really cheered me up.

I suppose, though, I will have to exercise a bit more care. If the Pakis become more vigilant, it'll make my job harder. Well, it would but for one little thing that Detective Inspector Gus McGuire and his motley clue are oblivious of ... one thing that's flown right under their radar. Idiots!

I press rewind and watch the whole sorry mess again. It's the best TV I've watched for years. A sudden thought occurs to me. It's a case of the stupid leading the even more stupid, isn't it? McGuire asking the thickos to help. Between the lot of them, they couldn't work their way round a plate of bangers and mash.

Well, his little appeal isn't going to help him. Not with what I've got in mind. He won't see this one coming. Not a chance! Whisky always makes me feel all warm and fuzzy inside, and tonight is no exception. That, and the thought of what I'm going to do next, gives me a warm glow. DI Gus McGuire may think he's onto the home stretch, though the truth is, it's only just beginning. I stretch out on the sofa, whisky glass balanced on my chest, feet up, and hit rewind again.

Chapter 69

19:40 The Fort

Gus had just about managed to watch the disastrous press conference, and despite Professor Carlton beaming his approval like a rotund toddler meeting Santa Claus, he was still fed up. His body ached with inactivity, and he had a tension headache coming on. He needed to get out of The Fort and do something. He jerked his head towards the door, and Alice sighed.

Glancing outside, she said, 'Why does it always piss it down when we have to go out? Why can't it be nice and dry?'

Gus grimaced. 'Yeah, well, at least you've not ripped your favourite trousers, been puked on and had to endure torture at the hands of Jez Hopkins' cronies.' He grabbed his coat. 'You can put your wellies on, and you'll be fine.'

Alice opened her mouth as if she was about to complain but was interrupted by Compo. 'I've got something.'

Dropping his coat by the door, Gus moved over to Compo's computer station. Wincing at the array of wrappers, near-empty mugs and coke cans, he glanced around for somewhere to lean his hand while he bent towards the computer screen. With a finger and thumb, he picked up a plate with the remains of congealed pizza and deposited it on the desk behind before placing his hand where it had been. Almost immediately, he yanked his hand away, with a 'Yeuch!' A smear of tomato sauce covered his palm.

Alice, who'd followed him over, shook her head before rummaging in her capacious bag and offering him another wet wipe. 'I'll be expecting reimbursement for these, if you keep this up.'

Ignoring her, Gus wiped his hand and then the table, before leaning over Compo's shoulder. Oblivious to the pizza incident, Compo was engrossed in the information on his screen. 'Don't know how this was missed before. Someone only did a half-arsed search, I bet.'

Jumping on the balls of his feet, he continued, 'Look, Christine Weston, Graeme Weston *and* Razaul Ul Haq all went to the same secondary school – Bolton Woods!'

Gus read the details from the screen. 'Weston was two years ahead of Ul Haq, but Christine and Ul Haq were in the same year group. That's a big school, still, they must have known each other. What subjects did Christine and Ul Haq study?'

Compo pressed a few keys, and Christine Weston and Razaul Ul Haq's A-Level results came up side by side on the screen. 'Looks like they both studied drama and geography.'

Gus straightened. 'If they both studied those two subjects, chances are they'd have come across each other. Why the hell didn't she mention that before?'

'I suppose it's conceivable Graeme Weston was oblivious to Ul Haq's existence, but you'd think she'd have told us she knew him at school.'

Gus shrugged. 'Don't recollect having the chance to ask her how she met Ul Haq. She was just so damn keen to get away from us.' He turned to Compo. 'If they all went to the same secondary school, chances are they lived near each other. Check out their addresses from then.'

'Already on it,' said Compo, pressing a key. 'The electoral roll will tell us where their parents lived at that time. Here we are!'

Gus and Alice craned their necks to read the information. 'Well, all three of them lived in Bradford Two postcodes.'

Gus pointed to Ul Haq and Graeme Weston's addresses. 'I'm sure these two streets are near one and other. Pin the three addresses on a Google map, will you, Comps?'

Compo did as he was asked, and Gus blew out a long breath of air. 'Those three must have known each other. It's too damn co-incidental. These streets are all within a couple of minutes' walk from one another. Check out their primary schools.'

'Bolton Junction First School followed by Bolton Junction Middle for all three of them.'

Gus sucked in his cheek and bit on it from the inside of his mouth. He didn't know what all this meant. Christine Weston, to give the woman her due, hadn't actually denied knowing Razaul Ul Haq from her childhood. Bit co-incidental they were having an affair now, though. Her husband, on the other hand, had categorically denied knowing him ... and *that* just didn't add up for Gus. Why the hell would he deny knowing him, if he had nothing to do with his murder? Was it just because of his wife's affair? Well, one thing was sure, he needed to have a little chat with Mr Weston, but that could wait until he came back from seeing the man's horse.

'See if you can come up with some friends from high school who might be able to link the Westons more closely with Ul Haq during those days. Get Sampson and the boy wonder to help you. I'd like a solid link before I re-interview the idiot.'

He moved over to the door. 'Get Christine Weston on the phone; I'll speak to her en-route. I want to see what she has to say about all this.'

Chapter 70

20:25 Canal Lane, Bingley

Gus got out of the car and stepped straight into a puddle. Closing his eyes for a fraction of a second, he cursed under his breath. *What the hell is it with me and bloody shoes today? This is the second pair I've soaked in the space of a few hours.* It hardly seemed worth putting on the wellies he'd grabbed from The Fort, but ignoring Alice's giggle, he walked around to the miniscule boot and took them out. Sitting on the front seat of the Mini, his legs sticking out, he swapped footwear and succumbed to his dark mood.

Christine Weston had been uncommunicative. She'd admitted to knowing Razaul at secondary school, yet refused to commit to her husband having known him. Whatever secret she had, she was clamming up big time.

Not only was it still raining, but it was well and truly dark now, and the last thing Gus wanted to do was traipse around a bloody quagmire to get a hair from a horse's mane. Apart from anything else, they were quite big fuckers, and the moonlight served to make their looming presence all the more menacing. It even smelled of farmyards, and that thought was enough to trigger memories – memories of big 'coos,' as his dad called them. The damn 'Hieland' ones, with their enormous horns, were the worst. *You could be impaled on those things. They could slice right through you! Lethal, that's what they were, lethal!* He risked another glance at the horses. Why couldn't they have been Shetland ponies? *They* were okay; small and dainty and mostly timid. Unlike these hulking bloody monsters.

Unwilling to reveal his trepidation to Alice, he flicked his mobile torch on and, trying to look nonchalant, headed over to the paddock at the side of the Hogg's house. He and Alice had already decided they could swipe a couple of horsehairs under the pretence of petting the animals, rather than ask permission of either Marcia or Michael Hogg. To be honest, the way Gus felt right now, he'd probably flatten the little scrote, if he saw him, so best to avoid that, if at all possible.

Two horse-shaped forms in coats cowered against the rain under a tree in the corner of the field. Great. At least they wouldn't have to climb into the field. That would have appeared decidedly dodgy if the Hoggs caught them. He motioned to Alice to hurry up. She'd grabbed some sugar from the canteen before they left and would use that to entice them close.

Looking all the while like a toddler, Alice seemed to take great pleasure in splashing through every puddle in her wellies. Gus shook his head, but couldn't quite prevent the grin from forming. Drawing level with him, she offered him a sachet of sugar. 'You just sprinkle it on your hand, and they'll lick it off.'

Gus shuddered. The very thought of those massive rough tongues rasping against his palm made him feel ill. He shook his head. 'No, you're alright, Al. Wouldn't want to spoil your fun.'

Casting a sideways glance to let him know she knew his game, Alice leaned against the fence and began to click her tongue in a kind of Morse code seemingly only known to horses. Two pairs of ears quivered in response, yet they remained in their sheltered position. Alice climbed onto the fence and clicked a bit louder, holding her arm at full length towards the horses. The black one shook his head and then took a couple of steps closer. Alice clicked again and spoke encouragingly. 'Attaboy ... come on then.'

Gus, about to roll his eyes, realised he used the exact same tone when speaking to Bingo. He restrained himself, instead took a couple of plastic bags from his pocket and opened one of them. The larger horse had edged closer and was nuzzling Alice. Sprinkling sugar on her palm, she offered it to him, and when his head dipped to snort it up, she ran her fingers through his mane. Trailing loose hair, she thrust her hand at Gus who enclosed it in the bag, sliding it down her fingers to trap the hairs before sealing and annotating it.

'One down, one to go.' Alice moved along the fence and reached out her hand to the brown mare that seemed a bit more hesitant than her equine friend. Coaxing words and her gentle tone seemed to work, as the horse dipped her head and licked the sugar from her hand.

Alice had just reached out her other arm to touch the mane, when the spotlight attached to the side of the house and aimed at the field illuminated them.

Fuck! Just a minute more, and they'd have had all the evidence they needed. Gus swung around, his heart sinking when he saw the door slamming open and a figure power from the house. The horses startled, retreated to their tree, as Marcia Hogg stormed across to them, her coat flapping as she ran.

Gus concealed the evidence bag he held in his hand and cursed under his breath before stepping forward. 'Hello, Mrs Hogg, we just wanted to have a quick word with your husband. Is he at home?'

The woman's eyes narrowed as her gaze moved from them to her horses. Alice stepped forward, smiling. 'Such lovely horses, Mrs Hogg. I couldn't resist saying hello to them. They remind me of my parents' horses. They live in Sussex, so I rarely get the chance to see them anymore. Beautiful animals, though.'

Alice's words seemed to mollify the other woman, and she moved forward, smiling slightly. 'The black one's Graeme's and the other one's my husband's, but it's me that looks after them in the main.' The black horse whinnied and pushed its head towards Marcia. She stepped forward, hand outstretched to the horse, and without warning, her foot slipped in the sludge.

Alice reached out with both arms and grabbed the woman before she landed in the mud. 'Oops, careful, it's slippy.' She pulled Marcia to her feet and accepted her thanks.

Gus cleared his throat, and Marcia turned towards him with a sneering look. 'He's not in. He's at a meeting. Don't know when he'll be back. You lot need to get off his back. Hounding him like he's a criminal.'

Gus smiled and dipped his head. 'Well, if he's not in, Mrs Hogg, we won't take up any more of your time.' And he and Alice walked back to the car. As they swapped their wellies back, Alice grabbed an evidence bag and scraped the horsehair from her hands into the bag. 'Slightly contaminated by Marcia Hogg's coat, but there's still some brown horsehair there too.'

'So, not a wasted journey then. Wonder if we'll get a match. Although, it's not as if Graeme Weston's the only one with access to the horses, is it? So, it won't be entirely conclusive, even if we do get a match,' said Gus.

'My money's on Hogg,' said Alice. 'He's more likely to fit the bill. I can see him wielding that tattoo thing and not blinking an eye.'

'Hmm, perhaps. I'm not convinced. I think he's more the 'beat 'em up, knife them in the gut' sort of thug. Mind you, I've been wrong before.'

'Talking of tattoos, how's yours coming along?'

Gus grinned. 'Scabbing over now. Not long 'til it's properly healed. I'll let you see it when we get back, if you like.'

Chapter 71

Michael Hogg was proud of what they'd built up over the years. As he viewed the main hall of Albion First Headquarters, the same pride he had experienced when they first dared to dream made his chest puff out. He and Graeme had started small. First, they'd courted those UKIP supporters who believed the party offered only an uneasy placebo rather than hard and far-reaching policies. These were ordinary people. Milkmen, labourers, doctors, businessmen and the like. Bradfordians who saw at firsthand the effects of spiralling immigration, diluted culture, and who wanted to see that trend reversed once and for all.

The BNP had sullied their copybook and lacked the political credibility in the mainstream, and so many of their followers had drifted to them, too. Albion First offered an alternative to Nick Griffin's hopeless efforts in the European Parliament. Graeme always said with clever politicking and tireless campaigning, Bradford Central constituency would be to Albion First what Brighton Pavilion had been to the Greens.

Donations from their various benefactors had furnished the building with plush conference tables and chairs, but what really brought a lump to his throat were the large swastikas mounted on flagpoles extending at angles from the wall. Each was interspersed by Union Jack and Saint George's Cross flags. A picture gallery spanned one wall, holding portraits of great leaders such as Adolf Hitler,

Benito Mussolini, Francisco Franco, Hendrik Verwoerd and Oswald Mosley in gilded frames. He thought Mussolini was a bit of a damp squib when compared to Adolf's achievements or those of Hendrik Verwoerd, the mastermind behind apartheid in South Africa. Nonetheless, some thought he'd earned his place on the wall. Pride of place on one wall was a huge TV used both for educating their members and monitoring current affairs. Underneath that was a wooden shelving unit containing hundreds of Albion First, British National Party, National Front and English Defence League propaganda DVDs. Hogg's gaze took in the double-sized bookshelf containing mainly illegally obtained publications. He particularly enjoyed leafing through the American Ku Klux Klan magazines, and the South African apartheid cum fascist newsletters on racial superiority and cultural purity.

Not long now, and the seemingly endless wait for a white Britain would be over, and he would be on the front lines of the attack. They'd nearly made it too. Nearly got their foot in the political door. Breaking away from the BNP had been beneficial for them. They'd been able to gather around them a blend of hungry youth and experienced elders. The ones with staying power who could lead them to political dominance. People like Graeme Weston.

He punched the table. What the hell was he supposed to do now? In a short while, he'd have to explain about Graeme Weston's wife and Graeme's sojourn, courtesy of Her Majesty's finest. What spin could he put on the fact those photos were on the front page of not only the local papers, but also national news. It had been bad enough convincing the Generals that if Nigel Farage, the UKIP leader, could have a German wife, then it was of no consequence Christine Weston was half Greek, because she *was* British, after all, and white. Now, she'd gone and whored herself with a fucking Paki all over the tabloids. And not just any fucking Paki, but a dead one at the centre of a serial killer murder investigation.

There was nothing else he could do, except try to convince them they could still pull themselves out of this. Of course, that would have been a lot easier if Weston hadn't got pissed and gotten himself arrested earlier, although that, too, could perhaps be used to bolster his reputation and give him credibility with the militants in the party – being in jail never hurt Hitler's reputation. This whole thing would need to be handled sensitively. After all, they wanted to appeal to ordinary voters too.

God knew when Graeme would get out. The only thing he'd been able to do was to send in the party lawyer with strict instructions to tell Weston to deny all knowledge of his wife's affair. The lawyer would also tell him to break off all ties with Christine on his release. The sympathy vote was the only one that could play out for him now. They needed to throw Christine Weston to the dogs for the duplicitous traitor she was, and Graeme would just have to put up with it. It was all for the greater good; and he'd have to convince him of it.

The thing was – Hogg had the distinct impression Graeme Weston would find it near impossible to divorce his wife. Whatever hold she had on him seemed unbreakable. Weston would hear nothing against her. He could understand that, to a certain extent. Christine was very attractive, and if the photo in the paper was anything to go by, she was also extremely flexible. He'd been tempted himself on a couple of occasions, though the snooty cow had turned her nose up. No, it seemed like she preferred to slum it with the Pakis.

He stood up, his face flushed, and paced around the conference room, considering each of the Generals in turn, playing out what he supposed would be their individual responses to the crisis. Jamie would no doubt follow Anthony Cairns' lead. Cairns would bluster like a pompous idiot for half an hour and then settle down to let everyone else make the decision, giving himself 'plausible deniability.' Rob Harrogate would insist on cutting Weston loose, regardless of how it would play out. He'd always been jealous of Weston's selection in the first place. Fancied himself as the candidate. The only problem with him was he couldn't string two sentences together. Tommy Bond was persuadable, more so if he could convince Brendon Hope to agree to brazening it all out.

Looked like it was up to him to paint a rosy picture of Graeme Weston as the duped husband with the traitorous wife; a man who took the moral high ground for the sake of his political party. Weston must be visible now, at all costs, constantly focussing on the important issues. The purification of Bradford, then Yorkshire, and then the whole of England. They must not be hijacked by Christine Weston's antics.

Then, of course, there was the other worry. Could the Generals control the foot soldiers? The last thing they needed was for one of them to go after Christine. He could understand their righteous anger. Christ, he was fucking angry himself. Still, right now, they had to play the long game. They needed to hold things together. Christine Weston could and would be punished later, of that there was no doubt. However, they couldn't risk the press swinging things in her favour. Making her look like a victim. No, they had to keep her safe, for the time being … until after the by-election, at all costs.

He'd spent the afternoon since the police arrested Weston, working on a statement for the press. In it, he'd portrayed Weston as the victim. Part of a conspiracy by the Asians and blacks supported by his wife who'd been brainwashed by working in City Academy which was full of 'ethnics.' He'd brushed away his arrest, saying Weston was helping the police piece together aspects of his wife's sordid past, in light of her lover having been murdered. He'd hinted at Christine Weston's culpability in the murder, revealing a time when she'd suffered from mental health issues that had jeopardised the wellbeing of their son.

Hogg looked out the window, his fists clenched by his sides. He could do with a cigar and a double brandy right now to steady his nerves. Didn't matter it was a pack of lies. The important thing was they turned the tide of doom away from their candidate. Didn't matter what it took, as long as they were smart about it. However, they had to be tactical.

Chapter 72

For the tenth time, Jez Hopkins read through the press release Michael Hogg had had delivered to him. He was nervous and a bit scared. It wasn't that he'd suddenly grown a moral compass or anything; he just didn't want to be a pawn in the hands of a racist political party who appeared to have a militia wing that were quite handy with a flick blade.

The message, delivered earlier by a large skinhead with muscles the size of baby elephants, had been clear. Publish this or else. The 'else' hadn't been specified, but it didn't take a genius to work out that broken bones and a liberal smattering of blood would be included ... his blood.

Deep down, he knew he had no choice. He'd have to submit the release, and, no doubt, it would make the front page tomorrow. That was all fine and dandy, except he knew if he did it once, he'd be expected to do it again ... and again. He regretted publishing the photos. Not for Christine Weston's sake ... no ... for his own. The nationals hadn't jumped for him, intimating Christine Weston's roll in the hay was a two-day scandal and further news, like the possibility of a general election in June leaked by a top Tory cabinet member, might trump that. Hell, Trump might trump it, for all he knew. That guy made headlines just by looking like he'd been Tangoed.

Now, he was stuck in Bradford, and it seemed like Albion First viewed him as their bitch.

Chapter 73

20:55 The Fort

The exhaustion of having been on the go for hours with little sustenance had kicked in. As Gus swallowed his anti-depressants with a sip of flat Irn Bru, he knew he should stir himself to go to the staff canteen for food. However, he also knew when he got there, he would be faced with a choice between a dried up yellowing jacket potato or a soggy salad sandwich on the verge of its sell-by-date. Sometimes, starving was better than the alternative. He frowned. What the hell was he thinking? There were loads of people in the world without food or even the promise of food, and here he was, moaning about a 'yella tattie.' He dragged himself to his feet, glanced around his team, who all seemed motivated and energised. Compo, head bobbing, was focussed on his screen, Sampson and Taffy were collating phone reports, and Alice was updating the murder board.

'Anybody want owt from the canteen?'

He wasn't surprised when Compo's head jerked up first. The lad had an uncanny ability to hear even the most obscure reference to food and to react like a Pavlovian dog. He rubbed his eye and then waved a hand at Compo telling him he'd noted his interest. With Compo, it didn't matter what was on offer. His strange metabolism seemed to guzzle all sorts and work it off, leaving him, if not slim, certainly *not* over-weight. Sampson and Taffy shook their heads.

Alice, head on one side, said, 'A Kit Kat?' She hesitated. 'Er, no … a Mars Bar, please.'

Gus waited. He was used to these conversations with Alice.

'A choc chip muffin. That's what I want.'

'Sure?'

'Definitely.'

He'd reached the door, when she said, 'Wait, actually, I'll have a white chocolate chip cookie.'

Gus nodded and left. He made it halfway down the corridor before Alice poked her head out the door and called after him.

'What, changed your mind again?' he said, laughing. 'Don't tell me it's the Kit Kat after all?'

She shook her head. 'No, still the white chocolate cookie, but I'll get it myself. Shamshad Ul Haq has just turned up wanting to speak to you.'

'Yeah?' He spun around. 'She in one of the kid's rooms?'

'Yep, Hardeep put her in the blue room.'

That was a turn-up for the books. Shamshad had been reluctant to talk to them about her dad, yet here she was at The Fort, asking to speak to him. Maybe she did know something that could shine a light on their investigation, although it seemed unlikely. How could she know anything about the Tattoo Killer?

'Come on, you're with me.'

Alice shouted back into the room. 'Hey, Taffy, nip down to the canteen and get Gus some tea. I'll have a chocolate brownie and get something for Compo, will you?'

Grinning, Gus waited for her, and they walked down two flights of stairs together. 'Any ideas what Shamshad wants?' asked Alice.

'Don't know, but I hope it's something useful. We're going around in circles with this one. All we've got is the forensics, and the hope Lewis Gore has something for us. I don't want there to be another victim before we catch this fucker.'

'Maybe Graeme Weston will give us something?'

Gus shook his head. I'm not sure he's got much to give; besides, he's lawyered up. I'll grab a bite after we've spoken to Shamshad and then tackle Weston.'

He pushed open the door of the child's interview room and saw Shamshad, black leather jacket discarded on the chair beside her and a large brown envelope on the table in front of her. She was tapping the fingers of one hand on her thigh. There were tension lines around her mouth, and the cheeky insolence that had radiated from her last time they'd met seemed somehow diminished.

Alice offered Shamshad a drink, which the girl declined, and then sat down opposite her. Gus pulled out the other chair and joined them.

From nowhere, Gus' stomach emitted a protracted rumble, making Shamshad grin. He returned her grin with a wave of the hand. 'I'm starving. Haven't eaten all day. My dad would say he could 'eat a scabby horse,' and to be honest, right now, that prospect is tempting.' Another rumble filled the room. Gus grimaced. 'You better tell me what you wanted to see me about before I start eating the furniture, Shamshad.'

She pursed her lips for a second, and a small frown dragged her sculpted eyebrows downwards. Gus wondered if she was re-considering sharing whatever it was she'd come to tell them. He leaned back and crossed his legs. 'We need help with this, Sham. If you have something that could shed light on your father's or the other men's murders, you need to share it.'

Exhaling, Sham closed her eyes revealing lined lids with a perfectly symmetrical black flick that gave the impression of a huge tick escaping the corner of each eye.

Who needs validation in the form of a tick for their eyeshadow? wondered Gus.

When she opened them, her eyes met his. 'This is big, Inspector McGuire,' she said and lifted the envelope. Holding it in one hand, she shook out a substantial pile of paperwork and handed the first document to Gus.

Alice leaned over so she, too, could see it. Gus scanned it. As he read, excitement rose in his chest. This had come right out of left field, and he wasn't quite sure how it impacted on his investigation. Leaning forward, he said, 'Where did you get this?'

Sham gave a teenager's shrug, which he interpreted as a nervous gesture rather than disinterest. She studied the ground in silence. Gus gave her the time to consider her words. The contents of the document he'd just seen needed explaining, and he suspected it wasn't going to be easy for Sham.

At last, she began to speak. First, she explained about Neha's admission to hospital and how she'd found the envelope in her bag. Her frown deepened as she described her sister's condition, and Gus' heart went out to the girl. It was easy, because of her bravado, to forget she had, in effect, lost both of her parents at a time when she would already be stressed out with her A-levels.

Shamshad went on to explain Neha was still in hospital, but that she had confronted her about the documents, and Neha had confided in her. The decision to bring everything to Gus, she said, had been mutual. Gus could tell by the way her shoulders slumped she still carried the hurt of her sister's secrecy with her. He hoped the girls could get over it, because they were going to need each other.

'I'm glad you did, Sham. This puts a whole lot of things in a very different light. Where did Neha get this? Did your father, Razaul, give it to her?'

'No, it wasn't him who gave it to her, although he'd told her all about it. You see, I wouldn't see him. I refused. Neha, well, she was more generous with him. She was seeing him behind my back, all this time.' Again, the flash of hurt in her eyes. She sniffed, so Alice pushed a tissue box across the table towards her.

Gus waited until she'd blown her nose and then said, 'So, who *did* give this to your sister, then?'

Biting her lip, Sham hesitated and then said, 'Look, I don't want to get him into trouble. It's already bad enough for his parents right now with all that stuff in the *Chronicle*. Neha and I don't want him caught in the crossfire.'

Gus frowned and studied the document again. 'Are you telling me *Jacob Weston* gave this to your sister?'

Sham grabbed a tissue and wiped her nose. 'Yeah.'

Gus rubbed his fingers and thumb over his chin in a stroking action as he considered what she'd said. 'You're telling me Jacob Weston, son of Christine and Graeme Weston, gave *your* sister copies of his own medical records?'

Sitting up straight, an indignant expression on her face, Sham nodded. 'Yeah, that's *exactly* what I'm saying. Believe it or not. I don't care.' She jumped to her feet, picking up the documents and began to thrust them back inside the envelope. She leaned over to grab the document Gus held, but he pulled it away and flapped it in the air. He was glad to see the return of the feisty Sham, however, he still needed to get to the bottom of this. 'Sit down. I do believe you. It's just quite … surprising, isn't it?'

With an exaggerated tut, Sham plonked herself back down and raked her fingers through her spiky hair. 'That's exactly what *I* thought.' Eyes wide, she eyeballed them. 'I've researched it, you know. Googled it. It's …'

'A blood disease,' said Gus. 'I know. My mum's a carrier, and so am I.'

Alice's mouth formed an O.

Seeing Alice's stunned reaction, Gus grinned. 'For me, it doesn't impact on my day-to-day life; unfortunately for young Jacob Weston, it does, because clearly both of his parents carry the gene, which he then inherited. Looks like he has Cooley's anaemia or, for the uninformed like yourself, Alice, thalassemia major. The implications on his health are quite severe. Blood transfusions every few weeks, lasting about four hours a shot. That's why he was at the haematology department today with his mum. It's all falling into place.'

Alice frowned. 'I thought only black people or Asians could inherit thalassemia.'

Sham glanced at Gus, and when he grinned, she said, 'Or those from Mediterranean countries. Mrs Weston's dad is Greek. I remember hearing that on the news on Monday. Someone was calling her husband another Farage with double standards because his wife is Greek.'

Gus frowned. Sham was fidgeting on her chair with a smile that said she knew something they didn't. 'So, Sham, are you trying to tell me that Graeme Weston is also of Mediterranean descent?'

Her smile became a wide grin, and her eyes sparkled. 'No ... I'm telling you *Jacob* Weston's dad is Asian.'

'Graeme Weston's of Asian descent?' Gus couldn't believe it. The man was fair with blue eyes and almost Aryan looks. That didn't make sense. And then, Sham rummaged in the envelope and pulled out a second document. 'No, not *Graeme Weston* ... His real dad!'

'What?' Alice and Gus spoke in unison.

Gus grabbed the birth certificate that Sham proffered. 'Shit, Al. It says here Christine Weston is the mother, and Razaul Ul Haq is the father of Jacob Weston.'

Gus fell back into the chair. This was mad. How could Razaul Ul Haq be Jacob Weston's father? Didn't Graeme Weston realise? How could he not? Surely, he'd have set eyes on his son's birth certificate before now. Why would he be party to a cover up of this magnitude, particularly with his political views? Why would he knowingly raise a mixed-race child as his own? It was all so confusing.

Gus watched as Sham extracted a third document from the envelope. This one was one of Razaul Ul Haq's medical records, and it confirmed that Razaul Ul Haq did indeed carry the thalassemia gene.

'Neha told me my dad confided in her because he wanted her to know our half-brother. Jacob and Neha have been meeting-up in secret for the past year.'

'In secret?'

'Well, in secret from his dad ... well, Graeme Weston. Christine and my dad knew.'

'Wow,' said Gus, thinking this put Christine and Razaul's affair in a very different light and opened up another possible motive for Graeme Weston to kill Razaul Ul Haq. It still didn't make it feasible Weston was the Tattoo Killer, though, and Ul Haq carried the same tattoo as the other victims. Perhaps Weston wasn't the killer, but he was certainly linked to this in some way. 'You did right to bring these in, Sham.'

She shook her head. 'There's more.' Tipping the envelope over the table, she allowed the last of the contents to spill out. It was photos of Razaul Ul Haq and Christine Weston having sex. Gus recognised one from Jez Hopkins article in the newspaper. There were many, and all of them appeared to have been taken without Christine and Razaul's knowledge.

'Did Jacob give those to Neha, too?'

Sham grimaced, 'Yeah. He told Neha someone sent them to his dad, well, Weston, and that Weston hit his mum because of it. Jacob found them and sneaked them out of the house. After he found out our dad was killed, he didn't want Weston destroying them.'

Gus knew Weston had hit his wife. He'd seen the evidence on Christine's cheek. 'Did you or Neha leak them to the *Bradford Chronicle* then, Sham?'

Sham gasped. 'No, I reckon that must have been Jacob. Neha says Jacob hates Weston. Don't know how he'd feel after finding out his real dad was dead.'

God only knew what Jacob Weston was feeling right now. Why would he publicly humiliate his mum like that though? Gus was sure the boy loved his mum, even if he behaved like a teenager at times ... he was entitled to; after all, that's exactly what he was.

He raised an eyebrow at Alice. 'Looks like I'll have plenty to talk to Weston about after all. Even if he lawyers up, he'll be hearing all about this. Get Sampson and Taffy to bring Christine in for questioning, too, please. I think the shit's really going to hit the fan for them when this goes public, and I don't want them at their home address when it does. Oh, and tell Sampson we may not need that CCTV from the *Chronicle* after all. I suspect young Jacob Weston will admit to delivering those photos.'

'Reckon the media will camp out there?'

Gus snorted. 'No, I'm more concerned about a possible backlash against Christine Weston from her husband's loyal supporters. Book them a hotel, and get a uniform to stay with them.'

Alice nodded, and Gus turned to Sham. 'I'm going to have to speak to Neha, you know? We'll do that tomorrow, and we'll be gentle with her.' He reached out a hand and placed it on the girl's arm. 'How are you?'

Sham shrugged, and despite her lopsided grin, her eyes were filled with tears. 'Well, I've gained a half-brother. I didn't know my dad. Didn't give him a chance. Guess my mum's poison worked on me. I've got Neha, so I'll be alright. *We'll* be alright. I'll make sure of that. Right now, though, I feel I only know half the story. Can you tell Christine Weston that when she's up for it, Neha and I would like to speak with her? Try to understand why she and our dad didn't stay together, when they clearly had feelings for each other.'

Chapter 74

21:20 The Fort

'Who the fuck leaked it then?' Gus was incensed. The nine o'clock news had just revealed Lewis Gore had been found alive and was in hospital at BRI. However, not content with that, they'd also leaked every detail they'd kept hidden about the tattoos … and all Professor Carlton's theories about the tattoo site possibly being symbolic of impotence or sexual confusion.

He slammed his palm onto the desk top, ignoring the smarting pain and yelled again, 'Well?'

Sampson, Taffy and Alice stood in silence. Gus knew they were waiting for his anger to abate before they said anything to him. He needed to calm down. It wasn't their fault the news he had so carefully omitted in his earlier press conference had found its way to the ears of journalists. They were insidious, deceptive and full of wiles. It could have been anyone from the paramedics to the hospital staff to a uniformed officer who'd let it slip … or, as Gus suspected, a combination of all of the above.

Running fingers through his dreads, he took a deep breath and focussed his mind on what he needed to do. 'Make sure Gore's room is policed at all times. I want an officer at the family home too. I won't have any of his family at risk. Carlton thinks the knowledge Gore isn't dead might make the Tattoo Killer escalate. We need to be prepared.' Time could be running out for the next unknown victim.

'Sampson, get the word out to uniforms to be doubly vigilant. Anything suspicious, and they act … got it? We've got no time for double-checking things. Get uniforms at known dogging sites, near the gay bars, on Thornton Road and Lumb Lane. Anywhere our killer might think of as being an area of deviant behaviour.'

He turned to Compo. 'Why don't we have a lead on how these victims interact with our killer? There's *got* to be an intersection ... a meeting point. Something in common between them that links them to the killer. We need to find it.

'Anything come through on the helpline? Come on. We need to go over and over what we know already. The answer must be in there somewhere.'

Compo shook his head. 'I've been running all sorts of permutations through my system, and I keep coming up blank. It's as if he's selecting them completely at random.'

'Just keep at it. Something will pop.'

'Gus, Graeme Weston's solicitor is asking when we're interviewing his client,' said Alice.

Gus snorted. 'He can wait. I don't think he can give us anything right now. My priority is either identifying the next victim or identifying the killer. Let's get cracking.'

Chapter 75

21:45 The Kill Site

'It's all going to hell, Tara, and it's all that stupid journalist's fault. I had everything so well planned, and now, he's gone and spoiled everything. Can you believe the things they were saying? It was disgusting. Making out I was a *pervert*. That I get some sort of thrill from what I do. Said I was a poof. Do you hear that, Tara … me, a poof? Well, that made me laugh! Idiots!

'I know who's behind it all. It's that Detective Inspector McGuire. He's got an agenda. He's the one who leaked all that filth to the press. Acting all innocent at his press conference, hiding that Gore was still alive, and then, behind the scenes, he leaks everything.

'He wanted to humiliate me, I reckon. That's why he released details of the tattoo. Revealed the tattoo site.

'AAAgh!

'It makes me so cross they've missed the whole point of them. Felt like shouting out loud 'IT'S A WARNING TO THEM NOT TO PROCREATE!'

'*Sexual?* Makes me want to vomit. As if anyone could get anything sexual from touching their wrinkled, brown slithery penises.

'Gus McGuire will have to pay … sooner rather than later. That's something that *is* on my agenda.

'Have an apple, Tara. There, there, you like that don't you?

'What shall I do? What shall I do? First, that ghastly photo in the newspaper, and now, it seems that the nigger's still alive. I was sure he was dead. He didn't come 'round like the others did. He was like a big lump of burnt meat ... a barbecued carcass, black and disgusting. Real waste of time, he was. Nonetheless, I had to stamp my mark on him, just the same. The whole point of the tattoos is they're a symbol of purity. What better place to put them than right there. Right on their sex. Right where it hurts. Anybody seeing that will remember and be warned against procreating impure genes.

'It wasn't the same tattooing a dead man, or as I've since discovered, an unconscious one. No screaming, no writhing against the ties. Made it a bit ... shall we say ... pedestrian. You won't understand, Tara. All you're interested in is sugar lumps, apples and hay and warm rugs, and someone to whisper sweet nothings in your ear. If only life could be so easy. If only humans were like you.

'He must be tough, though, that Lewis Gore. Mind you, those wogs are, aren't they? Big and beefy with no brains ... just brawn. That'll be what saved him, I should think ... his leather skin. Tattooing him was more difficult than usual. Darkie skin's tougher than Paki skin ... of course, I had to shave him. And that was quite vile. Coarse, filthy hair all curly and vile. You know, Tara? I couldn't even see the ink, because he was so dark. Makes my skin crawl touching them. Unclean animals.

'Doubt anybody would've missed him, either. That wife of his would've been glad to see the back of him. Wonder how many STIs he brought home from his 'business' with the whores.

'Wonder what state he's in. Doubt he can tell them anything. It was dark when I grabbed him, and I had my hoodie on. Anyway, I was careful. I always am, and he was out of it.

'Did I tell you he wasn't really dead, Tara? Yes, of course I did. I'm forgetting. I thought he was dead, whereas he was really just unconscious. Must have misjudged the Propofol. Haven't been able to store it properly either … maybe that's affected it. Next time, I'll increase the dose a tad – make sure. I'll have to get more. My stock's running low, and I don't know how I can get more from the vet. I'll think on that. Don't worry, sweetie, that Gore person will never be able to tell them anything.

'My job is even more important now, though, Tara. I've got to take the heat off Graeme so he can rise to the forefront again. Need to minimise the impact of his wife's actions. Won't go after her, though. Not this time. Got to play a long game. I'll get her in the end, though, but for now, I know who I'll go after.

'Impotent! How dare they? Maybe I'll leave an extra message next time … just to make it clear.

'Yes, and *that* will give me the greatest amount of pleasure.

'Time to go now. I'll be back, Tara. Don't worry. I'll be back later on tonight.'

Chapter 76

22:15 The Fort

Graeme Weston had been brought up from the cells ten minutes previously. Gus, with Alice, watched him through the mirror. He was dishevelled, and judging by the bags under his eyes and the way he guzzled the bottle of water he'd been given, he also had a hell of a hangover.

Good! Gus didn't want the smarmy little prick firing on all cylinders. Weston sprawled in his chair, scratching his stomach and grimacing every time he moved his head. He was a real sight, and Gus was glad. They were nearing something momentous, and he was keen to prise whatever gem of information Weston had been keeping to himself. Perhaps the pressure of keeping all those secrets about his son's real parentage and his wife's continued affair had proved too much for him. Everyone had a breaking point, after all. He couldn't rule out the possibility the first two victims had been a practise for the main event – Razaul Ul Haq – and maybe Lewis Gore was just to keep them guessing.

He grinned at Alice. 'Come on.'

When they walked in, Weston barely moved. Gus tossed another bottle of water at him and was pleased when the man's reactions made him move his upper body upwards to catch it. His face creased, and he released an 'Ow.'

'Hungover, are we?' Gus' tone voice was solicitous.

'*We?*' said Weston. 'You'll never be one of *us*. So, there's no point in pretending. Folk like you know deep down

343

inside that they're inferior. That they're not capable of the things *we* are.' He waved his hand in a nonchalant way. 'Doesn't matter how PC the goody-two-shoes try to be; you lot will *never* get there.'

Gus smiled and, placing the folder he carried on the table, pulled a chair out and sat down. He turned to Alice, who joined him at the table. 'There speaks the racist with blood down his shirt, stinking of vomit and sweat, with a wife who screws Asian men.' He flipped open the folder and spread the photos in front of Weston.

Weston averted his eyes. 'I want my solicitor. I also demand to be released. You're no doubt aware by now no harm has befallen my wife, so let me go.'

Alice smiled. 'Aw, that's a shame. If that was all we'd arrested you on, then we could, of course, let you go. Unfortunately, there's that small matter of assaulting a police officer. That doesn't go away as easily.'

'However,' Gus gathered up the photos and put them back in his folder, 'if you were to co-operate, perhaps that could be forgotten too. How about it?'

The door opened, and a suited man with white hair and a stoop walked in.

'Ah, here's your solicitor now, Mr Weston. Let's crack on, Alice.' He gestured towards the recorder, which Alice set up, leaving Weston's solicitor no option other than to sit down.

Introductions over, Gus began, 'We've received some information which gives a whole new perspective on things. It seems there is some question over your son's parentage.'

Weston jolted upright and glowered at Gus. 'What the fuck are you talking about?'

Pleased to have gained a reaction so easily, Gus smiled. 'Is there no question over the parentage of your son?'

'None of your business.'

Weston's solicitor leaned over and whispered in his ear. Weston glowered and shook his head.

'So,' said Gus, bringing Jacob's medical records from the folder. 'It says here your son suffers from the blood disease beta thalassemia. He has the thalassemia major strain, which means unequivocally that *both* parents must carry the thalassemia gene. Do you carry that gene?'

The solicitor made to intervene, but Weston growled, 'Shut up, I'll deal with this. How did you get my son's medical records? Do you have a warrant? You can't use this sort of thing against me when it's been obtained illegally.'

'Actually, it hasn't been obtained illegally. It was given to us by a relative of your son, and I wonder if you could answer my question. Are you a carrier of the thalassemia gene?'

Weston shot a glance at his solicitor, who then whispered in his ear. He leaned back and folded his arms across his chest. 'No comment.'

Although Gus had hoped Weston would break straight away, he hadn't counted on it. So, not betraying his disappointment, he continued, 'Are you the biological father of Jacob Weston?'

'No comment!'

'Do you know who the biological father of Jacob Weston is?'

'No comment.'

'Is Razaul Ul Haq, Jacob Weston's biological father?'

Despite the inevitable, 'No comment,' the twitch at the corner of his eye betrayed Graeme Weston's increased anxiety.

'Did you kill Razaul Ul Haq because you were jealous of his continued relationship with your wife?'

As Weston spat, 'No comment!' his fists clenched round the plastic bottle, bending it out of shape.

Gus smiled. 'Did you kill Asim Farooq and Manish Parmar, and abduct and seriously injure Lewis Gore to misdirect the police enquiry away from Mr Ul Haq's murder?'

The solicitor laid a hand on his client's sleeve, but Weston jerked his arm away. 'This is a fucking set-up. This is you lot being lazy. That's what this is. No fucking comment.'

Gus noted Weston's increased use of swearing with satisfaction. This was a sure sign he was getting to the man, and he fully intended to keep the pressure up. 'Did you kill Razaul Ul Haq because he threatened to expose your son's true parentage to your Albion First cronies, thus affecting your subsequent selection chances?'

'No comment.'

The odour of sweat from Weston wafted across the table, making Gus want to gip. Nevertheless, he continued throwing questions at the other man. 'Do you know which of your party members ordered the City Park bomb?'

Head bowed, voice tight, Weston said, 'No fucking comment.'

Gus turned to Weston's solicitor. 'We will be applying for an extension to further keep your client in custody. In the meantime, he will be returned to the cells. If you need time to consult with your client, you can use this interview room for now.'

Looking at the clock on the wall, he stood up. 'Where do you go on Wednesday afternoons every six weeks, Graeme?'

Weston's eyes narrowed, and a slow sneer spread across his face. 'No comment, brown boy.'

Gus held the other man's gaze for a long moment, then he turned and nodded to the solicitor before terminating the interview and leaving the room. Glad to be away from Weston's stench, Gus, with Alice, walked along the corridor only to be met by Taffy running towards them. 'Have you heard, sir? Christine Weston's house has been fire-bombed. The fire brigade is there, and Christine Weston and her son are en-route here.'

'Shit,' said Gus. 'I should have got her in protective custody earlier. Are they okay?'

Taffy shrugged. 'As far as I know, they smashed the living room window and tossed in a Molotov cocktail, yelling 'Paki lover,' before running off. Christine was in the kitchen, and Jacob was upstairs. She grabbed him, and they ran into the back garden where she phoned 999. No injuries reported, though they'll be in shock. The fire brigade doused the fire, which was contained in the front room.'

Gus' stomach gurgled, reminding him, yet again, he still hadn't managed to grab anything to eat. 'Right, Alice, we need to talk to Christine Weston as soon as she comes in. I need something to eat first. Give me ten minutes, will you?'

Chapter 77

22:55 The Fort

Feeling marginally better after a warm coffee and a Kit Kat that Alice had hidden from Compo at the bottom of her desk, Gus was all set to speak with Christine Weston and her son. He had no intention of going in guns blazing as he had with her husband. He suspected by now, after grieving for her lover and being frightened of her husband and his party, Christine Weston would be eager to work with him. After all, she still had Jacob to think about.

Christine and Jacob waited in the room where Alice and Gus had spoken to Shamshad Ul Haq in earlier. They had fish and chips brought in for Christine and her son, and smelling the tangy vinegar in the air, Gus wished he'd had the foresight to order some for himself. The tuna sandwich had barely hit the sides. His stomach growled, and smiling, Christine pushed her half-eaten packet towards him. 'I'm done, Inspector. You have them.'

A blush warmed his face. He really needed to stop interviewing people on an empty stomach. Knowing he still had a good few hours of work before him, he said, 'Don't mind if I do, Mrs Weston. Not eaten properly all day.'

With a rueful head shake, Alice snaffled a chip and laid the folder containing the documents Sham had given them earlier on the table.

'Shamshad Ul Haq came in to the station earlier and gave us some documents.' She turned to Jacob. 'Documents and photographs you gave to Neha Ul Haq.'

Christine gasped and frowned at her son. 'You gave Neha documents? What sort of documents, Jacob?'

Gus felt sorry for the lad. He remembered facing similar scrutiny from his own mum at that age, and his reaction had been similar to Jacob's now.

Shrugging, the boy averted his eyes. 'Just stuff.'

Alice smiled at him and turned to his mum. 'Look, Mrs Weston, perhaps you could discuss this with Jacob later, but right now, we need to ask you both a few questions.'

When Mrs Weston nodded her agreement, Alice continued, 'Neha has been ill and is in hospital.'

It was Jacob's turn to gasp at this news. He sat up straight, a frown drawing his brows together. *So, he really cares about his half-sister,* thought Gus, as the boy's voice rose.

'She's ill? Neha's ill?' He turned to his mother. 'We need to go see her, Mum.'

Alice shook her head. 'She'll be fine, Jacob. Maybe you can visit her tomorrow. For now, though, we need to talk about the things you gave her, okay?'

'You mean my birth certificate and my medical records and my dad's medical records?'

Oh, oh! Gus saw the shock flash across Christine's face. Judging by her reaction, she'd had no idea her son had done that. Christine blinked. For a few seconds, she said nothing, just stared at him, her mouth half-open. 'You gave those things to Neha?' She shook her head. 'Why? Why would you do that, Jacob?'

Jacob, eyes averted, studied his chips. As if hating the sight of them, he rolled the greasy packets together and flung them onto the table. His chest began to heave. Gus wondered if he should intervene. A shimmer of tears glistened in the boy's eyes, and his mother was pale, her face taut and anguished. The last thing he wanted was for things to get out of control. He wasn't sure he could cope with a hysterical teenager at the best of times.

However, from somewhere, Jacob appeared to gain some self-control. He glanced at his mother, his expression pleading. Gus noticed he clenched and unclenched his fists as he spoke, and a weariness sank to his stomach and threatened to overtake him. Why did some families seem to set themselves on this self-destructive mode?

Sounding defiant, if scared, Jacob said, 'I was scared *he'd* destroy them, now he's standing in that stupid by-election.' Rubbing a hand over his eyes, he continued, 'Thought he'd try to get rid of all the evidence. I couldn't have him doing that, Mum. Not when Dad's dead.' And tears streamed down his face.

Christine put her hand on her son's arm. 'Oh, Jacob!' She leaned forward and cupped his head with her hands. With her thumbs, she rubbed the tears away as they fell from his eyes. Her hands trembled as she did so, and she swallowed hard before saying, 'I love you, Jakey ... so much.'

Her words seemed to strengthen the lad's resolve, for he took a deep breath and rubbed his tears away with the back of his hand. 'I'm sorry, Mum.'

Poor sod. He was trying so hard to be a man, but he was really still only a boy. It was hard to deal with stuff when you were on the cusp of manhood, hormones all over the place, and to top it all, Jacob Weston had all the trauma of losing his biological dad and being at odds with his mother's husband. Not an easy situation for anyone.

Christine shook her head. 'It doesn't matter. We just need to help the police now. Sniffing, she sat up straight. 'How can we help?'

Gus dabbed his hands on a bit of soiled newsprint, whilst Alice rummaged in her bag before handing him another wet wipe, saying in a resigned tone, 'Here.'

Wiping his hands, he said, 'First of all, are these documents all genuine? Is Razaul Ul Haq Jacob's biological father?'

Christine nodded. 'You know it's almost a relief to admit it all now. It seems like I've been carting this like a weight around my neck for years. It'll be a relief to share it at long last.'

She pulled her son close. At first, he baulked against her, and then, he gave in. It was as if he sensed his mother needed his strength in order to tell her story. The two of them, Christine Weston, bruised and battered with her teenage son cuddled into her arms, made an incongruous sight, leant back on the sofa, looking as if they were about to share a bedtime story. It was unfortunate this particular story didn't have a fairy tale ending.

'I've known Razaul since primary school. At Bolton Woods, we became close for a while.' She smiled. 'Of course, reality got in the way. You didn't date outside your own culture much in those days. His family were traditional, and they arranged a marriage for him to a young girl from his parent's village in Bangladesh. Razaul didn't want to get married. He was young, though, and the pressure was extreme. My parents wouldn't have been happy for me to date a Muslim, so it seemed easier for us to split up. Razaul got married, and I went to university. When I got back, we bumped into each other. He was desperately unhappy, which is no excuse for what we did.'

Gus had heard from his parents how hard it had been for them thirty years ago; seemed like attitudes hadn't changed much. His mother had, as a mixed-race black woman, gone through the foster system in Scotland ridiculed and bullied. She'd struggled through abusive foster families and had, against all odds, managed to get the necessary qualifications to get to Edinburgh University where she met his dad. The way the auld man told it, it had been love at first sight for him ... not so much for his mum, who was doubtful of everyone's intentions. Gus smiled at the thought. His mother was still independent, although his parents depended on each other with a ferocious love Gus hoped one day to emulate for himself. His parents' relationship had been fraught with difficulties, judgements and negative expectations from the start. Yet, they were still strong together.

Christine, wiped her hair from her brow with a trembling hand. 'His wife had a series of miscarriages and suffered from depression. His parents had both died, and he was grieving for them. We began to meet in secret. Then, one day, he told me his wife was pregnant, and he had to stop seeing me. I agreed. This was his chance to be happy, so we split up again.'

Gus saw the sadness in her eyes, as her hand smoothed her son's hair. They were so alike. Yet, at close quarters, he could also discern Jacob's likeness to his dead father. What a hopeless situation to be in.

'A couple of years later, we bumped into each other, and Razaul confided how difficult things were with his wife. They had two beautiful twin daughters of whom he was so proud, but his wife was unstable. She threatened suicide repeatedly, and eventually threatened to kill the children if he didn't leave.'

She lifted the glass of water Alice had brought her to her lips and took a long sip before continuing. 'Razaul went to live with his brother, but he was concerned for Shamshad and Neha's safety. Eventually, he asked his brother to take his wife and daughters in, and he moved out. We continued to see each other. His wife's behaviour became more extreme, and she was admitted to Lynfield

Mount Psychiatric Hospital. This continued on and off for years. Razaul continually tried to make the marriage work. They'd live together for a while, and then, she'd become ill. Finally, she managed to poison the girls against him.'

'Only Shamshad, Mum,' said Jacob.

'Yes, that's right, only Shamshad.' She took another drink. 'Neha became ill, and he visited her regularly, but Shamshad would have nothing to do with him. However, before that, when the twins were around three, I became pregnant. I didn't know what to do. My parents are strict Catholic, and although I was in my twenties by then, I didn't want to disappoint them. For years, Graeme had pursued me, and on occasion, I'd gone out with him for a few months at a time. When he discovered my predicament, he proposed. I wasn't keen initially, because I knew his political views, however he was insistent, and he was besotted.'

Her shoulders lifted dismissively. 'He wasn't so awful then. He used to treat me like a princess … like something precious. He cherished me. Of course, as his involvement with the BNP, and then later, Albion First increased, that all changed. He resented me; yet, he wouldn't let me go.'

Gus found it difficult to imagine allowing someone else to bring up his child, and he found it equally difficult to imagine Graeme Weston bringing up a child with a Pakistani father. 'Did Graeme know who Jacob's real father was?'

'Yes, he did. I think he thought it gave him one over on Razaul. He'd always been jealous of him at school. Razaul was handsome and popular. Graeme was chubby and not so popular. I think he enjoyed the power he had over both me and Razaul. He knew how awful he could make things for Razaul. He made Razaul sign an agreement to have nothing to do with Jacob. When Jacob was old enough, and it became clear that Graeme was not going to be the father to Jacob I'd hoped for, Razaul and I decided to ignore the agreement. I introduced Razaul and Jacob. My son deserved to know the father who loved him.'

'And was Razaul happy to sign his son away?'

A flash of red spread across Christine's cheeks, and she scowled at Gus. 'Of course he wasn't happy with the situation. Neither of us were. What else could we do? We had to just get on with it ... none of us knew things would end up like this.' She balled her hand into a fist. 'We wouldn't have done it, if we had.'

Oh, for a crystal ball.

Unclasping her fist, Christine exhaled. 'When we registered Jacob's birth, I couldn't bear to put Graeme's name on the birth certificate, and as he was disinterested anyway, he didn't check. Well, not then, anyway. Later, when we discovered Jacob had thalassemia, Graeme insisted we cover it up. He was heavily involved with Albion First by then and didn't want anything to jeopardise his progress. I think the business with Razaul made him more ardent, if anything.'

Although this was pretty much what he'd expected to hear, it was beyond him how Christine had been able to live with Weston when his views were so vile. 'That must have been hard for you.'

'It was, although I had Jacob and I had Razaul ... and for a while, Graeme was happy to just cover up. In hindsight, half of the attraction was the fact he wouldn't be outdone by an Asian. He couldn't comprehend how I could have allowed myself to be with Razaul. It gave him a hold over me. Gave him control.'

That Gus could understand. Graeme Weston liked to be in control, and he would do anything to maintain his power. The question was, would he fabricate such an elaborate plot to get rid of Razaul Ul Haq? Gus didn't think so. He'd no doubt Weston would eventually have disposed of Razaul one way or another, but not this way. Besides which, it didn't fit with Sebastian Carlton's profile of a narcissistic male with issues with his sexuality.

'So, you carry the thalassemia major gene too?'

Christine gave a hollow laugh. 'Would you believe it? What were the odds of a lass, with a Greek dad and a Yorkshire mum, and a Bangladeshi man *each* carrying the same genetic flaw that could lead to Jacob's condition? Most times, you'd expect a broadening of the gene pool to have only benefits.'

Gus contemplated this. It was a complete fluke both Razaul and Christine carried the gene. Gus knew about it, being a carrier himself. Until now, he hadn't really thought of the implications of it. Now, he most certainly would. Although Jacob was doing well, the condition was a serious and restrictive one. The boy would not have an easy life. 'Couldn't you get a divorce? After all, by the time Razaul's wife was sectioned, you and he could have settled down together. You could have left Graeme.'

Christine flinched. 'I was too scared. Albion First are violent, and I'd seen the sort of things they'd done to other wives who'd tried to get out. So ... I stayed. I protected Jacob, and we stayed. When he was old enough, I made sure Jacob understood the situation, and he spent time with his dad ... his real dad.' She ruffled his hair. 'Had Graeme been a real father to Jacob, things would have been very different. I would have kept away from Razaul, and Jacob would have known nothing about this.'

Jacob pulled away from her. 'No!' His eyes flashed. 'How could you say that? I'd never have known Dad or Neha ... or Shamshad.'

'You're right, Jakey. You've got two sisters out of this mess, and that's good.'

Gus couldn't begin to imagine being married to a racist. How had Graeme treated Jacob? From the boy's disparaging comments, it seemed not very well. What a bloody fiasco, and now, everything was going to end up in the public eye. 'You do realise that some of this will hit the media?'

Christine lifted her chin. 'I've got Jacob, and he's got his sisters. We'll muddle through somehow, Inspector.'

Gus observed the mother and her boy. He knew they would survive this, if Albion First would let them, and if the media would cut them some slack. 'I don't suppose you know the answer to this. Graeme books a Wednesday afternoon off every six weeks, regular as clockwork, any ideas where he goes?'

Christine snorted. 'Oh, yes. I know exactly where he goes. He comes with us. Jacob needs a regular transfusion, and Graeme never trusted us to go alone. He comes with us every six weeks to make sure I don't reveal anything I shouldn't. He'd prefer to go to the Yorkshire clinic, but the specialist clinic is at BRI, and it eats him up being there with blacks and Pakistanis.' Her eye took on a steely glint. 'I enjoy seeing him suffer whilst we're there.' She lifted her fingers to her bruised cheek. 'Mind you, he gets his own back.'

The extent of the control Graeme Weston exerted over his wife made Gus more determined to let the man rot in the cells for as long as he could. It was no more than he deserved.

Alice leaned forward and looked directly at Jacob. With an apologetic smile at Christine, she pulled the photos from the folder and showed the top one to Jacob. 'Jacob, did you also send these to Jez Hopkins at the *Bradford Chronicle*?'

Christine's face paled. 'What? No? You didn't, did you, Jacob?' Apparently, the expression on his face was enough to tell her he had. Her voice wobbled when she spoke. 'Where did you even get those photos, Jacob?'

Gus held his breath as he watched the interplay between mother and son. How horrible for them this had to be discussed in the presence of strangers. Jacob was near to tears, and Christine wasn't faring any better. At times like this, he hated his job.

Jacob, head lowered, spoke. 'I found them in the living room. I'd heard you arguing with *him* on Sunday, and I saw what he'd done to your face on Monday. I was so angry, Mum. He'd no right to hit you. When I found the photos, I didn't know what to do, so I took them, and then, we found out Dad was dead ...'

'Oh, Jacob!' Tears flowed unheeded down Christine's cheek as she reached for her son.

Gulping back his own tears, Jacob allowed himself to be gathered in his mother's arms. 'I'm sorry, Mum. I really am. I just wanted to do something to help you ... to stop him. What if he killed my dad?'

Christine met Gus' eye. 'I don't think he would, but if he did, then Inspector McGuire will make sure he's punished for it.'

Feeling like he'd just been issued with an ultimatum, Gus held her gaze and nodded. If Graeme Weston was responsible for the deaths of three men, and the abduction and torture of another, he would be held to account and punished for it. Maybe it was time to consult with Sebastian Carlton again. See how recent developments had affected his profile of the Tattoo Killer.

Chapter 78

23:35 The Fort

Watching the CCTV footage from Mother Hubbard car park was beginning to do Gus' head in. They identified Mr Blackhurst's vehicle driving into the area, and they saw him getting out and heading into the fish and chip shop. His vehicle stayed in vision the entire time, unfortunately the vehicle that pulled in behind it, bearing the other old man's number plate, was partially obscured. They couldn't get a clear vision, although they could identify a figure exiting the vehicle and moving to the rear of Blackhurst's car. The person seemed small, and because their physique was concealed by baggy clothing, it was difficult to get an idea of their exact size and shape.

Compo had tried everything to enhance the footage to no avail, and the moving images were exacerbating Gus' tension headache. He should call it a day, but he had the uneasy feeling this person was unravelling. The apparent carelessness with Lewis Gore made it look that way. A snatched conversation earlier with Sebastian Carlton had supported this theory. The leaked information to the press would accelerate this unravelling, Sebastian had no doubt. Like Gus, Carlton had his reservations about Weston being their man. The shadowy figure on the screen could, at a push, be Weston; however, they had nothing to link the vehicle to him. In fact, all of Compo's searches of their prime suspects hadn't thrown up a vehicle to match the killer. Now, all Compo could do was try to crunch numbers and try to narrow down the number of Vauxhall Vivaro panel van owners to the target zones.

With Weston in custody, Gus had put a watch on Michael Hogg. The truth was, Gus would have liked to put an officer on each of the Albion First members, but with the recent swell in their numbers, it was impossible. All he could do was keep an eye on the key players.

He was missing something, and time was running out. Sebastian Carlton reckoned the error with Lewis Gore would enrage their killer even more. He reckoned he would take it as a personal affront and would hate the idea of a black person having one up. The only problem was because they hadn't yet come across a link between the victims, other than the Weston-Ul Haq one, they couldn't even hazard a guess as to who the next target would be. Sebastian Carlton had closeted himself in a spare interview room and was re-working his profile. Maybe he'd come up with something definitive, and Compo was still working on trying to find links between the victims.

'Take Razaul Ul Haq out of the equation for now, Comps,' said Gus, envying the other man's energy. 'He might be the anomaly. Focus on a link between the other three victims. They must have crossed paths with our killer at some point. All we need to do is find out when and where.'

Gus had sent the others home. He saw no need for everyone to be knackered the next day. So, for now, only he and Compo were left in the room. He'd thought Alice seemed tired and knew she wouldn't go home if the others were still there. Despite Sampson and Taffy's protests, he'd insisted. Anyway, Gus could just as easily *not* sleep here as he could at home. Compo, on the other hand, often pulled all-nighters and never seemed phased by it. He once told Gus he could cat-nap anywhere.

With the gentle buzz of Compo's computers and the occasional scrape of furniture as Compo wheeled his chair from side to side, Gus scrunched down in his chair, propped his feet on the table and closed his eyes against the harsh fluorescent lighting.

Thursday

Chapter 79

02:15 Doe Park, Denholme

His headlights barely pierced the cloying darkness of the winding lane down to Doe Park reservoir. Jez Hopkins had left the streetlights of Denholme village behind when he passed the children's playing field and took a left down the pot-holed track leading down to the reservoir. Through his rear-view mirror, he glanced at the lights behind him, ever conscious of the sinking feeling in the pit of his stomach as they faded in the distance. This felt off to him. The text message from a withheld number ordering him to drive here had, in the bright lights of his flat, seemed strange but not ominous. He'd assumed it was from Michael Hogg or one of Albion First thugs wanting to check he'd done as they'd asked and submitted the press release.

Now, though, in the dark, it seemed weird. He was used to getting strange requests to meet in outlandish places. Once, he had to meet a drug dealer on top of Ilkley Moor in the middle of a damn blizzard, and he'd been glad he had. He'd nearly contracted pneumonia, and it had taken him hours to defrost, yet it had been worth it. The scoop he got about failed police drug raids throughout the region and police incompetency had graced the paper's front pages for nearly a fortnight.

Then, there was that homeless guy who insisted he meet in his 'camp' in the bushes next to the Boating Pavilion café in Lister Park at midnight. That, again, had been worth the discomfort. Turned out the bloke had bought a lottery ticket and won fifty grand on it. He wanted to give it to his wife and children anonymously, so he could continue to live under the radar ... stupid, really, to have come to Jez about that. He had a moral obligation to report, and that's what he did. The emotional stories resulting from that article had kept going for weeks, and then, when the fella committed suicide in the boating pond a few weeks later, Jez's initial news articles had got a second, regurgitated, airing.

The random appearance of a horse bucking its head, inches from his passenger window, followed by the melancholy bray of another animal nearby, gave him the jitters. Clutching the steering wheel tight, he pulled his body forward and peered through the windscreen. The moon had disappeared behind a cloud, specks of rain dotted the glass, and his wiper's rhythmic scrape all combined to freak him out.

What if it wasn't one of Michael Hogg's crew who had texted? After all, they didn't need to meet him to find out if he'd submitted their whitewash of their führer's wife's bedroom romp. They could wait until the morning edition. His head almost banged off the window as he hit a large pothole and was nearly catapulted from his seat. Shit, this was madness, what was he doing? Maybe they had an exclusive interview for him? 'Behind the Scenes at Camp Nazi' or some such. He grinned. That would make a great headline, though he suspected all he was going to get from them was more of the same claptrap about Graeme Weston being a maligned cuckolded innocent, and, of course, who was to blame? The Pakistanis, blacks or gays, of course. Jez didn't actually hold with all that racist shit, but a story was a story at the end of the day.

The more he thought about it, the less likely it seemed they'd arrange a meeting in quite such a remote place. Thinking of remoteness made a thought spring into his mind. Could this be something to do with the Tattoo Killer? A fox ran in front of his car, and, instincts on high alert, he braked. The fox paused, its disdainful eyes catching the headlights, as, with a swish of its tail, it sidled under the fence and disappeared into the night. Jez released a long slow breath. He was getting spooked. He knew he was nearing the entrance to the reservoir itself, and thoughts of the Tattoo Killer still uppermost in his mind, he allowed his car to roll to a stop, engine idling as he considered. Shuddering, he glanced around him. He'd worked himself up so much, he half-expected a monster to loom out of the shadows.

Reaching over, he flicked the switch to lock all his doors, and then, with a strangled laugh at his stupidity, he flexed his fingers and prepared to drive on. What was he thinking? He wasn't in the Tattoo Killer's target group; he wasn't gay, black or Asian. Nah, the Tattoo Killer wasn't his mysterious caller. He edged forward, eyes searching for the hidden entrance, and then, as he swerved a degree to the right, his headlights caught the outline of a van nestled behind a tree. A figure in baggy clothing was wheeling something down the ramp from the back of the van. It looked like a trolley of some sort. In that instant, all of Jez's instincts screamed at him to drive past, not to stop, to get the hell away from there as fast as he could.

Glad his Corsa was small and nippy, he screeched into the entrance, all set to do a U-turn. The gate to the parking area was padlocked shut, so he rammed his steering wheel to the right, narrowly missing the van, as his Corsa screeched forward sending stones flying under his spinning wheels. An abrupt left yank, and he was moving back to the entrance, ready to head back up Foster Park View to Denholme. Thankful he'd not made the mistake of continuing on the road, which he knew was a dead end,

Jez put his foot on the brake, and tyres barely touching the road, he all but flew back.

In his rear mirror, he saw a shadowy figure wheel the trolley back into the van, slam the door, and then run to the driver's door. Thankful the van had been facing away from the road, Jez was sure he'd gained a few seconds lead as the larger vehicle would surely have more difficulty getting out of that tight spot.

Breathing heavily, he'd just reached the horse, who seemingly sensing his anxiety cantered beside the car to the end of the field. He could hear the van's acceleration behind him, and despite its lack of headlights to show its position, he sensed it was gaining on him. Muttering prayers to a God he generally thought little of, he approached the bend near the swing park and the welcome sight of streetlights. Breathing more easily, he risked a glance behind him and saw the van had now switched its headlights on full, making it impossible for him to see the driver or the number plate. He got to the end of the road and turned left, heading towards Thornton, where he knew he'd be on main roads most of the way.

Chapter 80

03:25 Lister Apartments, Manningham

Punching the steering wheel makes me feel slightly better. I imagine it is Hopkins' smarmy little arrogant face. How I'd love to see his nose squelch open under my fist, blood flying everywhere ... and his teeth? He'd have nothing to smile about when I'd finished with him. Maybe I'd make him eat every one of them. He's got it coming to him.

Wonder what spooked him? I knew he'd come. He is always greedy for a story, always wanting to be in the limelight. *That* had been the easy part. Soon as I'd seen his lights turn the bend at the top, I knew I had him. Wonder if he saw me getting the trolley out. Doubt it. The tree was in the way. That's why I parked there ... so I could get my stuff together, without being seen.

Don't know what he was playing at. I had it all planned. The road down to Doe Park has no cameras, and neither does the little lay-by leading to the car park. It was perfect, just perfect, until that idiot Hopkins got all skittish like a new-born foal and made a run for it. I was really looking forward to getting him. It was no more than he deserved. I was looking forward to hearing him scream, and I bet he is a screamer ... probably a poof as well. Well, he might imagine he's gotten away from me. He should think again. I'm not letting a little gay boy like him off the hook.

Glancing in my side mirror, I see the entrance to the Lister Mills car park. He thought he'd out-manoeuvre me by driving round via Thornton. Thought all the street lights and cameras would protect him, but all that will do is delay the inevitable. I drove back into Bradford via the back roads. Now, all I have to do is wait. It's not perfect, though I'll make it work. A bit of determination goes a long way in this world, and I am determined. Jez Hopkins needs to be punished. I'm not letting him get away with all his sordid little accusations. How dare he accuse me of being gay? Tonight, Jez Hopkins will die.

Chapter 81

03:55 Marriners Drive

Gus missed Bingo. The house always seemed empty without him. However, he knew that when he caught a case, Bingo was better off with his mum. Good for Bingo's mental health … not so good for his. He glanced over at Ringo, his canary with the Beatles haircut. His cage was covered with a cloth, and Gus, much as he was tempted to, had no intention of waking him up. Just because he was lonely didn't mean he should upset his pet's sleep rhythms. His dad had left him a bottle of Talisker, and although it was not his favourite malt whisky, Gus was drawn to it. The sleeping pills hadn't worked, yesterday's morning jog hadn't worked, so maybe the whisky would. With heavy limbs, he pulled himself to his feet and grabbed a glass and some ice from the kitchen, before pouring himself a liberal measure – a bit more than the two fingers he normally allowed himself at night.

He knew he was fading away. In his desire for sleep, he was exercising too much and not eating enough. No wonder he was in a damn state. Every time he fell asleep, the flashbacks about Alice jolted him awake. Only last night in the office, he'd dozed off for five maybe ten minutes tops, only to wake up screaming – with Compo's scared face looming over him. He had to get a fucking handle on this. Last thing he needed was to substitute Alice for Greg in his dreams.

He'd hoped when she came back to work he'd feel better, that the nightmares would stop. If anything, they had intensified. Between those and the panic attacks, he was losing it big time. He knew he had to let go of his guilt regarding Alice, and Greg too.

He raised his glass to the Bob Marley painting on the chimney breast. 'Slainte, Greg!'

Pushing his sleeve up, he studied his tattoo. He'd bloody shown Mo! He'd gone and done it, and now, he was the proud owner of a brand-new tattoo. Idiot thought he was a wuss and wouldn't go through with it, but he'd shown him. However, it was still raw and needed more Bepanthen. Tempted to scratch it, Gus quickly let his sleeve fall back into place. Last thing he needed was to scratch it and end up with it blotchy. It was a work of art, and he'd no intention of spoiling it. It was *his* reminder of his friend.

Pulling a blanket over his lower body, he savoured the last of his whisky, before lying back and resting his head on the pillow he'd brought down from his bedroom. He went over everything they'd have to do today, whilst at the back of his mind, the thought someone else could already be in danger was never far away.

Chapter 82

04:20 The Fort

'I'm telling you. I want to see McGuire, and I want to see him right now!'

The Desk Sergeant watched as Jez Hopkins postured in front of him, spittles of saliva spraying from his mouth. In all his time as an officer, Hardeep Singh had experienced more than his fair share of awkward customers, and he'd no intention of letting a scumbag like Jez Hopkins intimidate him. 'If you don't calm down, sir, you'll be seeing DI McGuire alright … in a cell.'

Hopkins ran his hands though his hair, and like a puppet with its strings severed, he seemed to collapse in on himself. All his bluster dissipated, and his body seemed to shrivel. In a small pleading voice, he said, 'Look, I need to see McGuire. I think the Tattoo Killer came after me.'

Hardeep studied the man, taking note of his appearance. Hopkins was dishevelled, as if he'd been dragged out of bed, *and* he looked frightened. He kept darting glances towards the door as if he expected the killer to burst through The Fort's entrance brandishing a tattoo gun. Sighing, Singh pressed a button to release the inner doors and signalled for the man to come through. It was too early to waken DI Gus McGuire on a whim, so he'd see what the little scrote had to say before contacting his boss. He'd seen how drained Gus was when he'd left only a couple of hours earlier. His blue eyes had been even more haunted than usual as he'd raised a hand in farewell. That was one guy who, no matter how much he tried, couldn't seem to outrun his demons.

He led Hopkins through to a side room, clicked on the light and bade him sit down at a cluttered table, before pushing a packet of digestive biscuits towards the journalist. Hopkins, eyes still darting round, took one and, as if he wasn't really conscious of his actions, began breaking it into small pieces. He inserted each one in his mouth, barely chewing before swallowing. As soon as he'd finished one, he started on another, and all the while, his right leg jogged up and down as if ready to run a marathon, minus the rest of Hopkins' body.

Hardeep didn't bother to ask what Hopkins wanted to drink. He just made coffee – strong and very, very sweet. If there was one thing he knew, it was when someone was in shock, and Hopkins was definitely in shock.

He placed the mug in front of the journalist and sat opposite, arms folded, resting on his large stomach, and sipped his own drink. He waited for Hopkins to take a few sips and calm down. Soon, the sugar worked its magic, and his leg slowed to more of a trot than a canter. When he saw a little colour return to the other man's cheeks, Hardeep spoke. 'Right, tell me what's got you all hot and bothered, lad, and we'll go from there.'

Jez put his mug down and rubbed the palms of his hands down his thighs. He cast his eyes upwards as if trying to recollect verbatim what had happened. 'Got a text about half one from a withheld number saying I should drive to Doe Park in Denholme straight away.' Jez glanced away, and his leg began to bob again.

Hardeep's eyes narrowed. Experience told him that by looking away, Jez was deciding how truthful to be with him. 'Look, lad. If you want our help, it's best you tell us everything. We can't help if you hold things back.'

Jez glanced around, and then, his eyes fixed on an old 'dob in a dealer' poster hanging by one pin on the wall.

He appeared to study it for a few minutes, and then, with an abrupt nod, he looked at Hardeep. Rubbing his hands down his trousers again, he continued. 'Okay. I thought it was Michael Hogg posturing on Graeme Weston's behalf.'

Hardeep had the pulse of The Fort at his fingertips and knew about Weston being arrested. He also knew Gus had raked Jez Hopkins over the coals earlier about those pictures in the *Chronicle*. So, why was Hopkins accepting texts from Michael Hogg? 'Michael Hogg? Firstly, why would he send *you* a text, and secondly, why would he withhold the number?'

Dunking a biscuit in his coffee, Hopkins lifted it, and it broke and splashed back into the mug, showering him with coffee. He cursed and picked up another biscuit which he began to crumble between shaking fingers. 'Yesterday, one of his Albion First thugs turned up at my door unannounced. He gave me a press release and –' His eyes flicked away. 'He threatened me. Not implicitly, you understand, but I got the message: get it in the paper … or else.'

Hardeep reached over and moved the packet of biscuits out of Hopkins' reach. 'So, did you submit it?'

With a shrug, Jez lifted his chin as if to say, 'So what if I did?' and then nodded. ''Course I did. Checked it for typos then submitted it.' He splayed his hands. 'The public's got a right to hear Weston's side of the story, you know. Besides which, I prefer to keep my bones intact.'

Hardeep snorted. He knew exactly the sort of spin Michael Hogg would put on it, and it would all be to beef up the Weston campaign with scant regard for the truth. He was sorry for Weston's missus. Hopkins was hunched over the desk, looking sorry for himself. Hardeep had little sympathy for the journalist. The amount of misery his irresponsible articles had caused the victims of the Tattoo

Killer, not to mention his unfair representation of the police. Well, he deserved some payback.

Keeping his expression neutral, Hardeep said, 'So, you're scared of Michael Hogg and think the text came from him?'

Regaining a modicum of his earlier arrogance, Hopkins snorted. 'Get lost! 'Course not. I wasn't scared. Been to all sorts of drug dens and whorehouses and all sorts. I thought maybe they had some sort of exclusive for me … maybe more images of Christine Weston or something?'

Not bothering to hide either his disbelief *or* his distaste, Hardeep said, 'So you went to the arse end of nowhere, in the middle of the night, in the hope of gaining some saucy images to grace your newspaper's front pages?'

'Well, not exactly. I went to see what they had to say, that's true.'

Hardeep stood up. 'Look, you're beginning to piss me off. You came in here all of a dither, saying the Tattoo Killer was after you, and now, you're waffling on about Albion First, I think you're pulling my strings, trying to get me to get DI McGuire over here so you can get an exclusive. Well, it's not gonna work, lad.'

'No, no, let me finish!' Hopkins pushed his mug away from him. His leg bouncing had accelerated.

With misgivings, Hardeep glared at him. He was in half a mind to toss him onto the street, but there was something in the journalist's eyes that stopped him. He thought it looked very much like real fear. Rolling his eyes, the Sergeant sat back down, glanced at his watch and said, 'Five minutes, and if you've not convinced me, then you're out.'

Not needing to be told twice, Hopkins told the officer what he'd seen in Denholme. By the time he'd reached the part where he headed towards Thornton, whilst the van seemed to head towards the country roads around Wilsden, Hardeep was interested. Very interested. It sounded as if Jez was right. It could have been the Tattoo Killer, although why, for goodness' sake, would he target Hopkins? From all accounts, he was a bit of a Jack-the-Lad with the ladies, but Hardeep hadn't heard rumours of anything 'strange.' Besides which, he was most definitely Caucasian. It didn't make sense.

Hopkins wasn't finished, though.

'I made sure I kept to the main roads and drove along Thornton Road, up to Duckworth Lane and along Lilycroft Road to here. I pulled into my car park at Lister Mills and parked up. Frank, the security guard, was having a cig, so I joined him for a quick fag, and then, he went to do his rounds, and I walked over to exit the premises. I was just crossing from the parking bays to the front of the complex, behind the safety barrier, when a van screeched up, heading straight for me. I jumped onto the kerb. It braked, then did a skidding reverse back towards me. It was the *same* van ... I'm sure of it. The bastard must have doubled back and waited for me to get home. It was the Tattoo Killer. It must've been. Anyway, I dived across the road and ran into here to tell you.'

'Don't suppose you got a good look at the bloke?'

Hopkins shook his head. 'Too dark.'

Hardeep picked up the phone and ordered two officers to check out the Lister apartment buildings. He knew the security guard, Frank – he'd once been a copper – so, Hardeep put in a phone call to him too. He suspected, though, that whoever had put the fear of God into Jez Hopkins would be long gone by now. It was all very intriguing, and one he'd have to pass further up the chain of command.

'Look, Jez, I'll get officers to check it out, and they can escort you back to your flat.'

Seeing that Hopkins was shaking his head furiously, Hardeep added, 'Or I can offer you a bed in the cells for what's left of the night.'

When Hopkins practically bit his hand off to accept, Singh knew he should call Gus. Yet, he was reluctant to overstep the mark. The lad was clearly petrified, if he was prepared to put up with a night in the cells rather than be escorted back to his luxury apartment. Instead, he phoned up to Compo, who he knew would still be fiddling about on his PC. Let someone else make the decision to call in the boss.

Chapter 83

04:45 The Kill Site

Iparked a couple of miles away. I know there's been police activity nearby, so I walked over the fields. I know them like the back of my hand by now, and tonight, I feel the need, despite the rain, to expend some energy. I was so angry ... still am. To be outdone by a half-wit ... makes my blood boil. Tara seems reluctant to come to me at first, so I grab her mane and pull her close. She whinnies and tosses her head. I smile as my fingers tighten, and she complies.

'Do you believe it, Tara? Twice in the one night he got away from me.'

I'm shaking so much, it's difficult to hold my hand still to offer Tara her treat. Poor thing looks puzzled. I release my hold on her and run my fingers through her mane. Her calmness engulfs me ... takes the edge off my rage. Tara always makes me feel better. I can always count on her. The anger begins to drain a little. I'm still angry. I can't quite believe stupid Jez Hopkins escaped me. I'd used a burner phone and expected he'd be too eager for a scoop to suspect anything. I wonder what spooked him. Right up until the last minute, he looked as if he was on board. Then, out of nowhere, he did that spinny turn, and I had to throw the trolley back in the van and take off after him.

Probably shouldn't have tried to get him at home. That was a mistake! Too close to the police station. 'I nearly got him, though, Tara. Pity he was so quick on his feet. I was livid, though. Really fuming, and truth be told, Tara, it affected my judgement a tad. Which leads to the big question: what should I do now?

'I *should* lie low for a while, really. Looks like Jez Hopkins has gotten a bit of a reprieve ... for now, anyway. I haven't crossed him off my list. However, for now, he is too hot.'

What went wrong? In spite of my anger, I smile as Tara's breath warms my neck. It is simple, really. I'd veered from my plan. Instead of continuing the way I had been, I'd deviated, and it was all that dreadful journalist's fault. Well, his and Gus McGuire's. If Hopkins hadn't published that despicable article, and if McGuire hadn't said those things at the press conference, I'd have continued purifying Bradford, one by one. The police haven't a clue. Not surprising, bearing in mind the one in charge is a half-breed. Not a hope of him cottoning on anytime soon ... not with his inferior intellect. Nonetheless, he needs to be taught a lesson ... and he won't even see it coming

So, the solution is easy. I'll move on to the next on my list and leave Jez Hopkins until the end. I've already studied this one for a while, and the reason I haven't acted before is they don't fully meet my criteria ... no deviance that I can find ... really family-orientated ... and that will be his downfall. He'll soon learn not to underestimate me. However, things have changed now. This target will be my *coup de maître*. This will really throw the cat among the pigeons. It will expose the flaws in their stupid profile; and, what's more, it'll be so, so easy.

I want to dance, I'm so excited. This is going to be brilliant. They'll never expect it, not in a million years. This one is an inspired choice. A bit more exotic than my usual targets, definitely different. Enough to keep the stupid police on their toes. It would launch at them like a bolt from the blue, and Detective Inspector Gus McGuire won't know what has hit him.

I stroke Tara's nose one last time and whisper, 'I won't be seeing you for a while. It's not safe for me here now. Too much interest in this place. I'll need to move somewhere else, and I've got just the place in mind. After all, it's just lying empty.'

Chapter 84

05:25 The Fort

Despite his lack of sleep, Gus was electrified. The attack on Jez Hopkins had given the investigation more impetus, a new direction. The big question was *why*. If it was the Tattoo Killer, had he changed his MO? Hopkins' description of the trolley he'd seen being taken from the van was similar to the sort of trolley Hissing Sid had matched the dog shit track to. The van itself matched the type of vehicle they were hunting. CCTV footage from Lister Mills Apartments had captured a snap of the vehicle, which again confirmed what they already knew. However, by tracking back ANPR records combined with CCTV, it seems the killer had swapped number plates again, and Compo was working on tracking similar vans entering Denholme the previous night.

Hopkins' statement regarding the route taken by the van indicated they'd be lucky to capture its image on the country roads, but maybe some of the bigger intersections, like The Ling Bob pub roundabout or Haworth Road might throw something up. The one thing in their favour was that traffic in those parts at that time of the night would be minimal.

He was expecting Professor Carlton to show up at any minute. The Professor had gone home late the previous evening, saying he needed to think about some things. When Gus had phoned to update him on Hopkins' suspected run-in with the Tattoo Killer, he'd screeched down the phone, and then, after a garbled few sentences, from which Gus understood he was on his way to The Fort, he'd hung up.

Sampson had been engrossed in something for the past hour. He'd been on the phone, and then back on his computer, and then on the phone again. Gus could tell by his face he was getting somewhere, so he left him to get on with it. He only hoped whatever it was would bear fruit. Alice was taking Hopkins' statement, despite his protests at having been asleep. Gus grinned, imagining the short shrift he'd have received from Alice, and continued to study the forensics reports that had come back from the labs. It appeared the horsehair found on Lewis Gore's clothes wasn't a match to either Michael Hogg or Graeme Weston's horses, which was disappointing. However, it was a match to the horse Alice had petted in the fields near the disused farmhouse opposite the Bay of Biscay. Brilliant!

He was just about to get Compo to pull anything they had on who owned both the field and the horse, when he read down and frowned. Apparently, a fragment of fabric taken from Lewis Gore's clothes had been matched to one found amongst the hair sample from Michael Hogg's horse.

Gus punched the air. 'Looks like we've established a link between Michael Hogg's horse and Lewis Gore. Taffy, find out everyone who has access to that horse, please, ASAP, and get uniforms to bring Hogg in for questioning. Do it now!'

Taffy scurried away, and Gus turned to Sampson, who was beaming like a Cheshire cat. 'Take it you've got something, Sampson?'

'Sure have. I've been going over and over the victims' histories, looking for possible intersections. You know, places where they could all have met?'

Gus rolled his eyes. 'Eh, yeah?'

Sampson flushed. 'Oh, yeah, em, sorry, Gus.'

'Just get on with it, Sampson. What have you got?'

Sampson grinned like a tame hyena. 'Well, I went over the histories we took from each of the victims' families and watched out for keywords like gyms and pubs and restaurant names. I got nothing.'

Wishing he'd get a move on, Gus responded in a sharp tone, 'Sampson! Cut to the chase.'

Swallowing, Sampson looked at his screen. 'Bottom line is, each victim, including Lewis Gore, and excepting Razaul Ul Haq, who we already think was an anomaly, had building work done, *or* was in the process of having building work done in the past eight months.'

Gus peered over Sampson's shoulder. 'Tell me they all employed the same builders or architect.'

Sampson shook his head. 'No. I phoned them all, and they all went with different builders, and none of them shared the same architect. However,' he paused, his face bright red with excitement, 'a throwaway comment by Asim Farooq's wife got me thinking, and when I checked with the others, it all added up.'

Gus was ready to strangle Sampson for going around the houses with this information, but he could tell the lad had worked hard and had really come up with something. So, with extreme difficulty, he kept quiet.

'Mrs Farooq mentioned how they'd got a quote from Weston's Builders in Bingley that was nearly triple the other quotes, so they didn't go with it. It got overlooked at the start when we only had one victim. Now, with everything that's been going on, I thought it was a bit too coincidental. Anyway, I phoned the other families, and they all told the same story. They'd all got quotes from Weston's, and when the quotes came back, they were all exorbitant. It's a link, isn't it?'

Gus strode over to the whiteboards and wrote 'Weston's Builders' in block capitals and drew a line from there to each of the victims. He stood back and studied it. The link was there, sure enough, however there was one massive problem. Graeme Weston had been in police custody when Jez Hopkins was attacked and had an alibi for each of the murders. Unless, of course, Hopkins was a red herring. He scowled. He'd never been convinced Weston was their man; now though, with the building quotes and the horses, there was definitely something going on there.

He turned to Compo. 'We need to find out how our killer got Propofol. See if you can link it to Weston. Sampson, re-check every vehicle owned by the Westons and by his business. We need to tighten this up. All employees, contractors, sub-contractors, builders, tradesman ... anyone who could have had access to those records.'

Before he had a chance to expand on his theories, the door crashed open, and Alice rushed in. Gus turned to beckon her over, but stopped when he saw her expression. In two strides, he was by her side leading her to a chair. 'What's up Alice? Are you ill?'

She shrugged him off and gripped his arm with a shaking hand, and then, her gaze found his. 'It's your mum, Gus ... the bastard's got your mum! Took her from right outside your parents' house.'

For what seemed like an eternity, there was silence in the room. Gus studied Alice, trying to process what she'd just said. He'd heard her. Of course, he had. His eyes searched her pale face, hoping against hope he'd mistaken her meaning. Then, he turned and stumbled away, pushing through the door and running down the corridor. Her words ringing in his ears, he burst through the toilet door, narrowly reaching the sink before he vomited. His stomach muscles protested, as lack of food meant all that came up was a stale coffee followed by a dribble of bile.

Raising his eyes to the mirror, he saw beads of sweat dotting his forehead. The acrid stench nipped his nostrils, so he turned on the tap, and washed it away.

He scooped some of the cool liquid into his hands and splashed his face, and again and again. The water didn't make any difference. In the distance, he could hear his name being called, then a frantic knocking on the outer door, as Alice demanded he speak to her.

Moments later, the door clattered open, and she was there beside him, wrapping her arms around his skinny frame and gripping tightly. It was only then he realised he was trembling, breath catching in his throat making him unable to speak.

She said over and over, 'It'll be okay, Gus, it'll be okay.'

Extricating himself from her grip, feeling as if he was watching from a distance, he replied, his tone dull, 'You don't know that, Al. You just don't know that.'

He took a deep breath to steady himself. His eyes stung. All he could think about was his gorgeous little mum. The feisty little woman. He hoped she was feisty enough for this. It wasn't as if she hadn't had enough hardship in her life. He remembered the last time he'd seen her. She'd been telling him and Mo off, as if they were still a pair of naughty school kids. He remembered Compo chomping through her overdone cookies, and in that instant, he made a promise to himself if he got his mum back, he would never ever disparage her lack of culinary finesse again. He'd give anything right now to be eating one of her burnt offerings.

He opened the door and turned to Alice. 'Update Nancy. She can lead from here. I need to go to my dad. He'll be in pieces.'

Chapter 85

07:45 Shay Farm, Shay Lane

Gus hadn't gone straight to find his father, as he had told Alice he would. He knew Graeme Weston couldn't be the Tattoo Killer, and he was unsure who it was. Nonetheless, the one thing he did know was there had been a match to the horsehair in the fields opposite the Bay of Biscay, and that's where he was heading. He knew his dad would rather he was searching for his mother than comforting him at home. Besides which, Katie was better at that sort of stuff than him. She'd look after Dad. At the thought of his big cumbersome dad's grief at having his wife abducted, Gus' eyes welled up. Honking on the horn, he shoved the thought to the back of his mind and accelerated.

When he got to the fields, he realised he had no coat, and he didn't care. He jumped out of the pool car and began to run over the fields. In the distance, he could see the big horse Alice had petted with its two mates in the little sheltered copse. Scanning the rest of the perimeter, he couldn't see any other living creature. He did a quick survey of the farmhouse, and as he'd expected, it was empty. With barely a glance at the horse who had shied away as he approached, Gus continued to run to the gate at the back of the field. As he reached it, two police cars, sirens blazing, pulled up, and Alice stumbled from one.

Storming over to him, she said, 'Did you think we couldn't work out he might bring her here, Gus? We saw you'd written it on the board and actioned officers to come here. Look, Nancy and I have got this. *You* need to go to your dad. He needs you. We'll leave a couple of officers here, just in case. I think it's unlikely now. Compo's on it.'

She placed her hand on his forearm and pulled him around so he was facing the bottom of the field. Giving him a gentle push, she said, 'Go. Go to your dad, and if you can't help yourself, give Sid, who is working the crime site at your parent's house, grief to find something, yeah?'

Realising how cold he was, and that the light drizzle had begun to soak though his jumper, he shivered. Alice was right. There was nothing he could do here. Maybe Sid would find something from the abduction site. Besides, it wouldn't hurt to see it for himself. 'Okay, Al. Okay, I'm off.'

Chapter 86

Unconscious, she appears smaller than she did when she was bustling around that farmyard with those yelping dogs and that big bumbling husband of hers. She was so full of herself. Proud she'd snared such an intelligent husband. Not so damn intelligent, if you ask me. If he is half as bright as he thinks he is, he'd have stuck to his own kind instead of diluting his genes with a half-caste ... breeding impurity into the world. Bad enough that she's given him half-breed children, one of them is a dirty dyke as well. Scum of the earth, that's what she is, despite her big house and her airs and graces.

I send a kick onto her stomach. I'm not looking forward to this bit, not like with the others. There is something a bit *off* about tattooing a woman ... needs must. Those are the rules, and no half-caste nigger is going to stop me. The only problem is, I can't do it right now. My new site isn't quite as remote as the other, so I'd better wait until later when there will be no-one in earshot. Maybe about half ten or so, just to be sure. Mind you, I could get the preparations underway right now.

Getting to work, I take out my flick knife and begin to cut her clothes off her body. This part I always find quite distasteful, although it has to be done. Her walking boots take a bit of pulling, but I manage in the end. She'd been out with those horrible dogs when I'd gotten to her. Our Corrine McGuire is a woman of habit, it seems. Every morning, at around 6:30, she'd set off with her two dogs, and often, she'd have that other dog with her too. It was easy for me to time it. I knew her husband would be in the kitchen at the back of the house. He's always there in the morning.

When I saw her climb the stile at the end of the field, I drove into their drive. The car I'd stolen was a C-Max with those slidey side doors. Stupid cow made it easy, coming right up to me, smiling. I just stuck the needle in and let her fall to the ground before jumping out and dragging her into the backseat. She was still unconscious when I got her back here. Took no time to drag her onto the trolley and cable-tie her in place. Stupid, trusting fool. No sense of self-preservation whatsoever.

Just because I can, I kick her again. She doesn't react, and her head lolls to one side with the momentum. I prise her eyelid open and her eyeball rolls back. Her chest rises and falls, so I knew she's alive. I don't want to make the same mistake I made with the other nigger. I'll be much more careful this time. Hmm, I don't want to stay here keeping guard, on the other hand, I don't want her coming-to and screaming her head off either … just in case. I look around and find just what I need. Yanking her head back with her hair, and using my elbow to steady it, I insert an oily rag in her mouth. If she wakes up, she'll not be able to make a noise, and into the bargain, the taste of that would be horrid. Win-win situation then. I move behind her and tip the trolley back at an angle and wheel her to the darkest corner of the garage. I'm not taking any chances this time. I still need to think about where I'm going to dump her body. Aah, I'll do that over a nice cup of tea.

I slap her face … just to double-check. No response.

'Bye-bye for now. I'll see you soon, and then, we can have *lots* of fun.'

Chapter 87

By the time Gus arrived at his parents' house, the SOCO team, led by Hissing Sid, was already there. The drive was large with enough space for at least four vehicles and still with room to sweep around, rather than do a three-point turn. Both of his parent's cars were most likely in the garage, and most of the drive was taken up by SOCO vans and a large perimeter sealed off with crime scene tape. His sister Katie's Range Rover was half on the grass verge outside the drive, as if it had been abandoned rather than parked. Gus wedged his car just behind it and got out. He knew Compo and the team were going through every builder, sub-contractor and employee Weston had on his books. Anybody who may have had access to their files. He wished Sebastian Carlton would get back to him with an updated profile. There were two anomalies to consider now. First, the attempted abduction of Jez Hopkins, and now his mum.

For once, Sid, his face serious, only nodded as Gus walked around the perimeter to enter the house, shouting, over his shoulder, 'I'll be out in a minute, Sid. Fucking find me something … anything to go on.'

The house seemed airless, as if all the joy had been sucked out of it, and Gus realised it was the absence of his mother that lay heavy in the air. Even the dogs hadn't respond to his entrance … a sure indication things were not okay in the McGuire house.

Taking a deep breath, Gus moved to the kitchen where he could hear his father's low rumble and the lighter tone of his sister talking. He pushed the door open and stood in the doorway. The faint smell of singed toast hung in the air, making his eyes well up. Shit, he'd give anything to have his mum come bouncing over, pulling him down for a kiss on his cheek. His dad sat at the end of the table, a mug of coffee untouched before him. Both of his dogs lay, ears back, at his feet, large eyes staring dolefully up at his father. Bingo was on his dad's knee, and as if sensing the older man's pain, he merely glanced at his owner before turning back and continuing his silent vigil.

Fergus McGuire's bulbous nose was redder than usual, and a pile of tissues scattered over the table told Gus he'd been weeping. His heart contracted as anger flooded him. How dare this bastard do this? His hands clenched into tight fists, his nails digging deep into his palms as he imagined what he'd do to the fucker when he caught him. He'd never seen his dad look so bereft, so broken, and he felt helpless … useless. What could he do?

The only thing he *could* do was find his mum and bring her back home. Once again, the killer had switched up the MO, and Gus knew this was now personal. A phone call from Sampson on the way over told him his parents had indeed gotten a quote from Weston Builders and had also rejected it for being too expensive. It had been for a utility room adjoining the kitchen and had been completed the previous year. It was clear that, even if Weston himself couldn't be involved in his mother's abduction, it was linked in some way to his business.

Sampson had also shared one other interesting piece of information about the profile, and as soon as he'd finished with his father, he intended to follow that up.

His father's bloodshot eyes, full of desperation, beseeched him, and Gus moved to his side, nodding briefly at his sister whose face betrayed her anguish. When he was sitting, his dad grasped his hand and held on as if it was the only thing anchoring him to real life. Maybe it was. His eyes, a darker blue than Gus and Corrine's, pierced right through Gus, and a small smile flicked his lips for a mere second. His accent was more pronounced with fear. 'Yer eyes are the exact same colour as yer mother's, Angus. That same piercing blue that sees everything. She's a wise woman, your mum … and a brave one, and *yer* her son. I know ye'll bring her hame tae me.'

Gus' heart clattered in his chest. He was sure the old man's faith was misplaced, and the very thought of what could be happening to his mum right now was clouding his brain.

His dad continued to speak, his voice low and firm, 'Ye've got tae find her, Angus. You ken you do. We cannae let those things happen to her … no' to yer mum.' He shook his head, and his gaze slid away, clearly trying to gain control. 'She's had too many bad things happen to her, and I swore when we married thirty odd years ago she'd never suffer again. Do you hear me, Angus? She's no' tae suffer.'

Gus swallowed hard and nodded. He could tell by the starkness in his father's eyes he was remembering the post-mortems he'd done on the Tattoo Killer's other victims. He tightened his grip on his dad's hand and pulled it slightly until his dad met his eyes. 'I'll find her dad. I'll bring her home. We're all working on this.'

He waited until his dad nodded and then turned to Katie. Her face was streaked with mascara, and despite her tremulous lip, she smiled at him. He reached over with his other hand and squeezed her arm. 'Make some fresh coffee and toast, sis. Dad and I need to go through what happened this morning, and we both need sustenance.'

As she busied herself in the kitchen, Gus, finding the domestic noises reassuring, asked his dad to tell him what had happened.

His dad's big hand stroked Bingo's head and two pairs of eyes; one brown and one piercing blue never left Fergus' face as he spoke. 'She went off with the dogs, like she always does at six o' clock or so. She was so happy. She loves that time of the morning when it's quiet. At around six forty-five, I heard them barking, so I knew she was nearly home. I popped the kettle on and set up the cafetiere. The thought she was taking a bit of a while to come in *did* cross my mind, but I assumed that this one,' he moved his hand to Bingo's head and pulled his ears, 'had rolled in something again and needed hosing off.'

He gulped. 'I should've bloody known. I should have gone oot tae see what she was up to. Next thing I know, I can hear Bingo outside there on the patio, barking and whining and scraping at the glass. I knew something was up straight away, so I opened the door, and he set off 'round the front, so I followed.' He glanced down at his old dogs and prodded them affectionately with his slippered toe. 'These two lumbering oafs were standing like a pair of confused schoolboys, and yer mum was nowhere to be seen. Down the drive, I saw a car, metallic red, I think, turn as if heading up to Cottingley.' His cleared his throat. 'That's when I saw the note, 'I've got her. Serves you right!"

Gus was surprised. The Tattoo Killer had never left a note before. Another change in MO. What the hell was going on? And his dad said he saw a car not a van. He supposed his dad could've been mistaken, but that was a long shot. There wasn't much traffic on that road so early in the morning.

He lifted a heavily buttered slice of toast that had appeared at his elbow and bit it. It tasted like cardboard in his mouth, still he knew he needed to eat, and that was about all he could manage. He was pleased to see his dad also take a slice. He slurped his coffee, nearly scalding his mouth in the process and, grabbing another slice of toast, stood up. 'Right, I'm off. I'll keep in touch.'

His dad stood and, knocking a protesting Bingo from his knee, said, 'Okay, I'm ready.'

Gus glanced at Katie who'd just walked back into the kitchen carrying a pile of clothes and hoped his face didn't betray the horror that was on her face. 'Eh, Dad, you can't come with me. I've got to do this on my own.'

Fergus' face took on a steely look. 'Och, nae chance, laddie. That's ma wife we're looking for. I'm coming wi' ye.'

Gus dragged his fingers through his dreads and sighed. He knew exactly what his dad was like. There was no stopping him once he'd made up his mind. 'Okay, but you do what I tell you, and you don't interfere.'

His father, nodding his head, was already heading over to slip his shoes on. Gus exhaled and said to Katie, 'Why don't I believe him?'

Kate smiled, and handed the clothes to him. 'You're soaked, Gus. You need to change. I found these in your old room. Put them on.' As Gus replaced his sodden clothes with dry ones, she continued in a quiet voice, 'He needs to do something, Gus. I just wish I could join you too.'

Gus, knowing how hard it was to do nothing bar wait, hugged her. 'You'll be fine, Katie. Get Gabriella to come over. You shouldn't be alone.' This was the first time he'd been close to his sister since her betrayal the previous year. And at the moment, none of that seemed important. All that mattered was getting his mum back. He raised his voice and shouted to his dad, 'I'll meet you out front. I need to talk to Sid.'

Outside, Gus struggled into a coverall and took a minute to phone Compo to tell him to see if he could trace the metallic red car. He'd take his dad into The Fort in a bit and get him to look through images of vehicles; hopefully, that would keep his mind occupied. He joined Sid, who was bent over something in the drive. 'Anything useful, Sid?'

Sid placed a gloved hand on Gus' sleeve and squeezed. 'A bit, not too much. Looks like he changed the vehicle.' He pointed to a flattened dollop of muck. 'This is a tyre tread, not big enough for a van. I'll be able to match it later. The note's been bagged, though I suspect our guy's too bloody smart to have left anything on that. Nonetheless, we'll go through it. One interesting thing is this. I found a small clump of horse shit just here.' He pointed to an area a few feet from the tyre track. 'Thought it was notable, what with the horsehair we found on Lewis Gore's clothes. Looks like it fell off someone's shoes. There's a tread mark there too. Mind you, it could've come from your mum's footwear. Do we know if she could have picked up horse poo on her walk?'

Gus shrugged. 'Not likely, she went through the woods usually … on the other hand, it's not impossible.' He glanced around. 'My gut tells me it's from our boy. Any chance you can send a tech up to the fields at the Bay of Biscay and see if you can match the print?' He stuffed his hands in his pockets, looking embarrassed. 'Mind you, I went up there this morning, and I know we sent some uniforms too. Fuck, I hope I've not obliterated anything useable.'

'Look, Gus, I heard you'd just got a match on the horsehair with the horse up there, and that you checked out the site but it was clear. Between you and me, I'd have gone straight there, too, if that sick fucker had taken my mum. It was worth a shot, and you did right.'

Chapter 88

'You can't be here, Gus. And you certainly can't, Fergus,' said DCI Chalmers, walking over in her stocking soles and encompassing first his dad and then Gus in a maternal hug. Despite one toe sticking through her tights, her blouse being creased, and her skirt looking like it had swivelled round her waist and was now on back to front, her eyes held a steely look, which immediately reassured Gus.

When she released him, he shook his head. 'You know I'm not going anywhere 'til my mum's been found, Nance, so you might as well stop wasting time. As for the 'Big Yin,' well, you're welcome to try. We both know you'll fail though.' He lowered his voice. 'I'll get him looking at vehicle colours and models. Keep him busy.'

For a second, he thought Nancy was going to object, then she gave a curt nod. 'The more of us on this, the better. Let me catch you up with where we are here.'

Glancing around the room, Gus saw Compo was busy on his PC, and Sebastian Carlton was working on a tablet in the far corner of the room. Presumably, everyone else was out doing follow-ups. Being in The Fort made him feel claustrophobic. He wanted to be out knocking down doors and searching properties; however, he knew that until they had something concrete, it was a waste of time. He needed to focus. There were answers here. His team was good, and he had faith in their abilities. They'd never let him down before, and he hoped they wouldn't this time. Not when the stakes were so high.

With determination, he brushed that thought aside and set his dad up with his task before moving over to Nancy who was sitting in his chair. He leaned his bum on the edge of his desk, folded his arms over chest and said, 'Right, what have we got?'

She snorted. 'Hmm, seems Propofol isn't very well monitored. Vets use it for operating on horses, and because it's not a controlled drug, it's not as well monitored as it should be. Other access points could be nurses, anaesthetists and doctors performing surgery. It's also becoming quite popular as a recreational drug. Compo's checking that out. I told him to follow the vet thing first because of the whole horses' link.'

Resting one leg over her knee, she pulled at her holey tights. 'Sampson and Taffy, with a whole load of uniforms, are trying to locate Michael Hogg. With Graeme Weston in custody, he looks like our next best bet, and he has access to the horses. His wife seems to have disappeared too. They may be together, but they're not at their home address, or Weston's business address. Hogg took this week off work at short notice, and apparently, Albion First are arranging a rally in support of Graeme Weston in City Park later on today.'

Gus slammed his fist into the table. 'Where the hell is he? Have they checked the party headquarters?'

Nancy nodded. 'We're on this, Gus. Alice is downstairs interviewing Graeme Weston, yet again, to see if he can give us any hints to Hogg's whereabouts. Compo's trying to track down any properties owned by the Westons, the Hoggs or Albion First. Uniforms have been despatched to each of the known Albion First Generals. We'll find him, ok?'

Gus had no doubt they'd find him, he just wasn't sure they'd find him in time. He glanced up as Sebastian Carlton approached. 'What you got, Prof? Why's he changed his MO?'

Carlton, glasses skew-whiff on his nose, said, 'The killer is unravelling, Gus. Unfortunately, he's nearing his endgame. The attempted abduction of Jez Hopkins last night was atypical. He doesn't want to target white people. *That* was personal. I think it was a reaction, possibly to Hopkins' article about Graeme Weston's wife. Abducting your mum today was more in keeping with his previous targets. Although the change of sex worries me.' He twiddled his glasses between his finger and thumb, frowning. 'I feel I'm missing something ... this is not an exact science, Gus.'

Ramming his glasses back on his nose, he continued. 'He watched your mother, knew her habits and chose an appropriate time, albeit not at night, when he normally strikes. Why choose a woman?' He shook his head. 'Hopkins had clearly not been stalked, hence the text to entice him out to neutral territory. I think with your mum he either brought her abduction forward ... or he has another reason. The note intrigues me, though. That makes it personal.' He turned and looked straight at Gus. 'I think he took your mum to get at you. Maybe because of the press conference. Maybe because you're getting close.'

Gus had an almost overwhelming urge to punch the Professor. The things that were leaked to the press – if they had endangered his mother, he'd never forgive himself ... and he'd bloody well find out who'd leaked it.

The Professor was still talking. 'Yeah, the note was a bold yet silly move. It was a taunt pure and simple, and it was aimed at you, Gus. I would suspect it's related to Weston's arrest, and the perceived slight regarding our killer's sexual orientation that was leaked. Compo told me your parents consulted Weston Builders for a building quote, so your mother was clearly in the killer's sights before now ... the note and the change in MO makes it personal. I've asked Alice to obtain permission from Weston to access his business records. I suspect he'll refuse, so when Compo told me the business was in joint names, I contacted Mrs Weston and got permission from her. Maybe we could send some people over there to go over his records for the past year. At least we'd know who else may be on the killer's target list.'

He peered at Gus over the top of his glasses. 'There is something else that bothers me, but I need to see the note first.'

Chapter 89

09:50 The Fort

It had taken Alice every ounce of willpower she possessed to smile at Graeme Weston, but smile she did. She needed something from him, and she'd play by whatever rules it took to get the information. Time was running out for Gus' mum, and they needed results fast.

'So, Mr Weston. We're looking for your campaign manager, Mr Michael Hogg. Have you any idea where he may be?'

Despite the fact that Weston had agreed to being interviewed without his solicitor, it appeared he wasn't going to give anything away lightly. He smiled when he answered, 'No comment.'

Alice hated his smug expression. She would give anything to shake a proper response from him, but she knew she needed to play the game. She inclined her head. 'You do know I'm not recording this, don't you? It's just between the two of us, and if you help us now, I'm sure DI McGuire will be happy to drop the assault charges.' She giggled in what she hoped was an endearing fashion. 'After all, I don't want my MP to have a criminal record now, do I?'

Weston raised an eyebrow. 'You're in Bradford Central constituency, are you?'

Alice, in a lifelong habit learned in childhood, crossed her fingers under the table and nodded. 'Yes, Little Germany. The flats above Shimla Sizzler.'

'Decided how you're voting, have you?'

Alice pretended to look coy and lowered her voice. 'It's a no-brainer, isn't it? The Tories can't do jack. The Labour Party's in chaos, and there's no Lib Dems I'd trust with my fart. I can't say too much in here,' she waved her hand in the air to indicate the wider police station, 'but, between you and me, I'm getting sick of it. Every single problem in this city is caused by them lot.' Hoping he'd misinterpret her flushed face for indignation, Alice swallowed down her disgust at what she was saying. 'As blacks go, McGuire isn't too bad, but some of the ones we come across shouldn't be allowed here. Half of them don't speak English even.'

Weston studied her face and then leaned across the table. 'What is it you need from me, Sergeant?'

Alice swallowed her grin, and instead, picked up her folder, as if she'd been given a list. 'What we need is to know where Michael Hogg is.'

Weston shrugged. 'If he's not at the party offices or at home or at his work, then I'm as in the dark as you. Mind you, he may well be 'visiting,' shall we say, the wife of a colleague. Michael is prone to sowing his oats in his own stable, so to speak. I have had words with him in the past about that.'

'You think he may be with the wife of one of your party members? Any idea which one?'

'No idea. Michael flits between them like the proverbial butterfly. Ask his wife; she generally knows who he's screwing, even if their husbands are too stupid to suss it out.'

'That's the thing, Marcia Hogg is also unobtainable.'

'Really? She should be at work. Isn't she at home either?'

Alice shook her head. 'Just one last thing, and then, we're done. You've been very co-operative. Did Michael have access to your business records?'

'I don't know where you're going with this. Of course, he did. His wife's my PA, for goodness sake, and Michael is a silent partner.'

This was news to Alice, and it made her heart speed up. If Michael Hogg was a silent partner, then he became an even more likely suspect. She smiled her most cloying smile. 'I don't suppose we could have access to your business records?'

Weston nodded his head, a huge smile spread across his face, and he extended his hands and did a slow hand clap. 'I wondered when you'd eventually get to what you really wanted. Well done trying to butter me up, but I'm not so green as cabbage looking, if you get my drift.' And he winked at her, before standing up. 'Interview terminated at …' he glanced at the clock and mimicked her voice, '10:01 precisely.'

Chapter 90

10:35 The New Kill Site

Can't believe the bitch is still unconscious. I thought she'd be awake by now. Alas, no. I don't want to, but I stretch out my gloved hand and touch her skin. It is freezing, yet I can feel the gentle rise and fall of her chest. At least she's breathing. Bet it's because she's smaller that the sedative's taking longer to wear off. Well, she'd better come 'round soon, or I'm going to have to leave her and come back later. The rally's starting at twelve.

I suppose I could just do the tattoo now, whilst she's unconscious. No, that's the bit I enjoy most, hearing them scream and feeling them strain against the ties. What the idiots don't get is that the more they struggle, the more it hurts. Mind you, with the size of their brains, I'm not surprised they can't work it out.

I suppose I could shave her now. Most of the others were already shaved down there. Some religious thing or other, I've heard. Bloody stupid, if you ask me. I like a bit of hair down below. The thought of shaving her makes my stomach roll, but I know I have to. If I get it out of the way now, when I came back at four-ish, I'll have about an hour and a half to enjoy myself, without having any dirty stuff to do.

Taking the aerosol, I spray shaving foam over her privates, and, trying not to gip, I shave the area. Dirty bitch had peed herself. The ammonia stings my eyes, so I press a bit harder. It doesn't matter, what are a few nicks amongst friends, after all? When I finish, I fill a cup of cold water and fling it over her to get rid of the foam. Then, I pour some Dettol into a bucket with some water and do a quick mop round. There, at least it doesn't stink now. Nice and clean for when I come back, that is, if she doesn't go and have another accident.

Angry at the very thought, I raise my leg and kick her in the side again. She already looks to be bruising from where I'd kicked her earlier. I don't care, though. She deserved it.

I push the rag more firmly into her mouth, and after a quick glance round the garage, I leave, locking everything up behind me, confident she won't be found. After all, the place is deserted now. Even the vehicle is gone. No-one will be back here. Not if they have any sense, anyway.

Chapter 91

'Where's Carlton gone?' asked Gus, glancing round the room. For the past ten minutes, he'd been pacing the room, waiting for Alice to return from interviewing Graeme Weston. Nancy had refused point blank to allow Gus to watch the interview. Deep down, Gus knew she'd been right. The mood he was in, he might have been tempted to charge the room and knock the arrogant little fucker out.

Compo glanced up from his screen. 'He headed off, muttering about a handwriting analyst at the university or something. Said he'd be back soon.'

Gus nodded and recommenced his pacing. His dad had identified a possible colour match for the vehicle he'd seen and narrowed it down to three different makes. Compo was scouring CCTV from the Cottingley junction in both directions, but without a definite make and number, it was difficult, if not impossible.

Christine Weston's list of buildings owned by the Westons was longer than Gus had anticipated, and he'd had to send three teams out with strict instructions to check the buildings out without being obtrusive. Each team had five properties to visit. So far, six properties in total had been cleared, including the field opposite the Bay of Biscay, which Weston sublet to the owner of the horse. For good measure, they'd sent two officers to check out the owner, and that, too, had come up empty. Tara, for that's what the horse was named, belonged to a forty-year-old woman who rode it regularly and hadn't even met the Westons. Her story checked out.

Nancy kept telling him they were narrowing, in but it didn't feel like it to Gus. He'd set his dad the task of going over all the forensics reports again, in case that threw up something, though more so to keep him busy. He dived for his mobile when it began ringing on his desk. 'Hello, Sid. Okay. Thanks.'

He turned to the expectant faces looking at him and shook his head. 'Sid just confirmed the tyre tread he found in the horse poo matched tyre treads around the Bay of Biscay field. That area was definitely visited by our killer, and I suspect this was his kill site. Tara's owner never drove in the field, but reported seeing tyre tracks for the past few weeks. That tallies with our timeline. The SOCO team are now going over the field with a fine-tooth comb.'

Alice came into the room, and the minute Gus saw her face, he knew she'd got nothing from Weston. Her shoulders drooped, and there was a tightness around her mouth, yet when she saw Gus and his dad, her face brightened. Without a word, she went over to Fergus and wrapped her skinny arms around his shoulders and hugged. The older man's eyes welled up as he patted her arms with his paddle-hands. Then, she came to Gus and repeated the gesture. Gus swallowed the lump in his throat, refusing to get tearful. There was too much to do.

Fuck, when were they going to get something? Where the hell was Michael Hogg? Alice began to contact the wives of the Albion First Generals. It was a slow process, but it needed doing.

Sampson and Taffy came in with bags of butties. 'Courtesy of DCI Chalmers,' said Sampson.

Gus wanted to scream that there wasn't enough time to eat, but he knew his team needed refuelling.

Sampson turned to Gus and said, 'The Albion First rally starts at noon, Gus. Surely Hogg will be there. He organised it, after all.'

Gus was tempted to say, 'Yeah, if he's not torturing my mum, he might show up.' Instead, he bit his lip. He couldn't take his fear and frustration out on his team. Instead, he said, 'Right, eat up, and then, we'll all head down there, except for Compo and my dad.'

Fergus McGuire was already on his feet, his huge frame looming beside Alice. 'I'm coming with you.'

Gus opened his mouth to object, however before he could, his dad said, 'You can't order me about, Angus. I'm not one of your team. I'd rather work with you, but if you ban me, I'll just go on my own.'

Gus knew when he was beaten, so he just grabbed his jacket and said, 'Taffy and Sampson, you go together, and Alice, you're with me and dad.'

Chapter 92

11:20 The New Kill Site

It was freezing. Corrine McGuire shivered, her entire body was cold, and she couldn't understand why. Had the forgotten to put the central heating on, or had the boiler broken again? She tried to open her eyes, but her lids were heavy, and her head pounded. She tried to swallow and realised there was something in her mouth. Something vile tasting and metallic. It rubbed against the back of her throat making her feel nauseous. What was wrong with her? Was she poorly?

She tried again to open her eyes, and this time managed a crack. It was dark. Not pitch black, rather a sort of shadowy grey sort of dark. A wave of dizziness engulfed her making her head swim, so she shut her eyes again and was relieved when the dizziness went. She tried to lift her hand to pull whatever was in her mouth out, again she couldn't. It was stuck. She tried her other hand and realised they were tied together. Her eyes flew open, and the vague fuzziness left her.

She remembered the car driving up to their house. She remembered approaching it to ask them what they wanted. She remembered the sting of something in her neck, and ... that was all. How long ago had that been? Was it hours ago ... or days ... or, God forbid, weeks?

This wasn't good. She knew it wasn't. Someone had drugged her, tied her up, gagged her and left her here. This was not good at all. It was then she realised she was naked, and at that thought, a familiar surge of panic rose in her chest. Tears rolled down her cheeks. *No! Not again! No! No! No! No! No!* I can't let this happen to me again.

Forcing herself to be calm, she breathed slowly through her nose, trying to ignore the oily stink that went up her nostrils. There seemed to be a faint Dettol smell too. She was aware now of the pain in her side and on her face. She tried to twist her body and realised she was lying horizontally on a metal structure. Its bars dug into her back and shoulders. Her legs appeared to be tied to the bottom struts, and her hands were tied around the vertical struts, behind her. They'd lost all feeling as the weight of her body and the metal crushed them. If she wiggled her fingers, spasms of pins and needles pricked her arm. She kept moving her fingers, little by little, to alleviate the numbness. It was agony, but she needed to be prepared, in case she got a chance to use them against her captor. She forced her eyes to stay open, and as they became more accustomed to the lack of light, she could make out her surroundings.

Turning her head to the left, she realised a small amount of light was coming from four very small windows just beneath the ceiling. She stared straight ahead and saw more light coming from the bottom of what looked like corrugated metal garage doors. At least she knew it was still daytime. She couldn't help thinking, *What if days have passed? I could have been unconscious for days.* Then, she thought of her husband. He'd be so worried ... beside himself. He was a big lummox, but he loved her dearly, and she couldn't bear to think of him in pain. Then, there was Angus, so tortured and full of guilt. She sighed ... and Katie. Her darling daughter full of a different type of guilt. They needed her.

That thought steeled her, and she continued to peruse her surroundings. It was definitely a garage. She could see a bench with tools along one edge. In the opposite corner stood a washing machine and tumble dryer, as if someone also used it as a utility room. Maybe that someone would come in and find her. Maybe that someone was the person who'd brought her here.

She tilted her head to one side, listening. All she could hear was the ominous tick of the old clock that hung, lopsided on the wall opposite. Closing her eyes, Corrine thought about her predicament. She realised her likely captor was the Tattoo Killer and, although Fergus didn't confide too many gory details from the morgue, she'd gleaned enough to know what was in store for her. Despite her pain, the thought of her husband made her feel better. She knew beyond a shadow of a doubt he'd be looking for her – and Angus would be looking too, of course. Her beautiful, damaged boy would move heaven and earth to save her. She knew he would. It was that thought that made her focus.

What could she do to help herself? She tried to manipulate her tongue around the rag to see if she could dislodge it, but that only made her feel sick, and she knew that would not be a good thing. If she could free her hands, she'd be able to pull it out. Right now, though, she could barely move them. Now she had some feeling back in them, she knew they were attached to something metal. She curved her back in an attempt to give her fingers some space and then stretched them as far as she could to assess what she was attached too. She caught her thumb on the edge of something sharp and moaned beneath her gag. She was sure she'd drawn blood. She sagged back onto the metal structure. Maybe it was one of those trollies they use in warehouses to transport stock around. Her muscles ached with the effort, and her breath caught in her throat, though at least it had warmed her body ever so slightly.

That was when it occurred to her. If she'd found something sharp enough to cut her thumb, maybe she could use the same thing to cut her ties. Taking a deep breath in, she curved her body upwards, again straining against the cables that held her. Clasping her hands, she stretched them over to her left, trying to find the sharp edge that had ripped her thumb. By the time she'd located it, she couldn't hold herself up any longer, and she collapsed back onto the trolley, the clatter making her bones rattle.

Closing her eyes, she promised herself she'd try again and again, until she succeeded in freeing her hands.

Chapter 93

S cowling, Gus flashed his ID at a traffic warden and got out of the car. He was beyond caring how he'd parked. All he wanted was to find Michael Hogg and beat him until he gave up his mum's whereabouts. With his dad labouring behind him, Gus and Alice sprinted straight for City Park. There was already a police presence on the ground in anticipation of the rally. The powers-that-be had decided banning the rally would give Albion First more coverage in the news. Gus couldn't have cared less right then. All he was focussed on was his mum.

Jez Hopkins appeared to have recovered enough to cover the rally. *Can't keep an evil little shit down, can you?* A substantial group of anti-Albion First protestors had turned up with banners and stationed themselves near City Hall, whilst Weston's supporters were gathering in and around the empty Mirror Pool and looking expectantly to the balcony above the café. Clearly the Albion First speakers were going to spout their hatred from an elevated position. Assuming that Hogg would be one of the speakers, Gus headed in that direction, his eyes moving from side to side, alert for a sighting of the barrel-chested thug.

Chants started from all directions, and Gus hoped it wouldn't be a repeat of the earlier demonstration. The police had begun to move among the ever-expanding crowd, stopping and questioning. Asking people to open their bags. They were on top of things, so far. Gus was

412

pleased with their quiet determination, as they methodically moved among the crowd.

There was still no sign of Hogg, however, and Gus was getting anxious. On the drive over, he'd tried to ignore the warning black shapes dancing in his eyes. His chest began to heave and tighten. *Shit, not now.* He couldn't afford to have a panic attack right now. He stopped and, ignoring Alice's questioning glance, closed his eyes and breathed slow and steady, like Dr Mahmood had taught him.

Alice gripped his arm and waited. Gus knew she understood what was happening and was giving him time to recover. He was aware of his dad standing next to him, as he continued to focus on his breathing. After what seemed like aeons, his chest began to loosen, and his heart rate slowed. A few more skipped beats and then a steady rhythm. He opened his eyes, and with a quick nod to show them he was okay, they moved onwards. To his right, he saw Imti and his girlfriend, Serafina, move towards their friends. There was no sign of Shahid. Maybe his political conscience was appeased after the last time.

As they got near to the ramp that would lead them up to where the speakers were beginning to congregate, Gus spotted Michael Hogg. He raised his arm and pointed. As one, he and Alice broke into a run. Taffy and Sampson, who'd appeared from the National Science and Media Museum side of the road, began to run too. As they drew nearer, Gus' progress was impeded by the growing crowd, so he yelled, 'Hogg? Michael Hogg? Wait there.'

Hogg's head jerked in Gus' direction, and then, he was off, running in the opposite direction. Gus increased his speed. His regular jogging meant Hogg was no match for him. As the other man reached the Imran Qureshi *Garden Within a Garden* floor painting in the space above the Mirror Pool, Gus saw his opportunity and dived. Wrapping his arms around Hogg's ankles, he wrestled him to the floor and yanked him around onto his back. Sitting on his waist, Gus snarled at him. 'Where is my mother, you nasty little racist fuck?'

Chapter 94

12:45 The Fort

'You're not doing it, Gus, and that's final. He's already mouthing off about police brutality and that's not going to help your mother, is it? We need him talking. You know that.'

Fergus patted his son's arm. 'You know she's right, Angus. Much as I want to smash the little scunnering bawbag into oblivion, we need to find your mum first.'

Shocked speechless by his dad's uncharacteristic swearing, Gus nodded. 'Okay, okay. But I'm watching the interview, and so's he.' He jerked his thumb in his dad's direction before saying, 'Come on, Da, this way.' He heard Nancy's loud sigh of relief as he left the room and smiled. She was probably relieved he'd given in so easily.

Alice sat opposite Michael Hogg in the interview room. Gus had cuffed him for resisting arrest, and if his face was anything to go by, he'd put up quite a resistance. Although he'd wanted to wallop him, Alice's arm on his shoulder had stopped him from slamming his raised fist into the man's face. All the damage had been done when Gus wrestled him to the ground. Unfortunately, his face had scraped along the tarmac as he fell. Gus felt no remorse and, in fact, was glad to have hurt him. When his dad had thundered up seconds later, Gus had stood in front of him as Taffy and Sampson escorted Hogg to their waiting car. Hogg had been cleared fit for interview by the police doctor, and his lawyer had turned up surprisingly quickly. Gus reckoned he'd been on standby, on account of the rally.

Alice went in gently to begin with, establishing his name and address and then introducing evidence after evidence. By the time she'd covered the horsehair and the building quotes and their link to all the victims, Hogg's confident expression had been replaced by look of anxiety. He'd pulled his tie loose and kept wiping his brow with a handkerchief. His lawyer demanded consultation time with his client.

Alice left the room and joined them in the investigation room.

'You need to offer him a deal, Al. Tell him we'll ask for a reduced sentence in a low security wing, if he co-operates. We need him to tell us where my mum is. The evidence is all circumstantial. We don't have DNA. The most we can hope for is him seeing sense. You have got to appeal to his better nature.' As he said it, Gus knew it was futile. What better nature did he suppose Michael Hogg had? He'd no sooner share information with the police than with Nelson Mandela.

Alice, however, agreed they should try, and they continued to work on their strategy. Then, Professor Carlton rushed in, panting slightly, luminous yellow trainers flashing as he moved. 'Don't you answer my calls any more, Gus?'

'Eh?' Gus pulled his phone from his pocket and realised he'd turned it off. 'Sorry, turned it off. What's up?'

Carlton caught his breath and said, 'I wondered earlier on. All that reacting to the article against Weston and then Weston's arrest got me thinking. After, when I saw the handwritten note, I was nearly sure, so I took it to my friend at the university. Had to hunt her down because she'd turned off her phone too. Anyway, I was right.'

Gus, impatient and feeling no desire to play Carlton's games, said, 'Spit it out then.'

'It's a woman.'

Gus frowned. 'What is?'

Carlton spread his hands out before him. 'The Tattoo Killer is a woman. One who wants to protect Graeme Weston, I'd say.'

Gus closed his mouth and spun away, raking his fingers through his dreads. A woman? Not Michael Hogg, despite the fact all the circumstantial evidence fit Hogg. He closed his eyes and went through everything they had: horsehair, building quotes, shadowy figure in baggy clothes, access to the kill site.

Shit, which one of them is it? Just then, Michael Hogg's lawyer came through the door. 'Your sergeant asked for a list of buildings owned by Weston's Builders, and my client has supplied this list. Now, can we re-commence this interview?'

Gus read the list and then, heading out the door, said, 'No, we're holding him for obstructing arrest. Take him back to the cells, Sampson. Come on, Dad, let's go get Mum.'

Chapter 95

13:30 The New Kill Site

Anger ripples through my body. I can feel it in the tension across my shoulders. What were they playing at, arresting Michael? Imagine that nigger laying hands on Michael like that. Wrestling him to the ground, like he was some sort of animal ... it was abhorrent. How dare he? Well, he'll be sorry now. His actions have just made it a hundred percent worse for his mum. First, he targets Graeme, now Michael. No way will I go easy on her now. No, she is going to suffer, and I am going to enjoy every minute of it.

I park up and get out. Faint wafts of smoke float in the air as I survey my surroundings. It's as quiet as it was this morning when I dropped her off. I usually park around the corner if I want to avoid being spotted; today though, there's no need. No-one will think it's suspicious. No-one is around. Humming to myself, I approach the garage. The rally was called off after Michael's arrest. The Generals tried to say a few words, but the Pakis had turned up, and they outnumbered us. It all fell to pieces. What do you expect, without Graeme and Michael to hold things together?

I roll the door up and walk inside, flipping it shut behind me. I switch on the light. Time to get everything ready. A quick glance tells me she is still unconscious, although her breathing is steady. I busy myself getting the ink and the wipes and the tattoo machine together. I pull

the workbench over beside her and place my things on it, and then, she opens her eyes.

For a second, I am startled, and then, I smile at her ... the fun is about to begin.

Chapter 96

Alice tagged along with them. Gus was sure Taffy, Nancy, Sampson and a squad of other officers were on their way too. One glance at the list told him the only building they hadn't checked was one belonging to Michael Hogg's parents. It had been transferred to Weston Builders recently. That was where his mum was. He was sure of it.

Screeching to a halt in front of the converted farmhouse, Gus rushed out followed by his dad and Alice. In the distance, police sirens approached. Gus reached the front door seconds before his dad, and, with a shared glance, they braced themselves and threw their combined weight at the door. It burst open, sending them flying inside. Gus started shouting, 'Mum! Mum!'

Whilst his dad's deeper voice yelled, 'Corrine! Corrine! We're coming, my darling.'

Gus ran through the house like a marauding Viking, crashing doors open, scanning the room and then moving onto the next. All rooms in the house exhausted, he headed back out to repeat the process on the out-buildings.

Alice's phone rang at exactly the same moment the police cars skidded into the yard. She answered it, and Gus saw her face pale.

'Shit,' she said and ran back to the car. 'We got the wrong place. She's at the Weston's.'

Chapter 97

13:45 Hawthorn Drive, Eccleshill

Two things happened within minutes of each other. The first was that Corrine McGuire brought her hands forward and grabbed her captor's head. The second was that, using her grip as impetus, she pulled herself *and* the trolley up, crashing her head onto the woman's face. A Glasgow kiss with a difference! When she heard the crunch of the killer's nose breaking, her spirits lifted. Warm blood spurting onto her face served only to give her a primal feeling that pumped adrenaline through her aching body. Still holding the woman, she brought her head back, and then with equal strength, pummelled it again onto the woman's broken cartilage.

Her screams gave Corrine more energy. She'd had enough pain, and this woman was the cause of it. Corrine McGuire was going to end it there and then. Moving her grip to the woman's hair, she yanked her head back and spun her around, making her yelp. Corrine transferred her grip until she had her forearm round the woman's throat. Using her other hand as counter balance, she exerted more and more pressure –

A ball of fire thrust into Corrine's stomach. A phew of air ricocheted from her lips, and her arms loosened their grip, as her assailant rammed her elbows once more into Corrine's tender flesh. Her attacker stumbled out of her reach. Her eyes, feral with hate, shone from her bloody face. Panting, she stood like a gorilla, knees slack, fists almost skimming the floor. Corrine, gasping raw breaths, glanced around. Her eyes flicking over all the possible weapons that were just out of reach.

Her teeth flashing through her mucus-covered face, the other woman snarled and took a step closer. She lifted her hand and picked up a crowbar from the workbench nearby.

Corrine knew she had to do something, so she began to wobble the trolley. Could she wobble it over until she was underneath it? Maybe the metal struts would provide her with some protection. She could hear the other woman's rasping breath and knew she'd elevated her arm ready to strike. Corrinne leaned her body as far as she could in a last-ditch attempt to move the trolley. Then, in her peripheral vision, she saw a flash of movement, and a waft of air touched her skin as the crowbar descended. Bracing herself, she closed her eyes and waited.

The loud sound of metal landing on concrete followed by a thump made her judder. She waited for the accompanying pain, but it didn't come. Instead, she heard a low whimper and a louder groan. Her eyes flew open, and she saw a woman with her hands covering her cheeks standing next to her, staring at a crumpled heap on the floor.

Taking a steadying breath, Corrine said, 'Thank God,' and fell back against the trolley at the same moment as the garage door shuddered upwards, and she could see her beloved husband and son dashing through. It was the most beautiful sight she'd ever seen in her life. And as they approached, great heaving sobs wracked her body.

Chapter 98

18:00 The Fort

Gus couldn't believe how resilient his mother had been in the aftermath of the rescue. He'd wrapped his coat round her naked body. Alice had cut the cable ties off her legs, and his father had lifted her up and carried her out to the waiting ambulance. She'd clearly been exhausted, and her body was bruised all over. Angry welts covered her wrists and ankles, and she'd lacerated her hands in her attempts to cut through the cable ties. She'd sustained a concussion and two broken ribs, but had no side effects from being drugged.

Gus had left her in the capable hands of his sister, his father, and his ex-wife Gabriella, who were fussing about her at home. She'd insisted on giving her statement at the hospital, and Alice had taken it, whilst Gus and his father listened.

When he'd heard his mum was being held at the Weston house, he'd wondered if he'd misread Christine Weston. Right up until the point when he'd hurled open the garage door and found his mum tied to the trolley with Christine Weston, staring wide-eyed at the woman she'd just hit with a hammer, he'd been unsure.

Turned out, Christine had returned home to see what damage had been done by the fire and to collect some clothes for herself and Jacob. When she'd pulled up outside, she'd seen Marcia's car in the drive. Assuming the other woman had come to collect something for her husband,

Christine had entered the house. When she couldn't find Marcia anywhere in the house, she was puzzled and had come back downstairs, which was when she heard sounds coming from the garage. She'd edged towards the door and listened. When she'd heard some of the things Marcia was saying, she'd moved into the living room and phoned the station.

Compo had immediately phoned Alice. Meanwhile, Christine had returned to listen in to what was happening in the garage whilst she waited for the police. When she heard the screaming, she couldn't stay outside any longer, and had opened the garage door and grabbed a hammer to help Corrine.

Having been cleaned up, Marcia Hogg was waxing lyrical about how she'd done it all to further Graeme Weston's political career. How Graeme Weston was the love of her life, and now that Christine had exposed herself as the trollop she was, he'd stand by her. She was clearly unhinged, and would no doubt spend the rest of her days in a psychiatric hospital.